Award-winning *USA TODAY* bestselling author **Yvonne Lindsay** has always preferred the stories in her head to the real world. Married to her blind-date sweetheart and with two adult children, she spends her days crafting the stories of her heart. In her spare time she can be found with her nose firmly in someone else's book.

USA TODAY bestselling author **Janice Maynard** loved books and writing even as a child. After multiple rejections, she finally sold her first manuscript! Since then, she has written fifty-plus books and novellas. Janice lives in Tennessee with her husband, Charles. They love hiking, travelling and family time.

You can connect with Janice at
www.janicemaynard.com
www.Twitter.com/janicemaynard
www.Facebook.com/janicemaynardreaderpage
www.Facebook.com/janicesmaynard
and www.Instagram.com/therealjanicemaynard

Also by Yvonne Lindsay

The Christmas Baby Bonus
Honour-Bound Groom
Stand-In Bride's Seduction
For the Sake of the Secret Child
Tangled Vows
Inconveniently Wed
Vengeful Vows
Wanting What She Can't Have
Little Secrets: The Baby Merger
Lone Star Holiday Proposal

Also by Janice Maynard

Christmas in the Billionaire's Bed
Second Chance with the Billionaire
How to Sleep with the Boss
Blame It On Christmas
A Contract Seduction
Triplets for the Texan
Hot Texas Nights
Million Dollar Baby
On Temporary Terms
His Heir, Her Secret

TANGLED WITH A TEXAN

YVONNE LINDSAY

BOMBSHELL FOR THE BLACK SHEEP

JANICE MAYNARD

MILLS & BOON

First Published in Great Britain 2019
by Mills & Boon, an imprint of HarperCollinsPublishers,
1 London Bridge Street, London, SE1 9GF

ISBN: 978-0-263-27194-2

1019

MIX
Paper from
responsible sources
FSC™ C007454

This book is produced from independently certified FSC™ paper to ensure responsible forest management.

For more information visit: www.harpercollins.co.uk/green

Printed and bound in Spain
by CPI, Barcelona

TANGLED WITH A TEXAN

YVONNE LINDSAY

To my fellow
Texas Cattleman's Club: Houston authors,
always a pleasure working with you, ladies!

One

As if it wasn't enough she'd had to hand over her additional casework to the rest of her already overloaded team, now she was headed all the way out to Royal, Texas. Zoe Warren was a city detective, hell, city girl, through and through. She already could start to feel her skin itch at the thought of cattle and cowboys and all that open pasture. Mind you, driving the three hundred or so miles to Royal had presented as a far more attractive option than facing yet another blind date set up by one of her four older brothers or her parents, who seemed to think she needed help settling down. And who said she wanted to settle down, anyway? She'd worked long and hard for her place on Houston P.D.'s detective squad, and her career trajectory was heading straight up. You weren't a third generation cop without some dreams and goals ahead of you—and at only thirty years old, she had plenty of dreams and goals to fulfill while quite happily still single.

Sure, one day it might be nice to get married, throw a couple more Warren genes into the pool of rapidly growing family her brothers and cousins were constantly adding to. But not right now. And not on her ever-loving family's timetable, either.

The open country that surrounded her had a raw beauty to it that even her citified eyes couldn't help but appreciate. But always, in the back of her mind, she was working. As lead detective on the homicide case that was sending her on this journey, she was beginning to feel like the more they uncovered about the deceased, Vincent Hamm, the less they actually knew about him, and for her, following down each and every rabbit hole in Hamm's life had become an obsession. The good thing about having this time on her own as she drove west toward Maverick County was that it gave her the opportunity for some thinking time. Time without the constant pressures that came with the responsibilities of her job.

Everything about this case was off. First, the vic had disappeared into thin air, then he'd never shown back up for work, and after the floodwaters had receded at the site of the new Texas Cattleman's Club being built in Houston, he was eventually found dead with his face destroyed. Whoever killed him had taken great pains to ensure he couldn't be visually identified—although the floodwaters had taken their toll, too.

Zoe took a swig of her water bottle and grunted in annoyance when she found it empty. Still, not long now and she'd be in Royal—she could stock up at a convenience store there. But first, a quick swing by the sheriff's office was in order to make a courtesy visit and let them know that she'd arrived in the county. Nathan Battle, the sheriff, had made a personal visit to Houston to lend his support to the case. Her vic was the son of a friend of his and she'd expected Battle to be loudmouthed at the very least, and difficult at worst. Instead, she'd been quietly surprised by his demeanor. Oh, there was no mistaking the determination behind his promise to Hamm's family to get to the root of who murdered their son, but he was a by-the-rules guy and his help here in Royal could prove invaluable to her investigation. She'd gone to great lengths to ensure she was doing everything in her power to bring the murderer to justice, and she was confident she'd earned the older man's trust. She liked the guy. Not pushy, just determined. She respected that.

About ten minutes later, guided by the GPS on her phone—without which she'd be totally lost anywhere, not having inherited the direction gene her brothers took for granted—Zoe pulled up outside the Royal sheriff's office. Three minutes after that she was back in her car. Turned out the good sheriff was out on a call, but she'd left a message for him to phone her when he got back.

She reprogrammed the GPS and found the midrange motel she'd booked just on the other side of town. It didn't take more than ten minutes to check in and unpack. She called for updates from her colleagues back in Houston and let them know she'd arrived safely, then decided to take a short walk around town to stretch her legs and familiarize herself.

Royal struck her as a prosperous town with a decent-sized population scurrying about their daily business. Being late afternoon, there were all kinds of people out and about. Business people, moms and kids, a handful of idlers loitering here and there, but overall the place had a good feel about it. She turned and headed back to the motel, her mind still churning over the facts of the case. Just as she reached her unit, her phone buzzed in her pocket. She slipped it out and looked at the screen. Nathan Battle.

"Sheriff, thanks for calling," Zoe answered.

"Thanks for coming by and letting me know you're in town. Did you want to meet?"

"How about tomorrow afternoon?" she suggested, mentally reviewing her plans for tomorrow morning, which included following up on the lead that had brought her to Royal in the first place.

She heard the flick of paper, followed by a grunt of assent. "Yup, works for me. I'll meet you at the Royal Diner for coffee and a slice of pie, say, three o'clock?"

Zoe's stomach growled in response to the mention of food. "Sounds like a plan. See you then."

That would give her plenty of time to make the drive out to the Stevens ranch in the morning and ask a few questions. Hopefully more than a few. That cryptic message left on Hamm's answering machine saying no more than "Thanks for nothing, Hamm" had spoken volumes when taking into account the tone of the speaker and the fact that Vincent Hamm had gone missing around the same time. They'd been able to trace the message to a local rancher, Jesse Stevens. Research had shown Stevens and Hamm had been friends at one time, but what had happened to drive them apart? Had it been enough to make Jesse Stevens want to kill his former friend?

Stevens was quite a force here in Royal. The wealthy rancher was very involved in the politics of the local Texas Cattleman's Club, and while Zoe may be grasping at straws, the fact that her vic had been found in the building currently being developed into a new Cattleman's Club might not be such a coincidence after all. Right now, she had to look at everything. Pressure from the chief of police and Houston's mayor was constant, and so far her team had little to show for their investigation. Her captain had pulled her aside just yesterday and asked her if she was getting stale. The question had made her bristle. Stale? When all she did lately was live, eat, sleep and breathe this case? Not likely. But he'd made it clear—he needed to see results or she might be stood down.

Thinking about it, Zoe reached a decision. She didn't want to wait until morning to go face-to-face with Stevens. She could drive out to his ranch right now. October sunset wasn't until around seven, which gave her three hours of daylight. Plus, the element of surprise would be in her favor if she just rolled up without an appointment. She opened her map app on her phone and pulled up the address she'd saved for Stevens's ranch before leaving Houston. The ranch was outside Royal and isolated. Nothing but pasture and cattle. Zoe ignored the itch between her shoulder blades and got into her car, set her phone in the hands-free holder and hit Start on the journey planner.

The drive took longer than she expected, but as she pulled through the gates of Stevens's ranch she felt a sense of triumphant relief that she had made it. People could tease her all they liked about her reliance on modern technology to get anywhere, but it got the job done, she thought with a small smile.

She was still smiling when she went up the front stairs of the impressive ranch house and knocked on the front door. But her smile slipped when no one came to answer. She knocked again and waited a couple of minutes before walking along the front porch to one of the side windows. She looked in. No movement, nothing. Zoe blew out a huff of frustration. Maybe a phone call would have been a better idea after all. Still, she had a list of his known associates here in Royal and she knew one of them was his neighbor. She walked back to the car and reprogrammed her app to the next address on her list.

This time she struck gold when she knocked at the door

of the neighboring ranch, which was no less impressive in size and structure than the Stevens property. She'd always known ranching was a prosperous undertaking when done right, but the two properties she'd been on so far were something else. She plastered a smile on her face and flicked her short dark hair back off her forehead as the steady sound of footsteps coming to the door echoed from the other side.

The words she was about to say dried on the tip of her tongue as the door opened, revealing a tall, imposing presence. While the guy wasn't heavily muscled, there was no doubting the latent strength in the shoulders that bunched beneath the checkered shirt he wore over a crisp white T-shirt. Zoe's gaze flicked up—something she wasn't always used to doing when wearing boots that, combined with her natural height, put her at around six feet. Instantly, her attention was captured by the man's eyes. Light brown and shot with gold, they were incredibly mesmerizing and were set in a face that was all sharp lines and angles softened by a generous dusting of five o'clock shadow that wrapped his jaw. There was an almost wolflike look to him—as if he were assessing her as prey.

Rather than getting put on the defensive, Zoe found herself reacting on a far more visceral level—each facet of her mind sharpening, while every cell in her body responded with pure feminine interest. A wave of physical need pulled from deep within her, robbing her of breath and making her nipples harden against the lacy cups of her bra. She drew her full lower lip between her teeth to stop herself from making the involuntary sound—something like a moan—that threatened to spill from her.

The man's hair was wet, as if he'd recently stepped from a shower and just slicked it back—its wet ends kissed the edge of his collar and left a damp trail. She drew in a sharp breath, only to discover how intoxicating the scent of him was. She was shocked at how deeply and suddenly he had affected her. She had trained herself from day one at the police academy not to show her emotions. Good things, bad things—it made no difference. She had learned to remain impassive, detached. But right now, she was anything but detached. In fact, right now, every instinct was screaming at her oversensitized body to plaster itself against his length and take his mouth in a possessive kiss that would leave him in no doubt of how much she wanted him. For a nanosecond she allowed herself the luxury of imagining where that might lead. To their two bodies, glistening with perspiration, tangled in tumbled sheets, gliding together, perhaps? She blinked hard and forced herself under control. This was utter madness. She couldn't even remember the last time she'd reacted to a guy this intensely.

Those intriguing eyes narrowed as he looked at her, and she realized that neither of them had spoken.

"Miss? Can I help you?"

His voice poured over her. Deep and strong and sexy as hell. This guy could recite a list of traffic infringements and make her knees turn to water.

"Detective," she corrected him, showing him her badge. "Zoe Warren, Houston P.D."

"You're a little out of your jurisdiction, aren't you?"

She wasn't mistaken. The warmth and pure male interest she'd seen reflected in his eyes had dimmed, his gaze sharpening warily.

"The boundaries of our investigation have stretched a little," she said carefully. "I'd like to ask you a few questions, Mister…?"

"Cord Galicia," he answered abruptly and thrust out his hand.

Zoe debated taking it. If her reaction to him on a purely

visual basis had been so extreme, how on earth would she react when she actually touched him? There was only one way to find out. She drew in a sharp breath, took the proffered hand and clasped it. A slow sizzle of awareness tracked along her skin. His hand was larger than hers, the palm firm, and she could feel the calluses that spoke of the hard work he did. The title of rancher wasn't simply some token. This man clearly worked, and worked hard. Did he apply himself to everything else he did with as much vigor? she wondered before giving his hand a quick shake and releasing it.

"May I come in?" she asked.

To her surprise, her voice remained steady. Quite a feat when her insides were jangling about as hard as they had in junior high when she'd been asked to prom by the captain of the soccer team. She was already head and shoulders taller than him but it hadn't bothered her—until she found out the whole thing had been a joke designed by the rest of the team. But that initial response, the delicious sense of anticipation and excitement, she'd never forget. She just never expected to feel it here on the outskirts of Royal, Texas, while working a homicide investigation.

For a moment it looked as if he'd refuse, but then he stepped back from the doorway and gestured for her to move inside. He closed the door decisively behind her, but Zoe didn't let it rattle her. She'd dealt with people with far fewer social graces than Cord Galicia.

"Can I get you anything to drink?" he asked as he led the way into a large open-plan living room.

"Water would be great, thanks."

"Take a seat," he said gruffly before heading through a doorway toward what was, presumably, the kitchen.

Zoe sank into a large leather sofa. In a smaller room the piece of furniture would have dominated, but not here. She looked around, taking in the high raftered ceiling—must be a bitch to keep clean, she pondered—and the tall windows that led to a paved courtyard outside. Large round ceramic pots in a jumble of bright colors, some with mosaics, were filled with flowers, and beyond that Zoe caught a glimpse of the sparkle of late-afternoon sunlight on water. A pool or an ornamental pond? she wondered.

"Here you are."

Cord Galicia stood before her holding a sweating tall glass of water in one hand. She reached up to take it.

"Thank you."

The man moved with the stealth of a wild animal, she realized. There weren't many who could sneak up on her like that.

"You said you had questions," he said as he settled onto the other end of the sofa.

"Yes, I do. Your neighbor, Jesse Stevens—are you well acquainted?"

She knew the men were best friends, but she was curious to see how Galicia reacted to being questioned. She kept her eyes focused on her host and didn't miss the way his body stiffened.

"What do you want with Jesse?"

"Please, Mr. Galicia, just answer the question."

"He's my neighbor, of course we're acquainted," Cord said begrudgingly. "But I don't see what he has to do with some investigation in Houston."

"That's my job," Zoe said with a grim smile. "Tell me, what's Mr. Stevens like as a man?"

"What do you mean?"

"Is he quick to anger? The type to follow up on a grudge?"

"I don't like where you're heading with this. Jesse is a decent man and an upstanding member of our community. If you're looking at him, you're looking in the wrong direction."

Zoe decided to take a different tack. "Do you remember Vincent Hamm?"

"Yeah, he grew up around here. We all did."

"Were he and Mr. Stevens particularly close?"

Cord shook his head. "No, I wouldn't say that. Jesse knew him, sure. But we all did. Is that who this is about? Hamm? Look, we were sorry to hear he'd passed, but it's not like we'll miss him. Seriously, we haven't moved in the same circles for years. Like I said, if you're after Jesse, you're after the wrong person. He's the most law-abiding and stand-up person I know."

"You'll forgive me if I don't immediately jump to believe you. That's pretty much what everyone says when asked about the people they think they know."

Two

"*Think* they know?" Cord didn't bother to keep the irritation out of his voice. "Since I've known the man most of my life, I can safely say I know Jesse Stevens pretty damn well, Ms. Warren."

"Zoe, please."

Oh, so she was attempting to play nice now? He let his gaze drift over her. He wouldn't have minded playing nice with her, if she'd been anything but a cop. She was exactly his type. Long and lean with sweet curves in just the right places. Even her short-cropped dark hair was sexy, and he bet it looked even sexier mussed up against a crisp white cotton-covered pillow. He shifted slightly in his seat as his body reacted in ways his mind was determined not to.

"The fact remains, I know my friend, *Zoe*," he said with emphasis. "And you're barking up the wrong tree."

She dragged in a deep breath, and he couldn't help but notice how her fitted shirt strained against the buttons across her chest. Oh yes, sweet curves all right. But off-limits, as was any woman serving in the police force. Cord let his gaze drift to the photo frame sitting on the antique sideboard across the room. Britney. God. Seeing her graduation picture from the police academy every day was a reminder of everything he'd lost. Her death two years ago, while on her first shift of active duty, had been soul destroying, and it was Jesse who'd kept him sane through that awful, dark time.

No, Jesse was not the kind of man to commit murder, and Cord would do whatever he could to ensure Detective Warren knew that. And, he reminded himself as he flicked his gaze back to the woman in front of him, if he ever embarked on a long-term relationship again, it wouldn't be with a woman who wore a badge and a gun and hunted down bad guys for a living. No matter how much his libido told him otherwise.

"Sometimes we're not always honest with the people we're closest to," she said in an obvious attempt to placate him. "Do you know when would be a good time for me to catch Mr. Stevens at home? I called on him earlier and no one was in."

"He runs a working ranch, so I guess it's safe to say there's never a good time. We have to make the most of the daylight hours available to us," Cord said, hedging, unwilling to give the woman more information than was absolutely necessary.

"Well, I caught you at home, didn't I? Mr. Galicia, are you being deliberately obstructive or is this just your charming way of treating all strangers?"

"Obstructive?" Cord felt a trickle of irritation at her insinuation. He wasn't being obstructive; he was being careful. They were two very different things.

"That's the usual terminology when someone deliberately withholds information."

He watched as she picked up her water glass and drained it. Her throat was long and slender, the muscles working delicately as she swallowed her drink. Damn if the sight of that pale column of skin didn't give him a hard-on. She snapped the glass back onto the table in front of her and rose on those enticingly long legs, then reached into her back pocket for a business card. She handed it to him as he hastened to stand.

"Call me if you suddenly remember how I can best reach Mr. Stevens," she said with a slight curl of her lip. "I'll be staying in Royal for a few days."

"Does the sheriff know you're in town?"

He could see she wanted to tell him that was none of his business, but instead she gave him a brusque nod.

"Of course," she said. "He's assisting in my inquiries."

Cord nodded. That made sense. The sheriff and the Hamm family went way back. "Maybe he can tell you how to get ahold of Jesse, since he's assisting you and all."

He couldn't resist goading her just a little. It rankled that she'd come out here without any notice on some jumped-up idea that Jesse was involved in Vincent Hamm's murder. The very thought was ridiculous. Jesse was the kind of guy to always bend over backward to help others, and Cord knew he'd gone the extra mile with Hamm on several occasions. And then the one time Jesse had to ask Hamm for a favor…

A frisson of warning prickled at the back of his mind. Was that what this was about? Had this woman unearthed something about Jesse asking Hamm a favor? A favor Hamm had refused to act on. Was that her angle? That Jesse had somehow been mad enough to exact revenge?

"I'm sure he will. Next time I talk to him, I'll be certain to get the lowdown on you, too."

"Me? Hey, you want to know about me, feel free to ask me anything." Cord spread his arms wide and quirked one corner of his lips up in a smile. "I'm an open book."

She sniffed. "Thank you for the water. No doubt I'll be speaking to you again."

The thought of seeing her again had its merits, but he doubted she meant what he was thinking.

"I'll look forward to it," he replied, imbuing into that handful of words enough innuendo to make Ms. Warren stiffen and give him a hard look.

"We'll see about that."

He led the way to the front door and watched her as she stepped onto the porch. There was a determined set to her shoulders, and he knew she wouldn't be deterred by him. One way or another she'd track Jesse down, and Cord didn't want it to be today. Jesse had enough on his plate with his sister's emergency surgery today. It had started out as routine to remove an inflamed appendix, but the dang thing had already ruptured, spilling infection through Janet's body. While she was receiving the best care possible, Jesse was beside himself with worry. Last thing Jesse needed was this detective visiting him in the hospital.

Maybe Cord could appeal to her good will, he thought. Just as the woman reached her grime-covered car, he called out.

"Jesse is at the hospital—that's why he's not at home right now. His sister had an operation today. There were complications. He's been there all day. A decent person would leave him be."

"Mr. Galicia, are you suggesting I'm not a decent person?" She cocked one brow as she raised the question.

"Well, that remains to be seen, doesn't it?" he challenged. "Give him a couple of days at least."

"And what do you suggest I do in the meantime? Paint my nails?"

He had to hand it to her. She didn't back down, not one bit. He probably shouldn't have told her about Jesse being at the hospital, but he'd hoped he could appeal to her sense of compassion. Surely she had one in there somewhere behind that blue-eyed deadpan stare of hers?

"Maybe we could have a drink or a meal somewhere?"

"Are you asking me on a date?"

The incredulity on her face would have been funny if it hadn't been so insulting.

"Sure, why not?"

For a second or two she looked totally at a loss for words. As a distraction tactic, asking her out clearly had merit, he thought with a quiet twinge of satisfaction. At least it appeared to have stopped her in her stride.

"What about it?" he pressed. "Tonight, just a drink. You can ask me anything you want."

"I can ask you anything I want anytime I want. I have a badge, remember?"

"What? Are you afraid of spending time with me?"

She snorted. "I'm not afraid of anything, Mr. Galicia. Especially not you. Sure, fine. What time and where?"

"Why don't I pick you up? Where're you staying?"

She named the motel.

"How about seven?" he asked, beginning to wonder what in hell he was letting himself in for.

"Seven is good."

Then, without another word, she got into her car and swung it around the circular driveway and back toward the main road. Cord watched until she went out of sight, then slowly closed the door to his house. His grandmother would have said he'd gone totally loco. Even he didn't understand fully what had prompted him to make the offer to Detective Warren, aside from the need to protect his best friend from her questioning. He flicked a look at his watch. Jesse said he'd be at the hospital until the nurses kicked him out. It would take the detective about forty minutes to get to town from here, then no doubt she'd want to fluff a bit like women did. She wouldn't have time to go to the hospital and bother Jesse, but just in case, Cord dragged his cell phone from his back pocket and thumbed a text to his friend.

How's Janet doing?

She's holding her own. They're talking about removing the breathing tube later tonight.

Cord felt a pang for his friend. Janet was the only family he had left, and to say he was protective of his younger sibling was an understatement. This hiccup with what should have been a routine procedure today had surely devastated him.

Good to hear. BTW, Houston detective in town asking questions about Hamm. I'm taking her out for a drink so she doesn't bother you.

Jesse's reply was swift.

LOL, taking one for the team? Such hardship. Is she pretty?

Trust his friend to ask the hard questions.

Yeah.

But she's a cop.

Yeah.

Do you know what you're doing?

Keeping her away from you, remember.

There was a pause, and Cord began to wonder if that was an end to their conversation, but then his phone pinged again.

Are you sure that's all?

You know my rules.

Okay. Don't do anything dumb.

As if. Hey, give Janet my love.

Will do. And let me know how your date goes.

It's not a date.

She's pretty. It's a date.

Cord rolled his eyes before texting his reply.

She's a cop. It's not a date. End of story.

He pocketed his phone and went to his room to get ready to head into town. But even as he changed into a good pair of jeans and a fitted shirt and splashed on a little cologne, he couldn't help but wonder why he was going to so much effort for the woman. Was it because he was trying to keep her distracted and away from Jesse, or was there something more? He snagged his car keys in one hand and headed toward the garage. There was only one way to find out.

Three

Zoe paced the confines of her motel room, wondering why the hell she'd agreed to this—whatever this was—with Cord Galicia. The man exuded pheromones like body odor. Both were equally unwelcome in her book. Galicia had been far too cagey about Stevens, and her own experience had shown that people don't generally hide something that doesn't need to be hidden. And even though he had said she could ask him anything she wanted, she doubted that would extend to more information about his neighbor.

She flicked a glance at the digital clock next to the bed. He'd be here any minute. As if she'd conjured him up merely by thinking about him, there was a firm knock at her door. She swung around and checked the peephole. Yup, just as sexy as the first time, she thought. She forced herself to take a deep, steadying breath before unlatching the chain and opening the door.

Even with the distance of a couple of hours, he still

packed the same punch. She'd never met a man before who had made her feel so darn feminine. She wanted to say she didn't like it, but there was something about the way the blood in her veins fizzed when he was around that she had to admit wasn't entirely unpleasant.

"Good evening," Galicia said, then bowed with a flourish. "Your chariot awaits."

"We're not walking?" she asked, stepping through the door and carefully locking it behind her.

"Nah, the place I'm taking you is on the other side of town."

"If you'd have said, I'd have met you there."

"What's the matter, Detective? Don't you trust me?"

She snorted. "I can handle you."

He gave her a sharp look that made her draw in a hasty breath. It was clear his mind had gone straight below the waist. Come to think of it, so had hers. Instead of giving in to the sudden roar of heat that flamed from deep inside her, she narrowed her gaze at him.

"Well, where's this chariot?"

He laughed, the sound a deep rumble that hit straight to her solar plexus. A delicious, lazy sound better suited to a bedroom than a parking lot beside a B-grade motel.

"Over here."

He gestured toward a classic F-150, and as they drew nearer, he opened the passenger door for her. She eyed the antique surface of the truck. Clearly left to go to rack and ruin at some point, the vehicle had been restored, but the paintwork remained aged and patchy—almost as if the rust was a badge of honor.

"Ranching not going so well?" she asked, casting an obvious eye over the multicolored hood.

"Let's just say I appreciate the patina of time. It's been

treated and clear coated. A testament to the age and longevity of the beast."

Zoe cast him a sideways glance. A somewhat romantic statement from a man who made his living from the land and the animals upon it. Eschewing further comment, she climbed up onto the front seat and waited while he closed her door and stepped around to the driver's side. The cab had seemed so spacious until he swung up beside her. Then his shoulders were suddenly too close to hers and the cologne he wore wove around her on subtle waves of body heat. She turned her head to the window, but it was no good. Her senses were powerfully attuned to him. She didn't need to see him to know that his leather jacket was so soft and worn that it fitted his shoulders like a second skin, or that the crisp denim of his jeans pulled across his hips when he sat at the wheel.

She also knew that no matter where she was, she'd never again smell that scent and not think of him. Of the raw masculinity he exuded in his simple stance, or the latent power in his hands, the teasing in his eyes, the sardonic curl of his lip. She gave herself a mental shake. What the hell was she doing, thinking of him in these terms? Right now, he was someone of interest in her inquiries. Someone to question, not drool over. She was not that weak nor that vulnerable.

But it had been a while since she'd been intimate with anyone, and, she reminded herself bluntly, a woman had needs. Needs, it seemed, that were hell-bent on distracting her from her job. Well, she owed it to her victim to get to the bottom of who was behind his murder—and to bring them to justice.

They hadn't driven long before Galicia pulled up the truck outside a small hotel.

"This is us," he said, getting out of the truck and walking around to her side.

To preempt him opening her door, she did it herself and dropped down onto the pavement. She'd keep her distance from him, get whatever information she needed and then she'd be on her way. She didn't want to stay here in Royal any longer than necessary. It might be a thriving town, it might even be civilized, but it wasn't her city. These weren't her people. Especially not the tall, commanding figure walking beside her as they entered the hotel and headed toward the bar.

If she wasn't mistaken, there was a brief flare of approval in his eyes. Not that she cared. She wasn't here to impress him. He gave her a brief nod and put a hand at the small of her back, guiding her toward the bar. As they entered, he gestured to one side of the room.

"We'll sit over there."

She noted he made it a gentle order, not a suggestion. Okay, so he thought he was in charge. It was his turf. She'd play his game. For now.

"What's your poison?" Galicia asked as they reached their seats. "No, wait, let me guess."

She played along, watching as he stroked his chin and eyed her thoughtfully.

"Something frilly to counteract the tough-cop act."

"I assure you, it's no act—and you'd be wrong. I'll have a beer."

She couldn't help but notice the attention paid to him by the waitress who hurried over to take their order, but aside from a polite "thanks," he paid the woman no heed. Instead, he kept his searing focus very firmly on Zoe. The waitress was back in a moment, two chilled glasses and two ice-cold longneck lagers on her tray. She set the drinks onto the table in front of them.

"So, Cord, did you want these on your tab or—" the waitress started.

"I'll take care of them," Zoe said, flicking some bills from her pocket and dropping them onto the woman's tray. "Keep the change."

The waitress looked from Cord to Zoe and back again, Obviously she wasn't used to Cord's dates picking up the tab. She left as Cord picked up a beer, poured it into Zoe's glass and did the same for himself.

"You're quick," Cord said with a quirk of his lips. "I appreciate it. Thank you."

"I pay my way."

"Gender equality and all that?"

"You drove, I bought the first round. Gender equality has nothing to do with it." She arched a brow at him as he chuckled softly. "Are you deliberately trying to irritate me? Because if so, you'll find I'm hard to put off."

"I'm definitely not trying to put you off."

He smiled again, the movement of his lips sending a sucker punch to her gut. How did he manage to have such a strong effect on her? This was crazy. She'd been out with plenty of men, had relationships with a few, but she'd never felt this intense, visceral response before. It made her feel vulnerable, as if she were cast slightly adrift, and she didn't like it one bit. Determined to maintain the upper hand, she took charge of the conversation.

"So, how long have you lived around Royal?" she asked.

"Ah, the inquisition continues," he drawled. He sat back in his chair, hooking one arm over the back, and gazed at her through narrowed eyes.

"Inquisition?"

"Yeah, it's what you do, isn't it? Grill people?"

"Like dressed in black leather with torture implements and stuff like that?"

His lips quirked again, sending a spiral of sensation curling through her lower body. Oh, that mouth. How would it feel against hers? How would he taste?

"I could see you in that getup."

She snorted a laugh. "In your dreams, buster. So, back to my question. How long have you lived here?"

His nostrils flared on an indrawn breath. "Am I wet off the back of the truck, do you mean?"

She rolled her eyes. He was needling her, twisting her words to sound like a veiled insult. That might be the angle some of her colleagues would have taken, given there was no mistaking Galicia's Mexican heritage. But she was not that kind of person. In fact, none of her family was.

"Look, I asked you a simple question. You're being deliberately evasive again." She lifted her glass and took a long sip of her beer, relishing the bite of hoppy flavor as it rolled over her tongue and down her throat. "I'm not sure what you call conversation in this neck of Texas, but where I come from, when we meet a person, we chat, ask questions. Y'know, get to know one another."

He nodded slowly. "We have similar customs here."

She fought back a laugh. "I wouldn't have guessed it. Maybe it'd help if I went first? I'm Houston born and raised. Youngest of five. Third-generation cop. Your turn."

"Royal born and raised. Only child. My grandparents came here, bought land, ranched it, expanded the ranch. My father took over, did more of the same."

She nodded. "And you? Still expanding?"

He shrugged. "Not in land, more in better ways to use it."

She sat back in her chair and felt herself relax as he began to open up and discuss a little of how he planned to diversify his business operations. She let his voice roll over her, enjoying the timbre and the slow, measured way in which he spoke. She gestured to the waitress for two more beers.

"Let me get those," he said.

"If you insist," she acceded.

Once the drinks were on their table, she decided to turn the conversation back to her investigation.

"So, you and Jesse Stevens. You guys grew up together?"

"Yeah. And he's not the man you're looking for."

Ha, so much for softening him up and then pouncing with a question, Zoe admitted to herself with a measure of reluctance. Cord Galicia may have relaxed with her, but it didn't mean his mind wasn't as alert as a fox's.

"Why are you protecting him?"

"Protecting him?" Cord laughed. "Nope, I'm just saving you time."

"You realize I have to question him."

"Why? Is my word not good enough?" Galicia challenged her.

She saw the latent anger that simmered beneath the surface. Was it because she wanted to question his friend, or because she was impugning his honor by not accepting his word?

"I'm sure your word is just fine." She sighed. "But that's not how we conduct an investigation."

Silence stretched between them, and for a moment Zoe thought the evening was over. She felt a pang of regret. If she'd met this man under any other circumstances, then maybe they could have explored this simmering attraction that burned between them. She watched Galicia's face carefully, but he gave nothing away. Eventually, he leaned forward and put his hand out.

"How about a truce, then?" he suggested.

"A truce? I didn't know we were at war."

"Oh, we're at something, but I'm not quite sure what it is yet. How about, while we find out, we agree that you won't ask me anything about Jesse and then I won't need to stonewall you?"

She hesitated a moment before taking his hand. If she did this, she was opening herself up for a whole lot of trouble. She could feel it in her gut. But then again, what was life if it meant not taking risks? She reached out her hand and felt a surge of awareness the moment their palms touched. He felt it, too; she could see it in his eyes. He wasn't smiling now; in fact, he looked serious—serious about her.

Her inner muscles clenched on a wave of pure lust. Right now, she wanted to do nothing more than lean across their table, sweep their drinks aside and reach for him, then drag his face to hers and plant her lips on his mouth in a deep, drugging kiss that would hopefully assuage some of this crazy pent-up tension he manifested in her.

Instead, she jerked her hand free and reached for her beer, downing half of it. When she looked back at Galicia, amusement reflected back at her in his gaze and she knew, in that instant, he was dangerous. Maybe not in the criminal sense of the word, but certainly in terms of her equilibrium.

She was a long, tall streak of trouble. He knew that as surely as he knew the head count of his herd. But he couldn't leave her alone. Even now, after that stupid handshake, he wanted to touch her again—and not just her hand. He wanted to see if those pert breasts he could see pushing against the fabric of her shirt would fit neatly into the palms of his hands. He wanted to trace the cord of her throat with his lips and his tongue, to taste her and inhale the very essence of her.

Damn, but she did things to him that twisted his gut in knots without even trying. Which meant he had to be doubly careful. He was breaking every single one of his own rules by taking her out tonight. Still, it wasn't as if he was going to marry her or anything dumb like that, he told himself. He was distracting her. Keeping her away from Jesse. She had no business with his friend, and the sooner she realized that and returned to Houston, the sooner he could get back to his normal life. Thank goodness things were a little quieter on the ranch right now. The calves had been dried out and had regained condition. His pastures were under control and his hands were onto the usual maintenance required before winter set in. He had time to spare and he'd make sure he used it well.

"Say, you want to grab a burger or something?" Cord asked before finishing off his beer.

"I could eat a burger," Zoe admitted.

"C'mon, the Royal Diner makes the best burgers in the state."

"That's quite a claim," she said, rising from her seat.

"It's no claim. It's a fact," he boasted.

Putting his hand at the small of her back again, he guided her to the door. He liked the way she moved, all smooth and lithe, her gait a match for his own. His mind flashed in an instant to how they would move together—on a dance floor, between the sheets of his extra wide bed. Damn if he didn't get a hard-on. He reminded himself that this wasn't just about him. This was about keeping Zoe Warren away from his best friend.

Cord knew Jesse had been in touch with Hamm before Hamm's tragic death. He also knew Jesse had been fired up about the guy. If Zoe figured that out, she'd likely put two and two together and make whatever the hell she wanted out of it. There was no way Jesse had killed Hamm. He might have been mad at the guy, but violence had never been Jesse's style, not even when truly provoked.

They reached the truck, and he held her door for her. She brushed by so close he could smell the scent of her shampoo or whatever it was she'd used in her hair. It made him want to lean in and inhale more deeply. To touch her short black hair and see if he could tangle his fingers in it as he brought her face to his. He must have made a sound, because Zoe stopped midway getting into the truck.

"You okay?" she asked.

"Never better."

"Hmm."

She swung up, giving him an all-too-brief glimpse of her sweet butt showcased in dark denim. He closed the door firmly and went around to his side, all the while wondering what on earth he'd let himself in for.

Four

The woman had an appetite, Cord observed admiringly as she tucked into a double beef burger with all the trimmings. He'd ordered the same for himself. He nodded at a few of the people he knew as they went by, but mostly his attention was on the woman seated opposite him in the booth.

"Nice place, even better food," Zoe said when she finished her first bite.

"It's a staple here in Royal. You're always guaranteed a good meal."

"I like it. Thanks for bringing me here."

The simple compliment with her thanks made him feel ridiculously proud.

"So, tell me more about yourself," he said. "You mentioned you're the youngest of five? Is that right?"

"Yeah. I like to tell everyone that my mom and dad tried five times before they got the mixture right. My brothers would disagree. If they ever listened to me, that is."

Cord smiled. "Wow, four brothers. I can't even begin to imagine what that was like growing up."

As an only child whose future running the family spread was clearly outlined from birth, he had often wondered what it would have been like to share the load with one or more siblings. But from what he'd seen with a lot of his peers, siblings were overrated. Zoe spent the rest of their meal regaling him with stories of the things her brothers got up to while trying to keep her in line. Emphasis on the word *trying*. Seems she'd been a handful as a kid, and Cord wouldn't mind betting she hadn't changed much.

They were lingering over coffee when he saw her fight back a yawn. It made him realize the time—nearly ten. While that wasn't late, when you'd done a five-hour drive, like she had, or in his case, been up since before the crack of dawn, it was definitely time to bring the evening to an end.

"It's getting late. I'd best get you to your bed."

His choice of words had color flaming in her cheeks. He felt an answering wave of heat pulse through his body, too. To distract them both, he signaled for the check and paid, without demur from his guest this time, and they went out to the truck. When they reached her motel, he got down from the truck and walked her to her door.

"Thank you for dinner," Zoe said after opening her motel room and flicking on the light. "I enjoyed the company. It can get lonely on trips like this."

"Happy to help you pass the time," he drawled in response.

Even though he'd chosen his words to tease, oddly, he meant it. He'd engineered tonight to keep her away from Jesse but found himself enjoying her company. Hell, if he was totally honest, enjoying her. The air grew thick and heavy between them as she looked up into his eyes. Without thinking, Cord raised one hand and slid it around the back of her neck as he lowered his face to hers and gave in to the impulse to see if she tasted as good as he'd been imagining all evening.

He felt the shock that rippled through her body as his fingers touched the bare skin at her nape. Felt the sense of hesitation before her lips parted and she kissed him back. He'd been wrong. She tasted far better than he could ever have imagined, and somewhere along the line their kiss went from a questing beginning to something hot and hard and hungry. It was as if they were combustible elements, drawn together into a conflagration that took them both by surprise.

Zoe made a sound, like a deep hum, and he was lost. He wanted her—all of her. Forget she was a cop, forget she was investigating his best friend and most likely him, as well. Forget everything but the sweet, spicy flavor of her mouth, the softness of her lips and the urgency that pulled them together.

He snaked one arm around her waist, hauling her to him. Being tall, she lined up against his body perfectly, her hips against his, her mound pressing on his erection. She rolled her hips, and he groaned involuntarily. The subtle pressure of her body against his was driving him to the brink of his control. If this was what she could do to him clothed, imagine what they could do to each other naked.

Her hands slid over his shoulders; her fingers clenched on the leather of his jacket as he deepened the kiss. When his tongue tasted hers, she shuddered from head to foot. He did it again. Ah yes, there was that little hum from deep in her throat. She wasn't a passive woman. She gave back as good as he'd given. Her tongue was now dueling with his. And then she was pulling him through the doorway. Together they shuffled over the threshold. He kicked the motel room door closed behind them and spun her to push her up against the door.

Lacing his fingers with hers, he lifted her hands up so they were against the door on either side of her head. Then he bent and kissed a hot trail of wet sucking kisses from her lips to her finely boned jawline and down the sweet cords of her neck. Beneath his touch he felt her heated skin jump as sensation transferred from his touch to her. He let go of one of her hands and cupped her breast through her shirt, groaning in frustration as he felt the pebbled nipple against his palm.

This wasn't enough. He needed to touch her properly, without the barrier of clothing. His hand was at her buttons before he knew he'd even formed the thought clearly. In his haste he realized he'd torn one button loose from her shirt entirely when he heard the faint sound as it hit the carpet at their feet. But even that couldn't stop him in his pursuit of the need to see her naked. The front of her shirt fell open and he tugged the tails from her waistband and shoved the fabric aside.

He sucked in a sharp breath. She wore a black lace bra under that almost-masculine shirt of hers. The woman was a total contradiction. Touch-me-not plain clothing and lingerie made for sin beneath it.

"What do you think you're doing?" she asked, her breathing ragged.

"What does it look like I'm doing, Detective? I'm undertaking an investigation of my own," he growled.

He reached to cup one of her breasts in his large hand. Yeah, she fit like she was made for him. Rubbing his thumb across her distended nipple, he leaned in and buried his face against her skin and inhaled deeply.

"You smell so good. I could lose myself in you, Zoe Warren. Fair warning."

The hand he'd freed stroked down the front of his body until she cupped his erection through his jeans. "Looks like I have something to scrutinize here, myself."

He flexed against her, enjoying her boldness. "You gotta do what you gotta do, right?" he chuckled.

The sound strangled in his throat as she tightened her grip on him. She wasn't shy, but then neither was he. He gently tugged down the lacy cup of her bra, exposing her breast to his mouth. Taking her nipple carefully between his teeth, he rolled the nub with his tongue. Zoe's head fell back against the door and she moaned. Letting her other hand go, he reached behind her back to loosen the hooks of her bra. He was still impeded by the straps remaining over her shoulders, but at least now he could shove the enticing garment up, exposing both her breasts to his starving gaze.

Her nipples were a dark raspberry pink, topping luscious creamy skin. He kissed one, then the other, his hands cupping her from underneath as he divided his attention between them. Zoe had let go of him, her fingers now knotted in his hair, holding him to her as if she never wanted to let go. That was fine by him, he decided as he let one hand drop to the fastening of her jeans. He swiftly undid the button and pushed down her zipper before reaching inside.

He felt the heat of her before he even reached the damp lace at the juncture of her thighs. It was a tight fit, his large hand inside her jeans, but it was worth the discomfort to feel how hot she was for him, how ready. His own arousal grew to painful proportions as he touched her through the lace, pressed on that spot that made her cry out in pleasure.

He took her mouth again in a deep, intoxicating kiss, his tongue probing her mouth in time to the pressure of his fingers on her down below. She pressed into him, as if she couldn't get close enough, and then, in a sudden rush of heat, he felt her climax against his hand.

It took every ounce of control not to come in his jeans as she shuddered beneath his touch. Instead, he used his caresses to gentle her, as he would one of his horses, with slow sweeps of his hands—drawing out her pleasure, prolonging his own torture. He knew it would take only a moment to unfasten his jeans, sheath himself and drive into her heat right here against the motel room door. But when he made love to her properly—and he knew he would sometime, hopefully very soon—it would be in a large comfortable bed where he could truly explore what they could achieve together.

Cord straightened her clothing and kissed her again. "I'd better go."

"Go?"

For the first time since he'd met her, she sounded unsure.

"Yeah, I'll be seeing you soon."

With that, he moved her bodily away from the door and opened it. He strode straight to his truck and got immediately inside, no mean feat when he had a hard-on that made his jeans uncomfortably tight as he settled himself into the drive home. He hazarded just one look at the motel room door before he backed out of the parking space. She stood there, holding the front of her shirt together with a bemused expression on her face.

Good, let her be bemused. While he might be in agony and his balls might be blue, he'd left with the upper hand. Let her think on that for a while.

Zoe rose the next morning still mad. She should never have let him kiss her, let alone touch her like that. And she'd climaxed, right there against the motel room door, she thought, staring balefully at the unassuming slab of wood. She never came like that—so quick, so intense.

Even now, thinking about it, she felt a tingle of anticipation all over again. Damn Cord Galicia for being so clever with his hands. *And don't forget his lips and tongue*, her subconscious oh-so-helpfully supplied.

This was hopeless. She needed to get out of here and do something, anything, to replace the memories Cord had instilled in her last night. She wondered how he'd felt as he'd left—whether he'd taken care of himself later once he'd gotten home. Perhaps in the shower, with hot water coursing over his body like a lover's caress. It was all too easy to picture in her mind and all too distracting, again.

She strode angrily to the bathroom. It was basic but, like the rest of the motel room, clean and functional. Besides, with how uptight she was feeling right now, there was no way she was going for comfort. Setting the shower to as cold as she could bear, she got under the spray and pulled the curtain across to encapsulate herself in the small space. She lathered up quickly and rinsed off, skimming her body with her hands and determinedly pushing back the memories of another set of hands on her pale skin. Of broad suntanned fingers touching and teasing her body, of those same fingers coaxing responses from her that had left her limp and sated and hungry for more at the same time.

It angered her that she'd been that easy. She'd come to Royal to further her investigation, not to have meltingly hot sex against a motel room door. And what was with that? Where had all her good sense gone? She'd been the one to drag him across the threshold and into her room. And when he kissed her, she kissed him back, as if she'd been starving for that level of attention. Okay, so maybe that bit was true, she admitted ruefully as she snapped off the shower and reached for her towel. It had been a while, and she'd never been the type to enjoy casual encounters. Her work made maintaining a relationship difficult at the best of times. She worked long hours, dedicated to both her team and to the victims whose stories she had to uncover. And that was what she was here for, she reminded herself sternly as she wiped her still-tingling body dry. Work, not play.

By the time she was dressed, she realized she was starving. She'd spied a coffee shop when she'd driven into town yesterday. It might be a good place for her to formulate her plan of attack for today. She still needed to get ahold of Jesse Stevens and actually talk to the man. She got into her car and, using the hands-free kit, called the number she had for the Stevens ranch. This time she got a staff member, but she still wasn't able to speak to Jesse. Frustrated, Zoe drove to the coffee shop.

She got a parking space right out front and walked up to the café, laughing under her breath at the name, the Daily Grind. Her nostrils were assailed with the delicious aroma of freshly roasted coffee beans the moment she entered. She ordered her coffee and a Danish and took a seat looking out the front window. Royal was a busy place, she realized, as people headed on their daily commute to work and school. The Daily Grind was no less busy as people stopped in for their morning coffee on their way to work, or settled in for a quick breakfast. When her coffee and Danish came, she took her time enjoying the flavors and skimmed the news on her phone. It looked like the Houston papers were still bemoaning the lack of progress in the Hamm murder.

She knew it wasn't personal—they had little to go on, but even so it irked her intensely that they hadn't been able to discover more by now. A heading regarding the Texas Cattleman's Club caught her eye. It looked like the official opening would be going ahead next month. No doubt that would be a glittering affair with all of Houston's who's who of anything important in attendance. She wondered about the guy who'd featured as an early suspect in the Hamm case—Sterling Perry. A leading contender for the presidency of the new club, he was an arrogant piece of work who wore his family's wealth like a second skin. She would have loved to have seen his ass nailed when her colleagues had arrested him on suspicion of operating a Ponzi scheme, but he'd been cleared of that. Even when he'd been suspected of being involved in Hamm's murder there'd been nothing to support the initial leads—the guy was like Teflon. Nothing stuck.

And then there was the other guy vying for the presidential role, Ryder Currin. Younger than Sterling Perry, Currin was far more charismatic and her research had shown he'd come into most of his money through sheer, hard work. Even now, despite his millions, the guy dressed as if he'd just stepped off the ranch. Zoe had wondered if the rivalry between the men had anything to do with Hamm's murder, but Ryder Currin had an airtight alibi for the window of time when Hamm was murdered. He'd been stranded at a local shelter when the storm hit and Angela Perry, Sterling Perry's daughter, had been there, too, and had vouched for him.

Zoe consumed her Danish and knocked back her coffee before leaving a tip and returning to her car. Maybe she'd have better luck tracking Stevens down at the hospital. Cord had told her his sister was there.

The Royal Memorial Hospital was easy to find, and visitor parking was relatively empty at this early hour. No doubt because visiting hours weren't until later in the day, she realized. She clipped her badge onto her waistband and went inside, knowing that the badge might give her access she would otherwise not get.

Sure enough, she was shown through to a ward where

Janet Stevens was recovering. The young woman was in a room on her own—apparently having been moved there not long before, after a brief stint in ICU post surgery. That was obviously why Cord had been so protective of his friend, knowing the other man must have been worried about his sibling. Galicia's protectiveness was, at its heart, an admirable trait, except for the part where he'd attempted to stall her investigation.

It made her wonder anew if that incident between them last night hadn't just been a distraction tactic. Something to blur her mind and keep her off Stevens's trail. Maybe he'd thought the little woman would be so blown away by what he'd done to her that she'd even hightail it back home.

Zoe discarded the thought almost as quickly as it bloomed in her mind. She'd been the one to pull him into her room, not the other way around. If anything, she was to blame for what had happened between them. And he'd been the one to walk away, unfulfilled. What did that say about the man? She shook her head. He was a conundrum, that was for sure. One she wouldn't have minded exploring further, if the circumstances had been different. But they weren't, and she had a job to do.

Zoe presented her badge to the duty nurse and asked if she could have a few words with Janet Stevens. The nurse was cagey, but after a quick call to Janet's doctor she said that Zoe was allowed five minutes, no more. Grateful for that, Zoe entered the younger woman's room.

Janet Stevens was pale but breathing without assistance. Walking farther into the room, Zoe watched the other woman as she opened her eyes.

"Good morning, Ms. Stevens. How are you feeling today?"

"Okay, I guess."

Janet's voice was groggy, as if she was still on some heavy-duty pain relief.

"I won't take much of your time," Zoe said quickly and introduced herself, explaining why she was there. "I'm sorry to bother you, but I can't seem to get ahold of your brother. I need to ask him a few questions."

"About Vincent? Whatever for? I know Jesse was mad at him, but he would never have hurt him," Janet protested.

"Can you tell me why your brother was mad at Mr. Hamm?" Zoe pressed, feeling a surge of excitement that she might finally be getting closer to finding some of the answers she needed.

"It's all my fault," Janet said weakly. "Jesse asked Vincent if he could return a favor and find me an internship at Perry Holdings. I've completed my MBA and Jesse thought Vincent would be decent about helping me. Turns out that while he was happy to accept Jesse's help plenty of times, he wasn't so keen to return the favor."

Would that have been enough to make Jesse Stevens commit murder? People killed over less. And it depended on the level of help Stevens had extended to Hamm in the past and what he thought the dead man owed him. She needed to meet the man to gauge for herself. A sound at the door had her looking up. Seemed she'd be meeting Jesse Stevens sooner rather than later, judging by the thunderous appearance on the face of the man entering the room.

"Who the hell are you and what are you doing in my sister's room?" he growled.

He was tall, blond like the girl in the bed beside her and he had piercing green eyes that looked as if they could cut through steel. His sister lifted a hand.

"Jesse, please," she implored gently.

"Detective Zoe Warren, Houston P.D.," Zoe said, gesturing to her badge on her waistband. "And you are?"

Even though she knew exactly who he was, it was important to her to establish who was in control.

"Jesse Stevens."

He answered bluntly, without offering his hand. It seemed she was persona non grata. A tiny smile curled her lips. Good, she liked knowing she'd riled him from the outset. Holding the upper hand was always her chosen starting point.

"Ah, Mr. Stevens. I've been trying to get ahold of you. Didn't you get my messages?"

A faint flush of color marked his cheeks. "I did."

She maintained her silence while raising one brow at him. His flush deepened. Just then, the nurse who'd directed Zoe to Janet's room appeared in the door and gave Zoe a stern look.

"Ms. Stevens needs to rest," she said pointedly.

"Thank you, I'm just leaving. Mr. Stevens, can I have a word with you outside?" Zoe asked.

"One minute, that's all."

Well, we'll see about that, Zoe thought to herself as she preceded him into the hallway outside his sister's room.

"Is there somewhere we could speak privately?" Zoe asked the nurse.

The woman gestured to a small sitting room down the hallway.

"C'mon," Zoe said to Stevens. "The sooner we get started, the sooner you can get back to your sister."

Realizing he had no reason to object, he fell into step behind her. Once they were in the room, Zoe closed the door behind him.

"What do you want?" Jesse asked, his voice and stance both belligerent.

"Just need to ask you a few questions."

"Ever heard of email?"

Zoe snorted lightly. "It's a strange thing," she said slowly. "We cops prefer to do things face-to-face. You can learn a lot about a person that way. So, tell me, why have you been avoiding me? Got something to hide?"

Anger flashed in his eyes for a moment before he visibly dragged himself under control.

"I have nothing to hide. What's this about?"

"Vincent Hamm." She threw the name into the conversation as if it were a gauntlet thrown in challenge.

"I knew him. What about it?"

"Been in touch with him lately?" she probed.

His gaze grew flat and cold. "Not for a few months. Why?"

"And when was the last time you spoke with him?"

"To be honest with you, I haven't spoken to him in a long time." Stevens huffed out a breath and rubbed his cheeks with one long-fingered hand.

Zoe grabbed her notebook out of her jacket pocket and flipped through a few pages before citing a date from a couple of months ago.

"Does that date sound familiar?"

"No more than any other date," Stevens replied.

"What about this—*Thanks for nothing, Hamm*. Do you remember saying that?"

"That's what this is about? A phone message?"

"Answer the question, please."

"Yeah, I remember saying that."

"You sounded pretty pissed off."

"Look, it isn't what you're thinking."

"And what am I thinking, Mr. Stevens?"

"How the hell would I know? You're a cop. It's bound to be bad, right?"

"Mr. Hamm is dead. I want to know how he came to be that way."

Stevens, to his credit, looked stunned. “You think I did it?”

“I’m not sure what to think right now,” Zoe said honestly. “But you’re not helping your case by being evasive with me. Let me warn you, Mr. Stevens. I am very good at my job, and I will get to the bottom of this.”

“Look, it wasn’t me. I wasn’t anywhere near Houston when he was killed.”

“So, you know exactly when he was killed?” she asked pointedly.

“Of course I don’t. Look, whatever happened to him, I had no part of it. In fact, I was at a stock auction, buying cattle. I’ve even got receipts to prove it.”

“Perhaps you would like to inform me what part you do have in my investigation during a formal interview to which you can bring those receipts.”

Stevens rubbed his face again. “Sure, when?”

“Let me talk to Sheriff Battle. I’ll work something out with him and I’ll be in touch. And this time…?”

“Yeah?”

“Answer your damn phone.”

Five

Cord's phone chimed to signal an incoming message. It was from Jesse.

Met your new girlfriend today.

Cord tapped the icon that would ring Jesse's phone. Texting was all well and good but sometimes you just needed to talk. This was definitely one of those times. His friend answered on the second ring.

"Is Janet doing okay now?" Cord asked.

No matter how mad he was right now, certain things needed to be taken care of first.

"Yeah, surprisingly well, considering how sick she was straight after surgery. They moved her onto the ward this morning before I got there. Gave me a heart attack to get up to ICU and find she wasn't there."

"I bet."

After Jesse and Janet's parents died, the two of them became even closer, since all they had left was each other. Cord could only imagine how Jesse must have felt to find Janet missing from the room where she'd been taken after surgery.

"I was surprised to see your girlfriend had beaten me there, though."

"I don't have a girlfriend," he enunciated carefully.

Even so, he knew exactly who Jesse was talking about, and the slow burn of fury rose from deep within. She hadn't listened to a word he'd said. Not only had she not stayed away from Jesse, she'd gone to the hospital and bothered Janet while she was at it. He rode the wave of anger for a few long seconds. Jesse was talking, but the buzz in Cord's ears made him sound like he was some distance away. Eventually Jesse's words sank in.

"She's a mighty fine-looking woman, even if she is a pain in the ass. Had some questions for me and wouldn't leave until she'd asked them."

"She questioned you? There at the hospital?"

She had nerve, he'd give her that.

"Yup, and I've agreed to an interview at the sheriff's office, too."

"You don't need to do that." Cord bristled. "And if you do, make sure you take your lawyer."

"I don't need my lawyer, Cord. No matter how much I wanted to wring the guy's neck, I did not kill Vincent Hamm."

"I know you didn't. Aside from the fact you're not that kind of guy, weren't you away around that time?"

Jesse made a sound of assent. "I've got nothing to hide, and the sooner your girlfriend realizes that, the better."

"Like I said, she's not my girlfriend."

Jesse chuckled. "But there's something going on, isn't there?"

The man was too damn astute. Yeah, there was something, but even he couldn't define the way Zoe Warren had crawled under his skin.

"She's a cop. Trust me, there's nothing going on," Cord said firmly.

"If you say so."

Their conversation drifted to ranching matters, and they eventually finished their call. Cord pocketed his phone and felt tension coil within his body. He wanted nothing more right now than to take his horse to the open pastures and go for a blistering ride. Anything to expend this pent-up energy that resided in a red-hot knot in the center of his gut.

He still couldn't believe the nerve of Detective Warren. The idea that the woman he'd left trembling last night had calmly gotten up this morning and gone straight to the hospital made him so mad he needed to do something to work it off. Preferably something to do with her. The random thought struck him square in the solar plexus, robbing him of breath. He strode through the house and out to the stables, the ride he'd been thinking of at the forefront of his mind. But then halfway through saddling up his favorite gelding, he hesitated and pulled his cell phone from his pocket.

Since he'd left Zoe Warren last night, he'd all but talked himself into staying away from her, but it seemed that would have to take a back seat. He needed to talk to the woman and set her straight about a few things. Clearly she hadn't been listening yesterday. He needed to ensure she listened to him today.

Zoe spent much of the middle part of the day back in her motel room working on her computer and going over all the information she had to date. No matter which way she looked at things, the answers she sought remained very firmly out of reach. She put in a call to her boss and apprised him of where she was so far. His response had not been heartening. Zoe's stomach grumbled, bemoaning the fact she hadn't picked up anything for lunch, when her reminder pinged to say it was time to meet the sheriff at the diner.

Her mouth watered the minute she set foot in the place. A wave from a booth near the front windows drew her attention, and she walked over to the sheriff and stuck out her hand.

"Sheriff Battle, good to see you again."

The sheriff stood and took her hand. "Call me Nate."

His grip was firm and dry, and unlike a lot of men she met in the line of duty, he didn't seem to feel the need to exert pressure and dominance over her by crushing the bones in her hands with the introductory gesture.

"Something sure smells good here," Zoe commented as she slid into the seat opposite him.

"I can recommend the pie. Of course, I am biased. This is my wife's business." He patted his firm stomach. "Hell of a job staying fit with that temptation in my life."

Zoe laughed. A waitress came over and poured her a coffee. She smiled her thanks and ordered a slice of pie to go with it. So what if it wasn't exactly healthy to eat pie for lunch this late in the day? A woman deserved a treat every now and then, right?

When the pie was delivered, she quickly sampled a bite and closed her eyes and made a blissful sound deep in her throat.

"Told you it was good," the sheriff said laconically as he leaned back against the red faux-leather booth.

"You weren't lying," Zoe agreed, quickly scooping up

another bite before putting her fork down and dabbing at her mouth with a paper napkin. It was time she got to the point. "What can you tell me about Jesse Stevens?"

"Jesse?" Nate Battle looked puzzled for all of two seconds. "I thought you were after Sterling Perry?"

"He's been cleared. So, Stevens?"

"You think he's got something to do with Vincent's murder?"

His tone was cautious, as if he was sounding her out, even though he clearly didn't believe she was on the right track. She explained about the voice mail message Stevens had left, then played the sound file from her phone.

"He sure sounds annoyed," the sheriff said mildly. "But that doesn't mean he did anything."

"You don't think he's capable of murder?" Zoe challenged.

"I didn't say that."

"But?" She knew he was leaving more unsaid.

"I just can't see it. The man's a hard worker, keeps to himself when necessary, steps up for the community through the Texas Cattleman's Club on a regular basis. But murder? No. Jesse's not the kind of guy to hold a grudge."

"Well, we'll see about that when I interview him."

Between her and the sheriff they arranged a suitable day and time. She wasn't worried that Jesse would run out of town. His devotion to his sister had been more than clear. He wouldn't be leaving her while she was in the hospital, and judging by how frail the young woman was, she'd probably need some continued care at home, too. There was no way Jesse was leaving anytime soon.

Thinking about Jesse led her thoughts to his neighbor. The guy had been defensive on his friend's behalf yesterday—and very distracting last night every time she'd tried to draw the conversation toward her investigation. Thinking about it this morning, once her mind had cleared from the unaccustomed haze of sensual fog he'd wrapped her in, she'd begun to wonder if his attention to her wasn't part of some greater scheme to distract her from her purpose.

"What do you know about Cord Galicia?" she blurted.

Battle gave her a strange look. Maybe because the instant she'd asked the question she felt heat begin to rise from her chest and up her throat. If she wasn't mistaken, she'd be breaking out in the nervous blotches of color that used to be her curse when she was a teenager facing a stressful situation.

"Cord? Well, he's Jesse's neighbor. They grew up together. Help one another out when necessary. They even learned to fly together back when they were in their late teens."

"But what about the man himself?"

The waitress came and poured the sheriff another coffee, and he took his time doctoring it how he liked it before he responded.

"He's a decent guy. You don't think he did it, do you? He and Jesse are tight, but Cord wouldn't commit murder for him."

"I don't know. Galicia was very protective of Stevens when I questioned him yesterday."

"You questioned him yesterday?" He blew out a breath. "You sure didn't waste any time upsetting the locals, did you? I thought we'd agreed to talk before you started questioning people."

She heard the note of censure in his voice. "I just wanted to get a feel for where people were situated on this thing. You can appreciate that my goal is to find whoever is guilty of Hamm's murder and charge them accordingly. I'm not here on vacation."

"I get that, but don't go off like a steer at a gate. Upset

folks and they'll close ranks and you'll get nothing out of them."

Zoe closed her eyes and breathed in deeply before opening them again. "I'm just doing my job. I've been living and breathing this case for months now. I want it solved."

"If it can be solved."

She didn't want to admit it, but he was right. "Yeah, there's that, too. The longer this takes, the harder it's going to be to find the evidence we need. Everything was compromised in the flood."

The sheriff's phone buzzed on the table in front of him and he glanced at the screen.

"I'm sorry, I'm going to have to take that."

"Go ahead."

She watched as he answered the call and got up to pace the sidewalk outside the diner. After a few minutes he shoved the phone into his pocket and came back inside.

"I have to go. Get in touch with my office to arrange a time to use the interview room. They'll make sure you have all the equipment you need."

"Thanks, Sheriff. I appreciate it."

"And call me before you go questioning my people, okay? You may actually get a better result if I come along with you."

"Noted, thanks."

She finished her pie and lingered over another coffee before heading to the sheriff's department, where she arranged to interview Jesse using their equipment. Apparently it would take a day or two to set up, because their camera and recording equipment were glitchy. While the news was frustrating, there was nothing she could do about it other than wait. There were probably worse places to cool her heels for a few days. The problem was she couldn't think of any right now.

* * *

Cord felt a whole ton better after a hard ride, but the irritation he'd felt over Zoe confronting Jesse at the hospital still prickled under his skin. He grabbed his phone and scrolled through his saved numbers, then punched the one he was looking for with a determined index finger. It rang three times before going to voice mail. Ha, she was avoiding him, was she? He contemplated hanging up without leaving a message, but where was the fun in that? Instead, he forced himself to smile as he spoke.

"I couldn't sleep last night for thinking about you. Call me."

Hopefully his message would rile her enough for her to call him. If not, well, he'd be paying her a visit. He was contemplating adding a hard swim in his pool to the ride he'd just had, when his phone buzzed in his pocket. A quick glance at the display brought a smile curling around his lips.

"Missing me?" he answered.

"Not at all," Zoe said breezily. "Did you want me for something?"

He hesitated, letting the silence play between them before speaking. "Now there's a leading question."

"Quit fooling, Galicia. Why did you call?"

"Come to the ranch for barbecued ribs tonight. Seven o'clock."

"What if I'm busy?"

"You gotta eat."

He could feel her indecision over the phone and chose his next words very carefully. "What are you afraid of, Zoe?"

"Not you," she answered swiftly.

He chuckled. "See you at seven."

He severed the call before she could respond. A smile

wreathed his face as he imagined her irritation at not having had the last word. It was kind of fun to keep her off-kilter just that little bit. To get where she was in her line of work, she had to be some kind of dogged control freak—turning over metaphorical stones and looking for clues every day. He'd bet she wasn't used to someone making decisions for her, and he really liked that, in this instance, it was him doing it.

She'd turn up tonight—he'd bet his newly weaned calves on it.

The entire drive to the Galicia spread, Zoe cursed under her breath. The arrogance of the man, ordering her around like that. *But you're going there, aren't you?* a voice in the back of her mind taunted. *You want to see him again.*

"Shut up!" she said aloud.

Or maybe you just want him?

The question rattled around in her mind as she rolled through the gates and up the long driveway to his house. He'd gotten her off so damn fast last night that he'd left her reeling. She hadn't even known she could feel so much so quickly. For her, lovemaking had always been a long, slow buildup, not always followed by release. But with him? It had been mere minutes. And every sensation he'd wrought from her had made her want more.

So, yeah, she was prepared to admit she wanted him. She couldn't continue to fool herself that she was coming out here to question him about Jesse Stevens, especially when Stevens himself had said he'd turn up for the recorded interview in a couple of days.

Zoe stopped her car and got out, staring at the house for the second time in as many days and admiring the stone exterior. The place looked solid, durable and reliable. *A reflection of its master?* she wondered. There was movement at the door, and Cord Galicia strode out, his presence commanding her eye from the second he came through the doorway.

Yes, *master* was the right term for him. Master of all he surveyed? *He might like to think so.* She smiled inwardly. But he was no master to her. She'd come here because she wanted to, not because he'd all but ordered her presence.

"I'm glad you came," he said as she approached the front entrance.

"Ribs are my weakness," she answered with as much insouciance as she could muster.

He showed her inside and then led her through the house and outside to a loggia. The scent of hickory smoke hung in the air and, combined with the aroma of barbecuing meat, made Zoe's mouth water in anticipation.

"What can I get you to drink? Wine?"

"No wine for me, not when I have to drive back to town," Zoe protested.

"You could always stay."

Her inner muscles tightened on a swell of desire at the simplicity of his words. She shouldn't have been surprised. She'd been half expecting it, hadn't she? Half *wanting* it, too?

"We'll see," she answered, keeping her words deliberately evasive.

"Wine it is, then."

She didn't argue when he poured two glasses of red wine and passed one to her.

"Thanks. The ribs smell good."

"They are good."

"Oh, you're so confident of your ability?"

"Abuelita's secret recipe," he said with a sly wink.

"Not so secret if you know it," Zoe felt compelled to point out.

"True, but she spent a lot of time showing me how to look after myself. She also told me that to win the heart of a good woman, a man needs to know how to do more than reheat a can of beans."

Zoe laughed. "Is that what you're doing? Trying to win my heart?"

As soon as she said the words, she realized they'd have been better left unsaid. A shadow passed over Cord's face and his light mood changed.

"Just offering some Royal hospitality while you're here," he said before taking a sip of wine. "What do you think of the wine?"

She took a sip, too. "Mmm, it's good, like velvet. I like how it doesn't leave a dry aftertaste on your tongue."

"It'll taste even better with the ribs."

He gestured for her to take a seat on the large outdoor rattan sofa, and she sank comfortably against the over-stuffed pillows. He lowered himself in the seat opposite.

"A girl could fall asleep here if she wasn't careful," she commented.

"Didn't sleep so good last night?"

A flush stained her cheeks. "Look, about last night."

"Hmm?"

He looked at her over the rim of his glass, and at the heat in his gaze Zoe felt her toes curl in her sensible low-heeled shoes.

She shook her head. "Never mind. Least said, soonest mended."

He laughed. "Is that something your grandmother used to say?"

She smiled a little. "Yeah."

"Zoe," he said as he leaned forward, his gaze intense. "Last night was merely an appetizer."

Six

Cord wasn't sure what devil of impulse had driven him to say that to her, but it was satisfying to watch the play of raw emotion that danced across her features. He could pinpoint the exact moment she decided to take control.

"Is that so?" she asked, arching a dark brow at him. "We'll see about that."

"Yes." He nodded. "We will."

Again he had the satisfaction of seeing her lose her tenuous grip on the conversation, and he decided to turn things to more general matters. He didn't want to alienate her entirely. It was enough, for now, that she was here.

"What do you do in your spare time?" he asked, reaching for the bottle and topping off her glass.

"Spare time?" She laughed. "What's that?"

"You're a workaholic?"

"Aren't you? You can't run a spread as big as this one without long hours, right?"

He tipped his head in acknowledgment. "But I have people I delegate to. An experienced foreman, ranch hands. Are you telling me your work is your life?"

"My work is a very important part of my life. I want to be the best."

"Better than your dad."

"Better than everyone in my family."

He looked at her a little closer. Being the youngest in a testosterone-heavy family had obviously left its scars. Zoe Warren felt she had something to prove to the males in her family, and it had to be proven on their battleground.

"What would you have done if you hadn't been a cop?"

"I never wanted to be anything else, much to my mom's great disappointment. After four boys she thought she could raise a kindred spirit. Someone who might enjoy shopping with her, attending high teas or getting pampered at the beauty shop. But that's not me. It doesn't mean she's given up on me, though," Zoe finished saying with a deep chuckle.

"Sounds like an intrepid woman."

"She is. I admire her, a lot. It can't be easy to see every person you love step out the door every day and have to wonder whether or not they'll come home safely."

Cord felt that unwelcome clench around his heart that he always got when reminded of Britney. He knew exactly what Zoe was talking about, and he knew just how much it hurt when that loved one didn't come home again. He put his glass onto the wooden table between them and got up to check on the ribs, anything to put a little distance between him and the reminder that while he may be powerfully attracted to Zoe Warren, she was first, last and always a police officer. He wouldn't go through that again.

The ribs were almost done. His grandmother would have been proud.

"I'm just going to grab the salad and corn bread. Be back in a minute," he said in Zoe's direction.

"Can I help?"

"Nope. You just stay right there," he said firmly.

As large as his kitchen was, he didn't want to be moving around it with her behind him. After last night he was struggling to keep his hands and his mouth to himself, and it had taken some effort to play the considerate host. To pass her a glass of wine without touching her fingers. To watch her sample the beverage without leaning forward to kiss the residue from her lips.

Damn, he was getting hard just thinking about it. To distract himself he went to the large double fridge and pulled out the bowl of salad he'd prepared shortly before her arrival. Setting it on a tray, he then grabbed the basket of corn bread he'd put in the oven to warm. He already had utensils and plates in an old painted wooden sideboard out in the loggia.

"You look very domesticated," Zoe commented as he quickly set the outdoor table and lit a bunch of squat candles in the center of the table.

"I'm a man of many talents. Come, take a seat," he suggested. "I'll get the ribs off the grill."

He plated up the ribs and brought the platter to the table.

"You mentioned your grandmother. Did she raise you?" Zoe asked as he settled into his place.

"Both my grandparents were still here with us when my father took over the ranch. My grandfather died five years ago but Abuelita is still fighting fit. She lives with my parents. When Dad retired, he decided he wanted to get away from ranching. Told me that if he lived here, or near here, he'd always be interfering in my way of doing things and he didn't think that was fair. They bought a condo in Palm Springs, but to be honest, I don't think he's happy there. Oh, he puts on a good face and all, but he's a farm boy at heart. Rounds of golf and cocktails at five?" Cord shook his head. "That's not his lifestyle."

"I guess he made his choice, though, right?"

"It worries me that he's unhappy. His pride won't let him admit he's made a mistake. I would welcome him back. His knowledge is invaluable, and God knows the house is big enough for us all to continue living here without tripping over one another. It worked for him and his parents. I don't see why it wouldn't have worked for us." He shrugged. "Whatever, it is what it is."

"I couldn't wait to move out of home and get a place of my own. Even though my brothers are all married, I just felt suffocated by my family's expectations of me."

"Their expectations?" Cord probed.

"I'm a girl. They want me to settle down and have babies."

"And quit your career?"

Her laugh was scornful. "They don't see this as my career. It's a placeholder to them, until I do the right thing and find a good man and settle down and let him support me. My family is fiercely traditional."

"Well, there's traditional and there's dark ages," Cord commiserated.

He picked up the wine bottle and held it above her glass without pouring, just waiting for her assent or refusal. There was no way she'd be legal to drive if she had another glass of wine. They both knew it. If she accepted the drink, she was staying. It wasn't until he allowed the thought to form again in his mind that he realized just how much he wanted her to stay. How much he wanted to explore her again. The moment Zoe's fingers lightly grasped the slender stem of the wineglass and lifted it toward the bottle, every particle in his body stirred.

Her blue eyes met his and locked. He saw the faint remnants of indecision fade and be replaced by something else. Heat. Need. Desire. He slowly tipped the bottle and poured.

"Thank you," she said, lifting the glass to her lips and taking a sip.

"No, thank you," Cord said, his voice no more than a rumble.

He dragged his focus back to their meal, to the succulent meat that, with a gentle bite, simply twisted off the ribs, then melted on the tongue in a burst of flavors. But right now his taste buds were flooded with the memory of Zoe's skin from last night, and the longing to repeat the experience—and more.

He couldn't say how he got through the rest of the meal or what they discussed. All he could think about was the fact that Zoe Warren was staying the night. Sure, she might yet take him up on the guest-room idea, but he had a feeling that she'd be sleeping with him. Actually, sleeping was the furthest thing from his mind. The anticipation of how the rest of their night would unfold settled around him, filling him with a sizzling buzz of excitement. Yeah, this was going to be a good night. He would put aside the reasons she'd come here and what she did for a living, and he'd make damn sure she forgot them, too.

Zoe felt herself relax in increments. It had to be the wine she'd unwisely drunk, she told herself. It would have nothing to do with the man sitting opposite her. The man who'd put together a meal that was worthy of any five-star restaurant, because even in its simplicity, it had been imbued with a myriad of flavors that varied in intensity but each of which created both craving and satisfaction. A bit like the man himself.

And just like that she didn't feel quite so relaxed anymore. She'd made a conscious decision here tonight. The moment she'd accepted his offer of wine, she knew she'd be staying—and forget about any guest room. The hum of her body had heightened to a persistent buzz of need, and the idea of taking care of that need on her own held little appeal when there was a warm and willing partner right here in front of her. She allowed herself to revel in the air of expectancy that built between herself and Cord Galicia.

When they finished their food, Cord began to clear their things away. Zoe swiftly rose to assist him.

"You don't need to help. You're my guest here tonight," Cord protested.

"Of course I'm helping you," she answered firmly, stacking plates and cutlery.

She followed him through to the kitchen, where she rinsed dishes while he stacked the state-of-the-art dishwasher. Clearly ranching was a profitable business for this family, not that money impressed her necessarily, but she liked seeing people enjoy the fruits of their hard labor—even if it was something as simple as a dishwasher. She made a passing comment, complimenting Cord on his choice in kitchenware. He laughed.

"You think I had anything to do with any of this?" He flung out his arms to encapsulate the entire room. "No way. When Dad declared his retirement, my mom and Abuelita took it as a chance to ensure that I didn't have to lift more than a finger without a woman here to look after me. Everything was changed. You just about need a software degree to operate the oven, let alone the microwave."

Zoe laughed along with him, but inside she felt something pull tight and close up like a clamshell. Clearly there was an expectation in this family that the women took care of their men. Not that looking after a household and all the multiple things that fell under that umbrella was in any way less important than what she did, but to Zoe her career was everything. She wouldn't give it up for anyone.

And no one is asking you to, that voice in the back of her mind reminded her tersely. *Basically you're here to satisfy an urge. Don't expect any more than that, nor any less.*

With that voice ringing clearly in her mind, Zoe cocked her head and watched Cord as he completed the cleanup. There was something very satisfying about watching a strong and capable man busy in the pursuit of domestic duties. Sexy even. Yeah, definitely sexy. Cord had big, strong hands with long, deft fingers. He kept his nails short and clean, but there was no denying those hands had calluses earned through hard work and determination. And yet they could be gentle, too, she thought on a shiver of memory.

"Everything okay?" Cord said as he turned to face her.

"Oh yes," she replied. "Just thinking about dessert."

"Dessert?"

"Yeah. You said last night was the appetizer. You've just fed me dinner. Which kind of leaves…" She let her voice trail away suggestively.

"Dessert."

He took a step closer, and Zoe felt the heat in the room skip up a few notches. When he reached out a hand to stroke her face with his fingertips, it was all she could do not to throw herself into his arms. Instead, she stood there, her eyes locked with his, her body all but visibly shaking as she waited to see what he would do next. She didn't have to wait long.

Cord moved fast, his arms going around her and one hand cupping the back of her head as he lowered his face to hers and took her lips in a searing kiss that all but turned her legs to water. Hot, steaming water, but boneless nonetheless. She reveled in the feel of his firm body as he hauled her against him, plastering her soft curves against his harder frame. And she lost herself in the taste of him—hot, sinful, spicy and sweet all at once.

Suddenly he was moving away from her, his hand clasping one of hers firmly as he tugged her after him.

"We're not doing this here," he said in a gravelly tone.

"As impressed as I am by your appliances, I concur with your decision," she teased in return.

He threw her a grin over his shoulder and headed for the staircase. She followed close behind as he continued down a carpeted hallway to the end, where he threw open a door and yanked her inside.

"I want you naked," he said in a voice that brooked no argument.

"How convenient. I want the same of you," she said bluntly and began to peel her clothing from her body.

Opposite her, Cord undressed just as quickly. She could barely keep her eyes off him. The sinewy strength of his arms showed in the way his muscles bunched and released as he dragged off his shirt with little respect for the buttons that tore free and bounced onto the carpet beneath their feet. He kicked off his boots and shucked his jeans and socks in a smooth movement, which left him standing there in front of her in only his boxer briefs. Clad in only her bra and panties, red lace this time, she eyed his very obvious erection constrained behind the cotton knit of his briefs. She sucked in her bottom lip and bit down hard to hold back the moan of delight that threatened to break free.

Cord, too, was taking a moment to feast his eyes on her body.

"Red lace? Ah, Detective, you slay me," he groaned as he moved forward to take her into his arms.

The shock of their skin touching made her draw in a sharp breath, which in turn made her breasts swell. The heat of his chest poured through her lacy bra, and she wished she'd been faster to disrobe so she could feel him more closely, without any barriers between them. She shifted, reaching her arms behind her only to feel him trap them in his hands.

"Not so fast, Detective. I think I want to enjoy the sight of you just a little longer."

He carefully walked her backward until she felt the softness of bed linen behind her knees.

"On the bed," he ordered.

"Are you always this bossy in the bedroom?" she asked.

But even as she said the words, she did as he'd commanded because she was eager to feel him against her again. Eager to feel him everywhere.

"Well, we'd have to do this more than once for you to have a basis for comparison, wouldn't we?" he responded.

She laughed. "Bossy and confident. What a combination."

"You forgot something else," he said as he hooked his thumbs into the waistband of his briefs. "I'm also very, very good at what I do."

Her mouth dried and her voice was little more than a croak when she spoke. "Ah yes, I'd forgotten. Perhaps you could refresh my memory."

His smile was feral and made every cell in her body clench on a wave of anticipation. Had she provoked the beast? It would seem so. He slid his briefs off his hips, freeing his straining erection to her hungry gaze.

"Mmm, dessert," she managed before he moved onto the bed.

"I'm not sure if you've earned your dessert yet," he murmured against her ear.

"Oh? Tell me what I've done wrong."

"Well, let's see. There's the matter of you pestering Jesse and his sister today."

"Not to have done so would be in dereliction of my duty."

"I'd asked you not to," he said, taking an earlobe between his teeth and biting gently.

Zoe squirmed as sensation shot through her.

"Actually," she said, breathless now, "you ordered me not to."

"You admit you were disobedient?"

He nipped a trail down her neck, while one hand brushed against her bra, rasping against her budded nipple before his fingers closed around the aching peak and squeezed just right. It felt like he already knew every intimate secret about her erogenous zones because he managed to zero in immediately on every one.

"I admit nothing," she gasped as he squeezed her nipple more firmly. "Besides, I have to wait until the sheriff's office equipment is repaired before I can interview him properly."

A spear of pleasure shot straight to the apex of her thighs and she squirmed again. She could feel her panties getting wet as her need for him increased in rapidly expanding increments.

"Equipment?" he asked, nuzzling against her skin, his hot breath making her feel even hotter.

"Yeah, video camera and recording equipment. Have to do things by the letter. But why are we talking about this? Haven't you got something more important to attend to?"

"More important?" He lifted his head and looked at her with a teasing glow in his eyes.

"Yeah—me."

He laughed. "Bossy, Detective. I see I'm going to have

to continue my investigation a little more carefully, just to remind you who's in charge here," he promised, his voice deadly serious.

His wet, hot mouth replaced his fingers at her breast.

"Cord, please," she begged, without even knowing exactly what she was begging for.

"Please—now that sounds nice. Please what? Please bite you?"

She groaned but nodded her assent.

"Your wish is my command," he said, his voice getting rougher with each touch he bestowed on her.

She felt his erection against her as he lowered himself and bit her gently through her bra.

"Naked, please. I want to be naked. This isn't fair."

"Fair? The detective wants fair?"

She felt his fingers at the clasp of her bra, felt her breasts spill free as the fabric mercifully fell away. Then there was nothing but sensation as he kissed and licked her heated flesh. She arched beneath him, desperate for her skin to meet with his, desperate for his touch lower down her body, where she ached with a hunger that was all consuming.

"Don't rush, Zoe. Some delights are best savored slowly," he teased as he spent more time first on one tautly beaded nipple and then the other. "Ah, you taste divine. I could do this all night long."

"Surely not all night… I may melt apart in your arms before that."

"Well, maybe not all night, then," he conceded with a chuckle. "Are you always so pedantic?"

"Details are my thing," she admitted on a rushed breath as he began to trail that wicked mouth of his down the center of her rib cage and lower to her belly button.

"I'm finding I like pretty much everything there is about you, Detective," Cord drawled.

"I have to admit I'm enjoying your journey of discovery."

He laughed again, and Zoe thrilled on the sound of it. Sex had been infrequent but good, but even so, she'd never enjoyed this level of fun in the process. Nor this level of aching demand that throbbed through her. If he kept this up, he'd have only to breathe on her clit and she'd be transported to the stratosphere. She could feel her body pulse as Cord continued his voyage lower, and lower still—but not quite low enough or fast enough for her satisfaction.

"I like what you've done here," he said, pulling back a little and stroking her neatly groomed body hair. "Intriguing. Hard to maintain?"

"Seriously, you're asking me about my personal grooming?"

"Why not? It hasn't distracted me from your punishment."

He pressed a kiss on her mound. Close, but still too far from her aching bud for her liking.

"Laser hair removal, and a regular trim." She ground out the words.

He kissed her again, a tiny bit closer to her clit, to her release. She shivered and pressed her head back into the pillow as he traced his fingertips up the inside of her thigh. Shivers rippled through her.

"Consider me punished," she begged. "Just please, touch me."

"Like this?" he asked, slowly pressing one finger into her wet core.

He stroked her, dragging a sound from her that spoke volumes to her level of need.

"More."

"And still the lady thinks she's in control." He sighed and withdrew his finger.

At her moan of distress he pressed two fingers inside

her and stroked her again, and then, at last, he closed his mouth around the aching, pulsing bead of flesh that had been his goal all along.

"Mmm, dessert," Cord said against her heated skin.

Zoe began to laugh, but then he changed the pressure of his tongue, moved his fingers, and all humor was suspended as he sent her soaring on a pounding wave of pleasure so intense she lost all sense of who and where she was. All she knew was the man who had delivered this pleasure was virtually a stranger to her, and right now she didn't care.

It was some time later before Zoe felt herself come back to any kind of awareness. Cord was lying on his side next to her, one arm bent under his head, his free hand softly stroking her belly.

"You're not going to leave me now, are you?" she asked, lifting a hand to trace the strong lines of his face.

"Nope," he said simply. "Not this time. Besides, we're at my place and I'm not letting you go anywhere."

"Good," she replied. "Because I want you inside me."

"Making demands of me now?"

"Yeah, got a problem with that?"

He flashed her a smile. "Not at all."

"But first..."

"First?"

"*My* dessert."

Zoe moved quickly to sit astride him. Beneath her bottom she could feel his erection, but that would have to wait awhile. First, she wanted to bestow on him a little of the same punishment he'd dealt to her. Cord's hands moved to grasp her hips but she shook her head.

"Uh-uh," she cautioned. "No touching. Not yet. Hold on to the headboard until I say you can move."

"Are you planning to frisk me, Detective?"

"I've told you, I'm conducting an investigation," she said with a playful curl of her lips. "A very important investigation."

She trailed her fingertips along the underside of his upper arms. His skin was softer there—deliciously so. As she traced around his armpits to the top of his rib cage, she felt his skin grow goose bumps at her touch.

"Do you like that?" she whispered.

"Oh yeah."

He shifted a little beneath her, and she lifted one finger to caution him.

"Don't make me get my cuffs."

"You brought cuffs to dinner?"

"And my gun. They're in my handbag along with my badge. I never leave home without them."

"Duly noted," Cord said with a slight frown.

Zoe hesitated in her movements, leaning back a little to study his face. His eyes still glittered with desire but his expression had become more closed, less playful.

"Does it worry you I carry a gun everywhere?"

She began to stroke his smooth chest, her fingertips tingling at the sensation of her skin on his.

"Not my place to worry about you."

"That's right, it's not. Enough talking. Now, just feel."

And she made sure he did. She smoothed her hands flat and skimmed the muscles of his chest, learning the dips and curves that made up the appealing shapes of his body, from his broad shoulders to his narrow waist. She bent down and kissed him before transferring her mouth from his lips to the flat discs of his nipples. They drew into small peaks against her tongue as she pinched and played with him. His hips shifted again and she clamped her thighs tight around him, halting his movement. Let him suffer the way he'd made her suffer—although it had been a delectable torment that he'd made her endure before bringing her to completion, and she had every intention of ensuring he experienced the same level of satisfaction.

And if he didn't? Well, she'd have to go back to square one and start over again. Her mouth curved into another smile at the thought, and she applied her attention to making him squirm beneath her as she tasted, licked and sucked at his skin. He wore a subtle cologne, but it was his own special scent that she'd quickly become addicted to. It made her want to nuzzle against him and draw in deep breath after deep breath. Never before had she felt this visceral level of attraction to another person, and it was intoxicating.

She rose up slightly and shifted her legs lower as she explored his torso, delighting in the way his skin jumped beneath her tongue as she followed the light trail of hair from his belly button down to his groin. His erection left her in no doubt as to his readiness, but she wanted to prolong this as much as possible. She let her tongue drift along the shadowed line of his inner hip—down, then up again. The hitch in his breathing told her that she was tormenting him, but to his credit he kept his hands firmly attached to the headboard, even though the muscles of his arms were bunched with tension.

Maybe it was time to take pity on him, she thought, and she turned her attention to his swollen shaft. She nuzzled at the base, breathing in the hot, musky scent of his skin, then trailed her tongue from base to tip. Cord groaned out loud at her actions, his hands suddenly letting go of the headboard and coming to cup her head, his fingers tangling in her short hair. She licked him again before taking the hot, silky head into her mouth and playing her tongue against the smoothness. His fingers tightened, and she felt his entire body clench as he fought against the urge to thrust deeper into her mouth.

Suddenly it became important to her to make him lose control, and she used every trick she'd ever read about as she licked, sucked and stroked him to a wild, shaking climax. When he was spent, she shifted until she was lying beside him, her head nestled against his chest, her arm across his waist. His heart beat like a herd of stampeding cattle in his chest and his body glistened with a light sheen of perspiration.

She'd done that to him, she thought with a touch of pride. She'd reduced this man—who had at first appeared to be fierce and determined, but who could cook like a dream, who could bring her to orgasm with a deftness she'd never known before—to one who'd put all sense of responsibility and control aside to revel in pure gratification. It was empowering to know she'd done that for him, liberating to realize that she could meet him on an even playing field where there were no specific roles based on gender. Only sensation, and pleasure and, she smiled anew, fun. Her time in Royal was shaping up to be very interesting indeed.

Seven

Cord waited some time until he could trust himself to speak again.

"That wasn't how I envisaged this evening happening," he stated bluntly.

Zoe continued tracing tiny shapes with her fingertips at his waist.

"Oh, disappointed?" she teased.

He felt something swell in his chest. Happiness? It had been so long since he'd felt anything like it, let alone trusted anyone with his body the way he'd trusted Zoe, that he found it hard to define.

"Definitely not disappointed," he growled. Cord rolled over so Zoe lay beneath him, his face directly over hers. "But I feel like we could do better."

She laughed—a deep-seated chuckle that made her whole body shake.

"By all means let's try it. You can never have too much dessert, after all."

She was a woman after his own heart, it seemed, and this time, when they made love, he made certain that, despite several delightful detours, they joined as one, thanking his lucky stars that the condoms in his drawer hadn't expired. He knew, because he'd checked before she arrived tonight, and while he hadn't wanted to assume this night would end with them both in his bed, he was so very glad it had.

Her long, supple legs hooked around his waist when he entered her, her heat and inner muscles drawing him in deep. Cord locked his gaze with hers, watched as her eyes became glassy as they rocked together in a dance as old as time. He felt her entire body clench on the first wave of orgasm as it hit her, and he allowed himself free rein, until they reached the summit together and hung there suspended in mutual bliss, before descending back to reality.

Morning came all too soon. In the distance, Cord could hear the sounds of his hands out on the ranch moving cattle, the lowing beasts voicing their thoughts on being brought in to a new pasture. He should be out there, working alongside them, but a certain tall, dark-haired detective was still entangled in his sheets. Not that he was complaining. She felt good—too good. Too easy to get used to and that sure wouldn't be a good thing. Not only did she live in Houston, she was a cop. A dedicated one at that. She wasn't in her career for a few years to pass time. No, this was a lifetime choice for her.

He hadn't been intimate with anyone since Britney, which probably explained why this thing with Zoe had flared up so quickly. There was no way it could be long-term. Fires that burned this brightly extinguished just as swiftly.

He thought about her bag downstairs, about the gun

she'd admitted was secreted in there. Even on a social visit, she was armed. It was part and parcel of who she was, and the danger that was associated with the kind of people she tracked down was equally a part of her every day.

He'd thought he could handle it with Britney. He'd supported her in her dream to become a cop, told her he'd be there for her 100 percent. But his support didn't equate to squat when she faced down a liquor-store robber only a few hours into her first shift. And being there as they pulled life support in ICU days after she'd been shot—well, that had been unarguably the darkest day of his life. He would not go down that road again. He simply could not.

Rebuilding himself had been hard, but his parents had put off their planned early retirement to see him back on his feet. His *abuelita* had been a strong, silent presence at his back, feeding his body and feeding his soul whenever he would let her. He'd resumed a life, of sorts. He'd dated once or twice, but things had never gotten to the stage they had with Zoe. Hell, he didn't even understand how things had moved this fast with her.

She was everything he never again wanted in a woman. Career focused, a detective and undoubtedly fiercely independent. She'd have had to fight her way into her position—past the expectations of her family that she fit into a more traditional mold, and past the obstacles that she no doubt had to overcome to be recognized in her working world. He'd always told himself that if he ever took the risk of another relationship again, it would be with a woman without career-focused ambition. One who shared the same dreams and goals as he had and who would partner with him in everything to do with life on the ranch. One who wanted stability, security and who had a desire to continue to build a legacy for future generations of Galicia children.

There was a sharp stab in his chest at the thought of

kids. He'd always taken for granted that he'd be a father one day, but now he wasn't so sure. That took a level of commitment he wasn't certain he was capable of anymore—not only to the children themselves, but to their mother, too. One thing was for certain, though—a woman like Zoe Warren was not on the same life path as he was. The whole city-versus-country thing would never work between them. He loved life on the ranch. He'd been born and bred into it as much as she'd been born and bred into her life in Houston. They were chalk and cheese, oil and water—and yet he couldn't seem to get enough of her.

Zoe stirred and stretched, untangling her limbs from his and rolling onto her back. Cord let his gaze slide over the lean lines of her body and then back to the surprising fullness of her breasts. Now that he knew how sensitive they were, he dreamed of ways he could tease them into the taut peaks that spoke evocatively of her depth of desire.

"Good morning," he said, his voice still a little gruff with sleep.

"How good is yet to be determined. On the meal basis we've covered appetizers, main courses and dessert. What's breakfast like around here?"

Never one to back down from a challenge, he showed her, and it was a full half hour later before he chased her into the bathroom, where they showered together. He would have taken her there again if he hadn't run out of condoms, but he had to satisfy himself with soaping her up and washing her hair and helping her rinse off. When she exited the shower stall, he switched the water to cold, determined to get his body under some semblance of control, but one look at her as she wiped her body dry with one of his thick, fluffy towels and he knew it was an exercise in hopelessness. The only way he'd return to any kind of normal was when she'd gone, and oddly, he didn't want her to leave.

She was dressed when he came into the bedroom with a towel wrapped firmly around his waist.

"I have to go," she said with obvious reluctance. "Thanks for dinner and…everything."

"Anytime," he drawled in response. "In fact, how about dinner tonight? We can go to the Texas Cattleman's Club."

"I've heard about it. Isn't the dress code pretty strict in the restaurant there?"

"I could lend you a suit," he offered only half tongue in cheek. In fact, the more he thought about her in one of his suits wearing that sinfully seductive lingerie underneath, the more he liked the idea.

"I'll sort something out. What time?"

"I'll pick you up at seven thirty."

"I'll be ready."

The second he heard her car start and head down the driveway, he grabbed his cell phone and dialed the number of an old school friend.

"Frank, you working on the sheriff's recording and video equipment?"

"Yeah, but how'd you know that?"

Cord's hand tightened on his phone. "That's not important. Tell me, how long do you think it'll take to get it all up and running again?"

Frank hemmed and hawed a little before speaking. "Should be done by the end of the day."

He started to get into some of the technical jargon that made Cord's eyes cross, so Cord interrupted him the moment Frank drew in a breath.

"Look, you remember how I bailed you out with Sissy when she thought you were having an affair. Gave you an alibi?"

"Yeah?" There was a note of caution in Frank's voice that hadn't been there before.

"You owe me one, right?"

"Sure do," Frank agreed.

Cord closed his eyes briefly. He hated having to do this. He knew Frank hadn't been unfaithful to his wife. Sissy had been feeling insecure when she was pregnant, and it was easier for Cord to say he'd been with Frank than for Frank's biggest secret—the fact that he was learning to read as an adult, so he could read to his newborn child—to come out to all and sundry.

"Could you take a little longer over that repair?" Cord eventually asked.

"Like a day or two more?"

"How about a week, maybe two?"

"And then we'd be even?"

"More than even."

"I could do that," Frank agreed.

"Thanks, Frank, appreciate it."

"You gonna tell me why you want me to delay on this?"

"No."

"Okay, then. Sounds like I'll be struggling to source a vital thingymabobwotsit."

"Darn hard things to track down," Cord agreed with a smile before ending the call.

Ryder Currin rode the elevator to Sterling Perry's floor determined to put this old rivalry to bed once and for all. The pain and damage it was causing had gone on long enough.

"Mr. Currin!" the receptionist gasped, recognizing him instantly as he swept out of the elevator and past the main reception area. "You can't—"

"Don't bother announcing me. I'll announce myself," he said over his shoulder as he strode toward Perry's office.

He heard the scuffle of activity behind him, but no one was going to stop him now. He'd had enough. The roll-on effect of Perry's bitterness, fed by years of lies and innuendo from everyone around them, had taken a toll far greater than either man could ever have anticipated. And, as far as Ryder was concerned, it stopped now. It was one thing for Perry to hold a grudge because of Ryder's close friendship with Perry's late wife, Tamara, but quite another for him to stand in the way of his daughter Angela's happiness. Ryder's relationship with Angela had been fragile from the get-go, but despite that they'd found a way to make it work—until the old rumors of Ryder's relationship with her mom had resurfaced. Ryder and Tamara Perry had never been more than friends back when he'd worked as a hand on the York ranch—close friends, sure, but nothing more than that. He'd been her shoulder to cry on when things got tough and when he'd questioned her happiness in her marriage to Sterling, she'd made it clear her loyalty to her husband was unswerving and she would always remain with him, no matter what.

In the face of the vicious claims that had begun to circulate Ryder knew there'd be a wedge driven between him and Angela or Angela and her father, and she'd have to choose between them. Out of respect for both Tamara's memory and for her daughter, who he loved more than life itself, he'd walked away from Angela and his promise to marry her because there was no way he was forcing her to make that choice. He'd regretted his actions every second of every day since. He couldn't work things out with Angela until he'd worked things out with Perry.

Perry's manipulation of those around him had done a lot of damage, but the older man's meddling had resulted in an unexpected bonus and thanking him would be Ryder's starting point. Thanks to Perry's anonymous labor complaint—one that unfortunately had a strong basis in fact and that Ryder had known nothing about until the complaint had been brought to his attention—he'd been able to institute worker reforms. Firing Willem Inwood had been unpleasant, but regrettably necessary. No one got away with treating his staff badly, especially not someone in a position of privilege and respect such as Inwood had held.

Just the thought of the man was enough to get Ryder's dander up, and he forced himself to shove his anger down deep before it could potentially damage the impromptu meeting he was about to have with Sterling Perry. Like he always told his kids—Xander, Annabel and Maya—never approach anything or anyone important in anger. He stopped in his tracks, squared his shoulders and took a steadying breath. At his destination, Ryder knocked twice, then pushed open the door to Perry's office. The older man was just putting down his phone.

"You'd better be quick," Sterling said with a sardonic curl of his lip. "I'm informed security is on their way."

"Tell them to stand down. I'm not here to fight with you."

"Really? Forgive me if I don't believe you," he taunted.

"Well, you can believe it. In fact, I'm here to thank you."

"Oh?" Perry's brows rose in genuine surprise.

"Yeah. Thanks to your anonymous—" Ryder made air quotes with his fingers "—complaint, I was able to cut the rot from my business and institute reforms to ensure such abuses never happen again. We'll be stronger than ever now, and it's all thanks to you."

He watched the play of emotions across Perry's face. It wasn't often the man let his facade down, and it was enlightening to see the short burst of confusion followed by reluctant acceptance.

"I see," Perry replied, leaning back in his chair. "You'd better take a seat."

Ryder sat in the chair nearest to him, just as security arrived in the room.

"Mr. Perry, we'll deal with your unexpected visitor right away."

"No need. It appears that Mr. Currin and I have some business to discuss. Please leave us." Perry waved a hand toward the door.

"You want us to wait outside?"

"That won't be necessary, thank you."

Ryder waited until Perry's muscle left the room. Had he really wanted to hurt the older man, there was no way his security detail had been here quick enough. Ryder made a comment to that effect, eliciting a burst of unexpected laughter from the man who'd become his nemesis.

"You're giving me advice now? What's going on? Has the world turned upside down?" Perry commented with his signature brand of cynicism.

"Not upside down, not yet, anyway. But we need to talk. Settle things once and for all."

"I have nothing to settle with you. As far as I'm concerned, you're nothing more than a burr under my saddle. Now that you and Angela are no longer engaged, I can rest happy in the knowledge that, aside from today, I need never face you again."

Ryder let the man's words roll over him. The bitterness in the other man's tone was deep-seated and went back twenty-five long and often unhappy years. Ryder didn't want the next twenty-five to be the same. Somehow they had to reach a reconciliation of sorts. If they couldn't, he'd never be able to go back to Angela and beg her forgiveness for walking away on their love, their life, their future together. That knowledge forced him to remain calm in the face of Perry's veiled insults.

He drew in a deep breath. "Look, I know you hate my guts—"

"That would require effort I wouldn't even bother expending," Sterling said as if the conversation bored him.

"You still resent my friendship with your late wife."

"Your relationship with Tamara was inappropriate," Sterling replied, biting back. "But she chose me. She always chose me."

"I know, but I want you to know that I never had an affair with her. I'll swear it on a stack of Bibles if it will help you to believe me, but as much as I admired and respected her, I never touched her. Not that way. We were friends, that's all."

Sterling shook his head. "Why should I believe you? You've not long come from my daughter's bed. What kind of man are you, anyway? First the mother? Then my daughter? That's just sick."

Disgust dripped from his every word.

"It would be sick if it were true. But I did not sleep with Tamara, ever. And my relationship with Angela is completely different. I loved Tamara, sure, as a friend, as a mentor in many ways, and I certainly didn't think you deserved her. Still don't, to be honest. But like you said, she remained with you and she remained true to her vows to you until her death, as well. For better or worse, Perry, she loved you and only you."

There must have been something in his words that started to sink in, because the hardened set to Perry's face began to soften. Not a lot, but enough for Ryder to begin to hope that maybe they could get past this at long last.

"So what if what you're telling me is the truth? It doesn't

change the things you've done since. The land you inherited from Tamara's father—the land that was so rich it oil it made your damn fortune—should always have been ours, not yours."

"You want it back in your family's hands?"

"Damn straight I do."

"Then give me your blessing to marry Angela."

The air between them crackled with barely restrained energy.

"Impossible. You broke off your engagement. She won't have you back."

"She will if she knows she doesn't have to choose between us. Angela loves me and I love her. We deserve to be happy. We deserve to be together."

"Why? You couldn't win her mother from me, so now you're settling for my daughter?"

"If I weren't a decent man I'd punch you in the mouth for that remark," Ryder growled through gritted teeth. "How dare you speak of your daughter so disparagingly. She deserves way better than that."

"I could argue that she deserves way better than you," Sterling spat back in return.

Ryder clenched his hands tight and then forced himself to relax his fingers. He had no doubt that Sterling was deliberately baiting him, seeking any excuse to call security back into this office and to see him escorted out of the building. He would not give the man the satisfaction.

"Luckily for you, I'm not the piece of crap you think I am. Look, we both love Angela. We both want her to be happy. I know that, as her husband, I can make her happy. I want to devote the rest of my life to her."

"And why should I believe you?"

"Because you can see it's true. I'm here, aren't I? I'm extending an olive branch. Deep down, you know Angela loves me, too. Despite everything you've ever done to try to turn her away from me. But I won't stand between the two of you, not the way you're standing between her and me. I loved her enough to let her go, but not having her in my life isn't fair to either of us. Now I'm telling you I love her enough to make a deal with you. If you agree to stand aside and stop trying to influence Angela against me, I will deed the land that her grandfather willed to me to her on our marriage."

There, he'd laid his trump card on the table.

"Obviously," he continued, "I would have preferred you to bestow your blessing on our relationship without what some may see as a bribe, but I prefer to look at it as an act of good faith. And Angela, well, she can make of it what she may. I'm sure you would rather your daughter see you through eyes that aren't clouded by the thought that you only gave us your blessing because it meant, in the long run, your family would get their hands back on land you've always considered should have been yours and Tamara's.

"Look, I love your daughter with all my heart. I will be a good husband to her and a fine father to any children we might be lucky enough to have. That land will eventually become theirs. Isn't that what you want in the long run?"

Sterling leaned back in his executive chair and pressed his fingertips together, studying Ryder carefully over their steepled peaks.

"Let me think about it," he finally said.

Ryder felt himself begin to relax. As progress went, that was a start. Certainly a better position than where they'd been before he walked into Perry's office today. Perry might have conceded to think about it, but Ryder could see that his stony visage had softened. By sweetening the pot with the land he'd inherited from Tamara's father, he knew he stood a far greater chance of winning the man's support.

"Which brings me to the Texas Cattleman's Club," Ryder started.

"I wondered when you'd bring that up. Don't push me, Currin. I might consider supporting your marriage to my daughter, but I will not relinquish my pitch for control of the TCC here in Houston."

"I'm not asking you to. But I do think we need to declare a truce and actually start to work together to find the killer. On opposite sides of the boardroom table we're formidable, but think how much stronger we could be if we worked together. Both for Angela's sake and for the reputation of the Houston club."

Again, silence stretched between the two men. After a couple of minutes Sterling Perry stood and came around to where Ryder had also risen from his seat. Was this where he ejected him from his office? Ryder wondered. He didn't know who was the more surprised when Perry stuck out his hand. Ryder didn't waste a second. He took it and shook it firmly.

"Truce," Perry said.

"Truce," Ryder agreed.

Eight

Zoe paced her motel room in irritation. Still no confirmation from the sheriff's office of a day when she'd be able to interview Jesse Stevens. Royal wasn't that antiquated. Someone was stalling; they had to be. In the meantime, she had an investigation to complete. She'd spent much of the day visiting places around town, asking random questions about Mr. Stevens and how the people around here saw him. So far all she'd heard were his praises sung from the rooftops. It was starting to get on her last nerve. No one was that perfect.

She'd begun to think she'd be better off hauling him back to Houston and questioning him there, but she knew if she did that, she'd likely get offside with Sheriff Battle, and she'd been at this long enough to know that you needed all the friends and solid contacts you could get. You never knew when you might need to call in a favor. So that left her cooling her heels, wondering what the heck to do next.

Take up horse riding? A course in cattle branding, perhaps? Both ideas made her skin crawl.

Zoe reached for her laptop and fired it up, scrolling again through the case notes she had on Vincent Hamm. It had all been so convincing, the way he'd left work after bitching about his job for weeks and vocally dreaming of a life in the Caribbean, spending his days surfing, then virtually disappearing into thin air before sending a text from the British Virgin Islands. But she knew he couldn't possibly have sent that text. Then who'd done it?

For a guy who had no enemies, he still managed to end up dead. Instinct told her it had to be connected to the building where he was found—the proposed Texas Cattleman's Club in Houston. But then there was this message from Jesse Stevens on Hamm's phone. As far as she knew, Stevens had nothing to do with the new club, but maybe there was a link she was missing here. Someone had tracked Hamm to the building. Was it Stevens? The crime-scene pictures were useless. After the flooding there'd been little chance of retrieving what could have been vital evidence. The forensic examination of his body by the medical examiner had also yielded very little, besides a grossly bloated body with its face gone.

"Argh!" she groaned out loud and closed her computer.

Maybe a run would clear her head. She glanced at her watch and decided she had time before getting ready for tonight. Across the room the garment bag hanging on the door of the cupboard that passed as a wardrobe in this place caught her eye. She'd splashed out on the new dress specifically with Cord's reaction to it very firmly in her mind. Together with the skinny-heeled black patent leather pumps, the emerald green cocktail dress with its plunging neckline was bound to excite him. Heck, it had excited her just trying it on in the store. And teamed with the green-

and-white crystal necklace she'd bought to go with it, and the white crystal studs the sales girl had told her were the perfect accompaniment to the outfit, she knew she'd knock his eyes out.

She thought for a second of how much she'd spent. Almost a month's salary. And for a guy? Someone she'd known, what, two days? She had to be mad. But that ever-present tingle that took over her body every time she thought of him reasserted itself, reminding her that this wasn't just about pleasing him or seeking his approval. It was about pleasing herself, too. She wanted to look good. So what if it wasn't the kind of outfit she'd wear to a family barbecue, which was pretty much the sum total of her social life. There'd be other men, other dates.

As soon as she thought of it, she pushed the idea out of her head. She didn't have time for dating. Not now. Not when a murderer still roamed free. But a dalliance with a handsome rancher? Yeah, she thought, smiling to herself as she subconsciously reached out to stroke the garment bag, she could squeeze that in.

Feeling as though she'd fooled herself into total justification for her shopping spree, Zoe changed into her running gear and slipped out of the motel, locking the door firmly behind her. An hour ought to do it, and maybe it'd help wear off the edge of sexual hunger that constantly badgered her every time she thought about Cord Galicia.

She was wrong. Two hours wouldn't have even been enough. Even though she'd pushed herself hard in the early evening heat, after returning to her room she still had that crazy itchy feeling that she knew only Cord Galicia could scratch. She was losing her grip. Normally at this stage of a case she'd be 100 percent focused on the job—no distractions. And yet with this one—and very possibly because there was so little to go on—she was all too easily distracted.

Maybe she ought to call Cord and cancel their arrangements for tonight. She even got as far as pulling his number up on her phone, but as her finger hovered over the call command, she backed out of the app and put her phone back down again. She groaned out loud and stomped one foot in frustration. She couldn't do it. She wanted to see him tonight. There, she admitted it.

Groaning again at her weakness for a man she should never have hooked up with, Zoe went through to the cramped bathroom and stripped off her running gear before stepping under the cool spray. She sucked in a sharp breath as the water hit her overheated body and goose bumps rose on her skin. It took a couple of minutes before the water came up to temperature, and it gave her time to get her thoughts in order and her raging libido under control.

Normally she'd be fine at this stage of a relationship. She snorted as she squirted some shampoo into her hand and massaged the liquid through her short, thick hair. Relationship? No way this was anything approaching that kind of serious. Besides, she didn't do serious. Didn't want to. Not yet, anyway. She had several more notches she wanted to achieve on the metaphorical belt that was her career with Houston P.D. She'd made it this far without distraction; she didn't plan on derailing her momentum any time soon.

Zoe rinsed out the shampoo and applied conditioner before using shower gel to wash herself clean of the grime she'd picked up during her run. Half an hour in one direction and she'd been out of town in open space. Sure, there'd been signs of civilization, like fences and the occasional car, but overall, there'd been a sense of openness and calm that she'd never felt before. Running in her neighborhood in Houston was always risky. Whether it was traffic or other sidewalk users, she always had to have her wits about her. She came home satisfied with the physical outlet but less mentally fulfilled than she felt today. Maybe the country had something to recommend it after all. Not that she'd ever live here, not with her work in Houston. But visit from time to time? Yeah, she could do that.

As she dried herself off and blew out her hair, tousling it with her fingers, she thought about her family. They'd hooted with laughter when she'd told them where she was heading, knowing how citified she was. And her sisters-in-law had chuckled alongside her brothers in total agreement. While Zoe loved the fact that her brothers had met their perfect matches, and that her parents were still incredibly happy together, she did wonder sometimes if she'd find that level of contentment herself.

When she thought about her future, contentment never really factored in, anyway. It was all about drive and progress and promotion. At a certain point, though, she'd have to stop, unless she wanted to find herself chief of police one day. She smirked at her reflection as she smoothed on some tinted moisturizer and dusted it with a light coating of powder. Her? Chief of police? She'd never handle the politics or the glad-handing required. But she wouldn't mind, one day, finding the balance between work and play and settling down with that special someone.

Her parents had fallen in love in high school and married the day after graduation. Her brothers had waited until they were a little older, but each had met his future wife and known what he wanted almost immediately. None of them had wasted time on long courtships or engagements. It seemed the Warren family were all about knowing what they wanted and going for it.

She'd never found that one person that made her feel certain that he was the one. Except for Cord.

She froze, her hand midway to her eyes and the mascara wand dangling uselessly in her fingers. Where the hell was she going with this? She wasn't ready to be married. She wasn't ready to settle down. Cord had made it clear, even if he hadn't used the exact words, that he was the kind of guy that wanted a woman who was all about home and hearth and family. She was definitely not that person. She was driven by her career. By the need to bring the bad guys to justice, by the determination to see that her victims wouldn't remain victimized for the rest of their lives. That they'd have closure.

Geez, she didn't even know why she was letting her mind flow down this track. That was the trouble with having to leave the city. It left you too much damn time to think and let your mind wander down ridiculous paths that under normal circumstances you wouldn't consider at all.

Giving herself a sharp mental shake, Zoe finished applying her makeup and stepped through to the main room to take the cocktail dress from the hanger. It was nothing to look at just hanging there; in fact, she'd been very ho-hum about it when the shop assistant had suggested it to her. But when she'd put it on, it was transformed—and it transformed her right along with it. Not just her appearance, but how she felt. In this dress she felt all woman. A woman with wiles.

The deep V of the neckline made wearing a bra impossible, and due to the silkiness of the fabric Zoe had accepted the suggestion she wear nipple covers with the outfit. Given her company for the night, and the way he made her feel, she thought she'd spare the rest of the restaurant the evidence of her perpetual desire for Cord Galicia. She chuckled as she put the things on, then slipped on a skin-toned thong before putting on the dress.

She smoothed it over her hips, then reached for the jewelry she'd bought to go with it. Finally she slid her feet into her shoes and picked up the small evening bag she'd bought to complete the ensemble. She went back into the bathroom to check her reflection in the floor-length mirror behind the door and barely recognized the creature who stared back at her.

A knock at her motel room door made her move away from the mirror and the stranger she'd seen there. Was this what seeing someone like Cord was doing to her? Changing her into someone she no longer identified with? But it was still her beneath the figure-hugging emerald green dress and the hair and makeup. Just a different her. And there was no reason why this version of herself couldn't have free rein right now, was there?

She swung the door open and felt her heart skitter in her chest at the sight of the man standing there waiting for her. Dressed all in black, from his boots to his shirt and jacket, and wearing a stunning silver-and-turquoise bolo tie, Cord looked about as dark and mysterious as a man could get. Until he smiled and her new lover shone through under his frank appreciation as his eyes skimmed her from head to foot and back again.

"Wow. You look amazing."

"Thank you. You look very nice, too," she answered and stepped through the door, making sure it was locked behind her.

"Nice? I'll have you know I went to a great deal of effort for you tonight."

His tone sounded wounded, but there was no doubt he was teasing her. It was another of the things she enjoyed about being with him. Nothing was too serious. Even when making love they could joke with each other.

"And I appreciate that," she said, patting him on the chest before fingering the bolo. "I especially like this."

"It was my grandfather's. I think he'd have liked you. He enjoyed the company of strong women."

Zoe felt a sense of accomplishment at the compliment. Sure, she knew that Cord found her sexually attractive, but underneath all that she'd sensed a reserve—as if she wasn't quite the kind of woman he wanted but, for the same reasons that drew her to him, he simply couldn't resist her.

"C'mon," he said, taking her by the hand. "Let's go."

The warmth of his skin permeated her own, sending that intriguing buzz of electrical current through her as they walked to his car. She took a step back.

"This is yours?"

She gestured to the sleek and shiny low-slung black Maserati that graced the parking lot next to her own dusty vehicle.

"Like it?" he asked before opening the passenger door and holding it for her.

"It's beautiful. I had no idea you had something like this. I was expecting the truck."

Cord smiled in response. "A beautiful woman deserves a beautiful form of transport."

He closed the door and went around to his side of the car. They completed the journey out to the Texas Cattleman's Club mostly in silence, but it didn't feel awkward. Cord had reached across and taken her hand, resting it beneath his own on his thigh as he drove. She enjoyed the intimacy of the action about as much as she enjoyed the man sitting beside her.

"So, the food is good here?" she commented as they

arrived out front of the club and pulled up next to the car valet who'd stepped forward. "It looks popular."

"*Popular* is an understatement. This place is a part of the fabric of Royal."

He put a hand to the small of her back and guided her through the front door.

Cord couldn't believe his self-restraint. Seeing Zoe framed in the doorway of her motel room dressed like she'd stepped off the cover of some glossy European fashion magazine had forced him to call on every ounce of gentlemanlike behavior to prevent himself from walking her straight back into the room and closing the door behind them. All he'd wanted to do in that instant was lose himself in her, and the truth of that frightened him. Sure, he'd started this in an attempt to keep her distracted and away from Jesse while he tended to Janet. But right now Cord couldn't say his motives were entirely philanthropic. In fact, they were the complete opposite.

Even now, with his hand against the small of her back as they entered the club, he was fighting with the base urge to turn her right around and back out to the car and take her home again. He wasn't in the mood for polite company and the conversation that he knew being seen with a woman here tonight would engender. What the hell had he been thinking?

"Mr. Galicia, good to see you this evening. Your table is ready. Please, come with me," the maître d' said as they entered the restaurant.

Cord let his hand drop from Zoe's back and gestured for her to follow the maître d' while he kept a circumspect two paces behind her. All the better to see the delicious curves of her butt in that dress, his alter ego reminded him. He clamped down on the thought but not before he felt the ripple of arousal the view before him wrought. The food tonight was going to have to be spectacular to distract him from what seeing her in that dress did to him. And the shoes… He felt another ripple shudder through him. Those heels were seriously sexy. He wondered, briefly, if she'd keep them on later for him, if he asked real nice.

You're not doing yourself any favors, he growled at himself. He watched as Zoe was seated at the table and felt a somewhat feral burst of protectiveness as the maître d's gaze lingered a second too long on Zoe's exposed cleavage as he shook out her napkin and laid it across her lap. Forcing himself to uncurl the fingers that had instinctively formed into fists, he took his seat and listened with half an ear as the man told them he'd send their waiter along shortly.

"Nice place," Zoe said, looking around.

"I'm sure you've seen similar in Houston," he said a little flatly.

Somehow seeing the way that guy had stared at Zoe had taken a little of the shine off the evening for him. In fact, he was beginning to question what he'd been thinking inviting her here. Showing off? Letting the city girl know he could give her as good as she was used to? *Idiot,* he told himself. They weren't even a couple in the true sense of the word. He had no right to feel possessive about her, no matter how intimately he knew her body.

"Not quite as sumptuous as this," she said with a smile and took a sip from her water glass.

The wine waiter came across and took their orders, shortly followed by the waiter bringing menus and letting them know the specials. Cord was grateful for the respite when they took their time selecting their appetizers and mains, and a little surprised, too, when he discovered they'd each chosen the same.

"Great minds think alike, hmm?" Zoe said with a warm smile that sent a wave of lust straight to his groin.

"Fools seldom differ," he countered, still a little surly.

Zoe reached across the table and took his hand. "Is everything okay? Would you rather we left?"

He shook his head. Of course she'd notice his change in mood. She was trained to observe these sorts of things. To study the human condition and ascertain the difference between the truth and the lies. Was that what she was doing with him all the time? Did she realize that while he'd started using sex as a distraction tactic, it had quickly become something else that he didn't want to define? He realized she was waiting for an answer and gave her fingers a squeeze.

"No, it's nothing. It's been a while since I've dined here is all."

In fact, the last time he'd eaten here was when he proposed to Britney, just before she left for training. The memory made his heart ache. Just two short years ago and yet it felt like a lifetime. And here he was, overlaying a new memory. He didn't know whether to be annoyed with himself or pleased that he was finally letting go. One thing was for sure, though—this thing with Zoe wouldn't go any further than the time she was here in Royal. He'd make sure of it. He couldn't handle the constant fear of living with a woman who carried a gun for a living again. His worst nightmare had already been realized once; there was no way he was tempting fate again.

The food, when it came, was sublime, and there was something inherently sensuous about the way Zoe enjoyed her food. He found he took pleasure in watching her, listening to the cadence of her voice as they talked, simply enjoying her presence. The last of his bad mood brushed away, and they were lingering over coffee and sharing a truly delicate serving of crème brûlée when he became aware of someone stopping beside their table.

"Cord, darling, how are you? We haven't seen you here in ages."

Cord rose to his feet, identifying one of his mother's Women's Institute cronies and her long-suffering husband hovering right behind her.

"Mrs. Radison, good to see you looking so well."

"Oh, you charmer, you. I received an email from your mom the other day. Seems like they're enjoying Palm Springs. And who is this?"

Just like that, the woman dispensed with the niceties and got straight to the point that he knew had led her to stop at his table. He had no doubt that the fact he'd been out with a new woman would be all around the gossips in town within five minutes of Olive Radison leaving the building. She put the word *social* in capital letters when it came to social media.

"Zoe Warren, please meet Olive Radison and her husband, Bert," Cord said, hoping this encounter would be over soon.

"Pleased to meet you, dear," Olive Radison purred. "So lovely to see Cord moving on. After all, it's been a while now, hasn't it, dear?" She patted Cord gently on the cheek, oblivious to the way his body had stiffened as if set in concrete. "Come along, Bert. We mustn't keep these young people from enjoying one another's company any longer."

And then she was gone, leaving behind a generous waft of her floral fragrance and a sense of discomfort settling on Cord's shoulders like a leaden cloak.

"Sorry about that. One of my mom's friends."

"No problem. She seemed friendly," Zoe commented lightly.

But there was something there in her gaze now that

wasn't there before. Questions that remained unasked and, on his part, unanswered. Suddenly he couldn't wait to get out of here.

"You done?" he asked abruptly.

Zoe's eyes flicked to his, and she stared at him a moment before giving him a quick nod. "Sure," she answered, gathering up her bag and rising from her chair. "I'll just go to the bathroom. Be back in a minute."

The dessert sat on the table, still unfinished, just like so many other things between them, he thought as he gestured for the bill. He'd settled the account by the time she returned to the dining room, and he rose to meet her halfway across the room. Together they went out to wait for the valet to bring his car around. The trip back to her motel felt a whole lot longer than the journey out. It was only as they neared the motel that they saw the flash of red lights and saw the fire engines and hoses lining the street.

"What the hell?" Zoe cried out as it became apparent it was the motel that had been on fire.

Cord pulled over and together they approached the area where the motel manager had assembled with a few of the occupants.

"What's going on?" Zoe asked when the woman turned to her to give her attention.

"I'm sorry, hon. But it seems someone's phone charger started a fire in the end unit. Once it took hold in the roof it spread quickly. There are fire walls between the units, but even so, there is a lot of smoke and water damage. I'm not sure they'll be allowing anyone back in to stay tonight. We'll have to reassess in the morning."

"Our things? Can we retrieve them?"

"I'll speak to the fire chief when he's free, okay, hon? Have you got somewhere else you can stay tonight?"

"She's staying with me," Cord said firmly.

"Thank goodness," the manager said with obvious relief. "The other motel near here is closed for renovations, and the hotel in town is able to put up a few people, but they're almost at capacity themselves, so we're short of beds."

Cord felt Zoe shiver as the manager moved away to where it looked like a command center had been established. He identified the fire chief there, and Nate Battle, too.

"My weapon is in there and my computer. I have to be able to clear my things from my room safe," Zoe said firmly. "I should go and speak to the sheriff."

That cold slice of reality cut through him again. Every time he let himself relax a little, forget a little, that one piece of hell-no-don't-go-there would come back and smack him clean in the face.

"Let's wait a bit. You're a registered guest. They know you're here. They'll come to us when they can," he said. "Are you warm enough?"

Before she could answer, he shrugged off his jacket and laid it around her shoulders. He could see she was at the point of protesting but thankfully she didn't. The night air was cooler than it had been, and she sure wasn't dressed for the climate.

It was another hour before the fire crew deemed it safe for those in units farthest from the burned-out room to enter their rooms and retrieve their belongings. Zoe didn't waste a second. Cord went with her, packing her toiletries in the bathroom as she grabbed her small case and her gun and laptop.

"This it?" he asked as he came through from the bathroom.

She gave him a brusque nod.

"You sure pack light."

"I wasn't planning on staying long."

Cord felt a twinge of guilt at her comment. She would be staying a whole lot longer now, thanks to him and his little discussion with Frank.

"Hey, don't worry about it. At least you know you can stay at my place."

"Your ranch is hardly the hub of activity here in Royal. What if I get bored?"

She gave him a challenging look.

"Then it will be up to me, as your host, to ensure you don't get bored, won't it? C'mon, let's go. The stink of this place is getting right up my nose."

Zoe followed the Maserati out to the ranch. She didn't want to be stranded when the call came to say she could conduct the interview with Stevens, and she couldn't see Cord letting her use the Maserati, although the idea had merit.

She pulled her car up outside Cord's house, swinging it off to one side of the driveway as he turned toward the multibay garage to the side of the property. He met her at the steps to the front door.

"You could have parked in the garage," he suggested.

"I prefer to be parked for a quick getaway," she said, only half joking.

He snorted, and she could see he wasn't entirely pleased with her response. *Well, so what*, she thought. This evening had gone from a very promising beginning to crash and, quite literally, burn in a very short space of time. And, she noticed as they entered the house, she had managed to get soot on her new dress into the bargain. There'd better be a decent dry cleaner in town.

She fought back a yawn. With last night's lack of sleep and the drama this evening, she felt exhausted.

"You want your own room this time?" Cord asked as they went up the stairs.

"Sure," she said, annoyed that he'd offered.

Something had crawled under his skin tonight, but she was too tired and irritated to try to figure it out. He showed her into a large room that, come morning, would be bathed in sunshine. The white bed linens reminded her of her somewhat-grimy state. Despite the fact the fire hadn't reached her unit, the soot and smoke had managed to permeate everything she'd touched or brushed against.

"Thanks," she said abruptly as Cord showed her the door to the connecting bathroom. "I can manage from here."

He stopped directly in front of her. "Are you sure about that? You look done in, and—" he paused to sniff "—your stuff smells of smoke."

She groaned in frustration. "I'd better put my stuff through the wash before bed."

"Don't worry about it. Leave it with me. Go." He tugged the bag from her hands and pushed her gently in the direction of the bathroom. "Shower. I'll leave something for you to sleep in on the bed."

He was gone before she could protest. All he'd left her with was her laptop case and her toiletries bag. Her gun was tucked into the side of the computer bag, and she'd seen his gaze flick past it. It was obvious he had some aversion to her carrying a weapon. Odd, when Texas was an open carry state. It wasn't unusual to see any adult carrying a gun. But, she'd noticed, he didn't carry one himself. She shrugged, putting the thought aside for now.

The shower was everything she longed for. She let the hot water sluice over her body and wash away the tension of the evening. What had that all been about, anyway? Something from Cord's past, obviously. And, just as obviously, something he hadn't wanted to discuss. Maybe she could probe a little more about that tomorrow, but for now, she needed rest.

She toweled off and padded through to the bedroom on bare feet. Cord had been back in here, she noticed. The drapes had been drawn and a deliciously soft T-shirt had been laid on the bed. She picked up the garment and held it to her face, inhaling the faint scent of his cologne. It felt sinfully wicked letting the wash-worn cotton skim over her body, almost like a lover's caress. And just like that, weariness fled from her body and a sensual tug of longing infused her instead.

He'd turned down her bed while she'd been showering, and she eyed the crisp white sheets with a mix of longing and aversion. It would take only a moment to head down the hallway to his room. She shook her head and yanked the sheets back a little farther. No, she was being strong. He'd clouded her mind quite enough for the very short time she'd known him. She needed to take charge of herself again.

She slid into bed and tugged the comforter up to her chin and lay there as stiff as a board, staring at the ceiling. It wasn't more than a half hour when she heard a soft knock at her bedroom door. It was so soft that if she'd been asleep, she probably wouldn't have heard it.

"Yeah," she called out.

The door opened a crack. From the soft light of the hallway she saw Cord standing there, his torso naked and a pair of pajama pants barely clinging to his hips.

"Everything okay?" he asked.

"I can't get to sleep," she admitted.

"Need some company?"

"Sure."

He was crossing the room before the word was fully

spoken, and she felt him get into the bed beside her. A few seconds later and his strong arms had pulled her against him, her back to his front. She felt him kiss the top of her shoulder where his T-shirt had fallen away to expose her skin.

"Go to sleep now," he said softly.

And, to her surprise, she did.

Nine

Zoe woke the next morning feeling like she'd had the best rest in a very long time. She rolled over to greet Cord, but he was already gone, and his side of the bed was cold, too, alerting her to the fact he'd been up for some time. Well, this was a working ranch, she reminded herself as she headed to the bathroom. When she came out, she was at a loss for what to wear and ended up staying in the T-shirt of Cord's that she'd slept in.

She made her way back downstairs and went to the kitchen, drawn by the aroma of freshly made coffee. Her mouth was quite literally watering by the time she found a mug in the cupboard and poured a cup from the carafe on the warmer.

"Good morning."

A voice from behind her made her spin around.

"Good morning to you, too. Good coffee, thanks," she answered, holding her mug up to Cord in a toast. "You're a man of surprising talents."

He smiled, the action sending a punch of heat straight through her body and making her all too aware that she stood here before him dressed in nothing but an oversize T-shirt. For all that it covered her butt and skimmed her thighs, she knew her nipples had to be prominent against the well-washed white cotton. She hazarded a glance downward. Yup, there they were. Perky as all get-out and happy as hell to see him.

And he was a sight this morning. Dressed in blue jeans, worn in all the right places, and a loose-fitting chambray shirt that was open a few buttons at the neck, he was a visual feast. Zoe took a sip of her coffee, sucking down the hot brew as if it wasn't burning the roof of her mouth and scalding her throat. Anything to distract herself from taking those few short steps across the kitchen and jumping up into Cord's arms and hooking her legs around his waist.

"Speaking of talents," he said as he grabbed a mug and poured himself a coffee, too. "Your clothes are dry and ready for you when you want to get dressed."

He made it sound as though getting dressed was optional, and for a moment she considered tormenting him by just hanging out in his T-shirt all day long. But she knew she would be the one to suffer. Already she felt as though she was at a disadvantage.

"Thanks, I'll grab them now."

"Would you like to look around the ranch with me today? I need to check some fences in the outer pastures."

"On horseback?" she asked, barely suppressing a shudder.

Sure, she could see the value of horses in this environment, but nothing and no one said she'd ever have to ride one. As far as she could tell, one end bit and the other kicked. She wasn't interested in what came in between.

"Not keen?"

"Not on horses, no. Got bikes?"

"I'm sure you'll enjoy what I'm planning. Why don't you get dressed, then we can have breakfast and get going."

"Yes, sir," she said with a mock salute. "Question."

"Yeah?"

"Where's the laundry room?"

He chuckled and pointed down a hallway off the kitchen she hadn't been down before. "Down there. You'll find it."

"Thanks."

She grabbed her things and went up to her room to dress. In no time she was back in the kitchen. She moaned out loud at the scent of breakfast cooking.

"Are those huevos rancheros?"

"Yup," Cord said, sliding eggs onto the plated tortillas topped with fried beans.

He spooned fresh salsa over the eggs and then crumbled feta cheese over the top and garnished it all with chopped cilantro. He took their plates over to the large wooden kitchen table and set them down.

"Eat," he said simply and gestured for her to take a seat.

Zoe didn't waste another second. She sampled the breakfast and moaned again.

"This is amazing. I think you must have missed your calling. Ranching? Forget it. You should have been a chef."

Cord smiled in return. "I did think about learning to cook professionally, but I was born to this ranch and its way of life. From the day I was old enough to walk, I was out there with my dad learning the ropes from the ground up, the way he learned from his dad."

"And the way you'll teach your children one day, too?"

He stiffened, his fork halfway to his mouth. "Maybe," he admitted before letting his fork clatter down onto his plate. "What about you? Planning to have kids one day?"

She shrugged, not entirely comfortable with the conversation being turned back to her. “Maybe,” she replied, mimicking his answer. “But the cooking? This is seriously good. If you ever decide to give up ranching, you could make a killing with your food.”

Cord helped himself to a little more salsa from the bowl he’d put on the table.

“They’re my grandmother’s recipes. I’ll be sure to tell her you’re impressed.”

“Please do. This is feta cheese, right?”

Cord nodded.

“I’ve never been a fan of it before, but this tastes divine,” Zoe enthused.

“I make it myself. I keep a few goats and like to dabble in new ideas. Who knows, maybe one day I can expand my herd some more and turn the goats and the cheese into a more commercial operation.”

“Seems I learn something new about you every day,” Zoe commented as she cleaned up her plate with the last scrap of a tortilla.

Cord shrugged. “I’m not complicated. If you want to know anything about me, just ask.”

Zoe leaned back in her chair and looked at him. “What went wrong last night?”

“With the fire?”

“No.” She pushed. “Before that. You were all good until we got to the club, and then when that woman stopped by, it was like you had been frozen in ice.”

“Old memories.”

Zoe waited for him to expand on that, but it seemed he felt that was quite enough on the subject because he abruptly rose from the table and cleared their plates away. Zoe rose to help him but he shooed her off.

“Go do whatever it is you women do before going out.

We'll be leaving in about fifteen minutes. Meet me by the garage."

Accepting she'd been summarily dismissed after touching on what was obviously a very raw subject for him, she did as he suggested and went back up to her room. After a quick trip to the bathroom she folded her clothes and stacked them in one of the empty drawers. They didn't take up a lot of room. Satisfied she'd killed enough time, she went downstairs and out to the garage. Cord was waiting by his truck. She could see he'd loaded some tools and a roll of fencing wire in the back of the truck.

As they headed down the drive Zoe asked, "Where are we going?"

"You'll see," Cord responded cryptically.

She fought back the urge to press him for more information, but they hadn't traveled more than five minutes before he turned off the road and drove toward what looked like a hangar. A wind sock hung limply at the end of what she worked out was a runway.

"You have an airport?"

"A private strip. Jesse and I share it, as it borders both our properties. We learned to fly together. He prefers to stick with fixed-wing and I prefer choppers."

"Choppers."

"Don't tell me you'd rather go horse riding?" he laughed.

"Actually, no, I wouldn't," she responded firmly. "Choppers are fine."

"So glad you approve," he teased. "Here, come and give me a hand with these."

He gave her his toolbox to carry while he grabbed the roll of fencing wire, then led the way into the hangar.

"We're going up in that?" Zoe asked, eyeing the small chopper settled on one side of the hangar.

"What, cold feet, Detective?"

"It's smaller than I'm used to, that's all."

"The Robinson R44 is perfect for around the ranch. We use it to monitor stock, find strays and check the fence lines. All sorts of things. It's highly maneuverable, so it's perfect for the kind of work we do."

"Sounds versatile."

"Oh, it is. You'll see for yourself in a few minutes."

"Where do you want this?" she asked, gesturing to the toolbox she'd set at her feet.

"I'll take it," he said, stepping toward her and picking it up with next to no effort at all.

She'd seen him naked so she knew he wasn't heavily muscled, but the man was very clearly strong. He hefted the toolbox into a compartment at the back of the chopper with ease and stacked the fencing wire in there, too, before attaching a pair of ground-handling wheels to the helicopter skids; then, grabbing hold of the back of the chopper, near the tail rotor, he tilted the machine and rolled it forward out of the hangar to the area marked on the tarmac with a large letter H.

Zoe followed, fascinated by the whole process. "I never realized it was as easy as that to move the thing."

Cord laughed. "There are all sorts of tools you can use. I prefer these," he said, gesturing to the removable wheels.

He bent down to remove them from the skids, and after stowing them away back in the hangar, he did a preflight inspection on the chopper. The sun glinted on the bright blue of the fuselage, making Zoe shield her eyes and wish she'd brought her sunglasses.

"There's a spare pair of sunglasses in the glove compartment in the truck if you need them," Cord said as he got to the end of his inspection.

"Thanks."

Zoe didn't waste any time. She went straight to the

truck and opened the glove compartment. The space was very full but she spied the sunglasses quickly and tugged them free. As she did so, a double-folded sheet of paper fell out with them. A funeral service notice, she realized. A stunningly pretty young woman smiled up at her from the front of the notice. She recognized her from a photo she'd seen at the house and assumed it was a relative. Zoe scanned the dates. The girl had died a couple of years ago. Was she the reason for the "memories" Cord had referred to? Instead of relatives, had they been a couple? Feeling as though she was prying into something intensely private, Zoe pushed the notice back into the glove compartment and swung it closed.

As she slid the glasses onto her nose and walked back toward the chopper, she thought about the young woman whose face had imprinted on her so firmly. There was something familiar about her, too, but she couldn't put her finger on when or where she'd seen her. Obviously she couldn't ask Cord. She didn't want to be accused of being nosy, for a start, but she sensed that the subject of the late Britney Collins was a sensitive one.

"Ready?" he asked as she drew closer.

"For sure. Thanks for the shades."

"No worries. I always carry spares."

Zoe's stomach lurched a little as they rose in the air and turned sharply to one side and flew away from the airfield. There was an incredible sense of freedom sitting here in this relatively small bubble and observing the ground racing away beneath them.

"All good?" Cord asked, his voice a little tinny through the headset he'd instructed her to wear.

"A-okay," she replied. "This is really cool."

He flung her another of those grins that made her toes curl. She watched as he competently handled the chopper, dipping and weaving along the contours of the land as they followed fence lines, until he found an area that looked to have been breached. He swiftly turned the chopper around, making Zoe's gut lurch again, before setting the machine down on a level patch of land.

"You do that as if you're born to it," she said after they'd exited the R44.

"I love it. There's a freedom that comes from being in the air that you don't get in a car or a truck. No matter how high performance."

She helped him carry his gear over to the breach in the fence line and watched as he competently made the repairs, handing him tools when he asked for them.

"You're good at this," he commented as she neatly packed his tools back into the box when he was done.

"I used to help my dad around home a lot. With my four older brothers, he had to do a lot of repairs," she said with a laugh.

"I can imagine. Did you enjoy growing up in a large family?"

"It has its drawbacks, but overall it's been good. My brothers are all married now and starting families of their own. It's a bit of a zoo when we all get together, but what can I say…it's family."

She stood up and stretched before leaning against one of the fence posts and surveying the land around them.

"Do you ever feel trapped by all of this?" she asked.

"Trapped? That's a strange way of looking at a large amount of space."

"Well, y'know. The responsibility you have to the land, to the herds, the people you employ. There's so much to consider every day of every month. You're never completely free of it, are you?"

He came and stood in front of her, and she could feel the warmth of his body as he came in close.

"Oh, city girl, you have no idea," he murmured before reaching up to pull something from her hair.

"Was that an insect?" she said with a wary glance at his hand as he tossed something away.

"Just a bit of grass. You're out of your element right now, aren't you?"

"It doesn't bother me," she said, defending herself.

"But you're not comfortable, either, are you?" he pressed.

"I'm never comfortable when I'm not in control. I don't know this world." She gestured around them. "Your world," she clarified.

"And you call yourself a Texan?" he teased, lowering his face to hers. "Let's see if we can't relax you a bit."

He planted his arms on the fence on either side of her and pressed his body against hers as he took her mouth in a sweeping kiss. He'd been thinking about doing this from the moment he first saw her in the kitchen this morning dressed in his old shirt. Last night had been difficult, but even so he hadn't been able to leave Zoe completely alone. He felt raw, as if his nerves were exposed and irritated, and the only thing that would soothe him would be to feel her warmth curled up against him as she slept in his arms.

That had been enough, for then. But now? Now was another story entirely. Now, with the clear fall light bathing the land around them and with the shade trees changing color and beginning to drop their leaves, the sheer satisfaction of being here in his element made him want to pull her into the spell, too.

Her mouth opened beneath his, her tongue meeting his and tasting him with the same eagerness he felt for her. It wasn't long before he knew that kissing her wasn't enough. Would likely never be enough. His desire for her was like a drug in his body, creating a need he couldn't, didn't want to control.

It was both exhilarating and terrifying in equal proportions. Look at how much he'd needed to be with her last night. Even with memories of Britney swirling in the back of his mind, he'd sought Zoe, convincing himself that she needed him more than he needed her. But as he'd lain there, holding her, listening to her steady breathing, absorbing the warmth of her skin, he'd admitted to himself that his need had been the greater.

He'd woken early, determined to put distance between them, but the second he'd seen her again all resolve had been blown to the four corners of the earth. He was glad she'd come out with him today. He'd wanted her to see this, his world, as she'd called it. To understand the call of the land, the beauty that lay before them.

What was the point, though? She was going to be here for only a short time longer. He doubted that Frank would be able to put Sheriff Battle off on the repairs to the equipment for much longer.

He'd take what he could get, he decided. Share with Zoe the perfect synchronicity of their bodies. And when she left, at least he'd have the memories.

Cord tugged her down to the ground and pulled her on top of him. He pushed his hands through her silky hair and cupped the back of her head as he continued to kiss her. She tasted so good, so right, and the way their bodies fit together was equally so.

"What's this?" Zoe asked, pulling slightly away. "Are we checking ground temperatures now?"

He laughed. She was amazing. He hadn't laughed during lovemaking this much, ever.

"Call it whatever you like. I thought it would be a shame to get your blouse all grass stained, hence me being on the bottom," he replied.

"Oh, so you don't want me to get dirty?"

There was a wicked gleam in her eye that totally undid him. "Oh yeah, get as down and dirty as you want."

"Did you bring a condom?"

"Do I look like the kind of man who'd forget something as important as that?"

She cocked her head and grinned. "I'm so glad you like to think of everything."

And then all sensible thought fled as she yanked his buttons undone and bared his chest. Her fingers spread over his skin, her nails lightly rasping over his nipples and sending shocks of delight through his body. He lay there, allowing her access to every part of him, lifting his hips in acquiescence as she tugged his belt free and undid his jeans. When her hands closed over his erection, he jerked against her.

"Whoa, there, cowboy," she murmured. "In some kind of hurry?"

"In some kind of something," he muttered in return.

He clenched his teeth and tensed as she stroked him, her rhythm perfect, and when she wriggled lower down his legs and took him into her mouth, he all but lost it. She licked and tasted him, drawing him into her mouth, then letting him slide free, in a tantalizing, teasing dance. The light breeze was a delicious cold shock against his wet skin. He couldn't take much more of this. He wanted—no, *needed*—to be inside her.

"Condom, front right pocket," he rasped.

Thankfully she was in agreement, because in a matter of moments she'd sheathed him and was pushing her jeans down and standing only briefly enough to remove them and her panties before lowering herself over him again. He could feel the heat at her center as she hovered over him, then reached for his shaft, guiding it to her entrance. And when she slid the rest of the way down he surged upward, meeting her halfway, again and again until the blue sky above them blurred and the only sounds he could hear were their labored breathing and the slap of their skin as she rode him to completion.

She sprawled across his body and he could feel the race of her heartbeat against his chest. He wrapped his arms around her, holding her close, knowing that this was only temporary but wishing it could be so much more. It was at least a half hour later that he felt her shift.

"We'll make a cowgirl of you yet," he teased as she got up and started to tug her clothes back on.

"Certainly has a few highlights to recommend it," she responded just as lightly.

But he could see the shadow that passed across her face. Yes, she was equally as aware as he was that what they shared was transitory. Well, given that fact, there was only one thing for it. They had to make the most of the time they had available.

And he did. Over the next three days he took her everywhere around the ranch with him, even going so far as to getting her up on his oldest, gentlest mare for a rein-led walk. And every night they lost themselves in each other. Of course, he never forgot who and what she was. Not even for a minute. Hard to when she checked her messages daily for updates on the Hamm case and spent a good portion of each evening on her computer. And there was her ever-present handgun. She hadn't worn it that first day they'd gone out in the chopper, but he couldn't avoid seeing its bulk nestled under her blouse every day since.

For now, he felt as though they were living in a bubble,

one where the outside world couldn't get to them. Which was just the way he liked it. Jesse had told him that Janet was coming home from the hospital this week—the infection she'd developed when her appendix burst was now almost clear. By the time she was firmly back on the road to recovery, and Jesse was relieved of the concerns he'd suffered on his baby sister's behalf, hopefully Zoe would have lost the bee in her bonnet about his best friend's possible involvement in the murder case.

He should have known better.

Ten

Zoe had taken control of the kitchen, with Cord supervising her breakfast-cooking skills. It was hard to focus with him standing there, leaning against the kitchen countertop with his hair still damp from the shower they'd just had together. Granted, he was dressed, which should have reduced the impact he had on her senses even after these past few days staying together. But to Zoe's surprise, her interest in Cord Galicia didn't appear to be waning anytime soon. In fact, the longer she stayed here, the harder she found it to focus on her case.

She was just removing bacon from the grill when Cord's cell phone trilled in his pocket.

"It's my dad," he said, checking the screen. "I need to take this."

"No worries, I'll keep everything warm for you."

"Everything?" he asked, stealing a quick kiss from her already swollen lips.

"Go, answer your phone call!" she laughed, giving him a playful shove.

She could hear him talking in the living room. Heard the sincerity and love in his voice as he spoke with his father. The bond was strong there, she realized. It surprised her in some ways, because Cord seemed to be so very self-contained. Not needing anyone or anything.

Zoe broke eggs into the pan and added cream, dill and seasoning before scrambling them all together with a spatula. She was just ladling them out onto warmed plates when the house phone started to ring.

"Can you get that please?" Cord called from the other room.

"Sure," Zoe replied and lifted the handset from the station in the kitchen. "Galicia residence."

"Is Cord available?"

"I'm sorry, he's on another call. Can I take a message?"

"Sure, it's Frank. Can you tell him I can't delay the repair of the sound and video equipment any longer? Nate's getting antsy and I really don't want to be in the sheriff's bad books. Tell Cord we're square now. I put it off as long as I could."

Zoe's brow furrowed in a frown. "Did you say sound and video equipment?"

"Yeah, yeah. Cord will know what I'm talking about. Can you just see he gets the message?"

"Oh, I'll see he gets the message, all right," she answered before severing the call.

Anger rose inside her like a storm surge, filling every nook and cranny of her mind and her body until it seeped from her pores like a palpable presence in the room. She replayed the conversation she'd just had over and over in her head. Each time it remained the same. Each time the result was damning. Cord had tampered with her investigation by deliberately delaying her interview with Jesse Stevens.

She heard a sound behind her and wheeled as Cord came back into the kitchen.

"Sorry about that. My dad sure can talk. He's missing the ranch." He came and stood beside her. "Hey, something's wrong. What's up?"

"You tell me," she said tightly.

"What do you mean? Who was on the phone?"

"Your friend Frank."

She watched his face as understanding dawned. "Ah."

Cord's expression closed up. Gone was the loving, playful cowboy who had occupied her days, and her nights. In place was the silent, careful man who'd greeted her the day she'd arrived in Royal.

"What you did was illegal. You deliberately hindered my investigation," she said bitingly through clenched teeth. "I should arrest you for that."

"Are you going to?"

"No. I don't plan to waste another second on you. Besides, the paperwork would be more than you're worth."

She shoved past him and headed upstairs. He was behind her a split second later.

"Where are you going?"

"To do my job."

She stormed into his bedroom, which they'd been sharing since that day out in the chopper, grabbed her bag and started throwing her things into it. Cord didn't try to stop her. Didn't so much as step in her way. She didn't know what upset her more—the fact he'd done what he had, or the fact that he didn't seem to care now that she knew. Then understanding dawned.

She wheeled to face him, hands fisted and planted on her hips.

"This was your intention all along, wasn't it?" she demanded. "Keep me distracted so I wouldn't question your buddy!"

To her utter humiliation he didn't say a word, but she saw the truth in his eyes.

"You bastard!" she spat.

She snatched her bag from the bed and hammered down the stairs. She paused only long enough to grab her laptop and case from the sitting room and then she was out the door. He didn't follow. He never said a word. And as bitter, angry tears started to track down her cheeks, she realized she'd been taken for a complete fool. Seduced by an oh-so-talented lover. Falling for all the stereotypes she'd sworn she'd never be caught by. Turned out she was just as fallible as anyone else. Worse, she'd been as stupid as some of her colleagues had always expected her to be. She'd lost sight of the case and all because a handsome man had paid her attention.

Well, she thought as she swiped the tears from her face and turned her car toward town, she'd learned her lesson, hadn't she? This interview with Jesse Stevens was happening today, one way or another, and then she was heading home.

She drove directly to the sheriff's office and parked outside. Thankfully Sheriff Battle was in when she asked for him, and he was quick to assure her that the interview room would be ready for her early in the afternoon. He also offered to contact Jesse himself and ask the guy to come in. All of which meant she had a few hours to cool her heels before she could complete her task here and then get the hell out of town.

Zoe headed to the Daily Grind and grabbed a coffee and something to eat. As she sat at the small table near the window and stared outside, she wondered if Cord had eaten the breakfast she'd just finished preparing before the scales had been torn from her eyes. Darn, but she'd been such an idiot. If anything, that hurt more than his lack of sincerity in starting their affair. And, yes, he'd started it. And she'd let him.

She suppressed the tingle that began in her body at the memory of that first night, of being pressed against the motel room door while he did incredible things to her. It had all been fake. A distraction tactic. And it had worked. But no more. She didn't trust anyone, especially not Cord Galicia.

Her mobile phone pinged with a text confirming the interview with Jesse Stevens at one o'clock. She texted back her agreement and finished her coffee. She still had hours to kill. Realizing she needed to burn off some steam, Zoe went for a long walk. While she walked, her phone buzzed. She looked at the screen. Cord. Damn him. She declined the call and shoved the phone back into her pocket, where it began buzzing again. She ignored it, only to have the darn thing continue to go off at regular intervals. In the end she turned off her phone, but she'd worked up a fine head of steam by the time she was shown into the interview room at the station. Sheriff Battle was already there, setting up the equipment. He looked up, his expression growing wary as she walked in.

"You okay?" he asked.

"I'm fine," she said sharply, then sighed. "No, actually I'm not fine, but my day will improve once I get this interview done and get back to Houston."

"Sick of us already?"

She cracked a wry grin. "I do have a job to do. Seems everyone has forgotten that fact."

Nate Battle shrugged. "Looked like you were getting

real comfortable with Cord the other night when he took you back to his place."

She stiffened. "He put me up for a few days, that's all."

He stared at her for a few moments, then nodded briefly. "Jesse should be here any minute. The recording equipment will upload a digital file to your email address when we're done. It'll be waiting for you when you get home."

"Good," she said. "Nice to know it's all working fine now."

"Yeah, about that..."

"Don't worry about it. The problem's sorted."

Yes, the problem was sorted, and she'd begun to accept that she'd had a narrow escape from a dirty, low-down snake. It would have been all too easy to fall for Cord Galicia. She'd deeply enjoyed her time with him on the ranch, had even begun to see the beauty that held him there, although her craving for hot asphalt and skyscrapers still lingered beneath the surface. She shook her head slightly. Nope, she wasn't going back down that memory track. She'd seal it up instead, for good.

A sound at the door made her turn and watch as one of the sheriff's deputies showed Jesse Stevens into the room.

"Good afternoon, y'all," he said, removing his hat and setting it on the desk between them.

Nate Battle didn't waste any time. He launched straight into the formalities, inviting both Jesse and Zoe to take a seat and then turning on the equipment and making the introductory statement for the record. Zoe felt her skin itch as she waited her turn to fire the questions she'd been hanging out to ask. After confirming it was Jesse's voice on Hamm's phone, she pushed him a little harder.

"You were extremely angry with Mr. Hamm when you left that message, weren't you?"

"I was."

Jesse's response was clipped, and she saw the glint of irritation in his green eyes.

"Could you state for the recording why you were angry with Mr. Hamm?"

"Sure. It's common knowledge that over the years I did several favors for the guy. When the shoe was on the other foot and I asked him for help getting an internship at Perry Holdings for my sister, he flat out refused. Seems the big city and his job there made him think he was too good for his old friends back home."

"I can see why that would have upset you," she said, baiting him.

"Upset me, yes. But not enough to murder the guy. I did not kill Vincent Hamm. I was mad at him, for sure, but I took it on the chin and moved on. I told you that around the time they say he was murdered I was three hours away from Houston, attending a stock auction." He reached inside his jacket pocket and drew out a folded wad of paper. "Here," he said, unfolding the papers and stabbing them with his finger. "As requested, my receipts. Motel, gas and copies of sale agreements."

Zoe looked over at Nate, who reached for the papers and carefully scrutinized them.

"It all looks genuine," he said carefully. "Covers the three-day window of time in which Hamm's murder most likely occurred, no question."

"Of course it's genuine," Jesse interjected. "I keep telling you. I'm innocent. Look, I'm sorry the guy is dead. No one deserved to die like that, but maybe he had it coming from someone other than me. Maybe he said no to just one person too many."

"Running my investigation now, are we?" Zoe added acerbically.

"I apologize, ma'am," Jesse said. "Not my place, I know.

But stand in my shoes for a minute and think about this. I would lose my family, my home—everything—if I were guilty of what you're suggesting. Look, if those receipts aren't enough for you, let me take a polygraph. I know you have one here, Nate. Hook me up. It'll prove my innocence."

Nate looked at Zoe with a question clear in his eyes. She took her time answering. On the surface, it would seem that Jesse Stevens was telling the truth. She sighed. Another dead end.

"Sure," she said to both men. "Let's do it.

It was close to four o'clock before the sheriff walked her out to her car. A sheet of paper flapped from under one of her wiper blades.

"Are you kidding me?" she groaned when she spied the parking fine.

Nate laughed and took it from her hand. "Let me take care of it."

"Thanks," she answered and opened her car door. "And thanks for your help today. I'm sure you probably had better things to do."

He shrugged. "There's always something to do around here. Might not be the bright lights and the big city, but it's never dull. You're satisfied now that Jesse's not your man?"

She nodded—a grimace twisting her features. "Yeah, but it puts us back to square one again. I'm sorry, Sheriff. I know you made promises to Hamm's family. I'd hoped we'd be able to bring them some closure by now."

"It's okay. I know you're not going to quit on this."

"Oh, trust me. Quitting is not in my nature. Obviously I need to shift focus. I've gone over and over my notes, but there's something I'm just not seeing. I keep coming back to the crime scene. It's gotta be someone connected to the building, or maybe even to someone connected to Perry Holdings. But where are the damn clues? Hamm must have seen or heard something that had gotten him killed, so why can't I find it?"

"You will. Eventually."

She laughed, but it lacked any humor. "Yeah. Maybe it'll shake loose on the drive back."

"It's getting late. You sure you don't want to stay an extra night?"

"No, definitely not. I need to get back," she said firmly. "I've been away too long as it is."

"Sure. You know, there were a lot of people surprised to see you with Cord at the club the other night."

"So glad I could provide entertainment for their evening," she commented cynically.

"He hasn't been seen out with anyone since Britney died."

"Britney?" There was that name again. Maybe now she'd find out why it had been oddly familiar to her.

"Yeah, they were engaged. Last time anyone saw them together was the night he asked her to marry him at the club a little over two years ago, just before she went to the police academy."

"She was a cop?"

"Yup, Houston P.D. Died on her first patrol. Nearly destroyed Cord when the news came through she'd been shot."

Understanding dawned. "I remember that. I didn't work the case myself, but everyone assigned to it was focused on finding her killers."

"It was a bad time for everyone who knew Britney, but most of all for Cord. His parents even delayed their retirement to help him out."

"And he hasn't been out with anyone since?" she blurted without thinking.

The sheriff shook his head. “Folks wondered if you’d be staying on.”

She barked a laugh. “No offense, Sheriff, but Royal’s just a little too tame for me.”

“That has its benefits,” he said with a smile that showed he wasn’t in the least offended.

Zoe held out her hand. “Thanks for everything. I’ll be in touch.”

“Thank you. And that file and the polygraph report will be waiting for you when you get to work tomorrow.”

After shaking hands, she got into her car and tapped her address into the map app on her phone. Then with a final wave to the sheriff, she headed out of Royal.

As she drove, her mind began to wander. So Cord had been engaged, and she’d been his first relationship since then. Not that it made any difference. He’d gone out with her only to stop her from interviewing Jesse. She thought back to the day she’d met him, to his dismissive attitude of her being a cop. All the pieces fit. But none of it excused him for using her the way he had.

Eleven

Her eyes were grainy with exhaustion by the time she pulled into her parking garage, but at least she was home. She'd taken only a short break about two hours out of Houston to grab some food and something to drink at a gas station. *Food*, she snorted as she grabbed her bag and laptop. *Cardboard with processed meat and cheese, more like.* She wondered if there was anything edible left in her apartment. Unlikely, but she'd take her chances when she got upstairs.

She exited the elevator and turned down the corridor to her apartment. All weariness fled and adrenaline flooded her system as she spied someone loitering near her front door. She dropped her things and reached for her gun just as the man turned around to face her. Shock replaced the adrenaline as she identified Cord.

"What the hell are you doing here?" she demanded, holstering her gun and snatching up her things again.

"And how did you know where I live, let alone get past security?"

How dare he be here? And ahead of her, too. She'd driven the maximum speed limit the whole way here. Unless he'd been here waiting for her for all the hours it took to interview Stevens. She felt a perverse imp of satisfaction at the idea of him cooling his heels for several hours tweak her lips into a half smile.

"You're not the only one with investigative skills," Cord said with a grin that flashed across his features, then disappeared just as quickly. "I'm here to see you. We need to talk."

"No, we don't. We've done all the talking—all the anything—we needed to do."

"Seems we differ on that topic. Perhaps I should have said, *I* need to talk to you."

"And why should I listen to you? You willfully obstructed my investigation."

"I did."

"We have no more to say," she said adamantly and brushed past him to insert her key into the lock. "Enjoy your trip back to Royal."

"I'm not leaving until we've spoken."

"Then I hope you'll be comfortable sleeping out here on the hallway floor because I have nothing to say to you."

She went inside and started to close the door, but Cord swiftly blocked her action.

"Look, hear me out. Please? I know I was a prize asshole. I apologize for that."

"Good of you, but it makes no difference. I'm investigating a man's death here. You impeded that investigation."

"So arrest me."

They stared at each other in silence for a full minute. Zoe couldn't tear her gaze from his. She could see her own reflection in the darkness of his pupils, saw the determination in every line of his face. His lips, which could do such wicked things to her body, were compressed in a grim line, and the humor that she'd so often witnessed in his expression was not evident today. He wasn't going to leave until he'd said his piece, that much was blatantly clear. She blew out a sigh of frustration.

"Fine, come in. Five minutes and then you're out again. How the hell did you get here, anyway?"

"I flew in."

She stopped halfway through to the kitchen and dropped her bags onto a chair.

"Just like that?"

"The beauty of flying."

"No five-and-a-half-hour drive? No toilet stops in questionable bathrooms?"

He shook his head.

"I hate you," she muttered as she entered the kitchen and opened the refrigerator to stare blankly at its meager contents.

"Even more than this morning?" he said, stepping up close behind her and peering over her shoulder.

She felt his presence acutely, even though he wasn't touching her, and caught her breath so she wouldn't inhale the appealing scent of him. Whatever he smelled like, however good he felt against her body or even inside it, he'd betrayed her.

"Yes, even more than this morning."

"What if I head to the convenience store around the corner and get us some food and cook you dinner? Would you hate me less, then?"

She closed the fridge door with a thud and turned to face him. "No, I wouldn't. It's late, I'm tired, I'm frustrated and I want to go to sleep. Say what you wanted to say and go."

"Not even a coffee?"

She rolled her eyes and moved to the coffee machine. "Fine, and then you go."

She went through the motions, not even fully aware of what she was doing. All she could think about was Cord and the fact he was here, in her world now. Not that it made any difference. She'd closed that door. It wasn't even as if a future together had been in the cards in the first place. Friends with benefits, that was all it was. Heck, not even friends, to be totally blunt.

"I hope you like it black. Milk's off, and I don't have any powdered creamer," she said, pouring him a mug full of the dark brew.

"Thanks, it'll do fine."

He took the mug, his fingers brushing hers. She hated the cliché of it, but there was no mistaking the jolt of awareness she felt as their skin brushed.

"You're not having any?" he asked.

"No, I need to sleep. Gotta get into the station early."

"Right, so I guess my time starts now?"

Cord watched as Zoe nodded and gestured for him to sit in the living room. Before sitting down opposite him, she removed her holster and slid her weapon onto the table between them. A reminder, perhaps, that she was trained in firearms and not afraid to use them. Or simply just a reminder that she was and always would be a cop.

He drew in a deep breath and began to speak. "What I did was wrong."

"Y'think?" she answered caustically and arched one brow at him.

"Not just from a legal perspective, but from a personal one. I've never been the kind of person to cause trouble with the police."

"And yet you did."

She crossed her arms and stared at him. Nope—she definitely wasn't going to make this any easier.

"Look, initially, when I knew you were investigating Jesse, it sent me into protective mode. He's been through a lot."

"And you don't think the Hamm family has been through a lot, too? That they don't deserve some answers as to who murdered their son?"

He shook his head. "I was wrong. I knew Jesse couldn't have been involved. I just didn't want you hassling him. But—" he held up one hand as she started to interrupt "—I had no right to do what I did nor delay your opportunity to interview him. I apologize for all of it."

"Great, I accept your apology. You can go now."

She started to stand.

"Look, just a few more minutes," he begged. To his relief she sat back down again. "I'm fiercely attracted to you, Detective. It scares me."

"Go on."

"I was engaged before, to a girl named Britney Collins."

"I know the name."

"Then you know what happened to her."

"I do."

"I can't go through that again. I can't face every single day knowing a woman I love is putting herself in danger." *Love?* Where did that come from? He was messing this all up, especially if the suddenly shuttered look on Zoe's face was any indicator. "I was never keen on her career choice. In fact, I have to admit that I never fully understood her need or her drive to become one of Houston's finest. But I couldn't hold her back. If I'd asked her, she wouldn't have done it. Instead, she'd have found work in Royal that satisfied her until we had kids, and then she would have stayed home with them. But I knew she wanted more than that.

"Part of me regrets not being selfish. She'd still be alive today if I had. But, in time, she'd have been desperately unhappy. Which brings me to you."

Zoe's eyes widened slightly. "Look, what happened to Britney was awful. It's something every cop and their family dread, but you can't compare her situation to mine. I've been raised in a police family. I've been a cop for nine years. I'm not saying I won't ever get killed on the job, but I am saying I am well trained, and in my role as a detective, I'm not exposed to the kinds of things a frontline officer is on a daily basis.

"But, all of that said, I'm not in the market for a relationship. Especially not a long-distance one. Hell, I'd probably stand more chance of being involved in a car wreck than I do getting hurt on the job."

"Does that mean you're not even willing to try? We have a connection, Zoe. You know it. I know it. Don't you think it's worth exploring to see what happens?"

She shook her head slowly, and he could see regret in her eyes. "No. Your life, everything, is in Royal. Mine is here. We might fit in the bedroom, but we don't fit when it comes to our lifestyles or our careers.

"I know you have an obligation to your family, and that's what drives you on your ranch. It's your home, it's what you do and, from what I could see, you're good at it. It fits for you. This city, the people in it, that's what fits for me. We're oil and water, Cord. We just don't mix. I think you should go now."

He stood, even though every cell in his body was telling him to fight harder, to tell her he could change, make adjustments, that if they both wanted it enough, they could make it work. But deep down he knew it would be futile.

In fact, it would probably only lead to more heartbreak for both of them.

"Thanks for hearing me out," he said, offering Zoe his hand to shake when she'd walked him to the door.

She took his hand and squeezed it gently, but before she could let him go he tugged her slightly off balance, pulling her against him. Without a second thought he cupped her jaw, tilting her face up to his and taking her lips with a kiss that both seared her flesh and said a bittersweet goodbye.

He stood outside the door after she'd closed it. He wasn't giving up. She might think it was over between them, but he had to be 100 percent sure they couldn't make a go of this. Life was too short and way too precious not to fight for what was important. He knew that better than most. And he had an ace up his sleeve that Zoe wasn't expecting.

Cord started walking to the elevator. This round was hers, but he was pretty certain he'd win the next one.

Cord pulled up outside the sprawling home in a suburban part of Houston the next day. The lots were a generous size here, the gardens well established and there was an air of quiet gentility about the area, with echoes of past families having been raised around here. He checked the address he'd been given and looked at the house across the street. So this was where Zoe had grown up. He could just imagine a younger, skinnier version of her shinnying up one of those giant trees or riding her bike along the sidewalk.

He reached for the large colorful bunch of flowers on the passenger seat of his rental car and the bottle of red wine he'd bought and got out of the car. The older woman who opened the door to his knock was smiling widely.

"You must be Cord," she said. "Welcome to our home.

We're so grateful to you for looking out for Zoe while she was out of town."

"Mrs. Warren, lovely to meet you, and it was a pleasure. Can I just say how like Zoe you look, or should that be the other way around?"

"Ah yes, people do say that. Come on out back. The boys and their families are already here. We're just waiting for Zoe."

"These are for you," he said, giving Zoe's mom the bouquet of flowers.

"They're beautiful, thank you. You'll make my husband jealous," she said with a girlish giggle.

"Well, I have brought him a gift, too," Cord said, brandishing the bottle of wine. "So I hope he'll forgive me."

She spied the label. "Oh yes, he'll forgive you, all right. Follow me."

Cord trailed behind her, his eyes catching on a series of family photos that lined the hallway in groupings that appeared to be by various eras within the family. He'd have liked to have lingered and studied the progression of Zoe's childhood to the woman she was today, but Zoe's mom was disappearing through a doorway ahead of him. He quickly followed her through the door and was met by a cacophony of sound. Kids, dogs, family. It looked like there were people everywhere.

This was what Zoe had grown up surrounded by. It was very different from his upbringing as the only child of a close-knit ranching family. Sure, they'd had extended family to visit occasionally, and some of the hands lived on-site. And there had been the Stevens kids as well, but this was something else.

"Jed, come and meet Cord, the guy I was telling you about."

A heavyset grizzled man in his late fifties put down the

tongs he'd been using on the outdoor grill and wiped his hands on the apron he was wearing. The pink frilly fabric looked incongruous on him, but that fact didn't seem to bother him at all as he came over to meet Cord.

"Jed Warren. I'm Zoe's dad. Pleased to meet you."

"Cord Galicia. Likewise. This is for you," Cord said, handing the man the bottle of wine.

"Well, thank you very much. We invited you here to thank you for looking out for our girl, not for you to bring us stuff," Jed said with a grin.

"My mom always said I should never arrive anywhere empty-handed."

"Well, I appreciate this. I really do. In fact, I might just put this on the rack so it doesn't get quaffed by the riffraff here." Jed gestured toward four young men in the backyard who, by their appearance, were obviously his sons.

Zoe's mom linked her arm in Cord's. "Come and meet the rest of the family, and please call me Sarah."

Cord made it through most of the introductions before completely losing track of which kids belonged to what parents, but there came a point when he felt a shift in the camaraderie of the moment to one of pointed observation. It coincided with an intense prickle of awareness running down his neck. Zoe was here. Slowly, he turned around and faced her. Fury and disbelief warred for dominance on her beautiful features.

Sarah Warren saw her daughter and bustled forward. "Zoe, darling. Glad you could get away from work. Come, have a drink."

"What's he doing here?" she asked bluntly.

Cord saw color infuse her mother's cheeks. "Zoe," she whispered fiercely. "We don't treat our guests like that."

"He's a guest? Seriously? You invited him?"

"Of course we did. He called us, trying to track you

down. Said you'd left something at his house when he put you up after that dreadful motel fire. You remember, the one you didn't see fit to tell your mother about?"

Cord stifled a grin. There was nothing quite like a mother's love and censure all rolled into one telling off. Zoe, it seemed, felt the same way.

"Mom, it wasn't that bad. But I still don't understand why he's here."

"Well, when he called and asked for your address, we just wanted to say thank-you for his hospitality toward you, of course."

The way Sarah spoke, it made her invitation to him so very matter-of-fact, but he could see Zoe wasn't having any of it.

"Right," she said, in response to her mom's explanation. "Well, I can't stay long. I'm waiting for a call to get back to the office."

"Surely you can take a couple of hours away from your work," her mother admonished and grabbed an ice-cold beer from a fridge on the back porch and shoved it into her daughter's hand. "There, now have a drink and play nice."

Sarah went back inside the kitchen, leaving Cord and Zoe mostly alone on the back patio.

"Great place your parents have. Must have been fun growing up here."

"With that lot?" she gestured with her beer bottle to her brothers, who'd lined up on either side of a picnic table to have a drink and a yarn while their wives supervised the children for a while. "Hardly."

"I bet it was fun," Cord said again, this time with a wistfulness to his voice that he hadn't expected.

"Are you stalking me?" Zoe said after a short silence.

"What? No!"

"It certainly looks that way."

"Look, I called your parents' house after you left because you left your computer cable behind. I wanted to know where I could send it. I explained to your mom why you'd been staying with me, and she gave me your address and then when I said I'd be in Houston, she invited me for dinner tonight. I could hardly refuse."

"Oh yes, you could totally have refused." Zoe took a swig of her beer and turned to face him. "And you still haven't given me my computer cable."

"Let's just say I got distracted yesterday. It's in my car now. I was going to leave it with your parents if you didn't show."

"You mean you didn't think I'd be here tonight?"

"Your mom wasn't sure if you'd make it. Seems you don't make it to a lot of family get-togethers these days."

Zoe groaned. "Don't you start. I get enough of that from Mom."

Cord shrugged. "Only repeating what she told me."

He looked at her. There were dark shadows under her eyes, giving them a bruised look and making her look more vulnerable than he'd ever seen her. He couldn't help himself. He reached out to touch her cheek. A slight buzz tingled through his fingertips as they grazed gently against her skin.

"You okay? You look tired."

She shook her head, breaking the contact. "I'm fine. This investigation is driving me insane, though. There's a whole ton of pressure from the top brass to wrap this up, like, you have no idea."

"And I made that worse for you, didn't I? I'm truly sorry. I wasn't thinking."

"Look, I accepted your apology," she said testily and took another sip of her beer.

"I know, but I meant it. Look, I won't stay. I can see that my being here is spoiling it for you."

Cord put his beer down on the table next to them and started to walk away. He was surprised when Zoe grabbed his arm.

"Don't you dare leave. It'll be more than my life is worth trying to explain it after you've gone."

He stopped and looked at her. She was glancing between him and her brothers, all of whom had turned to watch them with varying degrees of interest.

"Okay," he said and picked up his beer again. "Again, my apologies—this wasn't a good idea."

"No, it wasn't, but you're here now, so let's make the most of it. I take it you've met everybody?"

"Yeah. I like your family so far."

She snorted. "Well, the fact that you're still alive probably means they like you, too. Either that or they've decided you're an experiment."

"How so?"

"They're probably taking bets to see how long it'll take me to screw this up."

He raised his brows at her. "You do that often?"

She punched him in the arm. "I get enough cheek from that bunch over there," she said, nodding in the direction of her brothers. "If you're staying, you're my ally, okay?"

He shrugged. "Sure. Does that mean I get to kiss you again?"

In an instant the atmosphere between them thickened and changed into something far more intense. The sounds of the kids playing in the yard, of Jed grilling the meat and Sarah calling her boys to help bring salads out from the house all faded into the background. All Cord could focus on was Zoe's mouth. On the way her lips glistened with a sheen of moisture on the remnants of the lipstick she must have applied a while ago but that had mostly worn away. He wanted to remove the rest of it—with a scrape of his teeth, a rasp of his tongue, with the pressure of his lips.

Heat poured through his body and arousal followed swiftly after. He continued to stare at Zoe, and she remained silent in response. Her eyes had widened slightly, her pupils almost consuming the blue irises that told so much and yet hid so much at the same time. Cord realized that while he knew exactly how to bring her to a screaming climax, he knew very little about Zoe Warren, the woman. And he wanted to. Oh, how he wanted to. What had started as a distraction had wormed its way deep into his psyche and gone way beyond the physical attraction that sparked like fallen power lines between them.

This was so much more, and it was equally as dangerous at the same time.

Twelve

Zoe's breath caught in her chest. One minute they'd been bantering, she on the point of asking him to leave, until he'd gone and offered to do so—and she'd realized that she didn't want him to go after all. In fact, he was the reason she looked so darn tired today. It had nothing to do with the early start back at the station and everything to do with cursing herself for making him leave last night.

The truth was he frightened her. He was intense about everything he did—from seeing to his ranch to stroking her body to flaming life. She couldn't handle it. Didn't want to. And did, all at the same time. Cord Galicia had turned her on her head and she didn't like it one bit. Worse, he was distracting her from her work even when he wasn't deliberately trying to hold her back from doing her job. He'd inveigled his way into every crevice in her mind, meaning thoughts of him—reminders of his scent, the way he moved, the way he tasted—would unexpectedly send ripples of desire through her body at the most inopportune moments.

Last night, after she'd closed the door on him and sent him away—for good, she'd believed—she ended up going to her room and collapsing onto her bed, clutching her pillow to her body like some lovelorn teenager. She wasn't that person, and yet, somehow, he'd made her like that. Made her want him. Worse, he'd made her need him. She'd been unable to sleep in anything more than short snatches, and she'd been short-tempered with her team when she'd gone into the station this morning and they'd ribbed her about her vacation in the country.

There'd been no further progress on her case. She'd reviewed the sound and video files and polygraph results sent through from Sheriff Battle's office, looking for a loophole she might have missed, but they merely confirmed Jesse Stevens was totally clean. She'd even had his alibi checked out, although his receipts had been conclusive in themselves.

And then there was Cord.

She realized that her family was beginning to give them strange looks, as if they'd both missed something going on around them. And they had. While she and Cord had been locked in their bubble, the world had continued around them.

"Aunty Zoe, are you in love?"

The piercingly innocent curiosity of one of her nieces shook her from the spell she'd fallen under.

"What makes you say that, Theresa?" she asked, bending down to the four-year-old's level.

"'Cause you're looking at that man like mommy looks at daddy when she says she wants to eat him all up." Theresa took a deep breath. "And mommy loves daddy."

"Out of the mouths of babes," Cord murmured from behind her.

"Don't encourage her," Zoe said over her shoulder before smiling at her little niece. She rose, taking the little girl's hand. "No, honey. I'm not in love. But I am hungry for dinner. Are you?"

The rest of the evening passed relatively uneventfully. To her relief, Cord gave her some distance and didn't stick to her side. Even so, she was constantly physically aware of his every move. Even the way he tipped his beer to his lips sent a pull of longing through her. By the time her brothers and their wives started to gather up their kids and head home, it was getting late and exhaustion dragged at her.

Cord had been busy in the kitchen, helping clean up, when she decided it was time for her to go. Her mom, bless her heart, shooed Cord from the kitchen, telling him she and Jed could manage just fine from here. As a result, Zoe and Cord walked out together, and instead of her parents standing on the front porch and waving at her until she was out of sight, she had to fight back a tug of humor at her lips when her mom grabbed her dad by his arm and dragged him back inside immediately and shut the front door with a bang.

"Nice touch with the flowers for my mom, Galicia," Zoe said as she walked to her car with Cord shadowing at her side.

"I like to pay my respects. You have a nice family."

"Yeah, as much as I like to complain about them, I love them dearly. I couldn't stand to be too far away. It's not often we can all get together at the same time. We're all on different shift rosters, so whenever there's a free Sunday, Mom puts on an evening like this."

"Family is important."

"It's one of the reasons I'll never leave Houston," Zoe said firmly.

She needed to make it clear that she'd meant what she said back in Royal. No matter how powerful this attraction between them, there was no way it could ever work. Her job aside, she'd slowly die inside if she was that far from the network of her parents and siblings.

"I understand," Cord said quietly, his hands shoved into his jeans pockets as if he had to confine them to stop himself from reaching for her.

A part of her wished he would. Wished he'd take her into his arms and kiss her, right here on the street in full view of anyone. Instead, he tugged his keys out of his pocket.

"Good night, Zoe. It's been great. But I get the message. I'd hoped we could figure it out—make us work somehow—but now, having seen your family and you with them, I truly do understand what keeps you here. It's not just your job, because I know you'd be a great cop anywhere, and it's not the city. It's them, and you don't need to make any apology for that. Family is the glue that holds us together."

"Well, they're a pain in the butt most of the time, but yeah."

"They only want you to be happy. To have what they have."

Unexpected tears sprang to Zoe's eyes. His words cut her to her soul. She wanted that, too, but she wanted to be so much more than that at the same time. Somehow she'd just never envisaged being able to juggle it all. Her job had defined her for nine years, and, yes, she'd put her work ahead of everything and everyone she'd met along the way. With her dad and brothers being in the force, it had made it easier for her to hone her focus, even though they'd always teased her about settling down one day. But, at the same time, they balanced their work and family life without any serious problems.

But it would be different with Cord if they ever did try to make things work between them. He'd already lost a woman he'd loved to her job and in the worst way possible. Zoe had pulled the incident report and skimmed it when she'd gotten into work today. The facts had been chilling. No wonder Cord was so put off by guns and the people who carried them in their line of work.

He was walking away now, and she felt as if she was being torn in two. One half of her urging her to let him go, the other begging her to make him stay, even if only for one more night. The flip side won.

"Cord!"

She was moving toward him before she even realized it. The moment he turned, she reached for him, tugging his face down to hers. She kissed him—hard and fierce and with every ounce of longing that pulsed through her body.

"Come back to my place, please?"

He stared at her a full twenty seconds before replying. She could see the battle that raged behind his beautiful sherry-brown eyes. He closed them a moment, his long lashes sweeping down. They should look ridiculous on a man like him, a man who was so lean and fierce and strong, but instead they only made him look that much more appealing.

"Yes."

It was one simple word, just three letters, and yet it had the power to make her feel as if she'd won the lottery ten times over.

"Follow me," she said and all but ran back to her car.

He tailed her the few short miles back to her apartment building, pulling into the visitor parking he'd used the day before while she put her car in the parking garage. She ran up the ramp to where he was waiting at the front of the building, and she grabbed his hand and tugged him through the front door. She barely acknowledged security when they greeted her; she had only one thought burning through her mind. If this was to be their last time together, it had to be perfect, because it would have to last her forever.

The ride in the elevator was interminable, but finally they spilled out of the car and down the hallway to her apartment. She just managed to wrestle her door open and tumble inside her apartment with Cord right behind her. She grabbed him by his shoulders and pushed him up against the wall the second the door was closed and secured behind them. She tugged at his jacket, then his shirt, exposing the warm, tanned skin of his chest to her gaze, her fingers, her mouth.

He groaned and tangled his fingers in her hair as she kissed him and dragged her lips down his throat, nipping at the cords of his neck, then soothing them with her tongue. Her hands were busy at his belt, unbuckling it and then unbuttoning his fly with a dexterity that amazed her under the conditions. She shoved his jeans down his lean hips and her hand cupped his engorged shaft through his boxer briefs.

Cord didn't waste any time. He tugged at the buttons of her blouse and opened her jeans with equal alacrity, and she toed off her ankle boots and stepped out of her jeans, standing now on legs that trembled. His heated palm cupped her between her legs, and she just about went ballistic on the sensation of heat, silk and moisture against her most sensitive skin.

And then he was lifting her up against him. She hooked her legs around him and held on tight.

"Bedroom?"

"First door on the right past the sitting room," she directed.

He walked them both to the bedroom and dropped her unceremoniously onto the bed, but the second he joined her on the mattress she straddled him again, smoothing her hands in hurried caresses over his shoulders, his chest, his belly.

"You feel so good," she murmured and bent down to kiss him, her tongue teasing his, her teeth nipping gently at his lower lip, tugging it before swiping it with her tongue and kissing him hard.

Her entire body hummed for this man, and she couldn't wait to feel him inside her, stroking her to another amazing crescendo of feeling and sensation, but she could prolong the agony of waiting just a little longer if she could feast her eyes on him and touch him in all the places she longed to. Zoe traced the lean lines of muscle that defined his stomach, letting her fingers edge ever closer to the waistband of his briefs. She skimmed the elastic, then started from the top of his shoulders all over again.

"Detective, is there anything in particular you're looking for? Because you seem to be examining my body of evidence rather thoroughly."

She chuckled and nipped him in the hollow just inside his hip bone. He laughed in response.

"Don't rush me," she growled and pinched the side of his leg in punishment.

"Wouldn't dream of it," he replied.

Cord bunched his fists in her bedcovers and lifted his hips slightly as she slid her fingers beneath his waistband and began tugging his briefs off. His erection sprang proudly free of its confines, and Zoe smiled as she anticipated what she would do next.

"Seriously, Detective? You're just going to look at it?"

Stifling another chuckle, she looked up at his face

and gave him a stern stare. "Like I said, Galicia, don't rush me."

"Or what?"

"Or you might live to regret it."

"Are you going to torture me? I could get used to that."

She ignored the pang his words engendered. Get used to it? Get used to her? That wouldn't happen. She'd made it clear outside her parents' place. And then she'd muddied the waters by inviting him back here.

"Zoe?"

She looked into his eyes, saw the concern there.

"Just dreaming up a suitable punishment," she answered lightly.

She turned her attention to Cord's very enticing body and in particular to one very demanding shaft of flesh. She closed her fingers around the hot, hard rod and stroked him from base to tip before taking him into her mouth. He groaned again, and she teased him with her tongue and her lips until she knew he was almost at the point of no return. She released him from the warm, wet confines of her mouth and blew softly against his skin.

"Detective, I think you need to take me into custody soon or I might not be responsible for my actions."

"Duly noted," she said with a smile as she stretched over him and reached for the bedside cabinet drawer.

She grabbed a handful of condoms and dropped them onto the bed beside them before selecting one and smoothing it onto his straining flesh. Then, without wasting another moment, she straddled him again and guided him into her body, slowly and deliberately taking him inside her inch by slow inch. The expression on his face was one of pure concentration and control, as if he could slip at any moment. She loved the idea that she did this to him and that he let her.

Zoe rocked her hips, taking him that little deeper, clenching against his hardness, then releasing him, setting up a rhythm that increased in tempo until she could control herself no longer. And then she was lost on that wave of pure bliss, her internal muscles spasming and pulling Cord right along with her on that journey to the stars and back again. She collapsed over him, her body slick with perspiration and every nerve shuddering with the power of her climax. Inside her, she could feel him swell and twitch as the last of his orgasm pulsed into satiation and, finally, calm.

Cord's arms wrapped around her and he rolled them onto their sides, and together they slid into sleep, only to wake two hours later and take each other all over again. This time it was Cord who led the way, tormenting her to a point where she felt as though she might shatter into a thousand pieces, before taking her to even greater heights of pleasure.

When Zoe woke in the morning, it was to an empty bed and an empty apartment—and an even emptier heart. She sank onto the sofa in her living room, wrapped in one of her bedsheets, and bent her head and cried for all that they'd shared together and all that they would never have again. She knew now that it went beyond sex. Way beyond it. Somewhere along the line he'd stolen her heart. But it was a love that could never work, she reminded herself. She wouldn't compromise on that which was most important to her. Her family. Her work. And he knew that. Accepted it. Because he'd left without a goodbye, and now it was up to her to deal with that.

Eighteen-year-old Maya Currin synced her playlist to her car and settled in for the drive. The baby of Ryder Currin's kids, she knew if she'd told her family she was coming home, someone would have flown to drive her down or at least accompany her on the long journey from Boston back to Texas. But she didn't want company because she had plenty of thinking to do along the way. Not the least of which was clearing her head of that waste of space she'd called her boyfriend.

How could she have been so stupid to have thought Dirk had truly loved her? All he'd loved was her last name and the kudos that came with being one of the children of the famed oil baron and businessman, Ryder Currin. But she wasn't a real Currin, was she? No, she'd been adopted, and apparently discovering that had been enough for her boyfriend to stop pretending to love her anymore.

She shook her head as she put her car on cruise control after entering the I-81. How could she have been so stupid, so gullible? It was the latter that irked her the most. Her dad had always told her that people would like her for their position, for their money. She hadn't believed him and, believing she was a good judge of character, had delighted in proving him wrong. When she met Dirk, she truly believed every word that fell from his lying lips. Well, more fool her. Her love affair with him, however intense and brief, had momentarily distracted her from her quest to find out the truth about her birth. She'd always known her father knew far more than he'd ever let on, and she'd stopped worrying about it when she'd fallen in love.

But no more. Now she was going to get to the bottom of it. To find out what her birth story really was. She deserved to know. She was an adult, after all. Her father had promised he'd tell her the truth once she was eighteen and he owed her that truth now.

Being rejected for not being a real Currin was one thing. She could get over that and the idiot who'd even had the nerve to say such a stupid thing. But suffering the perpetual sense of disconnection from her father and her older siblings, Xander and Annabel—that was something else.

Yes, she'd known and accepted that Ryder Currin had chosen to raise her with Annabel's mom, Elinah. Elinah, Ryder's second wife, had, until her death when Maya was only five, been the only mother figure Maya had known. As a kid, she'd never questioned why they'd adopted her and brought her up as their own. Her adoption had been private and closed—which had sent up some flags when she'd tried to investigate exactly who her birth parents were. She had a right to know. A right to her history.

Every time she had a question it seemed as though there was yet another secret barring her from knowing the truth. Her father had told her over and over that the truth had no bearing on their relationship, that he loved her and that was all that mattered. But how could she continue to believe him and trust in his love for her when he wouldn't tell her who she really was?

The thought of walking away from the only family she'd ever known sliced through her like a physical pain. It was almost unthinkable, but if she didn't find the answers she sought, she didn't know if she could continue to pretend to be a part of them all. She needed to know the truth, and her father was the only person who could give that to her.

She'd decided this was important enough now to give up a week or more of her classes. Maybe she'd even take a break for the rest of this semester and return to Boston College again in the winter—with the truth in hand and her place in the world all the more secure.

Maya changed lanes and passed a long rig before easing back into the right-hand lane again. While she was eager to find answers, she wasn't exactly in a mad hurry for this confrontation. After all, she'd waited her lifetime to hear what her father would have to say, if he'd even say it, and she wanted to arrive safely and in one piece.

Thirteen

Cord kicked off his boots in the mudroom and walked into the house, heading immediately to the kitchen refrigerator. He snagged a beer by its neck and strolled back outdoors into the loggia. Damn, even here he couldn't rid himself of memories of Zoe.

The entire past week he'd been working every hour he could, even going so far as to repaint the sheds. Anything to keep busy and keep his mind off that woman. Thing was, nothing was working. No matter how tired he made himself, she'd inveigle her way into his thoughts.

He threw himself onto one of the outdoor sofas and leaned back to take a long pull of his beer. He grimaced as he swallowed it. Even that didn't taste any good. A sound from inside the house drew his attention, putting all his senses on alert. He wasn't expecting anyone, and thieves didn't usually bother this far out of town. He put his beer down on the table and rose to his feet, carefully opening the kitchen door and moving swiftly and silently through the lower floor.

He heard a sound again. This time there was no mistaking it. It came from the suite of rooms his grandmother had used. He doubted she'd left her valuables behind after the move to Palm Springs, but, either way, he hated the thought of someone pawing through her stuff. He reached for a tall brass candlestick off the hallway table and gripped it firmly in one hand as he carefully pushed the door open.

"Argh!" his grandmother screamed, and she dropped the clothes she'd been lifting from her suitcase on the bed.

She broke into a voluble stream of Spanish, telling her grandson in no uncertain terms precisely how many years he'd just shaved off her life. Cord threw the candlestick onto the bed and stepped forward to grab his grandmother and hug her tight. She was so tiny she barely even reached his chin, but her strong arms folded around his waist, just the way they had always done, and he felt her begin to calm down.

"What are you doing here?" he asked, still stunned to have discovered she was his intruder.

"Bah, Palm Springs. It's not for me," she said, tugging herself loose and bending to pick up the scattered clothing. "Maybe it's nice for a holiday, but I can't live like that. There's nothing to do!"

"Isn't that the point of being retired?" Cord said as he picked up a stray pair of his grandmother's voluminous underwear and passed them to her.

She snatched them from him with a sniff of disdain. "Retired? That was your father's idea. Not mine. He's my son and I love him but…" She shook her head vehemently. "Palm Springs is slowly driving him loco. I don't know how your mother stands it."

"But wasn't Palm Springs her idea?"

His grandmother made a dismissive snort. “Only after your father started talking about it. You know how he always needs to be led. Oh, he’s a hard worker, but he has to be allowed to think things are his idea. When he talked about Palm Springs and retiring, I don’t think either of them had the slightest idea of what it meant. Sure, they’ve made new friends, but it’s not—what is it you people say? Their scene?”

Cord sat on the bed and watched as Abuelita moved around the room, putting her things away.

“Anyway,” she continued, “I’ve had enough of being retired. So I came back to take care of you.”

“I’m a grown man, Abuelita. I can take care of myself,” Cord pointed out with a rueful grin.

His grandmother settled onto the comforter beside him. She raised a gnarled hand to his face, cupping his cheek and forcing him to look deep into her eyes.

“If that is so, my boy, then why do you carry so much pain in your eyes? Is it a woman? Let me talk to her. I’ll fix it for you.”

Cord laughed, the first genuine joy he’d felt since he’d slipped from Zoe’s bed and disappeared into the early strains of morning. The thought of Abuelita fronting up to Zoe and giving her a piece of her mind would be worth the price of ringside seats, for sure, but this was his problem and since it couldn’t be dealt with, it would simply have to be left to fade away.

“I see all your easy living hasn’t softened your edges,” he teased her, bending down to kiss the top of her head.

“Don’t try to distract me, Cord. I know when something isn’t right here.” She pressed a fist to her chest. “Tell me.”

“Talking about it won’t fix things,” he said firmly. “We’re too different. We knew it wouldn’t work from the start.”

“But you still got burned, yes?”

He nodded.

"It's good that you were prepared to open your heart again. I was scared that when you lost Britney, you would never trust yourself to love another woman." She sighed and patted his cheek before taking his hand. "Tell your *abuelita* about this woman. Tell me everything."

"She's a cop," he said on a deep sigh and felt his grandmother's fingers tighten almost painfully around his own.

"Go on," she prompted.

He told her the story of how they'd met. How unhelpful he'd been, how he'd deliberately distracted her from being able to meet with Jesse.

"And she still agreed to see you? Is the girl mad? I would have run a mile from you."

"As I remember, you did run several miles from Abuelo. Didn't he have to come and fetch you to the church on the day of your wedding because you said you'd changed your mind?"

"Pah!" She waved a hand contemptuously. "I needed to be certain he loved me, that is all."

"And he did."

Her face softened on a memory. "Yes, he did. But he would have been ashamed of what you have done to this girl. What did you call her? Zoo-ee?"

"Zoe," he corrected her. "And I was pretty ashamed of myself, too."

"So did you not apologize?"

"I did."

"And she didn't accept it?"

"She did."

"Then I don't understand. What is wrong?"

"She lives in Houston. Her whole life is there. Her family, her career. Everything that is important to her."

"Are you not important to her, too? You young people

today. You want it all your own way. You don't understand compromise. I did not want to leave Mexico, my family, my whole life, to come here to Texas. But your grandfather had a dream, and as his wife it was my role to support him in that dream."

"I know, Abuelita, and he loved you all the more for that. But I don't see how Zoe and I can work this out. I went to her, but she made it very clear that her life is in Houston. She won't budge on that. And I can't leave all this. You and Abuelo built it up for Dad and for me and future generations of Galicias. I can't just walk away. I have a responsibility to our name and to the land."

His grandmother was silently shaking her head. "Your *abuelo* never wanted this to be your prison, my boy."

"It's not a prison. I love my home. I love what it means to our whole family. I'm honored that it now falls to me to look after the legacy."

He said the words with vehemence, but the passion behind them was no longer in his heart.

"That might have been true before your Zoo-ee," his grandmother said with her usual uncanny insightfulness. "But it is not true anymore. I can see why you are unhappy."

"I'm not unhappy," he protested automatically, but even as he did so, he felt the sharp sting of regret pierce his heart. Regret for what might have been had the circumstances been completely different.

But then again, if circumstances were different, wouldn't he and Zoe be different people, too? Would they have come together as hastily as they had? Experienced the heights they'd shared? For all that they had no future together, he couldn't regret a moment of the time they'd had.

Cord had spent a lot of time thinking since Abuelita's return a couple of days ago. And he'd come to a decision.

After his grandmother had gone to bed, he lifted the phone and called his parents.

The sound of his father's voice as he picked up the phone in Palm Springs was instantly calming in the way that only a parent could soothe a child, no matter their age.

"Dad, we need to talk," Cord said after the obligatory greetings had been dealt with.

"This sounds serious. Should I sit down?"

"I can hear the bedsheets, Dad. I know you're lying down already," Cord said with a grin.

"What's up, son?"

"I think you and mom should come back. Take charge of the ranch again. No, hear me out," Cord interjected as his father started to object. "It's not that I can't manage, but I think you left too early. Tell me you're not bored stupid at the end of every day. Tell me you don't miss the herd, the land, the work."

"I don't miss getting up at dawn every damn day," his father grumbled.

"So you start your days a little later. But, Dad, come home where you belong."

"Did Abuelita put you up to this?" Cord's father demanded.

"No, not at all. It's been on my mind awhile. You know I've been diversifying the herd, raising goats, making goat cheese. I want to expand that side of the business, and I can't do it on my own, especially if I'm managing the beef herds and breeding program, too. I need you to come back and work the ranch again. Obviously the choice is yours, but there's a business opportunity that's opened up for me closer to Houston. To make it work, I need you here. If you're certain you don't want to come back, I'll let that opportunity go, because I could never leave this place without ensuring a Galicia is at the head of operations. I respect my heritage too much to do that. What do you think?"

Cord held his breath as he waited for his father's response. His dad's voice was choked with emotion when he spoke.

"I have a good many years left in me, and, yes, while I like the idea of calling my time my own and doing what I want when I want, it took coming here to make me realize that what I want most is whatever's happening on the ranch. But I made my choice, son. I walked away. The ranch is yours now."

Cord gripped the phone so tight he thought he might break it. He forced his hand to relax.

"Dad, walk back. *Mi casa es su casa*, you know that. I never wanted you to go in the first place. When can you get here? Tomorrow?" He laughed, feeling as though a massive weight had been lifted from his shoulders.

"Not quite so fast. We have some things to wrap up here, sell the apartment, pack. Maybe the day after tomorrow," his father joked. In the background, Cord could hear his mother's excited voice. "Your mother is looking forward to seeing you, too, by the way."

"I've missed you guys. We have a lot to talk about when you get back. You see, I've met a girl."

"A girl? What's she li—"

In an instant Cord's mother was on the phone.

"You've met a girl? What's she like? Tell me everything. Well, not everything. But tell me about her."

Cord fought back a smile. No, he would definitely not be telling his mother everything, but he knew it wouldn't hurt to have his mother's perspective on what he planned to do. His feelings for Zoe were too deep for him to take any risks. This had to be perfect, and getting his family on board with the idea was only the first rung on the ladder.

Fourteen

"Flowers for you, Detective," one of Zoe's colleagues announced as he brought a large colorful display of blooms to her desk. "Have to say, they brighten things up around here. Maybe they can lift some of that sour expression you've been wearing these past two weeks."

"My expression is none of your business," Zoe snapped. "Aren't there some follow-up interviews you're supposed to be doing?"

Her fellow detective snapped to attention and executed a sharp salute. "Yes, ma'am. Right on it, ma'am."

She heard him laughing as he left the squad room and fought back a smile of her own. He was a damn fine detective, but he also knew exactly which buttons to push to get her ruffled. You'd think after nine years on the force she'd have developed a tougher hide for this kind of thing, but all it took was something that essentially reminded her she was female to make her even more hard-assed than ever before.

Sour? Really? She was just doing her job. The scent of the flowers tickled her nose and reminded her of what had triggered her current less-than-wonderful mood in the first place. Flowers? Seriously, who sent flowers these days? And why to her work? It wasn't her birthday or any special anniversary of anything. She eyed the arrangement as if it hid a venomous snake somewhere in the cheerful collection of buds and blossoms and spied the envelope that was buried in their midst.

She yanked the envelope out and flicked open the flap, which already bore evidence of having been opened and read by at least one of her colleagues before being brought to her desk. She groaned. She'd never hear the end of this.

I miss you.

The message was short, sweet and unsigned. She felt a flush of heat tinge her cheeks as she read the three words again. There was only one person who could have sent these to her. Cord Galicia. Well, she'd give him a piece of her mind. She snatched her phone off the desk and started to punch in his number before realizing that she actually knew it by heart. What did that say about her?

Slowly, she put her phone back onto her desk, then rose to her feet and grabbed the flowers and walked out to where the captain's personal assistant was sitting.

"Here, Josie," she said, leaving them on the older woman's desk. "These are for you. A mark of appreciation for all you do for us."

The woman eyed them carefully before looking up at Zoe. "Weren't these the flowers that just arrived for you?"

Zoe shrugged. "Busted. But they're no good for my allergies. Would you like them or should I just toss them?"

Josie looked horrified at the very thought. "You will do no such thing. I'll drop them at my mother's care center on the way home. They love a splash of color in their main living room. At least they'll be appreciated there."

Zoe didn't miss the censure in Josie's voice. It was clear the woman didn't believe her excuse about allergies and felt she ought to be grateful someone had sent her such an extravagance, but Zoe didn't do guilt. Life was way too short.

Even so, as she walked back to her desk and shredded the note into confetti before putting the pieces into her trash bin, she couldn't help but cast her eye back at Josie's desk for one last look at the flowers.

The flowers were only the beginning. Over the next few days it seemed that Cord had begun a seduction on her, sending small gifts with a thoughtful message each time. A part of her loved them. Who wouldn't love the sinfully expensive body lotion he'd sent, which paired with her favorite perfume so perfectly, she argued against the inner voice that told her to throw it away. And the small basket of gourmet goodies had been highly appreciated in the squad room at morning break yesterday. In fact, her team was beginning to look forward to the daily deliveries with more anticipation than she did.

But the parcel that arrived today had been the last straw. Despite her best intentions to keep secret the sinfully seductive sapphire-blue silk underwear he'd sent her, the lacy bra and matching thong had slid from their wrapper and onto her desk before she could hide them.

The catcalls and hoots of laughter brought even the captain from his office to see what the fuss was. By then, Zoe had scrunched the pieces into the tissue and summarily dispatched them into her trash bin. Regrettably, the note with the words *I would give anything to see you in these* had been snatched from her hands and circulated around the squad room before she could grab it back.

At this rate she'd never be taken seriously at work again. It had to stop, and very soon she'd make that call to Cord that she'd been putting off. Tonight, she told herself. As soon as she'd followed up with the crime-scene techs on a piece of evidence they'd finally been able to get to that had been extracted from the Hamm murder scene.

She let herself into the lab and went straight to Kane, the tech who'd asked her to come.

"What is it?" Zoe said, coming straight to the point. "Tell me it's good news."

"Well, there's some good news. We're finally working through the last of the evidence that was collected at the murder scene. Obviously you know the scene was severely compromised by the flood—"

"Kane, don't waste my time by telling me what I already know. I need something to go on."

"Well, there's this."

Kane turned his computer screen toward her and magnified the picture displayed there. "As you can see, it's a human hair."

"You've examined plenty of human hair found at the crime scene. What makes this any different?"

"Well, it's not like the others in that it's naturally wavy and, get this, naturally red."

"So we're looking for someone with long, naturally wavy red hair?"

"Very possibly. Now, of course you know we can't determine sex from a single hair, unless—"

"Unless there is a root attached. Tell me there's a root attached."

Kane's face lit up. "Yup. This is definitely from a woman. Obviously we can't determine age, but we can narrow it down to an adult versus a child."

"Did you run the DNA? Did we get any hits in the system? A name, anything?" she demanded, trying her level best not to get excited at the news.

She hoped this could potentially lead her to Hamm's killer, because goodness only knew everything else at the scene had driven them from one dead end to another.

"Not yet. We only just uncovered this information in the last few hours. I thought you'd appreciate knowing straightaway."

"I do. I definitely do. Thanks, Kane. Let me know the minute you have anything else."

"Will do."

Zoe was almost in a good mood as she reentered the squad room, right up until the moment she saw the lingerie she'd thrown into the trash displayed on a crime-scene board behind her desk, with the heading Wanted… by Someone. A slow-burning rage filled her, but she knew better than to let any of that show to her team. She wouldn't give them the pleasure, but she'd sure as heck give Cord Galicia what was coming to him the second she got home tonight. She planned on leaving his ears so blistered he wouldn't bother her ever again. She pulled the lingerie off the board and furiously scored out the heading, then settled at her desk, acting as if nothing of importance was going on. Eventually, this would all settle down. It had to, because there was no future for her and Cord.

"Stop stalking me."

The smile that had been on Cord's face when he'd seen Zoe's caller ID on his phone began to fade. She sounded really pissed.

"I'm merely expressing my affection," he responded, fighting to keep his voice level.

There was one thing about this woman—she could get him from cold to burning hot in about three seconds flat.

The fact that this time the heat had everything to do with irritation and nothing to do with sexual attraction was neither here nor there. No one had ever had the ability to excite or incite him so effectively.

"Well, stop it. It's gone far enough. I thought I made myself clear when I said we have no future."

"You did," he agreed and leaned back against the fence railing behind him.

It was getting dark, and he probably should head inside soon but he enjoyed the peace of the late evening. Would enjoy it even better if he had someone special to share it with.

"Then why do you keep sending me stuff?"

"Tokens."

"What?"

"They're not stuff. They're tokens of my—" He paused for a moment before he said something he'd really rather say face-to-face and not over a phone connection.

"I don't care what they are, and I don't want them. Cord, really, this has to stop. You're making me a laughingstock at work."

Ah, and there it was. There was genuine pain behind her words. It wasn't the gifts she was objecting to—well, maybe not completely—it was where he was sending them. He hadn't thought through the ribbing she'd be getting at work. He'd seen them in a display in town and couldn't think past the mental picture of seeing her on his big, wide bed wearing them.

"You want me to send them to your apartment?" he offered, knowing exactly what the response would be.

She didn't disappoint. For the next several minutes, Cord held his phone away from his ear while Zoe went on a tirade that showed a far more inventive use of expletives and instructions of where to put certain things in a person's anatomy than he'd ever heard before. He was seriously impressed, although there was pretty much nothing about Zoe Warren that didn't impress him. When she finally settled into silence, he put the phone back to his ear.

"I'm sorry. It wasn't my intention to distress you, Detective."

"I'm not distressed," she snapped back. "I'm angry. You're not respecting my wishes. I don't want to see you anymore."

He felt the words like each one was an individual blow straight to his chest.

"But you don't hate me, right?" He couldn't resist digging at her one more time.

Her growl of frustration filled his ear until it was abruptly cut off as she severed the call. He nodded to himself. Yeah, she didn't hate him. She was just driven to do her job to the best of her ability, and she didn't see how she could make time for anyone, let alone him. Well, it was up to him to show her he could fit in her world, and maybe, just maybe, she'd change her mind.

It took a lot less time than he anticipated to get all his plans in motion. Turned out his parents had little emotional attachment to the things they had in their Palm Springs apartment and were happy to leave the place staged with all their new appliances and furniture and leave everything in the hands of the real estate agents. They'd arrived back home a week after his phone call, tired after the road trip but joyful to be back. And he welcomed them with open arms. Abuelita couldn't be more in her element with all her family under one roof again, and Cord wondered how she'd take the news of what he planned to do. To his surprise she'd merely nodded, patted him on the cheek and told him that a man needed to do what a man needed to do.

So now it was a matter of convincing the woman of his heart that she needed him, too. How hard could that be? Cord grimaced as he readied the helicopter for the flight to Houston, in no doubt this would likely be the most difficult thing he'd ever done. He stowed the package he'd painstakingly wrapped for her, one last gift in an attempt to win her heart, and towed the chopper from the hangar.

"You're really doing this, then?" a voice asked him from behind.

Cord turned around and smiled at Jesse. "Damned if I don't."

His best friend raised his brows in surprise. "Seems all rather sudden, don't you think?"

"When you know, you know," Cord said. "And I know if I don't try this one last time, I'll regret it for the rest of my life."

Jesse stepped forward with his hand outstretched. "Then I can only wish you the best, buddy."

Cord clasped his best friend's hand firmly. "Thanks. I need all the help I can get."

He climbed aboard and fired up the chopper as Jesse took the ground-handling wheels back inside the hangar for him. In a matter of minutes he was skyward and headed toward Houston with hope and trepidation warring for dominance deep inside him.

Cord hangared the chopper just outside Houston, the way he'd done on his last visit, and picked up his rental car. Sitting in the parking lot at the small airfield, he dialed Zoe's number.

"I'm going to block you," she said upon answering.

"Then I'm glad you answered this one last call," Cord replied smoothly. "I'm also hoping you'll agree to see me one last time."

He heard the weight of her sigh through the phone.

"Cord, really, stop flogging a dead horse. We can't work. You know we can't, and you know damn well why. Nothing's going to change that."

"One last time, Zoe. Please. We owe it to ourselves," he cajoled her.

"I thought the last time was the last," she answered.

He could tell by her tone she was thinking about it.

"I promise you, this will be the last time I bother you. No more gifts, no more calls, no more touching you—"

"All right!" she interrupted in a fierce whisper. "You win. One last time. When?"

"Can you manage a few hours off today? Say I pick you up at your apartment about two?"

"Cord—"

"Please," he all but begged. "Just this one *last* time, Zoe."

He held his breath as she hesitated.

"Fine, pick me up at two. I'll be ready."

She severed the call before he could say another word, but inside he felt his heart begin to beat again and felt the air around him refill his lungs. He'd never wanted anything as much as he wanted the rest of today to go right.

Zoe paced her living room, waiting for the buzz from security downstairs to say Cord had arrived. She'd left explicit instructions for him not to be let up to her apartment. If she was being totally honest with herself, she didn't know if she could trust herself around him. Since their last night together she'd missed him with a physical ache that no amount of overtime could assuage.

Her apartment phone buzzed, making her flinch. She picked up the receiver.

"Your guest has arrived, Ms. Warren."

"Thank you. Tell him I'll be right down."

Her heart was fluttering in her chest as she entered the elevator to head to the lobby. She clenched her hands into fists and deliberately relaxed each finger in turn, telling herself this reaction was ridiculous. This was their final meeting. The last goodbye. She felt a twist of sorrow deep inside her and pushed it ruthlessly away. This was what she wanted. Closure. An end to the restless nights and the unexpected and totally unbidden memories that flooded her mind at the most inopportune moments. An end to seeing a dark head on a tall, rangy body everywhere she went and wondering if it was him.

And then the elevator doors were sliding open and her eyes were searching for that figure that never seemed far from the periphery of her thoughts. The second her gaze alighted on him, she felt his presence with a physical impact that robbed her of breath and made a hot flush of need rise slowly through her body. She tugged at the front of her leather jacket and strode toward him as if she were totally in control and not at all feeling like she was on the verge of wrapping her arms around him, absorbing him—everything from his heat to his breath to the flavor of him—so she could tuck it away forever.

She came to an abrupt halt about three feet away. He gave her a nod.

"Thanks for making time for me today. I know it probably wasn't easy, especially at such short notice, but I want you to know I appreciate it. Shall we go?"

Wow, heavy on the formal, she noted as he gestured for her to precede him from the building. Not even an attempt to take her hand or kiss her? What was with that, and why the heck was she so upset about it, anyway? It was what she wanted, wasn't it? She came to a stop on the sidewalk and felt him come up behind her, stopping mere inches from her body. She sensed everything about him with a heightened awareness that was going to drive her absolutely crazy if she didn't wrestle it under control.

"Where to?" she asked, fighting to keep the tremor from her voice. Inside, her nerves skittered as he drew up beside her.

"My car." He gestured to the nondescript sedan parked in the visitor's area.

She saw the lights flash as he unlocked it and then stepped forward as he held open the passenger door. She got in, glancing at him as she settled into the seat. He hadn't smiled yet, not so much as a glimmer. That wasn't like him, and the firm set to his jaw made her nervous. This was ridiculous, she told herself. She knew this man, intimately, she reminded herself with a curl of desire licking its way through her body. Whatever he had planned for her, she had nothing to fear except maybe the loss of her own self-control.

And maybe that was what she feared most. She knew he affected her on levels she had never experienced with any of her previous lovers. Heck, even that word—*lover*—was enough to make her entire body tighten in a wave of lust so intense it almost made her cry out.

Cord settled into the driver's seat and started up the vehicle.

"How've you been?" she asked, desperate to break the silence that filled the car so awkwardly.

"Not great. You?"

She sighed. So much for that gambit. "Same," she answered and fell silent again, at a total loss for words.

What did you say to a man whose very presence turned you into a melting puddle of mush, desperate for his touch and to touch him in return? A man you'd turned away from your bed, your life. A man whose absence left a gaping hole in every single day. She turned her head and stared out at the road, watching as they headed out of the city.

"Where are you taking me?" she asked, her nerves stretched to breaking point.

"Airfield."

"What's with the short answers?" she demanded, letting her anger begin to rise in the vain hope it would quell the insecurity that plagued her.

"I'm saving myself," he answered shortly.

"For what?"

He took his eyes from the road ahead and flung her a searing glance. "You'll find out."

"What if I don't want to find out?" she said, taking refuge in belligerence.

This time it was his turn to sigh. "Zoe, just be patient, okay? You granted me this time, and I promise you it won't tax or harm you in any way. For now, we're headed to the airfield. What I want to show you is a short way from town, but I want you to see it from the air, rather than the ground."

"Fine." She crossed her arms over her. "Thank you for at least telling me that much."

She didn't have to wait much longer. At the airfield, Cord pulled into a restricted zone and swiped a card at the security gate before driving alongside the tarmac to where she recognized his helicopter sitting just inside a hangar. Questions tumbled through her mind, but she resolved to hold her tongue as they walked to the chopper, and he dragged it to the helipad and prepped it for takeoff.

Before she knew it, she was feeling that delicious lurch in her stomach as they took to the air. She loved the sensation. The only thing better was sex, and she sure as heck wasn't going to go there. Not when she was doing her level best to remind herself of all the reasons why she and Cord would never work. She began to list them in her mind, taking strength from each one. He lived too far away. He hated her job. He hated the fact she carried a gun. He was traditional and wanted to take care of her, when she was eminently capable of caring for herself. He… Her thoughts trailed off. Okay, so there were four reasons, but they were important enough to be deal breakers as far as she was concerned.

Her headset crackled to life.

"Look down there, to your left."

Zoe did as he suggested. "Looks like a ranch."

"It's a goat ranch. Angora, mostly."

"And the reason you're showing me this is…?"

"It's mine."

She swiveled to face him. "It's yours? But what about your spread in Royal? Who's going to look after that?"

"My parents, and some extra hands."

"But why?"

"Well, you remember the cheese, right?"

"Sure, it was delicious."

"I've been wanting to diversify for a long time, but Dad's a cattleman through and through. So we had an honest talk. Turned out he wasn't enjoying retirement but didn't want to step on my toes by coming back home."

"But why not run the goats on your existing family property, or buy more land closer to home?"

"Because you're not there."

His words hung in the air between them.

"But—" She started to protest, but he cut her off.

"Just hear me out. I can do what I want to do anywhere, especially now that I'm no longer tied to the family spread. Sure, I'll help Dad when necessary, but I don't have to live there."

"But your family, your history. That ranch is everything to you, isn't it?"

"It's not you."

Zoe felt her stomach dip again as he took the chopper down and settled it in an empty field at the top of a rise. Once he'd shut down the engine, they alighted from the chopper, and Zoe stomped after Cord as he moved away from the machine to where there was a great vantage point over the land they'd flown over.

"What do you mean, it's not me?" she demanded, poking him in the chest for good measure.

"Exactly what I said. I've fallen for you, Detective. You have my heart in your custody, and that's where it's going to be for the rest of my life."

"You can't say that. You barely know me," Zoe protested, fear threatening to choke her.

This was all too intense. This was supposed to be goodbye, and here he was, telling her he'd walked off his family's land and bought a ranch close to Houston so he could be nearer to her. Who did that? What craziness had crawled into his brain?

"That's true, but what I do know is that you're a prickly pear with a soft inside. You're diligent in your work, you're a fierce advocate for the underdog, whether they're a good person or not. I know you have the softest lips of any woman I've ever met and that you make love as fiercely as you defend your independence."

"That doesn't tell me why you did this. I made it clear we had no future. I'm not giving up my work to set up house with any man."

"I'm not asking you to give up work, Zoe. I'm asking you for a chance at a future together. I love you."

All the air left her lungs in a massive whoosh. There it was. Those three words. Words she'd craved and yet dreaded at the same time. Words that bound and trapped. She started to shake her head, but Cord closed the distance between them and caught her by her shoulders, forcing her to look at him.

"I love you, Zoe Warren. I want to make a future with you, if you'll let me."

"No," she whispered. "I can't. You want all the things I can't give you. My career is everything to me. You want a family, you want a stay-at-home wife who'll raise your kids and work alongside you on the ranch. I'm not that woman."

"Oh, Zoe, don't be scared. Yeah, I thought I wanted those things. But most of all I just want you. I'd be happy if we never had a family, as long as I knew you loved me and could live here with me. The commute isn't so far into Houston from here. We could make a future together."

"I can't do it, Cord," she said as her eyes glazed with tears. "You hate my job and everything related to it. Yes, it can be dangerous. Yes, my life can be on the line. But I have to keep doing this. Eventually, you'd ask me to give it up. I know you would. Eventually, you'd want to have kids. I don't know if that's ever going to be on my radar. I can't do that to you. I carry a badge and a gun pretty much every day of my life. It's who I am."

"And that's who I love. Don't you see? I *want* to make compromises so we can be together. What we have is incredible and special, and we deserve to be happy together. Please, Zoe, at least give us a chance."

Zoe continued to shake her head. "No, it'll never work. Eventually you'd expect me to change, and I won't do that."

"Or maybe it's just that you're too scared to try," he challenged her. "Too scared to reach for what you know is good. Too scared to be seen as anything but bulletproof

Detective Warren, who feels no emotions but always gets her man. Trouble is, Zoe, your man is standing right here in front of you, but you're too scared to take a chance on me."

"Maybe you're right, but that's who and what I am," she said, lifting her chin and staring him straight in the eyes. "Take me back. It's over, Cord."

Fifteen

Even as she said the words, it was as if a .45-caliber hollow-nose bullet tore through her heart. Cord just continued to look at her, as if unable to believe she was still saying no to what he offered. How could he not see how impossible it was? Sure, she could commute to work from here, maybe even keep her apartment in town for those times she pulled an all-nighter, but she was certain he still hoped that eventually she'd leave her work, put aside the potential danger, and settle down and play happy family. And even if she did that, she knew eventually she'd come to hate it—maybe even hate him. No, it was easier to stand strong, to ignore the allure of what he offered and to let him walk away.

As they transferred from the aircraft to his rental car, she saw him grab a parcel and stow it behind the driver's seat. It was only when they got to her apartment building and she opened her door to get out that he reached for it again.

"Hang on a second," he said, his voice gruff with emotion. "I bought this for you. You should have it. My last gift to you, okay?"

She didn't trust herself to speak. His voice was so desolate, so devoid of hope or joy, and it scored her heart into a million pieces to know she'd done this to him. She accepted the parcel from him and got out of the car, closing the door behind her and walking as quickly as she could back into the lobby. She punched the elevator button with a shaking finger and rode the car up to her floor, her eyes blurring with unshed tears.

When she let herself into her apartment, she gave in to the hideous pain that had begun back at Cord's new ranch and grown in intensity each time she'd said no to him. Her legs buckled and she knelt on the floor of her entrance hall and wept as she'd never wept before.

Once the first wave of the emotional storm had passed, Zoe realized she was still holding the parcel Cord had given her. She plucked at the tape and tore the paper away from a case. One she identified immediately. With shaking fingers, she opened the snaps on the case to expose the brand-new SIG Sauer handgun inside. She recognized the model because it was one she'd been planning to upgrade to. With its reduced-reach trigger and one-piece modular grip, it was a far more comfortable weapon for her to use, when she was forced to.

But it wasn't the gun that made her begin trembling all over again. It was the fact that he'd bought it for her. She knew how much he hated weapons and why. But he'd gone out and bought her the exact model she was planning to buy for herself. More than anything he'd said as he'd tried to persuade her at the new ranch, this spoke volumes as to just how far he was prepared to compromise to have her in his world.

Could she even dare to hope that they stood a chance? That he'd meant exactly what he'd said back there? That they could make a future together? The enormity of what he'd done, of the things he'd said back at the new ranch rained down on her like giant hailstones. She'd been such an idiot. Caught up in her rut of fierce independence, she hadn't stopped to see that she was ignoring everything her heart was begging for. Everything she'd always told herself she'd make time for when the time was right. But when would that time be if she never allowed the love of a decent and good man into her life? If she threw up walls at every opportunity? If all she ever did was take and give nothing back in return? She had to make this right.

Zoe was up on her feet in seconds, and after shoving the new pistol into her gun safe, she grabbed her car keys and headed down to the parking garage. But where would she go? The airfield? What if, by the time she got there, he'd taken off again? The new ranch? Had he even taken possession of it yet? And what if he was flying back to Royal? She had a responsibility to her job to turn up tomorrow. But wasn't Cord more important? For the first time in her life, she put the needs of someone else ahead of her job. She'd start with the airfield, then head out to the ranch, if she could find it on a map. Hell, she was a detective. If she couldn't find an address with the resources available to her, she may as well hand in her badge right now.

And if he wasn't at either place? What then? She started her car and peeled out of the parking garage, driven by a desperate sense of urgency. She'd tackle that when she'd exhausted her local resources, she decided. But one way or another, she would find him.

This wasn't how it was meant to turn out, Cord thought after he'd handed in the rental car and taken a cab to the airfield. He prepped the Robinson for takeoff automatically, trying to ignore the deep sense of loss that had settled inside him. He'd put everything on the line and it had still turned to dust in the wind. All his hopes, all his dreams, shattered. He knew he couldn't do this again. Couldn't put his life and his heart on the line a third time. This was it. The thought of telling his parents and Abuelita that he'd failed was a bitter taste in his mouth. He should have known better than to trust in love again.

The sound of tires screeching to a halt behind the security fencing to the airfield caught his attention and made him look up from his preparations. Then there was the sound of a woman's voice, shouting—no, pleading—with the guy at the security gate. Cord walked to where he could see what all the fuss was about. As he did so, recognition dawned and with it an ember of hope stirred in his chest.

"It's okay," he called out. "She's with me."

"Sir, you know this is an operational airfield. We can't just let people in all over the place."

"I understand. My apologies."

Cord planted his feet firmly on the ground and watched as Zoe pushed past the guard and through the gate, actually running toward him with a look of desperation on her face that fanned that ember to a warm glow. Even so, he didn't plan to make this easy. She'd crushed him. If she truly was back for him, as hard as it would be, he might actually let her fight for it.

"You haven't left yet," she said breathlessly as she drew up in front of him.

"Your powers of observation are on point, as always, Detective," he drawled, not letting an ounce of the emotions that crashed through him surface in the sound of his voice.

"I need to talk to you."

"I thought we were all talked out."

She slid her sunglasses off her face, and he was shocked to see the ravaging evidence of tears there. Zoe was one tough nut. He'd never have expected tears from her. Not in a million years. His every instinct urged him forward, to take her into his arms, to console her and make everything right, but instead he locked his knees and stood firm right where he was.

"Cord, I'm sorry," she started. "I made a stupid mistake."

He kept his peace, not trusting himself to speak.

"Look," she continued, "can we go somewhere a little less out in the open?"

"Nope."

"You want me to do this here?"

"Yup."

"Fine, then." She chewed her lower lip for a second. "I want another chance. I want to take you up on your offer. I want to tell you I was a stupid, prideful, frightened fool who thought she knew what she wanted. But when I walked away from you," she admitted, "I realized how much I really wanted you after all. I'm sorry, Cord. I love you. I guess I was fighting it because it all happened so damn fast. Heck, a few weeks ago I was prepared to arrest you for obstruction and now I want to spend the rest of my life with you."

Every cell in Cord's body shuddered as the impact of her words sank in.

"The rest of your life, you say?" he finally managed to enunciate, hardly daring to believe her words.

"Forever, Cord. I know a love like this doesn't come along often. My parents have it. My brothers have it. I want it, too, with you."

"So, um, marriage? And kids?"

"Yes, marriage and kids…eventually."

He nodded and looked away to the distance so she wouldn't immediately see the gathering moisture in his eyes as the realization of his dreams began to take shape again.

"Today wasn't easy for me," Cord said carefully, still not looking at her. "The last woman I wanted to spend a future with died in the line of duty. The same duty you take on every day you roll up to work."

"I understand that," Zoe said, taking a step closer and reaching out with both hands to turn his face toward hers. "I promise you that I will always do my level best to be as safe as I can possibly be. Beyond that, I have to trust my fellow officers to do their jobs to the best of their abilities, too. You can live with that?"

He allowed his gaze to meet and mesh with hers. "I have to, if I want you in my life, and I do want you, Zoe. I want to build a family with you, the way our parents did with us. I want to grow old with you. I know it's never going to be an easy ride—we're both too strong willed for that. I could never make a life with a biddable woman, anyway. I love your sass, your determination, your strength. Quite simply, I love you."

"Then you'll forgive me for being an idiot this afternoon? For nearly crushing us forever?"

"You may need to make that up to me," he said with a slow, teasing grin beginning to wreath his mouth. "For quite some time."

"I'll do anything you want. Come home with me now. We can make plans."

"Plans?"

"Well, after we…y'know."

"So you liked the gun, then, huh?"

"I love the gun, Cord, but even more than that, I love

what it symbolizes between you and me. And, Cord, I love you even more."

He grabbed her then and kissed her with all the pent-up hope and joy and relief and love that had surged through him the second he'd identified her behind the security gate. And he knew that while they might weather some storms, they'd do it together—stronger for all they'd fought for, better for having each other.

Epilogue

The hot breath of the police was a tangible sensation down my neck. They were getting closer and it was making me nervous. My hands kept sweating, I'd lost weight, my hair was falling out. Thank God no one had noticed yet. I was holding it together when it counted—just.

This craziness wasn't me. It wasn't my fault. I had no choice. Surely they'd see that, wouldn't they? The Sterlings and the Currins, they were the ones to blame. They had everything, and they took even more—the land that should have been my father's, the land that Ryder Currin had coerced out of Harrington York and that he'd made his fortune on.

I thought I'd properly put a spoke in Currin's relationship with Angela. The golden child. The woman with everything. Her daddy's right hand. None of them deserved happiness. Not at my expense.

And then there was that bitch cop who kept poking and

prodding where she shouldn't. It made me laugh when I heard she'd gone out of town on some goose chase to Royal when I'd been right under her nose all along. But she was back now, and more determined than ever.

I had to find my baby before they found out it was me. My child was the only thing keeping me going now. But I'd never find her if I was in prison. Please, don't let me lose my last chance to find my child, to hold her, to love her. To put right the wrongs of eighteen years ago.

Ryder Currin watched as Willem Inwood entered the boardroom and settled at the table with his lawyer by his side. Slimy bastard. He still couldn't believe that this feeble excuse for an executive had abused Ryder's staff and pretty much gotten away with it. And to think it was Ryder who'd given Inwood every opportunity to get ahead at Currin Oil. He'd believed the man to be loyal. The discovery that Inwood was the complete opposite had left a nasty bitter taste in his mouth.

He stared at Inwood, determined not to be the first to speak, taking in the slightly less-than-perfect dark auburn hair, the lanky frame and the dark brown eyes hidden behind his wire-framed glasses.

Ryder had never understood why a man such as Inwood, as insecure as he'd turned out to be, had to turn that insecurity on to his subordinates, instead of learning and growing. Inwood had been a complete failure as an executive on his payroll and it irked Ryder greatly that he hadn't noticed sooner and thereby had a chance to minimize the damage Inwood had wrought.

Inwood tugged at the tie at his collar and stretched his neck. It gave Ryder no small amount of pleasure to see the other man was uncomfortable in his presence. Inwood cast a glance at his lawyer, who nodded as if encouraging him to speak. *Great*, Ryder thought, *let the show begin.*

"I asked you to meet me here today to apologize for my actions. I should never have rekindled the rumors that you had an affair with Tamara Perry, and I apologize for the way I conducted myself while working for you."

"Is that so?" Ryder drawled. "Strange that you didn't seem to think that necessary when I fired you. Nor did you seem to think it necessary when you were haranguing staff and forcing them to falsify paperwork a couple of months ago when it became clear you were incapable of performing your duties properly, let alone adequately."

Hot color flushed the man's face, and his lips twisted into a feral grimace, showing him for the weasel he truly was.

"Look, I didn't need to come here today and put up with your insults!"

His lawyer leaned across and whispered urgently into his ear. To Ryder's surprise, Inwood settled down in his seat.

"I came here to clear the air. I've said I'm sorry. I didn't mean for any of this to go this far. Whether you accept that or not is up to you. But I also need to make something absolutely clear. I didn't kill Vincent Hamm. I never even met the guy. My lawyer will present you with the results of a polygraph that I voluntarily took to prove my innocence."

Ryder watched as the lawyer removed a sheaf of papers from the folder in front of him and slid it across the table. He picked up the data and scanned it quickly before reading the summary at the end.

"So this proves you didn't kill Hamm. But I have a sneaky feeling you know who did, don't you?" Ryder pressed.

Inwood's face paled. The red hue that had suffused his skin earlier now faded to a sickly gray. He shook his head.

"No, you've got it all wrong. In fact—" he pushed up from his chair and stood facing Ryder "—you can go to hell. I'd never give up my—"

Inwood closed his mouth with a snap, as if realizing that he was on the verge of saying something incriminating.

"You'd never give up your what?" Ryder prompted.

Inwood just shook his head and turned for the door. As it slammed behind him and his lawyer, who'd scurried out after him, Ryder leaned back in his chair and whistled softly through his lips. What was it that Inwood had been on the verge of saying? Was it a *who* or a *what* that he would never give up? One thing was for certain—Ryder would soon find out.

* * * * *

BOMBSHELL FOR THE BLACK SHEEP

JANICE MAYNARD

For Kathy and Patti:

Families are complicated at times—*understatement*!
Thanks so much for being the best sisters ever.
Love you both!

One

Hartley Tarleton had made a lot of mistakes in his life, but walking away from Fiona James—twice—had to be the dumbest. He'd had his reasons. Extenuating circumstances. Familial obligations. Still, he'd handled things badly. The woman in question was not likely to be in a conciliatory mood. Even worse, here he was—proverbial hat in hand—to ask for a favor.

Despite a host of misgivings, he parked across the street and a few cars down from her neatly kept bungalow-style home. The middle-class Charleston neighborhood had aged gently, preserving the best of the city's Carolina charm in a price range single people and young families could afford. Fiona was a landscape painter. A very talented one with a quickly burgeoning reputation. Hopefully, her starving-artist years were behind her.

Drumming his fingers on the steering wheel, Hartley rehearsed his speech. The home and the woman drew him, creating a burning ache in his chest. He'd spent two nights in that house, though not in succession. For reasons he wouldn't examine too closely, he recalled every detail.

On difficult days this past year, he had calmed himself by remembering the vintage dinette set in Fiona's tiny breakfast nook. The table was yellow, speckled with gray. He had imagined Fiona, with her naturally curly red hair and wide-set gray-blue eyes, sitting in one of the chairs with the chrome legs, a sketch pad in front of her.

Slowly, he got out of the car and stretched. This momentary procrastination was unlike him. If anything, he erred on the impulsive side. When he was a teenager, people criticized those tendencies as a sign of immaturity. He preferred to think of himself as grabbing the bull by the horns. He liked controlling his own destiny.

A trickle of sweat ran down the center of his back. The day was ridiculously hot and humid. Maybe he had been gone too long. Charleston was his home. Why then, did he feel like an interloper?

His heart hammered in his chest as he crossed the street and walked up the path. He had worried that Fiona might be out and about, but her carefully restored VW Bug sat in the driveway. The car was cotton-candy pink with tiny blue seahorses scattered across the hood. It was a whimsical vehicle, and perfectly suited to the imagination of an artist.

On the porch, he loosened his tie and told himself he wasn't going to lose it. Grief and a host of other emotions bombarded him. His throat was desert dry. Grimly, he reached out and rang the buzzer.

Fiona heard the doorbell and sighed with relief. She had ordered several hundred dollars' worth of new paint—oils and acrylics. The overnight rush fee made her cringe, but it was her own fault for not realizing sooner that she didn't have what she needed to begin a newly commissioned project.

She was wearing a paint-stained T-shirt and ancient jeans with holes in the knees, but the delivery guy had seen her in worse. Her back protested when she sprang to her feet. Sitting in one spot for too long was an occupational hazard. When she was deeply involved in her work, she could paint or draw for hours and never notice the passage of time.

Sprinting through her small house to the front door took a matter of seconds. The only thing that slowed her down was stubbing her toe on the back corner leg of the sofa. *Damn, damn, damn.* The pain had her hopping on one foot. She had to hurry, because the package required a signature.

She flung open the door, breathless and panting, momentarily dazzled by the bright sunshine. The man standing on her porch was definitely not a delivery man. Nor was he a stranger.

It took her a full five seconds to process the unimaginable.

"Hartley?" Her shock quickly changed to anger. "Oh, heck no." This man had bruised her ego and maybe even broken her heart.

She slammed the door on instinct. Or she *tried* to slam the door. One big foot—clad in a size-twelve Italian leather dress shoe—planted itself at the edge of the door frame. The foot's owner grunted in pain, but he didn't give up his advantage.

"Please, Fiona. I need your help."

There it was. Her weakness. Her Achilles' heel. Growing up in a succession of pleasant but unexceptional foster homes had taught her that becoming indispensable to the family in question secured a roof over her head.

She'd been self-sufficient for over a decade now—ever since she had aged out of the system. She had money in the bank, and her credit rating was unblemished. This perfect little house was almost paid for. Pleasing people was a habit now, not a necessity. A habit she had vowed to break.

But when she actually peeked at Hartley's face, her resolve wavered. "You look terrible," she muttered, still with her hand on the door blocking his entrance. Her statement wasn't entirely correct. Even haggard and with dark smudges of exhaustion beneath his eyes, Hartley Tarleton was the most beautiful man she had ever seen. Muscular shoulders, slim hips and a smile that ought to be outlawed on behalf of women everywhere.

They had first met more than a year ago at the wedding of mutual friends, Hartley a groomsman and Fiona his matching attendant. He had escorted her down the aisle during the ceremony. Later that evening, after a raucous reception that involved copious amounts of extremely good wine and plenty of dancing, he had removed her ghastly fuchsia bridesmaid dress…in her very own bedroom. Where she had invited him to join her.

That night, their physical and emotional connection was immediate and seductive—impossible to resist.

When she woke up the following morning, he was gone.

Today, his coffee-colored eyes—so dark as to be almost black—glittered with strong emotion. "Please, Fee." His voice was hoarse. "Five minutes."

What was it about this man that tore down every one of her defensive barriers? He'd walked out on her not once, but twice. Was she a masochist? Normally, she didn't fall for stupid male flattery. But she had actually believed Hartley had been as caught up in the magic of their tantalizing attraction as she'd been.

Sighing at her own spineless behavior, she stepped back

and opened the door wider. "Fine. But five minutes. Not six. I'm busy."

It was a pitiful pretense of disinterest. When he stepped past her, the familiar crisp, fresh scent of his shave gel took her back to a duet of nights she had tried so desperately to forget.

Hartley crossed the room and sprawled on her sofa. She remained standing, arms folded over her chest. The first time they met, he had worn a tuxedo befitting his inclusion in the wedding party. Nine months later when he had shown up on her doorstep without a word of explanation for his long absence, he'd been in faded jeans and a pale yellow cotton shirt with rolled-up sleeves.

Today, his hand-tailored suit screamed money. Despite his almost palpable misery, he looked like a rich man. In other words, not the sort of person Fiona should date. Or sleep with. Or include in any kinds of future plans.

The silence stretched on. Hartley leaned forward, elbows resting on his knees, head bowed. He was a man who always knew what to say. The kind of guy who could summon a woman's interest with one mischievous, wicked quirk of his eyebrow.

Now that she had let the big, bad wolf into her house, he was mute.

The uninterrupted, empty silence finally broke her. "What do you want, Hartley?"

The five words were supposed to be inflected with impatience and disinterest. Instead, her voice trembled. She winced inwardly, hoping he hadn't noticed. If ever there was a time for a woman to seize control of a situation and play the hand on her terms, this was it.

He didn't deserve her sympathy.

At last, he sat up and faced her, his hands fisted on his thighs. There were hollows in his face that hadn't been there before. Unmistakable grief. "My father is dead," he croaked. The expression in his eyes was a combination of childish bewilderment and dull adult acceptance.

"Oh my God. I'm so sorry." Despite her anger, her heart clenched in sympathy. "Was it sudden?"

"Yes. A stroke."

"Were you in Charleston?" They had discovered at the wedding that they both lived in the beautiful low-country city, but clearly they moved in different circles most of the time.

"No. But it wouldn't have mattered. He was gone in an instant."

"I don't know what to say, except that I'm very sorry, Hartley."

"He was old but not *that* old. It never occurred to me I wouldn't get the chance to say goodbye."

She wanted to sit down beside him and hug him, but she knew her own limits. It was best to keep a safe distance. Sliding into Hartley Tarleton's arms made her reasoning skills turn to mush.

His jaw firmed. "I need you to go to the funeral with me. Please." He stood and faced her. "I wouldn't ask if it weren't so important." The muscles in his throat flexed as he swallowed. He needed a haircut. When one thick lock fell over his forehead, he brushed it aside impatiently.

She had seen him naked. Had felt the gentle caress of his big, slightly rough hands on every inch of her sensitive skin. That other Hartley made her body sing with pleasure...made her stupid, romantic heart weave daydreams. But she didn't know him. Not really.

"I don't think it's a good idea, Hartley. We're nothing to each other. You made that abundantly clear. I don't *want* to go with you to the funeral," she said firmly, trying to sound tough and no-nonsense and not at all like the type of woman who let a man disappear for days and weeks on end with no explanation and then three months ago took him back into her bed…again.

"You don't understand." He moved a step in her direction, but she held him off with a palm-out stance.

"No touching," she said, reading his playbook. She wouldn't let him soften her up.

He shrugged, his expression harried. "Fine. No touching. But I need you to go to the funeral with me, because I'm scared, dammit. I haven't seen my brother or sister in over a year. Things have been strained between us. I need a buffer."

"Charming," she drawled. "That's what a woman wants to hear."

"For God's sake, don't be difficult, Fee."

His scowl would have been comical if his behavior hadn't been so atrocious. "*I'm* perfectly reasonable and rational, Mr. Tarleton. You're the one who seems to have lost your mind."

He ran a hand across the back of his neck, a shadow crossing his face. "Maybe I have," he muttered. He paced restlessly, pausing to pick up a nautilus shell a friend had brought her from Australia. It had been sliced—like a hamburger bun—with a fine-gauge jeweler's saw to reveal the logarithmic spiral inside. Hartley traced the pattern with a fingertip, the gesture almost sensual. "This is beautiful," he said.

"I just brought it out of my studio. I've been working on a series of four watercolors…a galaxy, a hurricane, this perfect shell. The pattern occurs in nature more often than you might think."

He closed his palm around the opalescent wonder and shot her a look. "And the fourth?"

Her face heated. "Oddly enough, it's a kind of broccoli… Romanesco."

For the first time, the tension in his broad shoulders eased visibly, and a trace of his trademark grin lightened his face. "I've never met anyone like you, Fiona."

She bristled. "What does that mean?"

"You're special. You see the world in a way us mere mortals don't. I envy you that."

The quiet sincerity in his voice and the genuine compliment reminded her of all the reasons she had fallen for his charms the first time. And the second. His habitual smile was an inexplicable combination of sweet and sexy. For a man who stood six three in his stocking feet and carried himself like an athlete, the hint of boyish candor caught her off guard again and again.

What could it hurt if she accompanied him to his father's service? It was an hour of her life, maybe less. She sighed inwardly, already losing the battle. "What day is the funeral?"

Now he definitely looked guilty. "Today."

She gaped at him. "*Today* today?"

"In an hour and a half."

Her temper ramped to a slow boil. "And you seriously thought you could simply waltz in here, demand my cooperation and get what you want?"

"No," he said forcefully. "No." The second denial was quieter. "I was *hoping*, Fee. Just hoping."

He shoved his hands in his pockets, and he didn't move. She gave him points for that. Everything in her past interactions with him suggested that he could indeed get what he wanted with little more than a kiss. But Hartley didn't try any funny business. All he did was ask.

Before she could formulate an answer, he grimaced. "I know I owe you explanations for my behavior. If you'll do me the kindness of standing beside me this afternoon, I swear I'll tell you whatever you want to know afterward. I won't run out. Not this time."

She searched his face for the truth. "Why are things awkward with your siblings? Isn't your brother your twin? I seem to recall you telling me that. Aren't twins supposed to be tight?"

"I did something to upset my father and Jonathan, my brother. I was written out of the will. And to be honest, maybe I deserved it. But I love my family. They're everything to me. I would like to heal the rift…if that's even possible."

He could have wheedled. Or flirted. Or even pressured. Instead, he simply stood there. Looking at her. So intently that her nipples tightened beneath the soft cotton of her bra. She hadn't imagined the physical connection between them. It was as real today as it was the other times he had blasted into her world. As real as the mantel clock that ticked a steady rhythm.

"Okay. I'll go with you." A platonic date to a funeral didn't mean she was capitulating a *third time.* "I can be ready in half an hour. Will that do?"

He nodded. "Thank you, Fiona." His gaze was sober. "I appreciate it."

"Wait for me here. If the doorbell rings, please answer it. I'm expecting some packages."

Hartley watched her walk away, wishing he could join her in the shower and forget that his life was imploding. It was nothing short of a miracle that she had agreed to go with him. Because of the situation he was in and the looming stress of seeing his family again, he had to slam the lid on all the erotic memories this small house contained.

His gut was in a knot, but the burning dread eased. With Fee beside him, he could get through this afternoon.

Before he could pull out his phone and check his email, a loud knock sounded at the door. The uniformed delivery man on the porch was beaming when Hartley answered the summons, but his smile faded.

"I have some packages," he said.

Hartley didn't call him out on the awkward, unnecessary explanation. "I see that," he said mildly.

The kid, barely twenty at most, tried to peer inside the house. "Fiona needs to sign for this delivery."

Hartley's territorial instincts kicked in. "*Ms. James* is in the shower."

The young man recognized the veiled rebuke. His face flushed. "You could do it, I suppose."

"I supposed I could." Hartley scrawled his name and handed back the electronic clipboard. "I'll tell her you said hello."

Three large boxes changed hands. Hartley gave the poor schmuck a terse nod and closed the door firmly. He couldn't blame the kid for having a crush, but Fiona deserved a man in her life.

The irony of that didn't escape him. In fact, now that he had Fee in his corner, he could spare a moment to wonder what she had been up to in the weeks and months he had been traveling the world. Was there a man somewhere who would protest Hartley's current involvement in her life?

His stomach-curling distaste for that thought told him he was more invested than he wanted to admit. It seemed impossible he could be obsessed with a woman he had known for less than a week, collectively. Yet of all the people in his life who could have been persuaded to accompany him to his father's funeral, Hartley had chosen Fiona.

The momentary peace he experienced deep in his heart told him he had made the right decision.

A lot of things were going to change in the next weeks and months. Even if his brother didn't trust him and his sister would reproach him for being gone so long, the three of them would have to work together to settle their father's affairs.

Only Hartley knew how very difficult that was going to be.

A noise in the hall brought his head up. His breath caught in his throat. "Fiona," he croaked. "You look amazing."

Her classic black dress was sleeveless and knee length. Sexy black sandals showcased slender legs. She had tried to tame her medium-length hair with two antique tortoise-shell combs. Now fiery curls framed her elfin face. "Is this okay?" she asked. "To be honest, I haven't been to a funeral in a very long time." She toyed with the simple pearl earrings that matched the necklace at her throat.

"You're perfect," he said.

Two

Fiona avoided funerals on a good day. Attending this particular one on the arm of the man who had treated her so shabbily didn't make sense.

Yet here she was.

Charleston, in all her low-country charm, basked in the summer sun. The city was a unique amalgam of Southern gentility and a lingering painful past. Palm trees and horse-drawn carriages. Elegant secluded courtyards. And everywhere, the patina of old money. Farther out from the city, pockets of poverty existed, but here in the historic district, wealth and social position held sway.

By the time Fiona and Hartley made it to the upscale funeral home in the heart of town, she knew she was in trouble. Hartley had barely spoken a word the entire time, but she was hyperaware of him at her side.

He drove with careless confidence despite the tightness in his jaw and his palpable air of tension.

It was impossible not to think about the other times they had been together. At least it was impossible for *her.* Presumably, Hartley was too distraught to think about sex.

She was having second and third thoughts about her role this afternoon. "So what do I need to know?" she asked. "I don't want to say anything I shouldn't."

Hartley shot her a sideways glance before spotting an empty spot down the street and parallel parking with ease. "Just follow my lead. My sister will be emotional. For several reasons. She doesn't know why I've been gone."

"Join the club," Fiona muttered.

Hartley ignored her sarcasm. "Mazie's husband is J.B. He's been a friend of ours since we were kids. He and Mazie reconnected recently and fell in love. And to further confuse you, J.B. is my brother's best friend."

"Got it."

"Jonathan, my twin, had serious brain surgery not too long ago, but he's made a complete recovery. His wife is Lisette. She's been working for Tarleton Shipping a long time."

"And your mother? I haven't heard you speak of her." Fiona got out and smoothed her skirt with damp hands. Meeting strangers was not her forte. In this situation, the stakes were much higher than usual. Hartley got out as well and closed his door, resting his arms on the roof of the car as he stared at her. "My mother is not in the picture. The only people you'll have to deal with today are my siblings and their spouses."

If his words were meant to reassure her, they failed. Hartley's air of mystery told her the Tarleton family had more than one skeleton in the closet. Why else would Hartley be so worried about seeing his brother and sister? It was beginning to dawn on Fiona that his brief though startling contact with her was not the only relationship he had abandoned.

They arrived at the funeral home early. Hartley wanted time to speak with his family before the receiving of friends began. When he took Fiona's hand in his as they mounted the steps to the red-brick and white-columned building, she wasn't sure he even noticed.

She tugged him to a halt before he opened the door, squeezing his fingers, trying to extend her support. "It's going to be okay," she said softly. "Every family goes through this. You'll make it. You all will."

His expression was grim. "Death is one thing. Handling the living is something else again."

His odd words stayed with her for the next half hour, illuminating the awkward family reunion.

Mazie was the first person to spot her brother. She ran up to him and threw her arms around his neck, her face wet with tears. "I swear I shouldn't forgive you, but I'm so glad you're here."

Fiona hung back as Hartley embraced his classically beautiful sister. Mazie's skin was fairer than her brother's. And though the family resemblance was strong, her eyes were more golden amber than brown. Her elegance made Fiona feel dowdy in comparison. Mazie wore emeralds that must have cost a fortune.

Hartley reached back and drew Fiona into the small circle. "Mazie, this is my friend, Fiona James. She was kind enough to be my date today."

Fiona grimaced. "I told him no one needs an escort to a funeral, but he wouldn't take no for an answer."

Mazie smiled through her tears. "That sounds like Hartley. Wait a minute," she said. "Fiona James the artist? My husband and I have a couple of your paintings. *The Salt*

Marsh at Sunset. The Bridge at Twilight. I treasure them. You're incredibly talented."

"Thank you," Fiona said. It still startled her to be recognized.

Mazie dried her face with a tissue. "Jonathan is just around the corner. You might as well get this meeting over with."

Hartley's gaze darkened. "Is he really going to be okay?"

"Right as rain," Mazie said. "He didn't even freak out when Lisette told him she had been keeping you in the loop. Apparently, staring death in the face mellows a man."

Hartley curled an arm around Fiona's waist. "Jonathan was misdiagnosed in the beginning, but fortunately, the mistake was caught in time."

"How scary," Fiona said.

Mazie nodded. "Terrifying. We thought we were going to lose him."

They turned down a hallway and more or less ran into the third Tarleton sibling. Jonathan had clearly overheard the end of their conversation.

He lifted a shoulder, his smile laconic. "Apparently, I'm hard to kill."

The two brothers sized each other up. The tension was painful. They were definitely identical twins. No hiding that. But even an outsider would have no problem telling them apart.

Olive skin. Dark brown eyes. Chestnut hair. Those were the commonalities. Hartley's hair was longer…untamed…sun-bleached. And he had the look of a man who spent a lot of time outdoors. Jonathan, on the other hand, was *GQ* handsome. Sculpted jaw. Expensive haircut. Conservative suit.

Two stunningly handsome men in their prime.

Hartley kept an arm around Fiona's waist. "Hello, Jonathan."

Mazie made a huffing noise. "For God's sake. Hug each other."

The brothers ignored her. At last, Jonathan held out his hand. "Welcome home, Hartley."

Even without being privy to all the details, Fiona knew this moment was epic. It was written in Jonathan Tarleton's wary expression and in the rigid set of Hartley's posture.

"Thank you," Hartley said quietly. "I'm glad to be back, but not for this reason. I'm sorry I wasn't here when it happened."

Mazie spoke up, her tears flowing again. "None of us were. Apparently, he died in his sleep. The housekeeper found him."

"Hell," Hartley said quietly. "I knew he wasn't well, but I honestly thought he would go on forever."

"So did we." Jonathan glanced at his watch. "Would you like to see him?"

Fiona felt the shudder that racked Hartley's body. "Yes," he said gruffly.

Moments later, the four of them stood around the casket. Gerald Tarleton had been a large man. But in death, he looked old and frail. Fiona knew he had built a far-reaching shipping empire that would now pass on to his children. Again, she wondered about Mrs. Tarleton. Was she dead or alive?

Soon they were joined by J.B. Vaughan and Lisette, Jonathan's wife. Mazie took care of the introductions. Her husband wrapped her in his arms and kissed the top of her head. "No more crying, honey. You'll give yourself a migraine." He dabbed his wife's cheeks with a handkerchief.

Fiona felt a fierce stab of envy. Would any man ever look at her with such naked devotion?

Her stomach curled with tension. Dozens of floral arrangements flanked the casket and filled the walls on either side. The heavy scent of carnations made Fiona feel ill. A cold sweat dampened her brow.

Could she leave? Could she simply run away? This wasn't *her* family crisis. Suddenly, she knew she needed a moment to gather her composure. But before she could make a break for it, the funeral home director appeared behind them and intruded with a hushed cough.

"Guests are arriving," he said, his tone sepulchral. "If you'll follow me, I'll escort you to an anteroom. We'll open the doors, and then I'll bring you in and arrange the receiving line."

This was Fiona's chance. In the transition, she darted down the hall and found the ladies' room. Once in the stall, she retched and dry-heaved. Oh, God. She felt terrible. Her life was usually placid and peaceful. She *liked* it that way. Damn Hartley for pulling her into the middle of this mess.

When the crisis passed, she put a cold paper towel on the back of her neck and touched up her makeup. All her life she had never done well with confrontation and stress. Lack of stability in her formative years had left her with issues. Duh.

Her psyche craved calm, the kind of steady, peaceful existence her art gave her. She was happiest when she could lose herself in a creative project. Seeing Hartley again and having to negotiate his family storms made her a nervous wreck.

Still, he said he *needed* her. That had been enough to coax her into accompanying him during this difficult afternoon. She'd spent too many years ingratiating herself with different foster families to change her personality overnight.

She was independent now. She didn't have to worry

about housing or food or even winning a kind word from a stranger. But the desire to fit in…to be useful…was never far from the surface.

Fortunately, the crowds of visitors had already overtaken the room where the Tarleton family stood to greet friends and business acquaintances. Fiona was able to slip in unnoticed and take her place at Hartley's side. He gave her a quick intimate glance, but immediately returned his attention to the seemingly endless line of men and women waiting to speak to him.

Fiona smiled and nodded, content to remain in the background. Occasionally, someone questioned Hartley about his long absence from Charleston. Each well-meaning query was deflected with a vague throwaway comment.

The man was a social genius, even if he did have more disappearing acts than Houdini.

At last, it was time to adjourn to the chapel. A couple of songs, some readings and a few words from Jonathan. Finally, it was over.

Fiona couldn't wait to leave. Her stomach still felt iffy, and her head ached. Before she could plan her exit, Mazie appeared at her side.

The other woman's eyes were red-rimmed, but she was calm. "A few of our friends have catered a dinner for us out at the beach house. We'll be headed that way in a few moments. Don't let Hartley escape."

"Oh, no," Fiona said. "This is your family time. I need to go home. It was lovely to meet you."

Mazie frowned and strong-armed Fiona into a nearby corner. "Please, Fiona. You don't know all the details." She paused and grimaced. "To be honest, I don't even know. But Jonathan and Hartley had a huge falling-out about something, something big. This is the first time they've been in the same room in over a year. They *have* to heal this thing. And we need you to be an impartial bystander."

"Why?" Fiona asked, searching desperately for a polite way to make her excuses.

Mazie's eyes filled with tears again, though this time perhaps not for her father's passing. "I adore my brothers. They've been my supporters and protectors my entire life. It kills me to see them so stiff and polite with each other. *Please*, Fiona," she said urgently. "Please have dinner with us."

Hartley walked up to them, overhearing his sister's invitation. "Of course she's coming—right, Fee?"

Fiona knew she was trapped. She gnawed her lip. "If you're sure I won't be intruding." She gave Hartley a pointed stare. "But I can't stay too late. I have a huge project to begin tomorrow, and I want to be in bed at a decent hour."

His gaze was inscrutable. "Understood."

Hartley was no more communicative during the drive to the Tarleton home than he had been earlier en route to the funeral. The silence suited Fiona just fine. She leaned her head back against her seat and closed her eyes.

Unfortunately, shutting Hartley out was not so easy. His masculine scent teased her nose. Her fingers itched to cross the divide between them and stroke his thigh. She *wanted* to help him. She really did. And she wanted to be with him. But her sense of self-preservation warned her to keep her distance.

Instead, she was accompanying him to a meal and a social occasion that was sure to produce strong emotions and any one of a dozen possible outcomes, from uncomfortable silence to vocal recriminations.

If she was lucky, the Tarletons would be on their best

behavior. Fiona would be able to return home and would never again answer her door to a tall, handsome lover.

Despite her misgivings, she was eager to see the beach house. Years ago, Gerald Tarleton had built a walled compound on the tip of a barrier island north of Charleston. Fiona knew of the property in general terms, but when Hartley steered the car through the front gates, she was both taken aback and enchanted.

The structure rested on massive stilts, of course. A sweeping staircase led up to the beautiful double-door entrance. Even from the driveway, Fiona could see the intricate stained glass that incorporated sea turtles, dolphins and starfish. As an artist, she was fascinated.

As a woman, she wanted to run far away.

Hartley shut off the engine and pressed the heels of his hands to his forehead. “This feels so damned wrong.”

“I’m sorry.” The words were inadequate, but she didn’t know how else to help him.

The early evening light illuminated his drawn expression. “I grew up here,” he said quietly. “After 9/11, our father was paranoid. He barely let us leave the house for the longest time.”

“I can understand that, I suppose. He wanted to protect you.” She gazed up at Hartley’s family home. It was a far cry from the houses where she had been bounced around.

Her longest tenure was twenty-five months—with a family who had taken in four other foster children besides Fiona. When the wife eventually became pregnant with her own *biological* child, Fiona and her de facto brothers and sisters were reassigned.

Fiona had begged to stay. At thirteen, she was the oldest of the lot and capable of being a help around the house. But the pregnancy was high risk. The doctor said too much stress and chaos would threaten the mother’s health.

Fiona's personality was quiet and self-abnegating. No chaos anywhere. But the doctor's orders prevailed.

Fiona's foster mom had cried and cried. She was too hormonal and stressed out to make a good decision. In the end, it was nobody's fault, but Fiona had never again invested so much of herself emotionally.

Hartley touched her hand. "Ready to go inside?"

Even that one quick brush of his fingers against her skin sent shivers dancing down her spine. Why did he have this effect on her? "Shouldn't I be asking *you* that question?"

His low laugh held little humor. "My brother and I are civilized people. You don't have to worry about fistfights."

"I wasn't," she said. "Until now."

Her attempt at humor took some of the darkness from his face. "C'mon," he said. "You'll like the house."

Fiona's sandals had spiky heels, so she didn't protest when Hartley held her elbow as they ascended the stairs. His touch made her knees weak. She had missed him… so very much.

She tried to remember how angry she was about his cavalier treatment of their budding relationship. But the bitterness of his absence winnowed away in the pleasure of having him near again. It was sobering to admit she was perilously close to letting bygones be bygones.

Though it was frustrating not to be able to resist his winsome charm, she liked the woman she was with him. He made her feel sensual and desirable.

Before Hartley was forced to make a decision about letting himself in or ringing the bell, Lisette opened the door and greeted them. Fiona wondered if that was deliberate, so his siblings wouldn't be in the position of welcoming him back to his own home.

"Everyone is gathered in the dining room," Lisette said.

"The food looks amazing. There's enough for half a dozen families."

When the six adults were settled around the table, the housekeeper began setting out the meal on the antique sideboard. The food had come from a top-notch restaurant in the city. Fresh seafood. Ribs. Roasted corn on the cob. The dishes were endless.

The meal and the accompanying conversation progressed in fits and starts. During one awkward pause as wineglasses were being refilled, Hartley leaned in and spoke softly to Fiona. "My siblings are both still relatively new to this marriage gig. Mazie moved in with J.B. after the wedding. Jonathan and Lisette are building their own place." His warm breath brushed her ear, making her shiver. The arm he curled across the back of her chair hemmed her in intimately.

Jonathan overheard the quiet exchange and lifted an eyebrow. "You're curiously well-informed for a prodigal son."

The edge in his voice was apparent.

Hartley shrugged with a lazy smile. "I have my spies."

Fiona forced herself to wade in. Someone needed to defuse the rising tension. "What will happen to the beach house?"

Three

Nobody said a word. As Hartley watched, Fiona's face turned bright red. There was no way to avoid land mines with *this* family around the table. To her, it must have seemed like an innocuous question.

Jonathan spoke up, his smile careful but kind. "It's a little early to be thinking about those decisions. This was our father's fortress, his safe place. He didn't ever tell me what he wanted to do with the house when he was gone, and I didn't ask. I'm sure the lawyers will guide us through probate."

Suddenly, Hartley had reached his limit. They were all on their best behavior because of the funeral, but one thing was certain. Jonathan wasn't opening his arms to let Hartley back into the fold. The unspoken message was clear. Hartley had walked away, and true forgiveness was in short supply.

He stood abruptly. "It was good to see you all. Thanks for the meal. I'd like to take Fiona for a walk on the beach, and then we'll head out."

Mazie looked stricken. "Are you leaving town again?"

Again, that awkward silence.

Hartley shook his head slowly. "No. I'm back for good." There was so much he wanted to explain…so many family secrets to unravel. But how could he upend his siblings' lives for no other reason than to justify his own behavior? It wasn't fair to anyone. Maybe he would *never* tell them.

Fiona stood as well. "It was lovely to meet all of you. Sorry it was not under better circumstances."

Moments later, the ordeal was over.

Outside in the driveway, Hartley looked down at Fiona's shoes. "You can't walk in those on the beach."

"Barefoot is fine." She slipped off her sandals and tossed them in the car, adding her small clutch purse as well.

Hartley removed his jacket, tie, shoes and socks, feeling as if he were peeling away layers of frustration and grief. He had always loved the beach, and this house in particular. "The ground is rough between here and the gate," he said. "Get on my back, and I'll carry you to the sand."

Fiona looked at him askance. "I can walk."

He ground his jaw. "It's a piggyback ride, not foreplay."

"Don't get snippy with me, Hartley. I'm not the enemy."

She was right. He couldn't let Fiona bear the brunt of his mood. "Sorry," he muttered. "Climb on."

He watched as she shimmied her skirt up her thighs. Maybe he was wrong about the foreplay. Fiona's legs were enough to keep a man awake at night. When she moved behind him, he hitched her up on his back and curled his hands beneath her warm, supple thighs.

Fortunately for his self-control, the path beneath the house and out to the gate was not far. Fee reached around him to disengage the lock, and soon they were at the water's edge. He let her slide off his back slowly, steadying her with one hand as she stumbled.

There was no moon. The water seemed dark and menacing. But the whoosh and roar of the waves was a familiar lullaby from his childhood.

He tried to empty his mind of all the sorrow and confusion that had consumed him since he heard the news that his father was dead. Gradually, the inexorable pattern of the tide soothed him.

Fiona stood at his side in silence, her presence both a comfort and a niggling frustration. Twice now, he had made love to her and walked away. The first time, he'd had no choice. The second, he'd been reluctant to embroil her in his family drama. Maybe he sensed that he was using Fiona as a crutch. Maybe he hadn't wanted to let her get inside his head. In both instances, his behavior was logical if not particularly admirable. But what was going to happen moving forward?

If he still wanted to sleep with Fee, and he did, most emphatically, then he needed not only her absolution, but also some notion of what was ahead for him professionally. Anything beyond that was more than he wanted to contemplate right now.

Almost as if she had read his mind, Fiona spoke softly. "What do you do for a living, Hartley? We've flirted and slept together, but I don't really know much about you at all."

Her question prodded an unseen wound. He cleared his throat. "Well, before I left Charleston for an extended period, I was a full partner in Tarleton Shipping. We were working on a proposal to add a boatbuilding arm...pleasure craft. That whole deal was going to be my baby."

"And now?"

He shrugged. "I doubt my brother has any interest in working with me after everything that has happened."

"Because of this mysterious *falling-out*?"

"Yeah." He sighed. "Jonathan is one of the finest men I've ever known. A straight arrow all the way. But as alike as we are physically, our personalities don't always mesh."

"Why did you not live at the beach house?"

"I got tired of butting heads with my father over the business. Jonathan had a knack for handling him with kid gloves. Dad and I only yelled at each other. Several years ago I bought an investment property at a premier golf community north of the city. I was the one who would wine and dine clients. Play a few rounds with them on the course. I liked being outdoors, even if golf wasn't really my thing. But I closed deals and grew the business."

"Who has done that while you've been gone?"

It was a simple question. Not meant to inflict pain. But it hit at the heart of his guilt. "I don't know." Fiona hadn't been the only one he hurt when he'd hared off to Europe. He'd left behind his family and the shipping business and cut all contact. He'd had his reasons. In retrospect, though, he honestly didn't know if he'd done the right thing.

Fiona moved restlessly. "The beach is lovely, Hartley. I really do need to get home, though."

"I promised you explanations. It's late. I don't suppose I could sleep on your sofa?" He threw it out there hopefully. Fiona's little house represented the peace and comfort he had lost in this last year.

"No," she said bluntly. Without another word, she started up the beach toward the gate in the high brick wall.

"Fair enough." He loped up the incline and scooped her into his arms. It was a tougher slog through the loose sand this way, but he persevered. He needed to hold her.

Fiona didn't fight him. As soon as they were back at the car, though, she insisted on wriggling out of his embrace.

After smoothing her hair and brushing the sand from her feet, she put on her sexy sandals.

Then she stood, hands on her hips, and watched him re-dress. “You don’t owe me explanations. I told you that.”

He rounded the car and cupped her face in his hands. Lightly. Gently. “I *want* to tell you, Fee. And in the spirit of honesty, I’d like to sleep with you again.”

“Sleep?”

She had him there. “Sex,” he muttered. Even to his own ears, he sounded like a jerk. But he wouldn’t dress it up. He couldn’t offer her anything more. His life was total chaos. Besides, Fiona would demand full-on honesty and intimacy from any man who shared her life for the long haul. That wasn’t him.

Her expression was mutinous. In the glow of the security light, the stubborn tilt to her chin was obvious. “*Sex isn’t the answer to all your problems*, Hartley.”

“Maybe not, but it would be damned good, and if you’re honest, you’ll agree. I know I messed up. I won’t do that to you again.”

“How can I believe you?” Her low laugh held a hint of dismay. “It’s a painful cliché, but I’m a kid who came through the foster system. Never got adopted. I have a few abandonment issues. Your recent behavior hasn’t helped.”

How many women would have the guts to be so vulnerable? He had a lot to answer for and no clear idea how to fix the messes he had created. “I want to kiss you, Fee,” he muttered. “But I’m trying my damnedest to respect your boundaries.”

Tears glittered in her eyelashes. She sniffed. “Shut up and do it, you aggravating man.”

It was all the invitation he needed. He wanted to snatch her up and take everything she had to give. Instead, he kissed her coaxingly, softly. Trying to tell her without words how much he regretted his missteps.

Fiona made a choked little noise in her throat and finally kissed him back. When her slender arms curled around his neck, he felt as if he had won the lottery. She was soft and perfect against his chest. He lifted her off her feet, desperate to make the kiss last.

"I'm sorry," he muttered. "So sorry I hurt you."

"You're forgiven. Doesn't mean I'm a glutton for punishment." She pushed away from him after a few seconds. Reluctantly, he let her go.

"So, what now?" he asked quietly.

"Nothing. At least not today. Or even tomorrow. *Twice*, I let you talk your way into my bed like I was a sixteen-year-old girl with her first crush. That was *my* mistake. I make no guarantees, Hartley. None."

He rolled his shoulders, realizing ruefully that he had been a little unrealistic about where this evening might lead. Even if he'd been saying all the right things, apparently his libido had jumped ahead to more titillating scenarios. "Understood," he sighed.

He started the engine and waited for her to climb into the front seat. The ocean breeze had tousled her hair. It stood up around her head like a nimbus, making her a weary goddess…or a naughty nymph.

Which did he want? The angel or the sexy sprite? In his imagination, she was both.

He turned the radio on for the drive back to Charleston. As they pulled away from his father's home, Hartley glanced in the rearview mirror. Jonathan stood at the top of the stairs, his arms folded across his chest.

Seeing his brother tonight had been surprisingly painful. After all this time, Hartley had been hoping Jonathan might have relented…that he had come to know instinctively that Hartley would never do anything to bring harm to his family.

But apparently, some hurts ran deep. Jonathan wasn't wiping the slate clean. In fact, he hadn't made any mention of the future at all. Hartley was on his own.

When they reached Fiona's street, she gathered her purse and started to climb out as soon as the car rolled to a halt. He took her wrist. "Wait, Fee. Please."

Her body language was wary. "What?"

"Let me take you to lunch tomorrow. I'll tell you the whole story, start to finish." He needed to tell *someone.* The secrets were gutting him. But his family was off-limits until he decided whether or not the truth would be too damaging. Fiona was a neutral player.

"I have to work tomorrow," she said.

"Dinner, then?" He was close to begging on his knees.

She hesitated for far too long. "Fine. But if this story is as convoluted as it seems, we should eat at my house. I'll fix spaghetti."

"I want to treat you," he said.

"You can't spill salacious secrets in the middle of a crowded restaurant. Besides, this isn't a date, Hartley. You seem to have a need to bare your soul, and I've agreed to listen. That's all."

"You're a hard woman."

"It's about time, don't you think?"

"I remember what it's like to make love to you, Fee. You can't blame a guy for wanting to re-create the magic."

"The magic is gone. You killed it."

Her words were harsh, but she was still sitting in his car. He took that as a good sign. "I love spaghetti," he said. "What time?"

"Six o'clock. Don't assume you'll be able to coax me into letting you spend the night. That's off the table."

"Yes, ma'am. You're cute when you're busting my balls."

"Grow up, Hartley. I'm immune to you now."

I'm immune to you now. Fiona had never told a bigger lie in her life. She slept poorly and woke up the following morning disturbed by the vivid dreams that had plagued her. Being with Hartley again kindled a hunger in her belly that no homemade spaghetti was going to fill. She wanted him. Still. After everything he had done. It was a shocking realization.

Despite her unsettled mood, she was a professional artist. That meant working regular hours even when her muse had taken a hike. Today was a case in point. It was harder than it should have been to concentrate on her new project…three massive panels that would hang in one of the main rooms of Charleston's visitor center.

Commissions like this one were her bread and butter. They paid the light bill and kept food in the fridge. But they weren't humdrum. Never that. She poured her heart and soul into every brushstroke.

Because of the size of the canvases, she'd had to buy a special easel that held the work in progress secure. At certain moments, she would have to stand on a ladder to complete the highest portions. Her sketch—the one the city had approved—included historical images all the way from Charleston's founding up until modern times.

A giant undulating current swept through the center of each panel, propelling the milestones of progress from decade to decade. Included in the visual telling were some very painful periods in time. She could see the finished product in her mind. The challenge she faced was being able to successfully translate her vision into reality.

It was her habit to paint for a couple of hours when she

first awoke and then take a break for coffee and a light brunch. After that, she would typically labor for another five or six hours and quit for the day. Hard work and determination had brought her to this place in her career. She was conscious that her success was based on a great many things beyond her control, so she was determined to make the most of her current success.

This morning, though, she found herself swamped with inexplicable fatigue and a draining lethargy that forced her to go in search of calories after only forty-five minutes in her studio.

In the kitchen, an unexpected déjà vu brought her up short. She and Hartley had stood in this very spot and made bacon and eggs amidst much laughter and many hot, hungry kisses.

She put a hand to her chest, trying to still the flutters of anxiety. Hartley wouldn't force her to do anything she didn't want to do. Her problem was far closer to home. It was *her*. Fiona. The woman with the deep-seated need for love and acceptance.

Hartley made her happy, but more than that, he made her wish and dream, and *that* was dangerous.

The fact that she had slept with him twice was no big deal. They'd had fun. Their sexual chemistry was off the charts. He was smart and kind and amusing, and she had never met a more appealing man.

But it was the long view that worried her. Like the deadly undertow out at the beach, Hartley had the power to drag her under…to tear apart the life she had built for herself. She was proud of her independence. She didn't lean on any man for support.

The danger lay in the fact that without even trying, he made her want to throw caution to the wind. When she was with him—and also when she wasn't—the smart, careful, cautious side of her brain shut down.

Even now, all she could think about was how much she wanted to share a bed with him again. Naked and wanton. Losing herself in the elemental rush of sexual desire. Hartley made her *alive*. And she loved it.

But with great joy came the potential for great heartbreak.

With the way she was feeling, it was too much trouble to cook anything. Instead, she opted for cereal and a banana. A cup of hot tea warmed her cold fingers. When she was done with breakfast, she carried a second serving of tea to the living room and curled up on the couch.

Cradling the china cup in her hands, she debated calling off tonight's dinner. Who was she kidding? If Hartley came over, she would sleep with him. Wouldn't she? Did she have it in her to say no?

Sitting here alone, it was easy to see all the problems.

The Tarletons were Charleston royalty. They and J.B.'s family, the Vaughans, had endowed libraries and funded hospital wings and sat on the boards of half a dozen philanthropic organizations across the city. Their bloodlines went back to pre–civil war times.

Fiona appreciated her own worth, but she was a pragmatist. Hartley appeared to have the attention span of a moth. He was interested in Fiona at the moment, because his life was in crisis. And because they had shared a couple of encounters that had all the earmarks of a romantic comedy.

Life wasn't like that, though. In the long run, the chances that he would actually come to love Fiona were slim. Maybe she was his flavor of the month right now, but when the novelty paled, he would be off on another adventure, with another woman, and Fiona might be left with a broken heart if she were foolish enough to fall for him.

Despite all her hashing and rehashing of the facts, she couldn't bring herself to text him and say *don't come*. How pathetic was that? She desperately wanted to see him. And then, of course, there was her curiosity about where he had been all these months.

He had never struck her as a liar. If he had explanations to make today, she had a hunch they would be true. Fantastical maybe, but true.

She finished her tea and stood, only to have the room whirl drunkenly.

With a little gasp, she reached behind her for the arm of the sofa and sat down gingerly. Had she poured bad milk in her cereal? Her stomach flipped and flopped. What was going on?

Five minutes later, she tried again. This time the familiar outlines of her furniture stayed put, but the nausea grew worse. At the last moment, she made a dash for the bathroom and threw up, emptying her stomach again and again until she was so weak she could barely stagger to her bedroom.

She curled up in the center of the mattress, shaking and woozy, and pulled the edge of the comforter over her.

Then it hit her. A possibility that had never once crossed her mind…though it should have. Was she pregnant? She'd had these odd episodes for several weeks now…had written them off as a virus or inner ear trouble or low blood sugar.

Her heart hammered in her chest. Her periods were not regular…never had been. At her gynecologist's urging, Fiona typically noted them on a paper calendar she kept in the bedside table.

When she thought she could move without barfing, she reached for the drawer, extracted what she needed and stared numbly at the unmarked boxes. Back one month. Then two. Then three. At last, she found it. A brief notation in her own handwriting. She'd had her period about ten days before Hartley last showed up at her house.

Dear Lord.

He'd used protection. Hadn't even balked at the idea when she told him she wasn't on the pill. In fact, he'd used protection that night after the wedding, too. He'd been a generous, thoughtful lover.

But no method of birth control was 100 hundred percent. And now that she thought about it, three months ago, they had made love multiple times during the night when they were both half-asleep. Had they messed up? Was there one of those times when his body had claimed hers skin to skin?

Her teeth started to chatter. She couldn't tell him. Not yet. Not until she was sure. He was going to be at her house in a few hours. With a moan of mortification, she buried her face in the pillow.

Yet even as she trembled with fear, excitement and happiness bloomed in her chest. A baby? Was she really pregnant? This could be the future she had always dreamed of...the family she so desperately wanted.

Hartley didn't have to be involved, but he *had* to be told.

Four

Hartley felt like a sailboat with a broken mast. He was home to stay. His time away had always been temporary. But his siblings hadn't known that, because he hadn't told them.

He'd left Charleston in order to be a hero. To fix things. And he'd succeeded in part. All the answers to all the questions had been found, thanks to his extended visit in Europe. Ironically, those answers were too dangerous and painful to explain to Jonathan and Mazie.

Had it all been worth it? Or had he ruined his relationships for nothing? On the day after his father's funeral, he found himself going in circles, or at the very least, becalmed.

What was he going to do with himself? If Jonathan wasn't keen or willing to have him back at Tarleton Shipping, Hartley was lost.

His enormous home adjacent to the world-class golf resort was not *him*. Never had been. At least that was one thing he could change. He spent the day taking care of small maintenance issues, and then called a Realtor and set up an appointment for the following morning.

He was going to sell his house. Immediately.

Maybe he would rent something in Fiona's neighborhood while he figured out his next step. She couldn't help him revamp his life—that was up to him—but sharing her bed would keep him sane. If she allowed it.

By the time four thirty rolled around, he was hot and sweaty but feeling pretty damn good about himself. He jumped in the shower, humming with more enthusiasm than expertise. With the prospect of seeing Fiona tonight, he had plenty of reasons to be upbeat.

His life had taken some unexpected turns, but he would get himself back on course. His siblings were all he had. Fiona was an alluring distraction from his painful family situation. Maybe it was wrong to pursue her. Maybe it was cowardly. Because if he used her and walked away again, he knew in his gut the damage would be permanent.

It would be smarter and kinder to stay away.

Even so, at ten till six, he pulled up in front of her charming home, grabbed the gifts he had brought and locked the car. He thought he saw the edge of a curtain twitch, but maybe not.

When he knocked, she answered almost immediately. "Hi, Hartley. You're right on time." She was wearing a daffodil-yellow sundress that bared her shoulders and emphasized her modest breasts.

He kissed her cheek. "These are for you."

She glanced at the label of his three-hundred-dollar bottle of wine and raised an eyebrow. "A little over-the-top for homemade spaghetti, don't you think? What if we save it for a special occasion? I made iced tea. And there's beer in the fridge…the kind you like."

He was ridiculously pleased that she remembered his preferences. A tiny detail, but a good sign…he hoped. "Sounds like a plan," he said. "Shall I put the flowers in water?" He'd brought her yellow and white roses, a summery bouquet that suited her home and her personality.

"Yes…thanks. You'll find a vase underneath the sink."

The conversation was stilted for two people who had seen each other naked. He wanted to say to hell with dinner and take her straight to the bedroom. "Did you have a good day painting?"

She whirled around, her eyes wide. "Why do you ask that?"

He cocked his head. "You told me you're starting a big new project."

"Oh." She flushed, her gaze skating away from his. "It was fine. Beginnings are always hard."

"Are you okay, Fee?" Now that he thought about it, she seemed pale…and nervous. She hadn't been this skittish the first afternoon they met. At that endless wedding rehearsal.

"Of course I'm okay." Her voice was muffled, because she had stuck her head and shoulders halfway into the fridge.

He glanced at the stove. "Do I need to turn off the heat? The spaghetti is boiling over."

"Oh, damn." She whirled around and rescued the pasta just in time.

He put his hands on her shoulders. "Fiona. Take a breath."

She shrugged out of his grip and put her hands to her cheeks. "Sorry," she muttered. "I'm a little nervous about having you here."

There it was again. That raw honesty. He winced. "I can go. If that's what you want."

They stared at each other across the small kitchen. "No," she said at last. "I don't want you to go."

Thank God. He reached for her hand and linked his fingers with hers. "I swear I'll be on my best behavior."

At last, she smiled at him. It was wobbly, but it was a smile. "I find that highly unlikely." She rested her head against his shoulder. "I'm glad you're here. Really, Hartley. I am."

His hands trembled with the urge to touch her. Coming here was wrong. He knew it. But he couldn't walk away from her a third time. Even if all they had was sexual chemistry, he wanted to erase his past transgressions. He needed to prove he could be trusted.

"Well, that makes two of us," he said heartily. "Now, tell me how I can help with dinner..."

Fiona was embarrassed and relieved at the same time. Hartley had taken her behavior in stride, it seemed. They consumed the simple meal and shared innocuous conversation without incident. Though she felt as if her secret was written on her face, she was clearly overreacting. There was no way for him to know the truth.

She had to get a grip.

"Let's go to the living room," she said when they had cleared the table and loaded the dishwasher side by side. "If you're going to bare your soul, I want a comfy spot."

Hartley followed her, chuckling. "I never promised that."

She curled up on a chair that was only big enough for one. No point in tempting fate. "You don't have to do this," she said.

Hartley shrugged. "You're the perfect listener. A disinterested bystander."

Fiona's heart sank. That wasn't what she wanted to hear at all. Hartley hadn't come to her tonight as a trusted confidante. She was about to be his therapist or his shrink. The distinction was painful.

She swallowed her hurt pride and reminded herself that Hartley wasn't her Prince Charming. Never would be. "Start at the beginning," she said.

Now he was the one to look uncomfortable. Maybe he hadn't rehearsed what he was going to say. "Well..."

"I'll refresh your memory," she offered helpfully. "After the wedding, I invited you here to my house. We both knew what was going to happen. It *happened* three times that night, and when I woke up, you were gone."

"Geez, Fiona. You make it sound so sleazy." He paced restlessly.

"How would you describe it?"

"I had airline reservations for the morning after the wedding. I was supposed to be on a flight out of Charleston at 7 a.m. You were a complication I never expected. I didn't know how to explain."

"Ah."

"It's true," he said.

She stared at him soberly. "Where were you going?"

"London first. I met with a private investigator who used to work for Interpol."

Fiona wrinkled her nose. "I think you've left out some pertinent details. Why would you need a PI?"

Hartley hunched his shoulders, his expression bleak. "Two days before the wedding, I received a blackmail note."

"Seriously?" Her skepticism was warranted, surely.

"The letter threatened to go public with a painful Tarleton family secret if I didn't give the blackmailer a million dollars."

"Hartley. This sounds like a spy novel."

"What you don't know is that my mother has been living in an inpatient mental health facility in Vermont since my siblings and I were preteens. A few people in Charleston know the truth, but not many."

"So you decided to do what?"

"My father's health was failing. Jonathan had been working his ass off at Tarleton Shipping, trying to keep the business afloat. My sister spent her adolescence without a mother. Our family has suffered more than our share of hard times. I didn't want the gossip."

"Everybody knows you can't pay off a blackmailer. Surely you didn't."

"Of course not. But I needed the money in hand just in case. I wasn't sure what else this mystery person might be willing to do. And I didn't know why we were targets."

"What did Jonathan say?"

Hartley's neck flushed. "I didn't tell him. I thought I could handle everything on my own. In retrospect, that wasn't too smart."

"I have to agree. Did you have a million dollars lying around in the bank?"

"Not exactly. I've told you about Jonathan. He's a play-by-the-book kind of guy. Never cut corners. Never bend the rules. If I had told him why I needed the money, he would have asked a ton of questions and then shut me down. I couldn't take that chance."

Her eyes widened. "What did you do, Hartley?"

He shrugged. "I took the money out of our account at work. It wasn't stealing. I own a quarter of the business."

"But you didn't tell Jonathan what was going on."

Hartley heard the criticism in her statement. "No. Like I said, he was under a lot of stress. I wanted to handle this grenade and defuse it. I never imagined that my brother and my father would jump to the absolute worst conclusion."

She shook her head slowly. "That's a lot to ask, Hartley. Blind faith?"

"They know me. Why would I take the money if not for

a damned good reason?" It still pissed him off that he'd immediately been painted the villain. Even worse, it *hurt*.

"Secrets backfire all the time." Fiona's expression was wry. "I can't say that I blame them, Hartley. You didn't trust them enough to believe you could all work together. Surely you see that was a mistake."

Maybe he did now. With the benefit of hindsight. "Well, I can't undo the damage, so it's a moot point."

"Mazie seems to have forgiven you."

"That's only because Dad and Jonathan kept her in the dark. If she knew the truth, she'd probably give me the cold shoulder, too."

"Let's circle back. So you took the money, and you went to London. What next?"

"Eventually, I tracked the letter back to a small village in Switzerland. The blackmailer was a relative on my mother's side. Her uncle, to be exact."

"Why would he want to hurt your family?"

"That's what I needed to know. As it turned out, he was only trying to get my attention. The letter he sent me served its purpose. It got me to Switzerland. Uncle Hans had fallen on hard times. An extended illness had wiped out his savings. He was in danger of losing his house and his dairy farm."

"Did you turn him over to the authorities?"

"How could I? He was a sick man in his late seventies. Frail. No family left. I felt I owed him something."

"So you *did* give him money."

"I paid off his house and put some cash in his bank account. Not much at all by our standards, but he was grateful and it made me feel better. I barely put a dent in the million. I ended up staying with Hans for a couple of months, filling in the blanks. He had a lot of stuff like family Bibles and heirlooms…things he wanted me to see. Items to pass on."

Fiona frowned. "There's something you're not telling me. Why did you come back to Charleston three months ago? And then leave again?"

"I came back to talk to my father and my siblings about why I had been gone. I had information they needed to know. But I chickened out at the last minute. Revealing everything I had learned in Europe was a potential bomb that threatened to blow up in my face. You were the only person I saw or spoke to. After that night in your bed, I went back to Switzerland to pack up my things."

"And then what?"

He shrugged, his eyes bleak with remembrance. "The uncle passed away. Rather suddenly. I found myself in the odd position of having to settle his meager estate."

"Even then, you didn't talk to your family?"

"I couldn't. The conversation was something that needed to be handled face-to-face. But with Hans gone, I began to ask myself if it wouldn't be better to keep everything I had learned to myself."

"What was this terrible secret, Hartley?"

His jaw was carved in stone, his profile no longer the affable man she had come to know. "The woman in that facility in Vermont—the woman who no longer recognizes us because she had a complete breakdown—the woman who is the only mother we've ever known—is *not* our mother."

Fiona couldn't sit still any longer. She jumped to her feet and went to him. Wrapping her arms around his waist, she rested her cheek against his chest, inhaling the pleasant laundry scent of his crisp cotton shirt. "That doesn't even make sense."

He eluded her embrace and continued to wear tracks in her rug. "Apparently, when my siblings and I were toddlers, my father took our mother to Switzerland to visit her family. She hadn't been back since they were married. They left us kids behind in Charleston with a trusted babysitter."

"Okay..." Her mind raced ahead, trying to guess the outcome. But nothing clicked into place.

Hartley's body language was agitated. "According to Hans, my mother committed suicide when they were in Switzerland. Apparently, she had been planning it for some time. There was a note. Hans still had it in the Bible. In her mind, it was better to do the deed where no one in Charleston would know. Maybe she thought my father would invent an accident. Hell, I don't know. She was a very sick woman."

"But I don't understand. Who is living in Vermont?"

He stopped his pacing and faced her. "My *aunt.* My mother's twin sister."

"Good Lord..." Her mind reeled.

"According to Hans, after my mother died, my aunt volunteered to marry my father, return to the States with him and step in as our mother."

"But surely someone would have noticed."

"I told you my father kept the family hidden away. Now all the security and the secrecy make a lot more sense. Maybe he was afraid. He knew keeping the business afloat was all up to him. Maybe he thought being a father was more than he could handle. Or maybe he was so distraught with grief, he wasn't rational."

"It's hard to believe..."

"Hans had pictures of the two women side by side. The sisters were identical. Any household staff here in South Carolina were vetted carefully. And maybe we kids were too young to know the difference."

"I don't know what to say."

"Pardon me for being flip, but being a foster kid doesn't sound so bad now, does it?"

She knew his angry sarcasm wasn't directed at her. "So you're telling me your father lost not one but two wives to mental illness?"

"Yes. And it also makes more sense, I suppose, that he sent the second Mrs. Tarleton so far away when she began to show signs that she might hurt herself or one of us. She wasn't the woman he loved. That tragedy—losing the love of his life—had happened long ago."

"The poor man."

"It's a lot to comprehend. Things were different back then. My father was much older than my mother. I don't think he would have ever considered raising us on his own. He would have been in shock when the suicide happened. Why did my aunt volunteer to take on a ready-made family? Perhaps her life in Switzerland was unhappy. We'll never know, because none of us can get through to her."

Fiona sank onto the sofa, her mind whirling with Hartley's story. Definitely a case of truth being stranger than fiction. "How long were you there after your uncle died?"

"About eight weeks. I sold the house and the farm and settled all the outstanding accounts. I had already shipped several boxes of memorabilia back to the States. I assumed Mazie would be interested one day, even if Jonathan wasn't. All I could think about was coming home, talking to my father, asking him a million questions. And then I got Lisette's phone call. Dad was gone. Now all his secrets are buried with him."

"You *have* to tell Mazie and Jonathan. You have to, Hartley."

He turned and stared at her, his face carefully blank. "I don't know that I do, Fee. I think the kinder thing is to leave well enough alone."

Five

Hartley felt empty…wrung out. Tonight—with Fiona—was the first chance he'd had to work through all of this. Hearing himself say the words aloud settled something in his gut.

He sat down beside her, his body limp with resignation and grief. Without overthinking it, he took her hand in his. Her nails were neatly trimmed but unpolished. Her fingers had calluses in certain spots. She might be small in stature, but she was tough in mind and body. Soft and sensual in bed. A force to be reckoned with when the sun came up.

"Think about it," he said, rubbing her palm with his thumb. "My siblings and I already knew our DNA carried the possibility of mental illness. But *two* sisters in the same family? Twins? That ups our chances of passing on whatever genetic anomaly took our mother from us. The medical community has made huge advances in treatment, but there are no guarantees."

"Isn't that all the more reason to warn them?"

He shook his head. "Mazie and J.B. have been battling infertility already. They may end up adopting. Lisette had a tragic miscarriage only weeks after their wedding and another one two months later. I assume they're trying again, but who knows? I can't be the one who makes those decisions for them. I won't play God. If I tell them what I know, it could change the entire course of their relationships."

"And what about you?" Fiona was milk pale. His story had upset her more than he had anticipated.

"I won't have children," he said bluntly. "All the secrets. All the lies? Families are supposed to love and support each other. I've paid the price for my father's failings. I won't put an innocent child through that."

Her eyes glistened with tears. "Don't you think your brother and sister and their spouses deserve that same clarity?"

He cursed beneath his breath, feeling put upon from all sides. If he'd been able to talk this over with his father, maybe he could have made the right decision. Now all he had were doubts and uncertainties.

"Don't push, Fee. I've been to hell and back. What do you want from me, damn it?"

She stood up slowly, her expression impossible to decipher. "So have I, Hartley. But life goes on. You've had a terrible day…a terrible year. Come to bed with me."

He jerked back, caught between exultation and the absolute certainty that it would be a mistake to sleep with her right now. "I don't need your pity," he muttered. "I'll go."

"Forget the past," she whispered. "Forget the wedding weekend when we met and the night we had after the reception. Forget the moments you spent in this house three months ago. Forget the funeral and the fact that your family is shutting you out. None of that matters right now. I want you, and I think you need me. Let's take tonight for ourselves."

Something about her urgent speech bothered him. Below the surface there was faulty reasoning in the words. But he was finally where he wanted to be, and she was offering him the chance for redemption.

He wasn't a saint—far from it. It was an invitation no mortal man could resist. Fiona. After all these lonely, terrible weeks.

"I came here for dinner, Fee. Nothing more. I swear."

Her smile was wistful. "I think we're both good at kidding ourselves. I can't explain this thing between us other than to call it elemental attraction. You said you wanted to have sex with me again. Maybe what we need is a chance to say goodbye and to have closure."

"Closure?" He mouthed the word with distaste, vaguely alarmed that she was giving him the brush-off in the midst of seducing him.

"I have two huge projects ahead of me," she said. "You have a lot of decisions to make about your life and your relationship with your family. If you're honest, being with me has been an escape for you, nothing more. Your life is one big train wreck right now. I forgive you. I'm not playing games."

He had a choice. He could stand here and argue with her about the future, or he could take what she was offering. In the end, emotional exhaustion won out. He needed her. He wanted her.

She was so beautiful it made his chest ache. Her pale, creamy skin was dotted with the occasional freckle. Those wide-set eyes were a combination of smoke and the sea. The wildness of her fire-kissed hair struck a marked contrast to the serenity she projected.

No woman had ever affected him so immediately, so

deeply. Something about her made him want to make love to her and bask in her peaceful spirit at the same time.

He felt cold inside. Fiona promised him warmth.

"Fine," he said. "Call it whatever you want. I won't say no to you. Not tonight."

She took his hand. He let her pull him to his feet. He was charmed and pleased that she was taking the initiative. In their earlier encounters he'd been the aggressor, the coaxer. Now, his sweet Fiona was staking a claim.

In her bedroom, they faced each other with odd hesitance. They had been virtual strangers before. Things were more *real* now.

"Should we check the doors?" he asked. "Set the alarm?"

She cocked her head. "The doors are locked. I don't have an alarm."

He frowned. "I don't like that. I'll buy you a new system. You need one."

"Hartley…"

"Hmm?"

"Shut up and kiss me. Before I change my mind."

"Yes, ma'am."

Three months. It had been three long months since he tasted her. The memories paled. She melted into his arms, stealing the breath from his lungs. Every part of him hard and taut with wanting. "I've missed you," he said huskily, nipping her lower lip with his teeth, sliding his tongue over hers. "So damn much. I used to lie in bed at night and calculate the distance between Switzerland and South Carolina."

Fiona wrapped her arms around his neck. "At least you knew where I was. All I had were a million questions. Actually, until you showed up on my doorstep three months ago, I didn't know if you were alive or dead. That sucked, Hartley. A lot."

"I'm sorry." His fingers fumbled with the zipper at the back of her bodice. "I'll make it up to you."

"See that you do."

Her teasing smile lit a fire in his gut. He sucked in a sharp breath when he realized that all she wore underneath the sundress was a pair of simple cotton undies. White. Unadorned.

No silk and lace confection could have been more titillating. He let the dress pool at her feet. "Damn, you're gorgeous."

"My boobs aren't very big."

The hint of uncertainty in her gaze brought tenderness into the mix. He kissed her nose. "They're perfect," he said. Carefully, he cupped her curves in his hands, teasing the pert tips with his thumbs.

Fiona's eyelids fluttered shut. She made a sound that was halfway between a purr and a moan. His erection flexed a centimeter more. "Look at me, darlin'. I want you to watch."

His big, tanned hands were dark against her white body. She sucked in a breath, but she obeyed. "I'll watch," she vowed. "It's my turn now." She unbuttoned his shirt and yanked it from his pants. "Get rid of this, big guy."

Sexual urgency told him to take and take until they were both satisfied. But tonight, he wanted to play another tune. Tonight, he wanted to convince her that he wasn't a bad guy. That there was more to him than the lover who ducked out in the night. Hartley Tarleton wanted to make a good impression.

Unfortunately, his patience for having her undress him was eroding rapidly. "I'll do the rest," he said, kicking off his shoes and bouncing on one foot and then the other as he removed his socks.

Fiona—naked but for panties and a smile—watched as he unfastened his belt and pants and shucked them to his ankles. When he lost his balance and nearly fell on his ass, she had the audacity to giggle.

"The man I remember was smoother than you," she said.

"Maybe I'm nervous," he deadpanned. She didn't have to know it wasn't a joke.

"Hurry up, Hartley. I'm getting cold."

It was still eighty degrees outside, even at this hour. And the AC system in Fiona's little house wasn't all that efficient. Perhaps she was nervous, too. She flipped back the simple yellow-and-blue quilt and climbed under the sheets. When she reclined on one elbow and crooked her finger, he was toast.

He was completely naked now. Unable to hide his need even if he had wanted to. Fee stared at his bobbing sex and licked her lips. The reaction didn't seem to be intentional. Her eyes had glazed over, and her chest was flushed.

When he made it under the covers and twined his body with hers in a skin-to-skin hug that fried his synapses, Fiona buried her face in his neck. "You are an impossible man, but Lord knows, you're magnificent. I love touching you." She ran her hands over his back and buttocks as if to make a point.

He found it hard to breathe. "Knock yourself out, Fee." She was warm and supple in his embrace. Her enthusiasm for his body made him glad he was a man. He would die happy if all he had to do was let her experiment with his various appendages.

She pulled back so she could kiss his collarbone. "I'm not even going to ask how many women you slept with while you were abroad."

"Not a one," he wheezed, trying not to come like an untested teenager.

When she zeroed in on the spot that was most eager for her attention, his vision went fuzzy. The sensation of her slender, warm fingers wrapped around his sex was indescribable.

She stroked him up and down, slowly enough to make his forehead damp and his muscles rigid. "I find that difficult to believe."

Was she torturing him on purpose? "I may have walked out on you, Fee, but I've never lied to you. After we met at the wedding, I've been too busy to look at other women."

Fiona wanted so badly to believe him, but she'd been a naive fool twice. Was he playing on her sympathies? Did it really matter tonight? He was here…in her bed. Very much alive. His masculinity was raw and erotic in the midst of her ultra feminine bed. The artist in her wanted to sketch him as he sprawled on his back and watched her.

The woman simply *wanted.* Period.

She reclined beside him and ran her hand from his throat to his hip. Warm golden skin was lightly dusted with just the right amount of hair. He was like a beautiful god, at the height of his physical perfection.

At the moment, her stomach was cooperating, thank heavens. Her earlier fears seemed ludicrous. Of course she wasn't pregnant. A woman would know something like that, right? She couldn't possibly be thirteen weeks along and have survived in blissful ignorance all this time.

Still, the possibility filled her with both anxiety and amazement. A child? A baby with Hartley's big brown eyes? An infant who would possess the best and worst of both of them?

Tremors came to life deep inside her body and spread

outward. She struggled with waves of fear and exultation and sexual arousal. How could she want this man so damn much when he had hurt her twice and had said recently—with perfect clarity—that he was *never* going to have children?

"Do you have a condom?" she asked, feeling her face heat. Hopefully, he would attribute her red-faced mortification to maidenly sexual frenzy. Until she knew for sure about the baby, she wouldn't take chances.

His gaze narrowed. A feral masculine smile accompanied his terse nod. "One second, darlin'." He leaned over the edge of the bed, giving her a stunning view of his tight butt. "Got it," he said triumphantly, brandishing his wallet.

While he was busy tossing the packet on the bedside table, Fiona raked his ass with her fingernails. The soft fuzz was golden, lighter than the hair on his head, as if he might have sunbathed in the nude while he was in Europe.

Thinking of Hartley naked on a beach somewhere made her dizzy. "I'm glad you came back," she whispered. "I missed you, Hartley."

At her words, his expression softened. "And I missed you, sweet Fiona." He moved between her legs and readied himself. "I don't even care if this is pity sex. I've been dreaming about you in my bed for weeks."

When he pushed steadily, filling her, driving himself home until she winced, it was as if everything in her world righted itself for a moment. And then she understood why. This was their pattern, their sexual MO. One frantic, unable-to-wait-a-second-longer coupling followed by a series of languid, self-indulgent second acts.

Hartley was a big man. Everywhere. Her body accepted his eagerly, straining to make the connection last. His urgency was flattering, his attention to detail admirable. Even as he took his own pleasure, he remembered every erogenous zone he had discovered during their earlier encounters.

A nip at her earlobe. A gentle grinding of his pelvis against hers, putting pressure where she needed it to climb even higher. Her breath caught in her throat. A wave of emotion staggered her, making her weak and weepy. He was so dear. So perfect for her. But he *wasn't* hers, and now he never would be. She had to remember that. Had to keep her heart out of this. Sex only.

She'd always heard people say that pregnant women were insatiable when it came to sex. Was that why she was already thinking about round two? Or was this wild urgency all for Hartley and no other reason?

He went still, his body rigid and trembling. "Fee? Are you with me?"

Her mental distraction hadn't gone unnoticed. "I'm here," she whispered. "Don't stop."

He took her at her word. Reaching between their linked bodies, he caressed the aching center of her need and sent her over the edge. The orgasm was off the charts. Incredible. Mildly astonishing.

The ripples went on and on.

Hartley chuckled hoarsely, wheezing as he attempted to speak while balanced on a sexual precipice. "You make a man feel damn good, Fiona. I'd like to spend the whole night reclaiming lost time. We've wasted months."

She smiled lazily, in an expansive, forgiving mood now that he had satiated her considerable needs for the moment. "*We?* Don't blame this one on me, Mr. Tarleton. I've been right here all along. You're the one who went missing."

His smile sent her buzzing again. "You can punish me later."

He withdrew almost completely and then went faster. Groaning, he thrust rapidly until he hit the peak, shuddering and panting in her embrace until he slumped on top of her, his body warm and damp.

She wrapped her arms around him, feeling his heart pound against her breast. As wrung out as he was, she could almost believe he'd been celibate since the last time they were together.

That was dangerous thinking. Such an idea made their brief dalliance more than it was. Why would a man avoid sex for the sake of two isolated one-night stands?

Believing in rainbows, pots of gold, unicorns and happily-ever-afters wasn't who Fiona was anymore. Over the course of her adolescence, she had stomped on her rose-colored glasses. She now viewed the world as it was. Broken. Hurtful. Uncaring.

Maybe that was harsh. She had wonderful friends. But the belief that a man and a woman could form a lasting bond on the basis of a few nights of hot sexual insanity was a fiction she couldn't embrace. She wouldn't.

Idly, she stroked the back of his head, feeling the silky hair slide between her fingers. The other Tarleton twin was a fine figure of a man, but she preferred Hartley's rough-around-the-edges masculinity. He could be brash and unrepentant and frustratingly stubborn, but he tugged at her heartstrings as no other man ever had.

When he could breathe again, he lifted his head. "Damn, woman. You're killing me." He kissed her slow and deep, his tongue mating with hers. "I don't want closure, Fee. I want you."

He punctuated his declaration with a string of kisses down the side of her neck, to her throat, to her breasts. Licking them. Nibbling. Forcing her to acknowledge his mastery of her body.

How could he do it to her so quickly? She was on the verge of climax again. Panic gripped her in a choke hold.

This had to stop. Her mornings were iffy now. She and Hartley couldn't be wrapped in each other's arms when the sun came up. "You should go," she said, blurting out the words with no finesse at all. "It's late." *I can't take the risk you'll stay until morning, see me barf and guess the truth.*

Six

Hartley jerked, stunned. He would have been less shocked if she had slapped his face. He'd been within an inch of giving his sweet Fee a second orgasm when she slammed some kind of door between them.

He gaped. "Are you serious?" Her raspberry nipples were puckered, begging for his attention.

For some reason, Fiona's gaze slid away. "I have to work early in the morning." She slipped out of bed and tugged the coverlet from the foot of the mattress, wrapping it around herself toga-style. "Thank you for telling me why you were gone so long. I hope you and your brother work things out between you."

He staggered to his feet, his brain racing to understand what had just happened. "Are you angry with me?" He frowned, knowing she had every right to evict him, and yet hurt that she could seem so unaffected by what for him had been cataclysmic.

As he reached for his clothes and reluctantly dressed, Fiona shook her head slowly. Smoky blue eyes stared at him. "Of course not. You did what you had to do."

"The past is the past," he muttered. "I'm more interested in what comes next. I'm not done with you, Fee."

Her eyes flashed. "It's not up to you, now is it? I didn't put my life on hold while you were gone. You can't drop back in and expect everything to be the way you want it."

Was this some kind of test? Was he supposed to work for absolution?

Screw that. He owed her an apology, and he had given it, sincerely and wholeheartedly. But he wouldn't crawl. First Jonathan and now Fiona. Was there no one who believed in him?

When he was fully clad, he shot her an angry glare. "I get it," he said. "You don't want to sleep with me anymore. Casual sex isn't your thing, is that it? No worries. Now that I'm home for good, I'm sure there are plenty of available women in Charleston. Good night, Fiona. I'll let myself out."

Even then he thought she might relent. She certainly *seemed* miserable. But she didn't say a word as he stormed out. He heard the *snick* of the dead bolt on the front door after it closed behind him. By the time he reached the sidewalk and headed for his car, the lights inside the house had been extinguished. He stood in the middle of the street… all alone.

In a year and a month and a week that had sucked big time, this was perhaps his lowest point. The investigation was over. Fiona no longer wanted him around. He had reconciled with his family…barely. But there was apparently no longer a spot for him at Tarleton Shipping. That ship had sailed.

He couldn't even laugh at his own stupid joke. Nor

could he face returning to the house that wasn't a home, the house he was going to sell sooner than later.

Instead, he drove aimlessly around Fiona's neighborhood. All her fellow Charlestonians were tucked in for the evening. No teenagers on skateboards. No sweethearts kissing good-night on street corners. Just peace and silence and the sense of a community at rest.

And then he spotted it. A small for-sale sign in front of a three-story brick monstrosity. The house was older than its neighbors and in bad need of repair.

Hartley pulled out his phone and looked up the specs on the Realtor's website. From the pictures, it was no wonder the house had been on the market over a hundred days. It probably had dry rot. Black mold. Maybe even termite infestation.

His spirits lifted. It was exactly the kind of project a man needed when he was looking for an anchor. And it had the added advantage of being under his lover's nose.

If he had genuinely thought Fiona was not interested in a sexual relationship with him, he would have walked away. After all, they had almost nothing in common beyond a visceral attraction. But *she* was the one who invited *him* to her bed tonight. Because the sex was great. Right? Up until that very last part, she had been a willing and eager participant.

It was a puzzle. One he was happy to study until he found the answers. For now, he would give her some space.

Unfortunately, not even a real estate agent hungry for a sale would appreciate a call after eleven at night. Hartley would have to be patient until morning. He decided to make a lowball cash offer, and then while he tried to woo his prickly artist, he would have a project to keep him busy.

Having a plan brought a measure of resolve. He hated

uncertainty…always had. Make a choice, even if it's the wrong one. That's how he operated.

It was late. He knew he needed to go home. But there was one more sore spot he needed to explore.

From Fiona's house, the drive to Tarleton headquarters took no time at all. The building was as familiar to him as his childhood bedroom. He parked right in front. Nothing to hide. Inside, there would be a night watchman somewhere.

At the main entrance, he entered a six-digit code in the electronic keypad and swiped his ID card. To his surprise, the door opened easily. Had Jonathan forgotten to revoke his credentials? Or had he believed Hartley would eventually come home? Either way, it soothed some of Hartley's rough-edged discontent to know he was able to walk inside.

His desk and his office were exactly as he had left them. For the first time, he began to understand how difficult his absence must have been for Jonathan. The questions. The work piling up.

A sound in the outer office had him whirling on his heel. Jonathan leaned against the wall, his expression inscrutable. Clearly, he had gone home after work and come back, because he was wearing old jeans and a T-shirt that had seen better days.

Hartley felt his neck heat. "I was just looking around. I wasn't here to steal the silver."

Jonathan shrugged. "I'm not accusing you of anything."

"Not at the moment." Hartley grimaced. Being at odds with his twin was a physical pain. He cleared his throat. "I'll go. Sorry to have bothered you."

Jonathan held up a hand. "You put the money back yesterday." It was neither a simple statement nor a question, but maybe a blend of both.

"I did, yes."

"Why?"

"I was *always* going to put it back. But neither you nor Dad cared to ask for an explanation. You just assumed the worst."

His brother frowned. "Don't turn this on me. *You* were the one who made off with a million bucks as if it were nothing more than Monopoly money."

"I had my reasons."

"Okay." Jonathan folded his arms across his chest. "Let's hear them. I've got all night."

It was a challenge. Plain and simple. A showdown. But Hartley was going to have to swallow his pride and walk away. He'd already told the story once.

No matter how much he wanted to erase the gaping void between him and his brother, he couldn't dump what he knew on Jonathan. Not without thinking it through.

Maybe Fiona was right. Maybe he owed his siblings the truth. But at what cost? They would both be hurt, as Hartley had been. Unsettled. Dismayed. And without their father to provide answers, this information Hartley had uncovered served no useful purpose.

Hartley cleared his throat. "It's late. The tale will keep for now. Good night, Jonathan."

When he went to slip past the president and CEO of Tarleton Shipping, his brother put a hand on his shoulder. For a moment, they both breathed the same air. Jonathan squeezed briefly, then stepped aside. "I believe you had your reasons. They may not have been good reasons. I'd still like to hear them."

Jonathan was reaching out. Making the first move. Being the bigger man.

Hartley was frozen with indecision. The irony of the situation would have been humorous if the stakes hadn't been so high. Here he was, a guy who believed in always stepping out, sure the path would appear from within the fog.

Now, when it mattered the most, he couldn't do it. The truth had hurt Hartley badly. Why inflict that pain on the man who shared his blood? The brother he loved.

He swallowed hard. "My reasons don't exist anymore. That's why I put the money back. I'm sorry I left you hanging, though. You've carried the brunt of Father's illness and the way that complicated the business. I'm sorry, Jonathan. I really am."

His brother's smile was wry but genuine. "You'd do the same thing again, though. Am I right?"

Hartley considered the question. Ignorance might be bliss, but not for him. He'd done what he had to do to protect his family. Maybe his ultimate task was to be the keeper of the secrets.

"Yes," he muttered. "I'd do it again. Why didn't you tell Mazie about the money?"

Jonathan raked a hand through his short hair, for the first time, betraying exhaustion. He looked beaten. Defeated. "Mazie adores you. I didn't know where you were or why you were gone. The missing money only made it worse. I figured you deserved whatever happened to you, but Mazie's big heart would have been shattered."

"Thank you," Hartley said.

"Don't thank me. I did it for her."

The snap in Jonathan's voice was both startling and depressing. Hartley's twin might have made an overture a few moments ago, but he was still very angry.

Nothing was going to be gained by rehashing old arguments. The untold truth lay between them, terrible and dangerous. It had unmanned Hartley, left him despairing and aching with hurt. Although it had been cathartic to unburden himself to Fiona, he hadn't even let her hear the worst of it. Unless Hartley was willing to tell Jonathan what had transpired in Europe, there was nothing left to say.

"I'll let myself out," he said dully. "Good night."

The morning after Hartley made love to her, Fiona knew without a doubt that she had made the right choice in sending him home. She awoke violently sick, unable to hold down either tea or toast until almost noon. Then, it was all she could do to drag herself to the studio.

She needed to buy a pregnancy test. That was how these situations worked. The thought of getting in a car and driving somewhere was more than she could manage.

So she painted. In short bursts of energy. Twenty minutes here. Thirty minutes here. Astonishingly, the project began to take shape. By late afternoon, she actually felt hungry.

She was cleaning brushes and tidying her work space when her doorbell rang. *Hartley.* Was she irritated by his persistence or flattered that he was back again?

When she opened the door with a neutral smile, the smile faded. Her caller wasn't Hartley. Instead, Mazie Tarleton Vaughan stood on the porch. "May I come in?" she asked, not bothering with social niceties like hellos or explanations.

"Umm…" Fiona felt awkwardly self-conscious, as if Mazie could see the possible pregnancy on her face.

The other woman vibrated with impatience. "I won't stay long."

There was nothing more to say after that, short of being unforgivably rude. "Of course…" Fiona stepped back, allowing her unexpected visitor to enter.

Hartley's sister surveyed the small house, at least the parts she could see from the foyer. "This is nice," she said. "It suits you."

"Thank you, I—"

Mazie interrupted. "We can do the get-to-know-you thing another day, but I'm here to talk about Hartley. Is he okay?"

"What do you mean?" Fiona winced inwardly. She had never been good at prevarication.

"Don't play dumb...please. My own brother has kept me in the dark. I don't need it from you, too. Hartley has a thing for you. Obviously. Which means he must have told you why he left. Right?"

Suddenly, Fiona could see beneath Mazie's imperious demand to the scared sister underneath. "Why don't we sit down?" She steered her guest toward the comfortable sofa and perched on the armchair that had seen better days. "I do know some of it," she said carefully. "But only very recently did he tell me anything. I was as much in the dark as you were. Yes, he's fine. A little lost maybe... after being gone so long."

"He needs to be back at Tarleton Shipping. He belongs there."

"I'm not sure he feels welcome."

Mazie's eyes widened. "What do you mean?"

"Your brothers have some issues to work out. According to Hartley, Jonathan is angry. And not inclined to welcome the prodigal with open arms."

Mazie burst into tears.

Well, crap. Fiona was not equipped to deal with all this family drama. It was why she lived alone. And worked alone. Still, she was not hard-hearted enough to ignore the other woman's distress.

She sat down beside Hartley's sister and handed her a tissue. "It will work itself out. Give them time."

Mazie wiped her eyes and sniffed. "You clearly don't

know my brothers very well. They are both stubborn as sin."

"Well, based on the one I *do* know, I have to agree."

Tears continued to roll down Mazie's cheeks. Somehow, Hartley's sister was as beautiful as ever. Hardly seemed fair. When Fiona cried, her face turned into a blotchy mess.

Mazie sniffed and scrubbed her cheeks with her hands. "Don't mind me. I've been on fertility drugs, and I'm a mess."

"That must be stressful," Fiona said quietly, keenly aware that her own body was out of her control at the moment. "Is there anything I can do for you? A cup of hot tea, maybe? I'm a bit of a connoisseur. Tea always helps me when it's that time of the month, so I keep plenty of bags on hand. I can offer you a wide range of choices."

Hartley's sister sat up straight, an arrested look on her face. She grabbed up her purse, took out her phone and opened a calendar app. "Oh, wow."

"What is it? What's wrong?"

"I've been so upset with the funeral and everything that I haven't paid attention."

"Paid attention to what?"

Mazie's expression was equal parts wonderment and bewilderment. "I missed my period, Fiona. I'm six days late."

Seven

Fiona smiled. "That's good, right?"

Her visitor was pale, her chin wobbly. "We've been disappointed so many times. I can't tell J.B. Not yet." She grabbed Fiona's arm. "Will you do me a favor?"

"Well, I—"

"Nothing big. Everybody in this city knows my family. If I stop in somewhere and buy a pregnancy test, word will get back to my husband before I return home. I don't want to get his hopes up until I know for sure."

Fiona felt like she was in the middle of a bad joke. "You want me to buy you a pregnancy test?"

Mazie's smile was sunny and cajoling, her tears forgotten. "Please. I'll drive. All you have to do is run inside the store and get it for me. Easy peasy."

"How can I say no?" Fiona wanted to laugh, but she didn't dare. "Let me change clothes. I'm speedy. Won't take long."

In her bedroom, she stripped off her jeans and T-shirt

and stared at herself in the mirror. At this particular moment, she didn't *feel* pregnant. Her tummy was flat, her body unchanged. Maybe she had the flu. The summer flu that only happened in the mornings. *Oh, Lordy...*

Mazie was snooping unashamedly when Fiona returned to the living room. She held out a small framed check for fifty dollars. "What's this?"

Fiona dropped her purse on a chair. "It's the first money I ever made as a professional artist. I was dead broke, and I needed so badly to cash it and pay my rent. But I decided to believe in my future and to believe there would be other checks coming. So far, I haven't had to break the glass."

Mazie nodded, returning the small frame to its spot on a bookshelf. "I know what you mean. Not the money part. My family has been fortunate in that way. But when I realized I didn't want to follow the boys into the family business, it was a struggle to decide what I was interested in—and then to make it happen. Now I sell jewelry in the historic district. I love my shop, and I do very well. It makes you proud, doesn't it? Women are always being underestimated. Drives me nuts."

Fiona grinned. Mazie was a firecracker. Fiona liked her. A lot. And although she had never had a real sister, Hartley's sibling was exactly the kind of female Fiona had envisioned when she wished for one.

Mazie handed over two twenties. "I don't know how much they'll cost at a convenience store. I've written down the brand I'd like to have. If you have to pick a second choice, I'll take what I can get."

"Then let's go."

Mazie insisted on driving. Her car was a current-year model that smelled of leather and a whiff of expensive perfume. Fiona settled into the passenger seat with a sigh of appreciation. Her own car was not a clunker, but as cute as it was, the little VW Bug was no match for high-end automotive luxury.

Mazie's driving was the real shock. She tended to talk with her hands, and though she didn't commit any traffic violations, her style was a little too kamikaze for Fiona's comfort.

They pulled up with a screech in front of a gas station mini-mart. Mazie gripped the wheel, her gaze anxious. "Hurry, please. I don't want to take any chances."

Inside the small shop, Fiona found the appropriate aisle quickly. Choices were limited, but the store did have the brand Mazie had requested. Instead of a duo, Fiona grabbed up four, then rounded the corner and plopped them down on the counter in sets of two. "I'll pay for these separately," she said, feeling the heat roll from her chest to her throat to her face.

It was ridiculous to be embarrassed, but this was her first pee-on-a-stick experience. The young store clerk didn't bat an eye. He rang up the two sales, dispensed change and Fiona's credit card slip, and went back to his phone.

Fiona had made a point of bringing a large leather tote instead of the smaller wristlet she often carried. Both women had valid reasons for keeping this little shopping excursion under the radar.

Fiona sauntered back outside as if she bought quads of pregnancy tests every day of the week. She opened the car door, slid into her seat and handed Mazie the white paper bag. "All set," she said breezily.

Mazie chewed her lip. "May I do this at your house?"

Weird. "Why?"

"I told you. I don't want to get J.B.'s hopes up. He hovers. And then it kills him when I'm sad."

"So how many times have you done this?"

"Not as many as you think. Twice maybe. Mostly it's just that my period starts, and then we know we have to wait another month. After this, I'll get out of your way, I swear."

"You're not in my way," Fiona muttered. Though she had to admit the entire scenario was freaking her out. What if Hartley showed up while Mazie was around?

Back at the house, Fiona showed Mazie the tiny guest bath in the hallway. Once Mazie was tucked away, Fiona darted into her studio bathroom and locked the door. Good sense dictated waiting until her guest had departed, but she couldn't.

Her fingers trembled as she opened the box and read the directions. This was a bad sitcom…right? The hero's sister in one bathroom. His lover in another. Both women possibly pregnant.

Fiona did what had to be done and waited. The message on the stick was swift and unequivocal. Positive. *Pregnant.*

She stared at it blankly. One part of her brain acknowledged she was in shock. The other more emotional compartment wanted to scream it from the housetop. She was having Hartley's baby!

Later tonight there would be time for the second test. To double-check. It wasn't really necessary, was it? Her body had already communicated the truth in rare form.

A sound from the other part of the house drew her back to the present. Though she was shaky and weak, she concentrated fiercely. *Wrap the evidence in tissues. Tuck it away. Stash the incriminating boxes in a back corner of the cabinet.*

Then she washed her hands, splashed water on her face and went in search of Mazie.

Hartley's sister was still in the bathroom when Fiona passed by. But moments later, she came out and joined

Fiona in the living room. Instead of being seated, she stood in the middle of the rug, her expression shell-shocked. "I did them both," she whispered. "They were positive."

Hartley had tried to give Fiona her space, really he had. But all day, missing her had been like a throbbing toothache. He still couldn't believe she had tossed him out of her bed.

He'd kept busy. The fixer-upper a few streets over from Fiona's charming bungalow would be his in less than two weeks—a cash sale. His own place out at the golf course already had several offers on the table. Hartley was leaving the minutiae up to the real estate agent. As long as he didn't lose money on the deal, he'd be satisfied.

The one detail he hadn't worked out was where he would live in the meantime. Even optimistically, it would take a couple of months to make his new three-story brick home moderately habitable.

Several of the potential buyers for the golf course house wanted to take possession ASAP. Hartley could go to a hotel, of course. For that matter, J.B. and Mazie would take him in. Still, they were relative newlyweds, even now. Besides, Hartley didn't want to make things awkward between Mazie and Jonathan.

Which left one obvious solution. Fiona.

He pulled up in front of her house and frowned. What was his sister doing here?

Indignation bubbled in his chest. Fiona wouldn't share secrets that weren't hers…would she? He thought he knew her that well, but then again, he hadn't bargained on being booted out of the stubborn woman's warm, comfy bed in the dead of night, so what did he know?

He banged on the door with his fist, unable to decide if he was suspicious or angry, or both. "Fiona! Let me in." When he reached for the knob, it turned easily. He opened the door and found two women staring at him, looking guilty as hell.

Both of them resembled kids with their hands caught in the cookie jar. "What's going on?" he asked.

Mazie and Fiona blushed. His sister looked happy. Fiona's expression was less easily defined. She wasn't smiling at him, and she didn't seem particularly glad to see him.

Mazie broke the silence. "Nothing's going on, silly. I dropped by because I wanted to get to know your girlfriend."

"I'm not his girlfriend," Fiona said quickly. "We're friends. That's all."

Hartley's sister waved a hand. "Friend. Girlfriend. Who cares about labels these days?"

Fiona went on the offensive, her gaze cool. "The question is, Hartley, why are *you* here? It's hard to have closure when you keep turning up like a bad penny. You walked right into my house."

Mazie snickered, her hand over her mouth.

Hartley closed the door and leaned against it. "You were the one wanting closure, Fiona, not me. Do you really want to discuss this in front of my gossipy sister?"

"Hey," Mazie cried. "That's not nice."

Fiona aligned herself with the fairer sex. "Mazie and I were sharing a moment. You're intruding."

Mazie flung herself at Hartley, wrapping her arms around his neck and threatening to strangle him. "No, he's not. I'm so *glad* you're home."

Her tight hug and the kiss on his cheek caught something in his chest and made his eyes damp. "I love you, too, sis," he said gruffly.

His eyes met Fiona's over Mazie's head. "What if I take the two of you to dinner? We can call J.B. and have him meet us at the restaurant. It'll be fun."

Inexplicably, his sister blushed again and looked at Fiona as if for help. "You're sweet to offer, Hartley, but I'll take a rain check. J.B. and I have plans tonight."

Hartley shrugged. "Fair enough. I'd still like to show you something before you leave. We can all three pile into my car. Won't take us long. Twenty minutes, tops."

"So mysterious," Fiona said.

He eluded his sister and curled an arm around Fiona's waist. Her hair smelled like raspberries. He loved raspberries. "I need your artistic expertise." He kissed her nose. She leaned into him. Progress…

Mazie glanced at her watch. "I'm in. But we need to hurry."

As the women climbed into his car, Fiona in the front, Mazie in the back, Hartley realized he was nervous. These two people were important in his life. Their opinions mattered.

When he pulled up in front of the huge dilapidated brick structure with the overgrown yard, he smiled inwardly. Attached to the small for-sale sign was another placard that said Sold. He'd done a lot in twenty-four hours. Moving ahead. Writing off the past.

Mazie leaned over the front seat. "What is this place, Hartley?"

Fiona stared through the windshield, her expression pensive.

He shrugged, gripping the steering wheel. "I bought it today. I'm going to fix it up and live here temporarily. Then sell it later for twice the price if I'm lucky."

"What do you know about renovating an old house?" His sister's concern was valid.

"Not much more than I've seen on TV," he admitted. "But I can learn. I have no illusions about doing all the work myself."

Fiona chewed her lip. "It looks like a wreck. Have you even been inside?"

She nailed him on that one. Perhaps she had already come to recognize his impulsive nature. "I saw lots of pictures," he said. "And I bought it for a rock-bottom price. It's a good investment."

Mazie pinched his arm. "And it's in Fiona's neighborhood…right?"

Fee frowned. "But you have a house. On a golf course somewhere. You told me about it."

"I listed it this morning. Had two offers before lunch and more this afternoon. I'll likely make a handy profit."

Mazie nodded. "He never really liked that house anyway. It served a purpose at the time." She patted his shoulder. "I think it's wonderful, Hartley. I have several friends in the construction business. I'm sure I can round up some experts here and there."

He squeezed his sister's fingers briefly, but his gaze held Fiona's, daring her to look away. "I was hoping Fee would be willing to help me from an artistic perspective. So I can flip it successfully."

Fiona stared at him, her chest rising and falling rapidly as if she were out of breath. "Work is really busy for me right now."

He brushed the back of his hand across her soft cheek, gazing at her with determination and sexual intent. "In the evenings, then. I'll feed you, and I'll pay you for your time."

Mazie fell back in her seat, beaming. "Of course she'll help you. Right, Fiona?"

Fiona felt pressured by the sibling duo. These two thought they could throw money at a problem and everything would break their way. They hadn't a clue what it was like to be hungry or alone or to lack confidence.

Instead of answering directly, she put a hand on the door. "Can we peek in the windows?"

Hartley's face lightened, his enthusiasm contagious. "Of course. Once the paperwork is further along, I'll get the real estate agent to give us a tour."

"Is it even safe?" she asked.

"I suppose we'll find out."

The three of them walked up the path, dodging plants that tried to grab their hair and avoiding broken glass where kids had tossed beer bottles while trespassing. Mazie wrinkled her nose. "How long has this place been empty?"

Fiona surveyed the three-story facade. "I pass by this way now and again. I seem to remember the owner dying a year or more ago. Maybe it's taken this long for the heirs to decide to sell it."

"I can't imagine they would want to keep it." Mazie frowned. "This place is kind of a dump, Hartley. I was imagining a diamond in the rough, not a total disaster."

He tried the front door, but of course it was locked. "The house has good bones. I have faith in her." He took Fiona's wrist and drew her closer. "Peek in this window here. Tell me what you see."

Even from the vantage point of a filthy pane of glass, Fiona was charmed. The house looked like a museum inside, a museum with chunks of ceiling missing and peeling wallpaper, but a museum nevertheless. The ornate cornices and hardwood floors hearkened back to an earlier time. If the double winding staircase at the back of the hallway was intact, Hartley might indeed have found a hidden gem.

"It's got potential," she said grudgingly. What she wanted to say was *Why are you buying a house near me?* It didn't make sense. Hartley was a man without a country, a displaced person. He had come back to his old life, but the world had moved on without him. So he was inventing a spot for himself.

If the only reason he was here with her was because he had no place else to go, she wasn't interested. She'd had a lifetime of not belonging. Now, her small house and her burgeoning career were all hers.

It wasn't that she didn't have room in her life for Hartley. The truth was, if and when she finally fell in love and got married, she wanted a relationship where her husband thought she hung the moon.

Hartley liked having sex with her. She was a handy distraction from his family woes. But she deserved more than that. If she really was pregnant, she *wanted* this baby. More than anything. Yet Hartley had said unequivocally that he wasn't interested in being a father.

If she told him and he tried to *do the right thing*, she couldn't bear it. He'd left her twice. Even if he tried to change his tune, how could she ever trust him or his motives?

Mazie squawked when she glanced at her watch. "Oh, heck. I've got to run. Take me back to my car, Hartley. I still have to go by the shop before I head home. J.B. will shoot me if I'm late."

"Since when is your husband a clock puncher?"

"We've both been working too much lately. We made a pact to have dinner together every night."

In the car on the way back, Fiona glanced over her shoulder. She and Mazie exchanged glances. Hartley's sister had shining eyes and a palpable air of excitement. This meal with J.B. tonight would be momentous.

As soon as Hartley pulled up at the curb, Mazie was out of the car and on her way. Hartley stared after her. "She sure was in a good mood."

Fiona nodded. "Of course she is. She has a husband who adores her. It's a gorgeous day. And her long-lost brother is finally home."

"I wasn't lost," Hartley muttered. "I simply chose to fly under the radar for a few months."

"Your silence hurt them," Fiona said. "If they stumble onto the other secrets you're keeping, it will be even worse this time. Surely you see they need to know what you found out in Switzerland."

Hartley glared at her. "You're not going to give up on this, are you? So what about you, Fiona? Shouldn't you be digging up all your family secrets, sordid or otherwise?"

She gasped, stunned by the attack. "Excuse me," she said carefully. "I'm going in the house now."

He reached for her arm. "Stop. Wait. Dammit, I'm sorry, Fee. I have a temper. You're only trying to help. I get that."

She trembled, close to tears. This was a bad time to fall apart. "Let's get something straight, Hartley. If you're telling the truth when you say you want to be with me, then I need to believe it. So far in our relationship, I've been either a convenient booty call or a buffer for your messed-up family dynamics. Since I'm not interested in either of those roles, I suggest you get your life in order before you come here again."

Eight

Mazie opened the front door of the gorgeous row house that was now *hers*, as well as her husband's, and slipped inside. She wanted to shower and change before running into J.B. Tonight was special.

Upstairs in her decadent walk-in closet, she perused her choices. After their wedding, J.B. had taken one of the smaller bedrooms and converted it for his bride. Now she had a tiny sitting area and plenty of space for her wardrobe.

He spoiled her.

She loved it.

Even now, it was hard to believe she was actually *married* to the handsome hunk who had been her teenage crush. J.B. had been a bit of a rascal in his youth. He'd broken Mazie's heart badly on one particular, memorable occasion. After years of keeping a careful distance from each other here in Charleston, they had reconnected when her little jewelry shop ended up right in the middle of one of J.B.'s big real estate projects.

One thing led to another, and now she was happily married to a reformed bad boy. She smirked as she grabbed a quick shower and changed into black pants and a royal blue silk top. She and J.B. worked hard. This commitment to having dinner together every night had not always been easy, but it was an intimate time they had both come to cherish.

She was ridiculously nervous. Mostly because she hadn't decided whether or not to bring J.B. in on her secret yet. It was too early to get excited. She knew that. She needed an appointment with her ob-gyn before she got her hopes up. No point in telling him when she wasn't absolutely sure.

Over-the-counter pregnancy tests weren't completely reliable.

In the dining room, she found J.B. scrolling through email on his phone while he waited for her. Immediately, he put the phone aside and drew her in for a long, slow kiss. "How's my best girl?" he drawled when she was flushed and breathless. The man was an Olympic-level kisser. World class.

"I'm great," she said. *Maybe really great.*

J.B.'s fiftysomething housekeeper was a Southern-style cook who had learned to tilt her wonderful recipes toward healthier options without sacrificing taste. Mazie might have gained five pounds since the wedding, but it was worth every ounce.

The first course was Caesar salad with freshly made dressing and shaved Parmesan. "I came by the shop this afternoon between site visits," J.B. said, "but you were gone."

"I went to see Hartley's girlfriend."

One masculine eyebrow lifted. "Mazie. I warned you about matchmaking. Hartley's a big boy. He can make his own decisions."

She stabbed a piece of lettuce. “He hasn’t done so well this past year,” she muttered. “I can’t stand to see the way he and Jonathan are with each other. It’s *wrong*,” she said, her eyes unexpectedly filling with tears. “They’re brothers. Twins, for God’s sake. Best friends.”

J.B. reached across the table and took her hand. “They’ll work through it eventually. Hartley’s home now. That’s a start.”

“Can’t you talk to them? Either? Both? Jonathan is being all *scowly* and buttoned-up and Hartley is…well, I don’t know. He’s acting weird. Did you know he bought a house today?”

J.B. blinked. “He has a house.”

“Not anymore. He listed it this morning. Already has offers.”

“So where is this *new* house?”

“Three blocks away from Fiona.”

“Ah. The plot thickens.”

“I dropped by to talk to her late this afternoon, and Hartley showed up, insisting that we look at his new toy. It’s a huge run-down place. Going to need tons of work.”

“Sounds expensive.”

She sat back and frowned. “Are you taking any of this seriously?”

J.B. grinned. “I take *you* seriously. They’re grown men, sweetheart. Give them time.”

“Did Jonathan ever tell you why Hartley left? Or what made Jonathan so angry he will hardly speak Hartley’s name?”

“He didn’t, my love. Whatever this is feels like a betrayal so deep Jonathan can’t get past it.”

Mazie chewed her lip. It didn’t take a psychologist to see that she was dwelling on this Hartley/Jonathan rift to put off telling J.B. what she suspected was true. It was so scary.

"Fiona knows."

Jonathan frowned. "Are you positive?"

"I asked her. She told me. Not the details," Mazie said quickly. "But that Hartley very recently confided in her."

"So she's important to him."

"Looks that way. But I don't think he knows it yet."

The housekeeper came in with the main course, and the topic was shelved for the moment. By the time dessert rolled around, Mazie had come to a decision. If she was going to wait for confirmation until she could see her doctor, then she wanted J.B. waiting with her.

While he drank his coffee, she watched him. He'd been almost a part of their family since they were all kids. It was impossible to imagine her life without him. He was funny and irreverent and never met a stranger. He would make a wonderful father.

Her stomach flopped and twisted. "J.B.?" she said.

His gaze met hers over the rim of his cup. "Hmm?"

"What if we go upstairs early tonight?"

A dark streak of red bloomed on his chiseled cheekbones. His eyes glittered with strong emotion. "Is that what you want?"

Their sex life had suffered in recent months. It was impossible to make love anymore without thinking about whether or not the baby they so desperately wanted was being conceived. And then every month when Mazie got her period, they both mourned.

"It is," she said.

He lurched to his feet, bumping the table. "I'll tell Mrs. P. to finish up tomorrow. That my dear wife wants my body."

Mazie covered her mouth, laughing. "You wouldn't dare."

"Watch me."

In truth, Mazie had no idea what he said to the housekeeper, but in less than half an hour, the kitchen was pristine and the older woman was gone.

Mazie wandered the living room aimlessly, praying for courage. J.B. found her there.

He paused in the doorway like a gunslinger walking into a saloon. “Alone at last,” he said, the words gruff.

She went to him and sighed when he immediately folded her close in his arms. There was no place she would rather be. Not ever.

“I need to tell you something before we go upstairs,” she said.

He kissed the top of her head. “I’m listening.”

She pulled back, searching his face. Wanting to judge his reaction. “I think I’m pregnant.”

His big frame went rigid. “Are you positive?”

“Not a hundred percent. I did a couple of store-bought tests. But I’ll need to see my doctor. I can’t get an appointment until Tuesday.”

He cupped her face in his hands. His eyes were damp. “God, I want this to be true. So damn much. I love you, Mazie.”

She swallowed hard. “I’m scared.”

His frown was swift. “About what?”

“Lisette has suffered two miscarriages already.” Tears she couldn’t stem spilled from her eyes. “What if that happens to me?”

“It won’t,” he said firmly. “We’ve had trouble *getting* pregnant. There’s no reason you should worry about *losing* a baby.”

She snuggled into his embrace a second time, drawing strength from the sheer physicality of his body. “I don’t *feel* pregnant,” she whispered. “Shouldn’t I feel something? Shouldn’t I know?”

J.B. stroked her hair. "You're gonna have to relax, Mazie."

"I know. I think it would help my stress level if you would play intermediary between Jonathan and Hartley."

"So that's how it's going to be, brat." He took her hand and headed for the stairs. "I get it."

"What?" she cried innocently.

He stopped halfway up to the second floor, his smile lopsided. "You think I'm going to say yes to you for an entire nine months."

"Is that a problem?" She gave him a smug grin, unbuttoning her shirt slowly.

His hot gaze started at her eyes and drifted lower, locking on the curves of her breasts, telegraphing his intent. "Not at all. Because I'm going to keep you on bed rest with me."

She giggled, shoving him in front of her. "That's not even a thing, J.B. Vaughan."

On the landing, he scooped her into his arms and carried her the rest of the way. "Whatever it takes, my love. Whatever it takes."

Fiona nearly called Mazie for advice, a woman she barely knew. That's how freaked out she was. After Mazie dashed away earlier, headed home to rendezvous with her husband, Fiona had made awkward excuses to Hartley and locked herself inside the cottage.

She couldn't face him right now. For all her big words about how wrong it was to keep secrets from his family, Fiona was doing the same thing. Keeping a huge plot twist from the man who might possibly be a father very soon.

That evening, she puttered around the house, dusting… tidying up. Since it was far too early for nesting, the only logical explanation was that she was losing her marbles. Popping her cork. Her well-oiled life was off the tracks.

How could she tell him she might be pregnant? Wouldn't it be smarter to find out for sure first?

And then what? He'd spoken his piece unequivocally. *I won't have children. I choose not to take that chance.*

Remembering his words hurt. Badly. It was as if he was repudiating everything that was happening to her. Of course he didn't know. How could he? That didn't make her anxiety and incredulity any less real and painful.

She managed to keep Hartley at bay over the weekend...barely. He called. He texted. He asked to come by and see her.

Her work was her excuse. She needed blocks of uninterrupted time. He claimed to understand. But each time they spoke, she felt his frustration increase. Worst of all, she missed him. A lot.

Having him in her bed each night would have been a wonderful comfort. Even feeling the way she did, she wanted him. As it was, she slept alone and awoke every morning barely in time to dash to the bathroom.

Her reflection in the mirror was appalling. Her hair was lank and dull. She had lost weight. Cooking was too much trouble. All she could tolerate, even later in the day, was chicken broth and dry crackers. When her stash ran dry, she used a grocery service.

Amid the stretches of feeling sorry for herself—and when she could stand for chunks of time—she worked on her paintings. Only then did she feel anything at all like normal. The repetitive brushstrokes calmed her. The colors that spread forth on the canvas filled the yawning chasm in her chest with purpose and joy.

In her heart, she knew she was pregnant. The doctor's appointment she had wrangled at the last minute for

Wednesday morning was only going to confirm her status as a mother-to-be. So what was she going to do about it?

She wanted the baby. Desperately. There was no doubt about that. Thinking about holding her own tiny infant in her arms made her heart sing. But uncertainty about Hartley's reaction tempered her excitement. Could she be a single mom?

Sunday night, she forced herself to take a shower and wash her hair. The nausea had finally subsided some. But her energy level was nil.

At eight, she put on soft cotton pajamas and curled up to watch a movie. Hartley's text came through before the first credit rolled.

Do you mind if I stop by for a few?

Ah, damn. The way her heart leaped in her chest told her the truth. She couldn't put him off any longer...didn't want to, for that matter.

I'm home. What time will you get here?

I'm in my car out at the street.

His comical emoji actually made her laugh.

Come on in.

She unlocked the door and watched him walk up the path. Everything inside her warmed and settled. Hartley made her world a little better. A lot happier. She could argue with herself all she wanted, but it was true. He was the one she had been waiting for...her knight in shining armor.

Could a black sheep prodigal make the leap to hero?

She gripped the edge of the door, white-knuckled. “Hello.”

He paused to kiss her gently. “Hello, yourself. You must have been working hard. Is the project coming along?”

“It is,” she said. That wasn’t entirely a lie.

“These are for you.” He’d brought more roses, blush pink this time. Without asking, he headed for the kitchen and dug out the vase. She followed, standing in the doorway to watch him. Were all women so emotional about the men who made them pregnant?

When he was satisfied with the arrangement, he dried his hands and set the vase on the table. “You look tired. I won’t stay long.” His smile was sweet, catching her off guard. “I missed you these last few days,” he said.

She swallowed. “I missed you, too. Come sit with me in the living room,” she said. “I want to tell you something.”

Not the whole truth and nothing but the truth. That conversation would have to wait for a few more days. After the official doctor’s appointment.

They perched on the sofa together. Hartley wrapped an arm around her shoulders as if it were the most natural thing in the world. Though arousal flooded her veins, it was more like a slow, warm river than licks of fire. Hartley was back in Charleston to stay. They had time. For now.

“How’s the new purchase?” she asked.

He yawned and leaned his head against the back of the sofa. “I may have bitten off more than I can chew. Although, I’m discovering that punishing physical labor does wonders for clearing a man’s brain. I’ve been working in the yard since I don’t have the keys yet.”

“Have you tried to talk to your brother?”

She felt him stiffen slightly. “I ran into him a few nights ago. It didn’t go well.”

"I'm sorry." The faint bitterness in his voice told her he was wounded by the rift with his twin.

Hartley rubbed the top of her shoulder with his thumb. "What did you want to tell me?"

"I know you disagree with me about whether or not you should tell your siblings about Switzerland. But I have some experience with secrets. It concerns my parents."

He pulled away from her and groaned. "Please don't make me feel worse. I never should have lost my temper. Your past is none of my business."

Her smile was wistful. "You've told me your *sordid secrets*. I think it's time for you to hear mine."

Nine

Sordid secrets. Hell. Now she was quoting his unforgivable words back to him. He felt like whatever was lower than pond scum.

Fiona stood up and wrapped her arms around her waist. Her pj's were not terribly thin, but he could see she wasn't wearing a bra. He was swamped by a wave of tenderness mixed with lust. It was an unfamiliar combo, and he didn't know what to do with the feelings.

"Please don't," he begged. "God knows, you don't owe me any explanations."

She stared at him, big gray-blue eyes filled with feminine emotions he couldn't decipher. "I spent my whole life wondering who I was. I lived in an actual orphanage… a children's home, until I was eight. After that, they had to move some of us out to make room for more. I was labeled *amenable*, so I went into foster care. It wasn't terrible. Some of the families were pretty wonderful. But it was all temporary. I knew it and everyone else did, too.

The odds of getting adopted at that age are like winning the lottery."

She'd barely started and already her story was tearing him apart, leaving him raw inside. While he'd been living in a veritable castle, Fiona had been tossed around by governmental red tape.

"I don't need to hear this," he said. *I don't want to hear it.*

Fiona was on a mission. "When I was seventeen and a half, they told me I could begin the process of applying for my records to be opened. Then, when I reached my eighteenth birthday, I would have the option of knowing or not knowing. My choice."

"And what did you do?"

"I filled out the paperwork, and I started dreaming dreams. Now that I was going to be an adult, I was sure my biological parents would want to know me. I wasn't on drugs. I had graduated near the top of my high school class. I was not going to *ask* them for anything at all. The only thing I wanted was to be able to look them in the eye and see where I came from. To understand why I was allergic to apricots. To know if it was my dad or my mother who gave me my artistic ability, or maybe a grandparent. To finally study my family tree."

"Ah, hell, darlin'—" This story didn't have a happy ending. He knew it before she even told him the rest.

Fiona ran her hands through her hair, her eyes scrunched shut as if she didn't want to remember. "When my birthday rolled around, everything was an open book. The details were sparse, but they were there. I came from a small rural county up the coast. Rampant poverty. Poor schools. High numbers of opioid deaths. My birth mother was fifteen when she had me. She hemorrhaged after the delivery and died before they could save her."

"Good God." The long-ago tragedy was stunning. "And your father?"

"He was in jail for drug possession the night I was born. The following day he was released, but on the way to the hospital, he crashed his car into a tree."

"Because he was high?"

"Yes."

"Surely you had grandparents."

"The official report listed four names. I followed up on each one. All deceased. At that point, I no longer had any interest in looking for cousins or aunts and uncles. I was done."

He went to her and held her, feeling the fine tremors that racked her slender body. "I'm sorry," he said.

Fiona rested her cheek against his chest. "It was wretched," she said. "I felt so foolish for all those silly dreams I had spun in my imagination."

"Dreams are not bad things."

"No. But despite everything I learned, I didn't regret seeking out the answers. I decided I wouldn't be defined by my origin story. There was more to me than that. I set goals, and I pursued my passions, and I made peace with my past. Knowing is *always* better than not knowing, Hartley. That's why you need to tell Jonathan and Mazie about their mother."

He hadn't expected her to turn this on him, but he should have seen it coming. "There's a difference," he said stubbornly, releasing her and going to stare out the window.

"How?"

He shot her a look over his shoulder. "Jonathan and Mazie don't have any 'blanks' like you did. They know who they are. They're *not* wondering and wishing. So they aren't struggling to find answers."

"But the truth they believe is a lie."

He ground his teeth. There was merit in what she was saying. Still, other factors made him leery of sharing the information with his siblings. "Our father just died. I think that's enough trauma for one season. Maybe you and I can agree to disagree on this point."

"I'm pretty stubborn about things that are important to me."

He found a smile, wanting to shift the mood to less volatile topics. "Duly noted." Pulling out his phone, he flipped to the photo icon. "I actually came tonight to ask about you doing a job for me. A commission."

"I've got a couple of big things in the works, Hartley."

"This will be small. Mazie's birthday is coming up in a few weeks, and I wanted to surprise her." He showed her a photo. "This is Mazie and J.B. at their wedding reception. See how he's looking at her. I know she would love to have you paint this for them."

"That's not really what I do. I focus on outdoor subjects. Landscapes. Birds. That kind of thing."

"But you *could* do it…right? Mazie would flip. She's been singing your praises to me. She thinks you're phenomenally talented, and I agree."

"Flattery will get you everywhere," Fiona said. Her laughter loosened the knot in his chest that had appeared when she told him about her parents. "Text me the photo. I'll fool around with a sketch and see what I can do."

"Thank you." He pulled up her number, sent the photo and set his phone on the coffee table. "How about a kiss before I go?"

Fiona didn't want him to go. Not at all. She wanted to burrow into his embrace and feel his hands on her body and forget for a few moments that she was in big trouble.

She cocked her head and stared at him. His innocent expression had to be at least 75 percent fake. He knew what his kisses did to a woman. "Are you asking permission?"

Hartley tugged her toward the sofa again and sat down, tumbling her onto his lap. "I want you, Fee. To a degree that's damn scary. What do you say to that?" Brown eyes stared into hers. The humor was gone now. In its place was pure male hunger. Or maybe not so pure. His expression promised all sorts of mischief. All sorts of pleasure.

Her body responded instantly, softening, yearning. She couldn't even barter for a short-lived fling, because she was growing a baby. A baby who was his. How was she going to tell him? For all her big speeches about the danger of secrets, she was scared spitless to expose hers.

"I want you, too," she said, no longer able to pretend that she didn't. There was no reason to dissemble. Soon enough he would find out that her body was fully prepared to welcome his. Damp heat at her core yearned for his rigid length to fill her and drive her mad.

That's what it was. Madness. She should tell him he didn't need a condom. Explain what happened on that night three months ago. Ask what they were going to do about it.

All the reasons not to make love to him tonight were valid, but she shoved them aside in the pursuit of happiness. Carpe diem. Worry about tomorrow another day.

He twisted one of her curls around his finger. "I care about you, Fiona. This isn't casual for me."

His sober promise should have made her heart sing. At any other moment in her life, that declaration would have been exciting and perfect. As it was, her anxiety ratcheted higher.

"There's nothing wrong with casual. We're both young and unattached. I'm not expecting any commitment at this point."

Her words seemed to bother him. He frowned. "Have you been with a lot of men, Fee? For some reason, I got the impression you were a bit more fastidious about your sexual partners. Am I wrong?"

Now she was caught in the crosshairs. If she said yes, he might ultimately wonder if the baby was his. But a negative response—an admission that he'd been her only sexual partner in the last three years—might reveal more than she was willing for him to know.

She reached up to stroke his masculine jawline. The shadow of a late-day beard gave him a rakish air. "What we stumbled into at the wedding last year and then again three months ago was definitely special. We have chemistry. I'm not denying that. But I have a life and a career that don't really intersect well with yours. Our goals are different." *I have a baby on the way, and I'm thrilled about creating a family.*

"Meaning what?"

"You and I are friends. Temporary lovers. I like plain speaking. I don't need flowery compliments or promises about the future."

"Is this because I'm homeless and unemployed?" His wry grin was boyish and charming and totally unfair.

She rolled her eyes. "You're a wealthy man. I can ignore your money as long as we're playing at this relationship."

"Hell, Fiona. I've never had this level of negotiation before sex. Then again, sex with you is worth a little extra trouble. So what you're saying is that your art and your career are more important than flesh and blood relationships?"

"Of course not. Don't twist my words."

"Then *you* explain it."

How could she? All Fiona wanted was a family and a home of her own. Hartley, on the other hand, was going to be furious when he found out about the baby. If he wanted the unvarnished truth, he could have it. "We had great sex, but that's all it was."

His face darkened with displeasure. "If a man had said that, he'd be pilloried. What are you so afraid of, Fiona? I won't ask for anything you aren't willing to give. We're good together. Admit it."

"I've already admitted it, Hartley."

"If we sleep together right now, are you going to let me spend the night?" His pointed question caught her off guard. Guilt turned her stomach queasy and her face red. He couldn't be here when morning came. Not the way things were with her right now.

She lifted her chin, meeting his gaze calmly. "No. I like my privacy and my personal space. There's nothing wrong with that."

"Okay then." Before she could do more than gasp and flail in his arms, he flipped her onto her back and started unbuttoning her pajama top. She was paralyzed by her need for him. When she was bare from the waist up, he paused and sucked in a breath. "You are so damned beautiful."

He stroked one nipple with a fingertip. His touch made her skin burn. "Hartley…"

"What?" He sprawled beside her, partly reclining beside the low sofa. When he leaned over her, took that same nipple in his teeth and tugged gently, she groaned.

"Don't stop," she whispered. Heat rolled through her body, making her shift restlessly. Had she closed the curtains? Rational thought fled when he dragged her pajama bottoms down her legs along with her plain cotton undies. Now she lay there completely naked, like a not-so-virgin sacrifice.

The look on his face threatened to incinerate her. His

words were ragged. "Each time I leave you I think I might have exaggerated this in my mind. And then we're together again, and I know it's all true. My hands are shaking, and I can barely breathe. That's not normal for a guy my age. I don't know what happens when I touch you…when we touch each other."

The trace of bewilderment in the midst of his arousal reflected her own conflicted emotions. Only now, she had the added bonus of worrying about whether she had a baby bump that would tip him off.

"Enough talking," she muttered.

He chuckled, but stood and ripped off his clothes. His sex was stiff and eager. Had he always been so…*big*? Maybe it was because the lights were on or because he loomed over her.

"Let's go the the bedroom," she pleaded.

A dark flush rode high on his cheeks. The skin stretched taut over the planes of his face. He was the conquering hero…the ravaging marauder. The intensity of his focus on *her* made her shiver.

"No," he said bluntly. "Can't wait."

He moved her like a rag doll, sitting down on the sofa and spreading her legs across his body. Before she could do more than gasp, he entered her with a forceful push. His back arched. He cursed softly. And then he captured her mouth in a frantic, hungry kiss.

This position made her feel deliciously vulnerable. Her hormones went wild, plunging her into a quick, sharp climax that didn't last nearly long enough. "More," she demanded.

"Whatever the lady wants."

Seconds later he tumbled them both to the floor. Her simple rug might never look the same to her again. He lifted one of her ankles onto his shoulder and thrust hard, all the way to her womb. The pleasure was a sharp-edged jolt, so searing, she wondered for a moment if they should be doing this. What did she know about being pregnant?

It was all theoretical until it happened to you.

Then he bit the inside of her thigh and she forgot to worry about anything but the magic they were creating together.

Hartley braced himself on his arms, slowing his movements until both of them were panting.

"Did you lose your way?" she asked, the words undeniably petulant.

Her pique made his masculine grin broaden. "It's called building the tension."

"Did you read this in some manual?"

"Are you criticizing my technique?"

She reached up and brushed the lock of hair from his damp forehead. It fell immediately back over his eyebrow. "This isn't casual for me either," she whispered, admitting defeat.

Her words stunned him visibly. She saw the shift in his gaze. The flare of heat. The exultation.

Gently, he disengaged their bodies and picked her up in his arms, a feat which took considerable strength considering she was on the floor.

"I wasn't done," she complained.

"Patience, Fee." In her narrow hallway, he bumped the bedroom door open with his hip and carried her to the bed. "I need soft sheets for the finale."

"Since when?"

He kissed her nose. "Since I decided to impress you with my romantic prowess."

It wasn't even funny, because it was true. Somehow he had managed to inject tenderness into their sexual insanity. That scared her so very badly. Because he was not going to be able to give her what she wanted and needed. He'd already told her that.

Sex, he could do. Family and forever, not so much.

She'd never had much luck with forevers. Even worse, this particular situation was snakebit from the beginning.

"Come here," she said, holding out her arms.

He settled on top of her with a groan, resting his forehead against hers. There wasn't room between them for a sheet of paper, much less a secret of the enormity of hers.

What was she going to do?

"You're amazing, Fee," he said, filling her again, igniting the flame that had been banked for a time. "Wrap your legs around my waist."

When she did, he slid his hands under her ass and lifted her into his thrusts, giving both of them that extra measure of perfection they craved. She was close, so close.

Hartley shuddered and found his release, his breath warm on her cheek. His scent surrounded her, marking her sheets, making it impossible to pretend he didn't belong here. He was everywhere, filling her feminine bedroom with the force of his personality.

Rolling to one side, he stroked her sex, drawing a quick ragged sigh from her parched throat...sending her over the edge into warm, drowsy completion. "I love how you do that," she said.

"Do what?" he asked, the words slurred as his eyes drifted shut.

"You know exactly how to touch me."

He yawned, turning her and spooning her from behind. "It's my superpower, Fee."

Ten

Fiona woke up some time before dawn. Three things became clear in an instant. A very large, warm man had her wrapped in the pure bliss of his muscular arms. She had to pee. And her stomach had begun its morning calisthenics.

Her choices were limited. She could wake him up and physically shove him out of her house. That seemed mean and cold. She knew he hadn't meant to stay in defiance of her wishes. The two of them had been exhausted, Fiona from being pregnant, and Hartley from working at his new property.

So, if she wasn't willing to kick him out, she had to somehow make it to the bathroom and conceal the fact that morning sickness was about to take its toll. Again.

It was still dark, though the clock on her bedside table told her dawn wasn't far off. Slowly, she began easing out of Hartley's embrace. Even those small movements made her forehead break out in a cold sweat. The timing didn't make sense. Most people were sick during the first twelve weeks and finally got better in the second trimester…or so she had heard.

Then again, she'd known women who struggled with nausea the entire nine months, so who knew? Surely that wouldn't happen to her. She had to work. No work meant no pay. She certainly didn't want to get a reputation for being late on commissioned pieces. That wasn't who she was at all.

How was Hartley going to react? She wanted him to be happy, but that wasn't going to happen. Would he stay away from the child entirely? Or would he want even a minor role?

She had to tell him soon, so they could make plans for the future. Or so *she* could.

How could she keep from breaking her heart again and again if she and Hartley were always connected by this unexpected baby?

Thankfully, Hartley never stirred as she extracted herself from her predicament. Because her house was old, the bathroom was in the hall, not attached to her bedroom. She was able to throw up—twice—wash her face and tiptoe to the kitchen without disturbing her guest.

She didn't turn on the lights. Instead, she heated a mug of water in the microwave, added a tea bag and sat at the table, cradling the cup in her hands. Though it wasn't cold in the house, her shivers came from the inside out. Getting sick so violently left her feeling weak and shaky.

How did women stand this?

Gradually, she sipped her drink and her mood stabilized. Females had been handling this situation since the dawn of time. Fiona, herself, was more resilient that most. She'd had to be. This pregnancy was a curve she hadn't seen coming, but she would deal with it. Somehow.

Hartley startled her when he appeared in the doorway. There was enough light filtering through the window now for her to see that he had pulled on his pants and nothing else. Broad naked chest. Big bare man feet. He was an alien presence in her neatly feminine environment.

He raked a hand through his disheveled hair. “Sorry, Fee. I didn’t stay on purpose.” His voice was gruff and low, roughened by sleep.

She shrugged. “I know. We were both beat.”

“I’ll let myself out in a minute. I wanted to say goodbye.”

Suddenly, she was teary and emotional. Stupid pregnancy hormones. She patted the table. “Come sit. Make coffee if you want to. Everything is there on the counter.”

He glanced at the empty coffeepot. “What are you drinking?”

“Hot tea.”

He put a hand on her shoulder and kissed the top of her head. “You doing okay, darlin’?”

His concern made her want to sob. She had to get a grip. “I’ve been pushing myself too hard lately. Not eating well. Feeling a little rotten today.”

Once the coffeepot was burbling, he sat down beside her, rubbing her back. “Poor baby. What can I do to make it better?”

Rewrite the past. Tell me you’d love to have a dozen kids. Go away and never come back.

That last one was a huge, wretched lie. She wanted Hartley, and she wanted Hartley’s child growing inside her. The kicker was, she didn’t see a way for all of that to happen at the same time. Or ever.

“I’ll be fine.” She finished her tea, wishing she had a second cup.

"Why don't you take a day off?" he said. "You're the boss…right?"

"Yes. But being self-employed isn't for sissies. I have to think about things like quarterly taxes and health insurance premiums and mortgage payments."

"Ah." He stood and poured his coffee.

Fiona had been afraid the aroma might provoke her nausea, but thankfully, the smell was more comforting than anything else.

When Hartley sat down again, he studied her face. "I have a proposition for you," he said.

"It's too early in the morning for propositions."

He stroked the back of her hand with his thumb, sending tingles all over her body. "I've noticed a few things on the outside of your house…maintenance issues."

She interrupted him, feeling defensive about her beloved bungalow. "I know. I have a gutter that needs repairing. The roof lost a few shingles in that last storm. And the eaves need painting. It's a question of time and money, Hartley. I'll get to it." *Somehow.*

"Hear me out," he said. "I was thinking you might take in a boarder."

"A boarder? I only have one bedroom."

"True. But you have a very nice sofa. My new place is three streets away. It would be damned convenient for me to be close during the renovation. I could pay you rent, *and*," he said, "in the evenings, I could do a few handyman projects around your house."

Fiona closed her eyes. It was too early in the morning to be doing battle with a charmer. "I've already told you. I like my privacy and my space."

"Your studio is in the back of the house. I'll stay out of your way. You won't even know I'm here."

Her brain was muzzy. She could smell the scent of his

sleep-warmed skin. All she wanted to do was go back to bed. *You won't even know I'm here.* Was he kidding? He filled up a room with his smile, which was exactly what got her into this mess in the first place.

From the moment she met the handsome groomsman who was going to walk her down the aisle at their mutual friends' wedding, she'd been a goner. Never had she met someone like Hartley. He was a combo of Viking marauder and Saint Bernard puppy. A stubborn alpha male who shaped the world to his liking but could laugh at himself and coax a woman into his bed with the twinkle in his eye. It was almost impossible for her to get mad at him, because he was so genuinely well-intentioned.

Hartley thought he could control the world, or at least his corner of it. That was why he was now estranged from his brother and why Fiona questioned telling him about the baby. He'd made up his mind not to have kids.

How would he react when she told him it was far too late?

She rubbed her temples. "You have plenty of money, Hartley. Find a hotel nearby. There are dozens of them."

"I lived on the road for over a year. I missed you, Fee. I missed having sex with you. I want to be here. Under your roof. Platonically if necessary until you can trust me again."

"Do you really think I'll sleep in my bed, and you'll be on the sofa? Come on, Hartley. I'm not that naive."

His thumb strayed up her arm, teasing the inside crook of her elbow. "That would be entirely up to you."

She pressed her thighs together. Now that her nausea had abated, arousal settled heavy in her abdomen. "I can't deal with this right now. Take me back to bed. It's too early. My brain doesn't work."

"Whatever you want, Fiona." He picked up her hand and sucked her pinky finger, his teeth raking her knuckle.

Holy hell. Had she always had that erogenous zone, or was pregnancy making her insatiable?

She jerked her hand away with a gasp she tried to turn into a cough. He had far too much ego as it was. No need for him to know he could reduce her to mush so easily. She fled down the hall. It wasn't even seven yet.

When she climbed under the covers, Hartley was right behind her. He nuzzled the back of her neck. "Do you want to sleep or screw?"

Her helpless giggle was mortifyingly girlish. "Do I have a choice?"

He leaned over her on one elbow, his expression dead sober. "You always have a choice, Fee."

"I'm sorry," she said quickly, feeling small. "I know that. I wasn't accusing you of anything. Well, except for being far too hard to resist."

A smile cracked his stoic expression. "A compliment? Wow, Fee, I don't know what to say."

She curled a hand behind his neck and pulled him down for a kiss. "You could say you'll give me a few days to think about this living together thing." *Maybe the morning sickness would subside soon, and Hartley's presence in her house wouldn't be such an issue.*

His tongue mated with hers, stealing her breath. "Fair enough."

Hartley didn't want to leave this woman or this bed at all. But he knew when to back off. If he couldn't win her over with cogent arguments, then he had to play to his strengths.

Though he couldn't take credit for whatever animal

attraction had bewitched them, he'd be happy to use it to advance his cause.

It had alarmed him to wake up this morning and realize he was in bed alone. Fiona had seemed *twitchy* or something when he'd found her in the kitchen. As if he were indeed intruding on her personal space. Gradually, though, she had relaxed.

Now she was warm and affectionate and very clearly inclined to get the day off to a good start. He sifted his fingers through her rumpled curls. "Have I told you how much I love your hair?"

She grimaced. "I hated it for most of my life. I wasn't allowed to go the movies very often, but one of my foster moms had a huge DVD collection. I adored watching Gwyneth Paltrow in *Emma.* Kate Hudson in *How to Lose a Guy in 10 Days.* I envied their blond beauty, because I was the antithesis of that. Skinny and freckled and bashful."

"Neither of them can hold a candle to the woman you are now." He could see that little girl in his mind's eye. She had grown into a stunning human being. "You have a fire in you—maybe it's the creativity, I don't know. The moment we met each other at that damned wedding, I could no more have walked away from you than cut off my own arm. I wanted you desperately. Beyond all reason. Why do you think that is?"

She toyed with the shell of his ear. "Is that a serious question?"

Her touch sent little tingles of fire down his spine to his sex. "I think it is. I've always been suspicious of things I don't understand."

"But…?"

He slid his hand inside her pajama bottoms and found her center. She was warm and wet. He shook with the need to take and take and take until he blacked out from the pleasure. "But I'm learning to live with not knowing."

"Wow. What a sacrifice."

"Has anyone ever told you you've got a mean streak?"

"Most people think I'm adorable." She turned up her nose at him, clearly inclined to make fun of herself.

He chuckled. "Can't argue with that."

Sex with Fiona was never what he expected. In the midst of aching arousal, he still wanted to play endlessly. Her body was soft and supple. Small and yet powerfully feminine, strong enough to make him weak.

He hadn't entirely grown accustomed to the power she wielded. And he was pretty damned sure she had no idea the power was even there. Perhaps for now it was best she didn't. *Because he didn't know what he was going to do about the situation.*

Before climbing into bed, he had shucked his pants and boxers. Fiona wrapped her hand around his erection. His vision blurred. He was breathing like he had run a mile, and they had barely started.

He held his hand over hers. "Easy now. Let me unwrap you first."

"I'll help," she said. "You're being kind of slow."

His laugh was little more than a wheeze.

Between them they ripped off her pjs and clutched each other, naked skin to naked skin. It was enough to make him forget his name and every last one of his troubles.

His world narrowed to this bed. This woman.

Crap. Condoms. Did he have any left? He reached for the floor and his mangled clothing and found one more. Thank God.

His hands shook as he rolled it over his erection. "Foreplay?" he croaked.

She grabbed handfuls of his hair. "Not a chance. Get over here."

He filled her with one wild thrust. It was heaven and hell and every level of torment in between. Burying his face in her neck, he tried to count her heartbeats, to memorize the taste of her skin right below her ear.

Her body welcomed him, drew him in, held him captive. He had never been more glad to be a man. Whatever his sins—and there were many—he must have done something right. "I can't stop wanting you," he groaned.

Fiona sucked his bottom lip, sinking her teeth in just enough to sting. "Works both ways. But we can't stay in bed all day," she said, panting. "We're mature adults. We have to set boundaries."

He braced his weight on his hands for a minute and studied her face. Her cheeks were flushed, her throat abraded by the stubble on his chin. The red hair that was silky and soft fluffed out around her heart-shaped face. Before today, he hadn't noticed how that sweet pointed chin could be so stubborn.

"I never met a boundary I didn't want to smash."

Her eyes widened. The flush deepened. "I always thought of myself as a good girl."

"Just think of me as your black sheep lover. Ready to do any naughty thing your heart desires."

She squeezed his sex with her inner muscles, drawing a ragged groan from his dry throat.

"Make love to me, Hartley," she said. "Now."

It was a demand he was happy to oblige.

The feelings racketing around in his chest were foreign to him, dangerously so. He shoved them away, choosing to concentrate on the physical. When he knew Fiona was at the edge, he reached between their linked bodies and stroked her intimately.

She arched against him and climaxed, whispering his name over and over, making him feel like a king. Seconds later, he lost the fight with his own galloping need and came so hard he actually saw yellow spots dancing behind his closed eyelids.

Without meaning to, he slept again. But when he awoke fifteen minutes later, this time he wasn't alone.

He watched Fiona breathe, her breasts rising and falling almost imperceptibly. Gently, he twisted a curl around his finger, a game that was rapidly becoming one of his favorites.

The springy red-gold strands clung to his skin, alive with the passion he felt in her. In one blinding instant of clarity he understood that he couldn't be the man to break her heart. Not with the disappointments and challenges she had faced in her young life so far.

Fiona was a fighter, yes. Fiercely independent. Generous and brave. The right man could spend a lifetime making her happy…making up for all she had lost.

The big-ass problem was, Hartley didn't know if he was good enough or smart enough or deserving enough to be that guy. He'd been plowing ahead with his laundry list of wants and needs, determined to find his way into her life. But what or who did Fiona need?

When he stroked her cheek with the tip of his finger, her eyelashes fluttered open. Her gaze was dreamy. "Wow."

He couldn't stop his smug grin. "Ditto."

She stretched, causing all sorts of interesting reactions beneath the sheet. "I have to *work*, Hartley. Really, I do."

He rolled to a seated position and held up both hands. "I know, I know. I'm gone. But before I leave, one more thing."

Her hand settled on his thigh, perilously close to his semi-erect sex. "You never give up, do you?"

The temptation was almost overwhelming. Instead of giving in, he tried to be the better man. Lurching to his feet, he dressed clumsily, conscious of her gaze on his naked body. "No, no," he said. "I want to take you out on a date Friday night. It's a charity gala, black-tie. My father is receiving a posthumous award. Apparently, despite everything, my family wants me to be there."

Fiona raised up on her elbows. "Well, of course they do. That's lovely, Hartley."

"I want you to come with me, Fiona. Dinner, dancing. The formalities will be brief."

"I'd love to," she said simply.

"Really?" His disappointment at having to leave her bed was appeased. "I thought we might stay overnight at a small hotel near the event site. So we can indulge in champagne and stroll through the summer night back to our love nest."

His teasing hyperbole made her smile. "That sounds delightful. What time will you pick me up?"

"Well, if I were already staying here…" He trailed off, gauging her mood.

She pulled a robe out of her closet, slipped it on and belted it with a double knot. "You are incorrigible. Not tonight. Not tomorrow. Not this week. After the gala, we'll talk."

He pretended to scowl. "You're a hard woman."

She rounded the bed and slid her arms around his waist. "Patience, Hartley. That new house of yours will take weeks of work. We have all the time in the world."

Eleven

As it turned out, it was *Fiona* who was pressed for time. Not in regard to her work. She'd actually had bursts of energy in the late afternoons and was finding herself wildly productive in those moments. Although her workday had shifted and morphed from her usual pattern, she was not as far behind as she had feared.

The real problem was her clothes. When she dressed Wednesday morning, the jeans that had fit her only the day before were suddenly and mysteriously too tight. She stared in the mirror and ran a hand over her belly.

There was no denying it. Even if the convex shape of her tummy was barely perceptible to the naked eye, her body was changing. Blossoming with new life. The barrage of feelings that knowledge evoked made her feel completely out of her element.

She'd never had a mother, not really. What did she know about giving birth or breastfeeding or how many times was too many to read *Goodnight Moon*? Scarier still was wondering how her baby's father was going to react to the news. Would Friday night or perhaps Saturday morning be the right time to tell him? In the midst of her panic ran a deep, mysterious vein of intense joy.

Though this was a situation she had never anticipated or imagined she wanted, now that her baby was becoming a reality, she was fiercely glad. No matter what happened with Hartley, this child was *hers*. Hers. A family of her own.

In the end, she left her jeans unbuttoned at the waist and chose a loose cotton tunic in navy and orange that would hide any telltale signs. The appointment with her ob-gyn would confirm what she already knew.

Now she understood how Mazie felt the other day… slinking around, hoping no one would see. It was as if she had a giant sign on her back shouting, "I'm pregnant."

An hour later when a no-nonsense nurse called her name, Fiona rose to her feet and followed the woman through a maze of hallways to an exam room. The obstetrician was a female, only two or three years older than Fiona herself. Dr. Anderson was thorough, kind and reassuring. "You're in excellent health, Ms. James. You shouldn't have problems, but of course, you know to call our office immediately if you have any concerns."

The doc handed over a prescription for vitamins and a handful of educational pamphlets, and soon Fiona was out on the street again. She had been certain she was pregnant, but hearing the confirmation from a professional made everything so much more *real*.

As she stood on the sidewalk, her limbs were shaky, and her emotions pinballed. It was impossible to decide which response was the correct one. Jubilation and trepidation seemed equally appropriate.

Since she had already broken up her workday, she decided to consolidate errands. Before leaving the house that morning, she had looked online for maternity shops. There was one nearby, so she stopped in…just to take a look.

She had several tops at home that would probably work for three or four months. What she needed were some stretchy pants on the dressier side. Sometimes she met with prospective clients, so she had to look professional, even if she *was* an artist.

The clothing in this particular shop was wildly expensive, particularly considering she would be wearing maternity pieces for only part of a year. She found one sleeveless shift that she could wear over short-sleeve T-shirts. It didn't look like a tent, so that was a plus. A couple of pairs of pants and she was done for the moment.

It was hard to imagine her body getting big and round. Maybe it would be smarter to wait for the rest.

A more pressing priority than maternity clothes was finding something to wear for Friday night. She owned three relatively formal dresses, but none of them were really exciting. One was a hand-me-down from a friend. Another was the dress she'd worn at the wedding where she and Hartley met, and the third was a heavy winter velvet.

She wanted to look like she was comfortable in his world, even if she wasn't. Since this was definitely a special occasion, she sought out a little boutique where, normally, she only window-shopped. Today, she marched right in and started perusing the racks.

Sequins weren't really her thing. Color was another challenge. Black tended to overwhelm her because of her extremely fair skin and her stature. She wanted something *floaty* and romantic…the kind of gown a woman wore when going out with the man she loved.

The random thought stopped her dead in her tracks. She

didn't *love* Hartley. She couldn't. Sexual attraction was a powerful force, but it wasn't the same as love.

Her stomach churned with nausea, though the baby wasn't to blame. For the first time, she honestly tried to imagine how Hartley was going to react when she told him the truth. She couldn't bear the thought that he would decide to care for her and the baby because he had no choice.

After being taken in by a string of well-meaning foster parents over the years of her childhood and adolescence, she'd had her fill of being someone else's *obligation*. She didn't need Hartley's money, and she didn't need his reluctant parenting.

He was worried about his mother's genetic legacy. Even more than that, his father had created such a mishmash of lies and deceit, Hartley was disgusted by the idea of parenthood. Hartley was determined not to recreate his unorthodox childhood. It made sense. It did. But there was absolutely nothing Fiona could do to alter the present situation. The only option would be to terminate the pregnancy, and that was out of the question.

This baby had already stolen her heart. Making plans for the future was scary and exciting at the same time. After the gala, she told herself. After the gala she would work up the courage to let Hartley know about her pregnancy. Who knows? Maybe the reality of her situation would change his mind.

"May I help you, miss?" A tall, statuesque saleswoman with exquisitely coiffed white hair interrupted Fiona's spate of worrying and gave her a warm smile.

"Yes, thank you. I have a function Friday night. Black-tie. Nothing I have at home will work. Can you point me in the right direction? I don't like anything too fussy, and I'd prefer the more casual side of formal. Am I asking the impossible? My hair clashes with some colors, obviously."

The woman took a step back and surveyed Fiona from head to toe, as if studying a mannequin. “White,” she pronounced. “Possibly ivory, but I think white is the shade for you.”

“Really? Isn’t that a bit too bridal?”

“You must be attending the Chamber Awards Gala Friday, correct?”

“Yes, ma’am.” It was hard not to feel like a little kid playing dress up when faced with this paragon of elegance.

“Come with me, young lady. The dressing rooms are this way. You may call me Clarisse.”

Fiona trailed in her wake, wondering if she had started something she would regret. Even the changing area was fancier than her bedroom at home. A small antique chandelier. Tall cheval mirrors edged in gilt. Thick, lush carpet underfoot.

Clarisse indicated a small cushioned chair. “Wait here,” she said. “Help yourself to fruit water and biscotti.”

When the other woman disappeared through plum satin curtains into the bowels of the store, Fiona sat down and pulled out her phone. She was increasingly worried about Hartley. After that first day, he had never again spoken about what he discovered in Switzerland.

Fiona was certain that if he simply told Jonathan the truth about why he had been gone and what he’d learned, his brother would no longer have a reason to be angry. Well, maybe because of the money, but Hartley had put it all back. That shouldn’t be a problem in the end.

Clarisse returned with an armful of gowns, effectively ending Fiona’s fretting, at least for the moment. The older woman ushered Fiona to a changing room. “Here are the first three,” she said. “We can move on quickly if none of these suit your taste.”

Fiona stripped down to her undies and surveyed the

haul. One of the ivory dresses caught her eye instantly. It was strapless and fitted from the breasts to the knees, where it flared in a cloud of tulle. The satin had a faux antique patina that appealed to her artistic sensibilities.

But the fit was so tight…

She tried it on, holding her breath.

Clarisse rapped at the door. “Shall I zip you up?”

“Yes, please.” Fiona couldn’t tell anything at all with the dress open down the back. She clutched it to her chest and waited for the imperious salesclerk to help her.

When everything was tucked and fastened, both women surveyed Fiona’s reflection in the glass. The woman looking back at them was wide-eyed and flushed.

Clarisse pursed her lips. “What do you think?”

Fiona touched her hair. Perhaps she could wear it up. “I love it,” she said slowly, stunned that a single item of clothing could make her feel so wonderful. Already, she was imagining Hartley’s face when he saw her in soft satin and bare skin. The dress made her feel sexy and sophisticated.

Clarisse nodded. “I believe it’s perfect for you. But I suggest you try on half a dozen more just to be sure.”

“Oh, no,” Fiona demurred. “I won’t change my mind, I promise. Are you sure I can pull this off? I’m not really accustomed to attending events like the gala. I don’t want to feel self-conscious.”

“If you’re worried about the pregnancy showing, don’t be. That tiny baby bump won’t be visible at all, even though the dress fits as if it was designed only for you.”

Fiona gaped. “You can tell I’m pregnant?” Her mood plummeted. “Maybe I should look for something looser.”

Clarisse’s expression softened. “I know women’s bodies. It’s my livelihood. But unless someone sees you naked, I assure you your secret is safe.”

Unless someone sees you naked… Fiona gulped inwardly. Not exactly reassuring words given how the evening was likely to end. Hartley in a tux and Fiona dressed to kill? It was going to be their wedding party introduction all over again.

"I'll take the gown," Fiona said firmly. If she was going to be Hartley's plus-one and mingle with his family and friends and business acquaintances, she wanted to look her best.

After paying for her purchase and laying it gently in the back seat of the car, she pulled out her phone and did a search for Mazie's shop. It was a jewelry store in the historic district. As luck would have it, All That Glitters was less than a quarter of a mile away.

Fiona set out on foot. Parking spaces were at a premium in this part of town; plus, she needed the exercise anyway. Though she was by no means a slug, the fact that she was pregnant meant making healthy choices all the way around. She might be inexperienced when it came to babies and mothering, but she was determined to give this little one every advantage.

When she entered Mazie's place of business, the premises were pleasantly cool and scented with the aroma of jasmine. Quiet music played unobtrusively. Can lights overhead illuminated cases of rings and necklaces and bracelets. The atmosphere was everything a weary, overheated female tourist could hope for. Consequently, the place was crowded and buzzing with conversation.

Fiona spotted Hartley's sister right away, but she hung back, not wanting to intrude. When Mazie passed off a happy shopper to the employee at the register who was waiting to ring up and wrap the woman's purchases, Mazie made a beeline for Fiona.

She beamed. "You found me," she said.

"This place is gorgeous. I love how you've used color and light to showcase your merchandise."

"Thanks. Coming from an artist, that means a lot."

Fiona lowered her voice. "How are you feeling? What did J.B. say when he found out you're pregnant?"

The other woman's face was radiant. "I feel amazing. And my husband is over the moon. He barely lets me out of the house, though. Being doted on is great, but I've tried to tell him I'm fine."

"Maybe he'll settle down when he sees how well you're doing."

"I hope so. I love the attention—who wouldn't? Still, I need to breathe." Her smug smile told Fiona that J.B.'s hovering wasn't really a problem.

Mazie took her by the arm. "I need to talk to you," she said. Without waiting for a response from Fiona, she steered her toward the back of the store. "My office is tiny, but no one will disturb us."

Behind the chintz curtain was a jumble of boxes and a nook barely large enough for an antique rolltop desk and a couple of chairs. Mazie motioned Fiona toward one of them. "Water?" she asked.

"Yes, please." The temperature was in the nineties. Her throat was dry. She was either nervous or dehydrated or both. "What's up?" she asked.

Mazie took the other seat and handed Fiona a bottle, then uncapped her own. "I'm worried sick about telling Lisette and Jonathan."

"And Hartley?"

"Him, too. But Lisette has miscarried twice. I don't want to upset her with my news."

"Don't be silly. You have something to celebrate. Lisette will be happy for you. She probably sees pregnant women every day."

"Maybe." Mazie wrinkled her nose. "J.B. and I thought that we'd have all of you over for drinks and hors d'oeuvres before the gala. That way we could tell everyone at once."

Mazie knew instantly this would be a test for her own pregnancy. If Hartley was delighted for his sister, maybe there was hope for Fiona. "We'll be there," she said.

"Excellent." Mazie hopped up and pulled a small box from the shelf behind her shoulder. "I've been meaning to give you one of these," she said. "Sort of a welcome-to-the-family gift. It's clear that my brother is nuts about you."

Fiona wasn't sure this was the time to say that she and Hartley were temporary. So she smiled weakly and opened the offering. It was a delicate seahorse charm, suspended from a beautiful eighteen-inch box chain. "Oh, Mazie. This is lovely."

Mazie hovered. "Put it on. It's white gold. If you'd rather have the more traditional yellow, we can swap it out."

"Oh, no. This is perfect." Fiona fingered the little sea creature. "But I think it's too much. We barely know each other."

"You bought me pregnancy tests. That advances the timeline exponentially."

Fiona chuckled. "Maybe so." She stood and used the small oval mirror on the wall to fasten the chain around her neck. The charm nestled in exactly the right spot. "I love it."

"It's the kind of thing you can wear with everyday outfits. And it suits you. Whimsical and unusual."

"Are you sure that's a compliment?"

Fiona's wry question made Mazie laugh. "Of course it is. That's why my brother is so besotted. No woman he's ever dated is anything like you. You're an original."

"And all those other women?"

Mazie shrugged. "Cookie-cutter debutantes. Rich. Confident. Boring."

"We should all be so lucky," Fiona muttered. "I should go," she said suddenly, feeling weepy for no particular reason except that the life growing inside her was playing havoc with her temperament. "I just wanted to say hello and see where you worked."

"Well, now you know, so don't be a stranger."

When they returned to the main showroom, the crowd had thinned. Fiona wanted badly to share her own secret. But a host of things held her back. This family had a lot of skeletons. For an orphan, it was hard to imagine the kind of blood loyalty that kept a group of siblings together over the long haul.

"Thank you for the invitation," she said. "I'm sure Hartley will be happy for us to come." It wasn't exactly the truth, but she didn't want to add to Mazie's worry about the big reveal. "What time?"

"Probably five thirty. I'll text you both when we nail it down."

"You do realize it's only forty-eight hours from now?"

Mazie grinned. "Not to worry. I'll put my feet up and let J.B. make all the arrangements."

Twelve

Fiona continued to be sick in the mornings. Fitting into the dress she had bought was not a problem. Fortunately, Hartley kept his distance, perhaps hoping his uncustomary reticence would cement her trust.

For two days, it almost seemed as if time stood still. That she had never met Hartley. That her whole life wasn't about to change.

She took advantage of the momentary lull to paint like mad. The work was a welcome distraction. Anxiety about the weekend made her queasiness worse. She had agreed to spend the night with Hartley after the gala. In a romantic, indulgent boutique hotel. What could possibly go wrong?

At the wedding where they first met, and again when Hartley showed up at her house unannounced, the sex and the budding relationship had been wild and thrilling, carried along on a wave of lust and adrenaline and some insane concoction of pheromones.

Friday night would be different. She and Hartley were

invited to socialize with his family. They were going to appear together in public. Neither of them could expect a spontaneous outcome. When a man and a woman dressed up, shared a fancy social occasion, and then checked into a room, what happened next was a done deal.

Fiona was both terrified and giddy with excitement.

In the end, she decided to leave her hair down. Her curls had a mind of their own, and they barely reached her chin. Taming them would take more energy than she possessed at the moment.

She was not a sophisticated woman. No point in pretending.

Friday afternoon she cleaned up her studio and took a shower. She'd bought new undies and a silky nightgown at the maternity shop. Ordinarily, she was more of a tank top and panties sleeper, but tonight she wanted to be someone different. The kind of woman who coaxed a man into bed and made him never want to leave.

She and Hartley had texted back and forth over the past few days, but only briefly. Was he playing games with her? He'd gone from bludgeoning his way into her life to respecting her boundaries. What did it mean? Why was she so suspicious of his motives?

After packing a small overnight bag, she did her makeup and stepped into the fabulous dress. Only then did she realize her problem. With no Clarisse at hand, Fiona couldn't zip up the dress on her own.

Damn, damn, damn.

Hartley was as jumpy as a bullfrog on hot concrete. It felt like weeks, not days, since he had seen Fiona. He was playing the long game, giving her the space she wanted. Had it helped his case?

The only way he managed to survive his self-imposed

separation was by working his ass off packing up his house and getting it ready for closing. All he could think about was whether or not Fiona was going to let him move in. Even if she made him sleep on the sofa, it would be a start. He'd made reservations at an extended-stay condo unit, just in case.

He had mixed feelings about showing up at J.B. and Mazie's house tonight. Lisette and Jonathan would be there, of course. Things were still frosty with his twin. Maybe avoidance was the best policy. Keep the width of the room between him and Jonathan.

Any worry about family squabbles took a back seat when Hartley pulled up in front of Fiona's now-familiar house. He shut off the engine, mentally calculating how many hours and minutes it would be until he and the lovely red-headed artist were alone together. His body tightened and ached as he imagined undressing her.

He had booked the best room in the swankiest, most exclusive hotel in the city. Pulled out all the stops. Tonight would be a slow, sexy buildup to the main event.

If he lived that long. The way he felt right now, he might go quietly insane.

She knew they were good in bed. Why couldn't she admit the benefits of a convenient living arrangement?

He wanted her day and night.

Truth be told, his feelings for Fiona were not entirely comfortable, because he didn't understand them.

When he strode up the path and knocked, no one answered. Seconds passed. He knocked again. "Fiona, it's me."

Suddenly, he heard the sound of the dead bolt being turned. The door opened. But no more than six or eight inches. Certainly not enough for a large man to squeeze through.

Two big eyes in a heart-shaped face peered out at him. "You're early," she accused.

He frowned. "Barely fifteen minutes. What's wrong, Fee?"

The part of her he could see turned bright red. Perfect teeth mutilated a plump bottom lip. "We have a situation."

"Are you sick?" Disappointment flooded his stomach. And then he felt like a jerk for being disappointed.

"I'm not sick."

"Let me in, darlin'. It's hot enough to fry meat on the sidewalk."

"Okay. But wait a minute. And be quick when I let you in." The door closed all the way. Something—maybe an elbow—hit the wood.

He didn't know what the hell was going on, but he wasn't going to get any answers out here. "Fiona…"

Before he could form an objection, the door opened a second time. A small, feminine hand grabbed his wrist and dragged him through the narrow opening. "I need help," she said breathlessly.

When she slammed the door, and he saw her for the first time, he took a blow to the chest. His sweet, usually unadorned Fiona was wearing makeup. She looked unbelievably fantastic. Hot and sultry and gorgeous.

Her eye shadow was smoky gray, a color that made those slate blue irises sparkle. Mascara darkened pale lashes, creating a vision of feminine sexuality. She wore red lipstick, the color of arousal. His mouth dried. "You look amazing."

"Thank you. But I…"

Then he saw it. She was clutching her dress to her breasts. Ivory satin caressed her body. The gown appeared to be undone.

Lord help him.

Fiona's gaze was pleading. "The saleslady fastened me at the store. I never thought about the fact that I'd be home alone. You'll have to zip me up."

He took a step backward. Lust zinged from his sex to his throat, drying his mouth. "Um…"

"It's not a corset," she said. "Just a zipper." Impatience mixed with embarrassment in her voice.

He couldn't do it. He absolutely couldn't do it. All he'd thought about since the last time he stood in this house was how soon he could make love to her again. Now he was hot and horny and frustrated. Dangerously close to the edge. "A neighbor," he croaked. "I can fetch someone."

Confusion darkened her gaze. "Mr. Fontaine on the left is eighty-seven and deaf. My other neighbor has three kids, and they're at soccer practice. What's the problem? We're going to be late."

Well, hell. He could try. He wasn't a slave to his baser instincts. He was a highly evolved, overly educated, twenty-first century gentleman.

She turned her back to him. "Do it, Hartley. Please."

Do it? Was she deliberately trying to drive him out of his mind?

His hands shook so hard he had to clench his fists. "Okay," he muttered. "Don't rush me. I don't want to ruin your dress."

Clearly, Fiona had no idea how she looked from behind. The zipper was a long one. Her soft, pale-skinned back was exposed from the nape of her neck to where her spine took a feminine curve at the top of her ass.

She wasn't wearing anything else but tiny underwear. And even then he got only a peek of lace. Mostly, the view was all Fiona. Naked Fiona.

Gritting his teeth, he took hold of the zipper and wrestled it upward an inch and a half, no more. Fiona made a noise that sounded remarkably like a moan.

He ignored the sexy provocation and tried again. The fabric was slippery. The dress was clearly meant to be fitted to a woman's body with little room to spare.

Suddenly, he had to touch her. Had to see if that magnolia-white skin was as soft as it looked. He traced her lower spine with both thumbs. "We could skip the gala tonight," he muttered, only half kidding.

Fiona shot him a look over her shoulder. "No, we can't." Her eyelids were heavy. The words lacked conviction.

He moved the zipper another inch. His self-control was shot. Wanting her was a living, breathing pain. How was he supposed to resist? He kissed the top of her spine. "Tell me to stop, Fee." His entire body was tense. Braced. As if being stretched on a rack. His sex throbbed beneath the confines of his tux pants.

"Stop what?"

It was a dangerous question, because in her voice he heard the truth. She knew exactly what he was asking.

"Fee…" He pleaded with her.

She dropped her head back against his chest, her curls brushing his chin. "I missed you," she muttered.

He snapped. Completely. His need for her sent him reeling off a cliff. Without conscious thought, he lifted her bodily, freed her from the puddle of satin and kicked it aside.

Spinning her to face him, he ground out the only words he could think of in his delirium. "Speak now or forever hold your peace."

She curled her arms around his neck, her eyes soft with arousal. "I'm going to let you do all the talking," she whispered.

The madness rolled over him like a tide. He shoved her against the door, feasting on one perfect spot at the curve of her neck—careful, though, not to mark her skin. He freed his erection, fumbled with protection and fingered her sex through her panties. She was wet and warm and welcoming.

There was no time to remove her underwear. He tugged at the elastic between her legs and gave himself enough room to maneuver. Then he lifted her and shoved hard, lodging himself all the way to the hilt. Her butt smashed against the door.

Hell and damn. His body was on fire, burning from the inside out. When he moved in her, Fiona whimpered as if afraid he was going to leave her. Not bloody likely. "I'm sorry," he muttered. The weight of his many failings threatened to drown him. She was an angel, and he was nothing but a man enslaved by his need for her body, her soul.

Fee leaned into him and nipped his earlobe with sharp teeth. "I'm not sorry," she said.

Things blurred a bit after that. He remembered hammering into her again and again, muttering words of desperation. Fee's legs tightened around his waist. "Don't stop," she begged.

Half a second later, her sex contracted around his, the sensation exquisite and inescapable. He groaned her name and came with her, burying his hot face in her neck.

When it was over, he set her gently on her feet and kissed her forehead. He was weak, embarrassingly so. He couldn't think of a single thing to say.

Fiona, ever practical, touched his cheek, patting him as if he were a child to be comforted. "I'll use the bathroom in my studio. You can take the one in the hallway."

When she bent over to pick up her dress, he nearly lunged for her again. Instead, he clenched his fists and tried to breathe through the pain. He was falling in love with her. The knowledge crushed him. Fiona was the kind of woman who wanted marriage and a family.

He would give her the moon if she asked, but making babies was out of the question for him.

When he had put himself back together, at least where his clothing was concerned, he went to her bedroom and stood in the open doorway. Fee was seated at the antique vanity adjacent to her bed tidying her curls and freshening her lipstick. With her arms lifted and her body still naked, she looked like a painting by one of the old masters.

Woman combing her hair...

"Did I ruin your dress?" he asked. It was tossed across the bed.

"I don't think so." Her gaze didn't meet his when she stood. She hadn't bothered with slipping into a robe.

They were lovers. No need to pretend otherwise. Even so, he averted his eyes when she picked up the heavy satin and stepped into it. Too much temptation. She gave him her back. He zipped her up carefully.

"You look beautiful, Fiona." He squeezed her shoulders.

She had wrung him out and used him up, but he was hard as a pike already and wanted her no less than he had before.

"Thank you," she said quietly. "We should go. We can still make it to Mazie and J.B.'s if the traffic is kind." She picked up a small evening clutch covered in seed pearls.

"Wait," he said, reaching into the pocket of his jacket. "I almost forgot. Mazie told me the two of you chatted when you stopped by the store about what you were going to wear tonight. I pumped her for the color and bought you this. I hope you like it."

He handed over a velvet box and watched her face as she opened it.

Her eyes widened. "Hartley…these are gorgeous. But it's too much. I'd be terrified of breaking them."

"Nonsense. Pearls are meant to be enjoyed. They warm with your skin…become part of you. Turn around."

Carefully, he slipped the long double strand over her head. The woman and the dress had been stunning before. Now Fiona looked like a princess. He stood behind her as she examined her reflection in the mirror. Their eyes met in the glass. "I love them," she said. "Thank you, Hartley." When she stroked the necklace with two fingers, he could almost feel her touch against his skin.

He swallowed against a startling lump of emotion in his throat. "I'm glad. I would kiss you, but I don't think we have time for more repairs."

Fiona glanced at the clock on her bedside table and squeaked. "We have to go. Mazie will kill us if we're late."

"What's so important?" He loved his sister, but he was more interested in being alone with Fiona than a round of appetizers and small talk.

Fiona's cheeks turned pink. "Who knows? Your siblings are complicated people."

"So true." While Fee turned off lights and checked doors, Hartley took her small suitcase and put it in the trunk of his car. Only the fact that they were spending the night together kept him in line. It would be far too easy to blow off this gala and let Mazie and Jonathan represent the family.

Truth be told, he still felt guilty about leaving them to do that the whole time he'd been gone. He'd borne a load of his own, but did that balance out the sin of abandoning the family?

In the car, he took Fiona's hand and lifted it to his lips. "Thank you for coming with me tonight. I'll be the most envied man in Charleston with you on my arm."

When he nibbled her knuckles, she jerked her hand back, laughing. "Behave yourself. And don't think ridiculous flattery will let you have your way about everything."

"It's only flattery if it isn't true, Fee. I'm not sure how a woman like you is still unattached."

His praise seemed to bother her. She wrinkled her nose and stared through the windshield. "What does that mean? A woman like me..."

He started the car. "Beautiful. Smart. Talented. Sexy as hell."

"I appreciate the vote of confidence, but I'm not anything special. Don't get me wrong. I have healthy self-esteem. I'm not fishing for compliments."

"Then what *are* you doing?" He frowned, bothered by the fact that she seemed clueless about how she affected him.

"Let's change the subject, please."

He bowed to her wishes, wondering how deeply her early years had marked her. What was it like to be a kid without a home? He couldn't even imagine it.

Yet, he'd *had* a home, and he possessed as many hang-ups as Fiona. Perhaps more. Warning bells sounded in his head. He was getting in too deep. He didn't need to psychoanalyze her to enjoy sex. He needed to back up and look at the big picture.

Fiona was silent for the remainder of the short trip. As always, he wondered what she was thinking. Was she looking forward to sleeping with him tonight? Really sleeping? He was vaguely astonished to realize that he wanted that almost as much as he wanted sex.

Maybe this relationship was temporary. In his gut, he knew it was. That didn't mean he couldn't enjoy it while it lasted.

Thirteen

Fiona was a pile of nerves by the time she and Hartley made it to Mazie's house. The two of them were a full ninety seconds early, a minor miracle considering how they had spent portions of the previous hour.

A uniformed maid met them at the door and escorted them to the dining room. The home was stunning. But Fiona had no time to gawk at the classic architecture and fabulous furnishings. Everyone else was already present. Jonathan and Lisette. And of course, J.B. and Mazie.

Hartley hadn't lost all of his reserve with his siblings. The round of greetings was cordial, but to Fiona's eyes, everyone in the room was carefully on his or her best behavior. She exchanged hugs, too… That seemed to be required. Only Jonathan and Hartley kept a physical distance.

The light appetizers set out on the sideboard were amazing. Fiona could have made a meal out of only this, but she worried about spilling food on her dress. Given how careless she had been with her beautiful new gown already, perhaps she shouldn't press her luck.

When everyone had been wined and dined, J.B. commanded the floor. Fiona expected Mazie to make the big announcement. Instead, her husband grinned widely.

"We're glad you came tonight. Mazie thought this would be a good time to get us all together."

Jonathan looked puzzled. "We're going to the gala—sitting at the same table. I'm not sure what you mean."

Mazie patted her husband's arm and nodded. She glowed. Apparently, that was a real thing. Except for the unfortunate ones like Fiona who were sick as dogs.

J.B. laid a hand on his wife's shoulder. The two of them exchanged a private look that was intimate and smug with happiness. Then J.B., former bad boy and now thoroughly content homebody, cleared his throat. "We're pregnant," he said. "Well, Mazie is. We wanted you all to know."

After a moment of stunned silence, Lisette was the first one to react. She jumped to her feet and smiled broadly. "That's wonderful news. I'm thrilled for you."

Mazie stood as well and embraced her sister-in-law. "I wasn't sure what to say to you, Lizzy. You and Jonathan have been disappointed twice. I feel guilty that I'm the one who's pregnant."

Lisette shook her head slowly. "Silly goose. Your happiness doesn't hurt me. Jonathan and I are fine. We don't know what the future holds for us, but we'll be tickled pink to welcome the first of a new generation of Tarletons."

"And Vaughans," J.B. said. "Don't forget the daddy."

In the midst of laughter and more hugging, Fiona sneaked a sideways glance at Hartley. He was saying and doing all the right things, but he was pale beneath his tan. Had his family noticed? They had all known him far longer than Fiona had. Maybe it was her imagination.

Jonathan picked up a flute of champagne from the sideboard. "To new beginnings," he said. "And to a healthy pregnancy and a perfect little baby—" He halted, an arrested look on his face. "Boy? Girl?"

"Too soon to tell," Mazie said. "Plus, there's always the possibility of multiples given the meds I've taken."

J.B. turned green. "Oh, hell," he muttered. "I forgot about that."

Mazie slid her arm around his waist and chuckled. "I wondered how long it would take you to remember."

Lisette glanced at her watch. "I hate to break up the party, but if we're going to make it in time for the presentation, we'd better head out."

Jonathan nodded. "You're right, sweetheart. One more thing, though. I'll make it quick." When everyone fell silent, Jonathan stared at his twin with a hard-to-read expression.

Fiona had sat down again on the sofa. Hartley perched on the arm beside her. She felt the fine tension in his body when Jonathan spoke.

The CEO of Tarleton Shipping addressed the room. His brown-eyed gaze, so like his sibling's, was focused on his brother. "We've all been through a lot in the past year. Changes and more changes. But one thing stays the same…family." The muscles in his throat worked visibly. "I want you to come back to work, Hartley. The company needs you. I need you. Whatever happened while you were away is water under the bridge. The important thing now is that you've come home."

Fiona was stunned. She squeezed Hartley's hand, silently urging him to accept the olive branch.

He stood up slowly. She had no idea what he was thinking. "I'd like that," he said gruffly. He reached out to his brother. "Thanks, Jonathan."

All the women were misty-eyed as the two men shook hands. There wasn't time to dwell on the tentative truce. Maybe Jonathan planned it that way. Everyone rushed to gather phones and car keys and purses.

Soon, Fiona was in the car with Hartley. "Well, *that* was awesome," she said. "I'm so happy for you."

When Hartley didn't respond, she put a hand on his shoulder briefly. "You okay?" she asked as she fastened her seat belt, taking care not to clip the delicate fabric of her dress in the mechanism.

Hartley pulled out into traffic, his big hands clenched around the steering wheel. "I'm fine." His jaw was granite hard.

"I don't think you are. I thought you'd be excited about returning to Tarleton Shipping."

"I'm pleased," he said tersely. The declaration was hard to believe.

Fiona chewed her lip. "No one is holding a grudge. No one is demanding answers about why you were gone. Your family is wonderfully intact."

"Maybe," he muttered. "He was my best friend. I doubt we'll ever get that back."

"Which is why you have to tell them the truth. You see that…right? Jonathan and Mazie need to know that their mother is not their mother. And that you didn't abandon them for no good reason. This is a critical time for your sister."

Hartley muttered a rude word beneath his breath. "Ignorance is bliss. Trust me on this."

"You are so damned stubborn," she cried. His intractability infuriated her. But they were already pulling up at the event site, so she had to drop the argument.

Crowds of impeccably dressed attendees poured into the building. The venue had once been a trio of row houses.

Careful renovation turned the historic structure into an upscale, sophisticated spot for weddings and other special occasions.

Tonight, the chamber of commerce was celebrating philanthropy in Charleston and honoring Gerald Tarleton with a posthumous award. He would have received the honor in person had he not died so unexpectedly.

As guests entered the building and gathered in a large, bright atrium, screens on four walls detailed the many programs and projects to which the Tarleton patriarch had been a benefactor. The photographs spanned a couple of decades. From the older images, it was easy to see that Jonathan and Hartley resembled their father in his younger days.

The chamber president quieted the crowd and summoned the three Tarleton siblings to the miniature dais. J.B., Lisette and Fiona lingered at the back of the room.

For the first time, Fiona truly understood the place this family held in the story of the port city. The Tarletons were low-country royalty. She was glad all the focus was on the stage. She felt queasy and out of her element.

Hartley was so damned sexy when he stepped up to the microphone and said a few words. She put a hand to her chest to still the ache there. She was such a hypocrite… insisting that he come clean about his trip to Europe. Insisting that secrets were hurtful.

Soon, the brief ceremony was over and huge double doors swung inward, allowing the crowd to progress to the ballroom where a fancy meal was waiting. When the Tarletons rejoined their respective partners, Fiona felt even more like a fraud. She was here under false pretenses. Hartley wanted her. He'd said so in a dozen different ways.

But their fledgling relationship wouldn't stand a chance when the truth came out.

The large room filled rapidly with conversation and laughter. The waiters and waitresses who moved between tables were a welcome distraction. Hartley was seated beside her, but he felt a thousand miles away.

Despite the intimacy he and Fiona had shared earlier, he was only going through the motions now. Behind his pleasant smile she saw a world of confusion. He was hurting, and she didn't know how to help him.

Who was she kidding? She didn't even know how to help herself.

Though the food was wonderful, she ate sparingly. She still had to get through the early morning hours without revealing her *interesting* condition. As much as she wanted to spend the night with Hartley, she was courting danger.

Tomorrow, she wanted to tell him calmly, rationally. Not have him find out about the baby because she was hunched over the toilet losing her breakfast.

Things improved when the lights dimmed and couples began moving onto the dance floor in the center of the room. Crystal chandeliers overhead reflected candle flames from the ornate centerpieces.

Hartley stood and held out his hand. "Dance with me?" he asked gruffly. When she twined her fingers with his, he tugged her to her feet.

"I'd love to," she said.

Hartley was an amazing dancer. She remembered that from the wedding where they met. Though he was big and broad and unabashedly masculine, he moved with confidence across the polished floor.

When she tried to keep a space between them, Hartley simply ignored her self-conscious behavior. "No one's watching us," he said, his breath warm on her temple. "Relax, Fee."

She was pretty sure he was deluding himself. A good

portion of the room—at least the single females from twenty to forty—were eyeing Hartley like he was dark chocolate and they had just finished a ten-day juice cleanse.

Hartley, on the other hand, was flatteringly single-minded. He held her close. His gaze never strayed to other women. His beautiful cognac eyes mesmerized her.

"This is fun," she said, resting her cheek against his shoulder. It wasn't what she *wanted* to say. She wanted to pour out her thoughts and her fears and her questions about the future. She wanted to tell him how he made her life brighter and better. How he made her feel desirable and sexy and *hopeful*.

She wanted to tell him she loved him. Her breath hitched. The knowledge had come to her gradually, but could no longer be ignored.

The words lodged in her throat. Like Cinderella watching the clock, Fiona didn't want to miss a single moment of the magic. She was racing against time, trying desperately to see a solution where there was none.

She *knew*, deep in her heart, that as soon as she revealed the truth about her pregnancy, Hartley would be long gone and she would turn into a fat orange pregnant pumpkin with nothing to show for this crazy affair other than a single glass slipper and a broken heart.

J.B. and Mazie were the first to leave the party. Like Fiona, Mazie had been battling exhaustion. Jonathan and Lisette soon followed.

As the room emptied, Hartley and Fiona remained on the dance floor, swaying from one romantic song until the next. Earlier in the evening, the band had played pop tunes. Top-forty hits.

Now, with the lights low and only two dozen couples still enjoying the music, the old standards were the best.

Especially as a prelude to a cozy overnight rendezvous at a nearby hotel.

Hartley stroked the back of her neck with a single fingertip, reducing her to a puddle of need. "I want you, Fee."

The hoarse words were not surprising. He'd been noticeably aroused for the past hour. She tipped back her head and searched his face. "I want you, too," she said softly. *So. Very. Much.*

They gathered their things from the table and headed for the exit. Numerous people interrupted their progress to say something to Hartley about his father, but finally, they were out on the street in the warm, muggy heat of a Charleston evening.

Hartley had parked the car in a two-tiered garage around the corner from the venue. They strolled there slowly, hands linked like teenagers on prom night. Despite everything that was wrong, Fiona experienced a totally illogical surge of hope.

Maybe Hartley did care for her more deeply than she thought.

Maybe he would be able to handle her shocking news with equanimity.

Maybe she would finally have the family she had always wanted.

At the car, Hartley insisted on carrying both bags. He tucked his smaller case under his arm and picked up Fiona's carry-on. "I'm still holding your hand," he said, giving her his trademark grin. "Tonight is a big romantic gesture. I'm impressing you with my strength and stamina."

She bumped his hip with hers. "Save the stamina for later."

His cheeks flushed. "Duly noted."

Their lodging was a brief walk away. The streets were mostly deserted. When they arrived, a sleepy desk clerk checked them in. Hartley had booked the rooftop suite with a view of the city.

They skipped the elevator and climbed three flights of stairs. Since her escort had his hands full, Fiona unlocked the door and walked in. “Oh, Hartley,” she said, delighted. “This is gorgeous.” The furnishings were soft and stylish but not too over-the top for a man to feel comfortable. A deep, inviting sofa upholstered in sage green suggested any number of alternatives for adult play. The huge four-poster bed dominated the room.

Beyond the bed, French doors opened outward onto a private patio. Fee kicked off her shoes and went to explore. When Hartley dropped the bags and followed her outside, she leaned over the railing. “This place is perfect.”

He wrapped his arms around her waist from behind, tugging her back from the edge. “*You’re* perfect.”

The absolute sincerity in his voice wooed her, turned her knees to mush. She spun to face him. “Thank you, Hartley. Thank you for thinking of this.”

He kissed her nose. “Sit right there. Don’t move.” The small table was flanked by two metal chairs.

Moments later, he was back carrying a bottle of champagne and two glasses. “This was our welcome gift.”

As he started to work on the cork, Fiona felt panic rise. Pregnant women couldn’t drink. “None for me,” she said. “I want to be awake for the next act. But you have some.”

He gazed at her quizzically, setting the bottle aside. “Whatever the lady wants.”

She reached across the table and took his hand. “I’ll ask it again. Are you okay?”

His expression altered for a split second and then settled back into his habitual lazy grin. Had she touched a nerve?

“Why wouldn’t I be?” he said, but his fingers drummed on the table.

"We haven't had a chance to discuss your sister's news. I was afraid it upset you."

His jaw worked visibly. The silence lengthened. "I don't think it's *good* news, if that's what you're asking. But before you start in on me, it wouldn't have changed anything if I had told them the truth. They wanted a baby. Mazie already knows that mental illness runs in our family."

Fiona sighed inwardly. Had she ever met a more stubborn man? "Genetics is a tricky business," she said. "Besides, their baby is half Vaughan. None of us can guarantee a perfect pregnancy ahead of time. It's a roll of the dice."

"Good thing I'm not a gambler."

She glared at him, completely frustrated, but unable to tell him why.

Suddenly, Hartley stood up and paced. "Do you really want to have this argument right now? I thought we were here to indulge ourselves."

He was right. Once she told him the truth tomorrow morning, everything would change. She wanted this one last night. She wanted Hartley. The other could wait. "I'm sorry," she said. She mimed locking her lips and tossing the keys. "From now on, it's all about you and me."

At last, his body language relaxed. "I'm glad to hear it." He moved behind her chair and played with her hair, sifting the strands, his fingers brushing her ears, making her tremble. He had barely touched her, and already she was wild for him.

When she tried to stand up, two big hands settled on her shoulders. "Don't move, darlin'. We're gonna take this slow. We have all night."

It was supposed to be a promise on his part, but to her ears, it sounded dangerous. *All night*? What was she thinking? Morning always came, and with it, a reckoning.

He reached around her and slid his slightly rough man-hands inside the bodice of her dress, cupping her bare curves. She shuddered, biting her lip to hold back a ragged moan. Sounds carried on the night air.

"What are you doing?" she whispered.

"Enjoying myself." The laughter in his voice made her smile, though she was too wound for amusement to take hold.

She exhaled shakily. "Carry on."

He played with her breasts, making her squirm. The nipples were more sensitive now that she was pregnant. When he kissed her neck and nuzzled the spot just below her ear—because he knew she liked it—she reached up and grabbed his wrists. "I want to go inside," she pleaded.

"Not yet." Without warning, he tugged her to her feet. "Let's look at the stars."

Fourteen

Fiona was confused. They were outside. All they had to do was look up. Apparently, that wasn't enough for Hartley. He tugged her toward the edge of the patio where a low stone wall topped with three feet of wrought iron marked a boundary. A century and a half ago, a gentleman might have coaxed a Southern belle up here to see the sights.

The hour was late. Few people roamed the streets below. The ones who did, didn't look up.

Hartley stood behind her, crowding her. "Hold on, Fee." He took her hands and placed them on the smooth, cool metal curlicues. "Don't let go."

Her heart beat faster. Could he see the way her chest rose and fell with her startled breathing? She wanted to question him, to demand an explanation. But another part of her, submissive, aroused, wanted to see how far this would go. Hartley was a modern-day pirate. An adventurer. A man unafraid to push the bounds of propriety.

Even so, she was shocked beyond words when she felt him lift her skirt. Despite the season and the temperature, the air felt cool on her bare legs and the backs of her thighs. "Hartley?" The ragged word was equal parts protest and slurred pleasure. Surely he wouldn't…

Once again, he kissed the back of her neck. "I'll keep you safe, sweet thing. You can trust me."

Her fingers clenched painfully around the unforgiving iron. She might have swooned had twenty-first-century women been given permission to do such a girly thing.

His big hands palmed her butt, squeezing. He made no move to take off her panties, but his thumb traced the crease in her ass through nylon and lace. Goose bumps covered her body.

Her voice was frozen, her breath lodged in her throat. Between her legs, her sex wept for him. She was swollen and hot and damp, unbearably needy. Would he unzip her dress? Here, where they were exposed?

The idea both frightened and seduced her.

Hartley continued to play with her backside as if he had all the time in the world. Just when she thought she couldn't bear another second of his lazy torture, he reached around her and, with a single finger, stroked her to a sharp, vicious climax. She shuddered and groaned.

Afterward, her forehead rested against the metal. She could barely breathe. His hand was concealed by layers of tulle and satin. If anyone on the street below was inclined to gaze upward, nothing would seem amiss.

Hartley moved closer. She felt his arousal at her back. "I told you we'd see stars," he muttered, his voice heavy.

Her body went lax, leaned into his. But still, she held the railing. "How much did you have to drink, Hartley Tarleton? You're out of control."

His laughter was strained. "Possibly." He covered her hands with his.

The visual was enticing and beautiful and painfully perfect. She wanted this man and this life. But she wanted more. She wanted a future full of love and laughter and family squabbles. She wanted everything.

Without warning, he scooped her into his arms. "I'd like to get horizontal now. Any objections?"

Fiona waved a hand, yawning. "Not a single one."

Hartley knew he had met his match. There had never been a female he couldn't walk away from. Not until Fee.

Lust and tenderness and determination swirled in a dangerous cocktail of emotion. He wanted this woman. Maybe forever. The knowledge should have stunned him, but oddly, he recognized it. The need to claim her as his own had been growing underground. He'd told himself he was having fun.

Instead, he'd been making plans.

Fiona had no family of her own. He could share his.

As he carried her over the threshold into their hedonistic bedroom and bumped the door closed with his hip, his heart beat faster, a syncopated rhythm that made him breathe too fast. Was there more to this thing with Fee than sex? Did he want more?

Now they were enclosed in a cool, private lovers' boudoir that smelled of roses and sin. He set her on her feet and kissed her roughly, his hands tangling in her hair, holding her head.

"I never seem to get enough of you, Fiona. Why do you think that is?"

Her sleepy smile was sweet and guileless. "I have no idea. But I'm a fan of your work."

His hands shook. "I may not be able to stop. I may have

to take you all night, again and again. Like that first time we met."

"Do you hear me complaining?"

The sass in her voice inflamed him. Something about this weekend was bringing out his caveman instincts. He backed her up against the carved post at the foot of the bed. Falling to his knees, he knelt between her legs and found his way under her skirt.

Her skin was hot and fragrant with a familiar scent. He nudged her feet apart. Though his body ached fiercely with the need to be inside her, he wanted to give her every ounce of pleasure possible.

When he tasted her intimately, she groaned. Her hands fisted in his hair, making him wince. This time, her orgasm was slower, richer. It rolled over both of them in an endless stream. Hartley felt the quivers in her pelvis, the sharp jerk when her body hit the top.

She collapsed in his arms. He eased her down onto the soft, luxurious rug, wrapping her tightly against him. While Fee struggled to breathe, he pressed kisses to her hot face. "I need you, Fiona James. Tell me you want me, too."

"Of course I do." She blinked at him, befuddled.

"What if we travel the world for a few months? Give you new horizons and inspirations to paint? We'll go wherever the wind blows us."

She flinched. The change in her face was so obvious a blind man would have seen it. While Hartley had been weaving dreams, Fiona had clearly been on a different track. Distress darkened her soft blue-gray eyes. "Your brother asked you to come back to work. You can't abandon him again."

Suddenly, he remembered Fiona's aversion to his spending the night at her house. What kind of fool was he? A woman who wanted her "space" clearly wasn't keen on spending a lot of time together.

The raw hurt in his chest was astounding. Had he really been so clueless about his own obsession and Fiona's ambivalence?

"Forget I said anything," he said lightly, tucking away the heartsick feeling in his gut. "It was the lust talking. You're a very sexy woman. I plead temporary insanity."

"Hartley…" She cupped his face.

He'd be damned if he'd let her see that she had bruised his ego. Jumping to his feet, he dragged her with him. "Enough talking," he muttered.

He stripped the dress and underwear from her body and then removed his own clothes rapidly. After folding back the sumptuous covers, he tumbled her onto the bed. He wanted to prove to himself that his emotions weren't involved.

But when he tried to be rough and impersonal like this was just another encounter with just another nameless female, he couldn't do it. Fee's bottom lip trembled. Her beautiful eyes welled with tears. "I care about you, Hartley. You know I do."

The lukewarm words were like alcohol on a razor cut. He held her wrists in one hand and loomed over her. "Let's put that to the test."

Deliberately, he held her down and pleasured her, made her come three times. Every time she tried to coax him to enter her, he resisted…even though the truth was, he was sick with wanting her.

Finally, his body betrayed him. He'd been aroused for a million hours, desperate to find solace in her arms, her soft, sweet body. He spread her legs and thrust hard, finding himself at the mouth of her womb, buried as deeply as he could go. Wanting to bind her to him. To demand that she acknowledge this incredible connection they shared.

It was over soon. Humiliatingly so.

He visited the bathroom. So did she. After turning out the lights, they climbed into bed. It would have been a fitting end to the evening if he could have turned his back on her. But he was weak in the way only a man could be. He dragged her close and spooned her, already yawning.

They fell asleep without another word.

Fiona awoke at dawn, groggy and needing to pee. It took a moment for her surroundings to register. And then she remembered. The hotel. Hartley.

Panic struck as she assessed her nausea. Unbelievably, her stomach was at rest. Maybe she was turning the corner. It didn't matter anymore, though, did it? Hartley would have to be told about the baby today, and then it was all over.

When she turned on her side to look at him, his eyes were open. He was on his back, arm slung over his forehead, staring at the ceiling.

"What do you want to do?" she asked. They had made plans to enjoy brunch, play tourist at the open-air market, spend a second night at the hotel, make love until they were satisfied.

Hartley didn't even look at her. "I think we should check out of the room. Head home. Separately. We need to back up and take a look at what we're doing. You're right, Fiona. If I'm returning to work at Tarleton Shipping right away, I'll have a lot on my plate."

"You're angry," she said, her heart sinking.

He shrugged. "No."

It was time for the truth. She sat up and wrapped the sheet around her all the way up to her neck. This wasn't an easy conversation to have naked. "I need to tell you something," she whispered.

Shivers racked her body. The nausea threatened to return.

Without warning, Hartley rolled out of bed. "I'm done with talking and listening, Fee. I'm calling a time-out. You in your corner. Me in mine. This relationship is too damn much work."

The next thirty minutes passed in a haze of misery. They took turns showering. Room service sent up coffee and croissants. When both Hartley and Fiona were dressed and ready to go, they carried their bags downstairs and turned in the keys. Fiona's overnight case held a satin gown folded up inside.

Hartley drove her home without speaking a word. He stopped at her sidewalk and left the motor running. There was no choice but to get out, yet something held her back. "Are you done with me?" she asked. "Done with us?"

His expression was inscrutable. "I don't know."

In the days that followed, Fiona lost herself in her work. It was a pattern that had served her well in the past. She felt the urgency of getting all her large commissions finished before the baby came. What did she have? Five months? Six? Babies could come early or late…

She had no idea how she would cope in the beginning. Caring for a newborn was a huge amount of work. And there would be no paid maternity leave for a self-employed artist.

Should she swallow her pride and ask for Hartley's help? He must have thought his travel-the-world plan hadn't interested her. Quite the opposite. It sounded like the most amazing honeymoon.

But preparing for the baby and getting her projects completed didn't leave any time for a months-long jaunt.

And still she hadn't told her baby's father the truth. Though it wasn't entirely her fault, she felt guilty. The longer she waited, the harder it seemed, particularly after the way their romantic weekend had ended.

Despite her distress over the way she and Hartley had parted and her worry about the future, each day brought new reasons to be excited about her pregnancy. Thankfully, she had made it through the worst of the morning sickness. It still caught her off guard at times, but not every day and not as badly as before.

Her breasts were bigger now. The little baby bump was growing more noticeable. Slowly but surely, her body was changing. Soon, telling Hartley would be a moot point. People would begin to notice her shape and draw their own conclusions.

Every morning she told herself today was the day. She would seek him out, give him the news and weather the explosion. After all, this baby linked them, no matter what. But every day she lost her nerve. Seeing the look on his face when he heard the truth would destroy her.

She *wanted* this baby. Desperately. Knowing that Hartley couldn't or *didn't* broke her heart.

Over a week after the gala, Mazie showed up unannounced on Fiona's doorstep. Because she was working, Fiona nearly didn't answer the bell. But her back was hurting, and she needed a break anyway.

She wiped her hands, peeked through the window and felt her heart catch with disappointment. It wasn't Hartley. Of course it wasn't.

Fiona opened the door. "Hey, Mazie. What's up? Come on in. Please excuse the fact that I'm covered with paint. Neatness is not one of my gifts."

Mazie tossed her keys in a chair and put her hands on her hips. Her usual sunny smile was nowhere in sight. "What have you done to Hartley?" She demanded an answer.

The pile of guilt smothering Fiona grew deeper. "Nothing," she said weakly. "I don't know what you mean." She wrapped her arms around her waist, feeling her face heat.

Hartley's sister paced, her stance agitated. "Jonathan is worried about him. He says things are going smoothly at work, but Hartley is distant."

"Well, that makes sense, doesn't it? You're all dealing with the fallout from his being gone. I'm sure it will take some time to get back to the way things were. I wouldn't worry about it."

"That's not all." Mazie scowled, her expression stormy and anxious at the same time. "J.B. is throwing a big party for my birthday soon. I asked Hartley to bring you, and he gave me some weird evasive answer about how you were super busy. It was clearly a lie. What's going on with you two?"

In another circumstance, Fiona might have confessed her pregnancy. She liked Mazie and felt close to her already. But to admit she was pregnant would bring a host of questions and problems. Mazie would rightly want to know why Fiona hadn't told Hartley he was going to be a father—and why Fiona and Hartley weren't living together.

Fiona couldn't explain any of that without divulging Hartley's secrets.

Those secrets weren't hers to tell.

"I'm sure Hartley can find a date for the birthday party. And I'm also sure it's not good for the baby *or* you to get so upset. Give Hartley some space and time to regroup. He'll be fine."

Mazie cocked her head, studying Fiona as if she could see inside her brain. "I was under the impression the two of you were pretty serious."

Fiona bit her lip. Hard. She refused to cry in front of the other woman. "I think Hartley and I want different things out of life. Besides, he needs a chance to get back in the groove at Tarleton Shipping."

"Did you have a fight?"

How was Fiona supposed to answer that? "Not a fight *exactly*. I suppose you could say we had words. But it's over. We're both fine."

Mazie scrunched up her face and ran her hands through her hair. "Why can't anything be simple, dammit? I thought you were perfect for my brother. I can't believe he let you slip through his fingers."

"It was my fault," Fiona said, not wanting Mazie to be disappointed in her brother. "I needed things that Hartley wasn't ready to give. So don't blame him. It's just that he and I are two very different people."

Mazie's face fell. "Well, that sucks. Can you tell me more? Maybe I can knock some sense into him."

"It's personal," Fiona said. "I'm sorry, Mazie. I love your family, and I would have liked to be a part of it. But it's not in the cards." She paused briefly. "I hate to be rude, but I really do need to get back to work."

Mazie's eyes glittered with tears. "He needs somebody."

"You're matchmaking, because you and J.B. are so happy, but not every relationship works out. Hartley will find someone else." Saying those words out loud was an actual physical pain.

"I suppose." Mazie's glum acceptance didn't make Fiona feel any better at all. "I still wish you could come to my birthday party," Mazie said.

"Perhaps you and I should have lunch one day. Just the two of us. A girl can never have too many friends."

"I'd like that. I won't let you slip away simply because my brother is dumb. I'll call you soon. Sorry to interrupt your work."

Fiona said her goodbyes, locked the front door, threw herself down on the sofa and cried…

Fifteen

Unfortunately, tears never solved anything. When her pity party was over, she was no closer than ever to finding answers, and now she had a headache and a stuffy nose besides.

She wiped her face with the hem of her T-shirt and sat up. Reaching in her pocket for her phone before she could change her mind, she sent Hartley a text.

I miss you.

When he didn't answer right away, she reminded herself that he was at work. The important thing was, she had made an overture. Not only did he need to come pick up his birthday gift for his sister, but Fiona needed to see him face-to-face and tell him the truth.

To make sure she didn't back out again, she added a second text.

Mazie's birthday present is ready. Let me know when you want to pick it up.

The dizziness and light-headed feeling she experienced when she hit Send had nothing to do with her pregnancy this time. She was so damned scared.

What would she do if he ignored her entirely? Thankfully, Mazie's painting was Fiona's ace in the hand.

A few hours later as she was fixing herself an early dinner of tomato soup and grilled cheese, her phone finally dinged. Now is good for me, the text said.

Her heart stopped. She wasn't ready. Her hands were clammy and shaky.

Can we make it 6:30?

I'll be there.

With barely an hour to scarf down her food, clean up the kitchen and take a quick shower, she had to hurry. Instead of a sundress, which was her go-to hot-weather wardrobe when she wanted to look nice, she found a pair of new jeans in her closet and paired them with a simple button-up shirt. White. Sleeveless. Nothing to say she wanted to look good in front of an ex-lover.

For courage, she added the seahorse pendant Mazie had given her. The little creature was cool against her hot skin.

Again and again she rehearsed the words she wanted to say when she revealed her pregnancy. All the things she had wanted to say when they were at the hotel but didn't have the chance. Letting Hartley off the hook. Telling him he didn't have to be involved with the baby at all.

All the practice in the world wasn't going to make this confrontation any less painful. What she really wanted to do was get down on her knees and beg him to love her *and* her baby. To plead with him to be happy.

When the knock came at six thirty sharp, she opened the door. Instantly, she knew that Mazie had been right. Hartley looked terrible. Still handsome, of course, but stripped of life. His eyes were dull. The usual joie de vivre that put a twinkle of mischief in his expressive face was gone.

"Come on in," she said. "The painting is on the sofa."

When she closed the door, he stopped in front of her and bent to kiss the top of her head. "Hello, Fee."

Silly tears sprang to her eyes. She blinked them away. His tenderness was more painful than outright hostility. Swallowing the huge lump in her throat, she led him through to the living room. "There it is."

Hartley stopped in his tracks, his expression awed. "My God, Fiona. This is phenomenal." He picked up the small canvas with careful hands and examined it closely. "You've captured the two of them exactly. Mazie will adore it." He turned back to look at her, where she had paused in the doorway. "I knew you were talented, but this is something else again. You're an amazing artist. I don't think I fully understood how gifted you are until now."

His praise warmed the cold places in her broken heart. "Thanks. I'm happy you like it. Shall I wrap it for you?" She had brought the supplies from her studio just in case.

"Yes, please."

He prowled the room for the few minutes it took her to enfold the framed canvas in thick kraft paper and tie it with a fancy golden bow. "There you go," she said. "All ready for the birthday girl." Some tiny part of her still expected him to invite her to the party, but Hartley didn't say a word.

Despite the awkwardness between them, a silly sprig of hope continued to push through her fear. She couldn't procrastinate any longer. "Hartley, I need to talk to you about something."

"Me first," he said. "I need a favor. I know we didn't part on the best of terms, but I need your help."

"With what?"

His expression was bleak. "My siblings and I have been summoned to the lawyer's office tomorrow morning at ten. Something about a letter from our father. Written to me. But the other two are supposed to be there to hear it read aloud. J.B. and Lisette will come with Mazie and Jonathan, of course. I'd like somebody with *me* who is in my corner."

"It's your family, Hartley. Of course they're in your corner. It wouldn't be appropriate for me to intrude."

"I'm going to have to sit there and let my father berate me from the grave. The others may have forgiven me, but my dad died before I even came home. This isn't going to be pleasant." He pressed three fingers to his forehead as if he had a headache.

She swallowed, feeling frustrated and emotional. Finally, she had worked up the courage to tell Hartley about her pregnancy, and he had rerouted the conversation before she could even start.

"You need to eat," she said. "It will make you feel better." There she went again. Trying to make herself indispensable.

In her small kitchen, she waved him to the table and found him a beer. While she made a second version of the meal she had eaten earlier, Jonathan brooded visibly. His masculinity dwarfed the modest room. Or maybe it was his expansive personality.

Hartley was larger than life. He had the family background and the adventuresome spirit to pull off any scheme he chose to pursue. Go racing off to Europe to uncover a decades-old secret. Buy an enormous wreck of a house and blithely decide to renovate it at a moment's notice.

Sweep a bridesmaid off her feet a year ago and make her fall head over heels in love. That last one was his most outrageous affair. Fiona had been an ordinary woman with an ordinary life until Hartley came along.

She sat beside him and sipped a glass of iced tea while he wolfed down the modest meal. He ate as if he were starving.

It was ridiculous to feel sorry for him. The man had plenty of money. Charleston was chock-full of fabulous restaurants that offered takeout. But she loved him, despite the impossibility of their relationship. She wanted him to be happy.

Suddenly, she knew she couldn't procrastinate any longer. She would make love to him one last time and then lay all her cards on the table. "Hartley," she said. She reached a hand across the table and held his wrist. "Would you like to stay the night?"

Hartley nearly choked on his soup. His body went on high alert, sensing danger. Is this why he had come? He could have asked Fiona to deliver the painting via local messenger service. He'd told himself the package was too valuable to entrust to other hands.

The truth was far simpler. He had wanted to see Fiona again. Her three-word text had been all the permission he needed.

Even so, he equivocated. "We always end up fighting afterward."

She lifted his hand and kissed his fingers one by one. "Don't be mean, Hartley."

"Would you rather me be *nice*?" He leaned toward her and curled a hand behind her neck, pulling her close for a searing kiss. The taste of her went to his head like 100 proof whiskey.

He had tried to stay away. He really had. But it was a losing battle. Until another man put a ring on her finger, he was going to fight for what he wanted. And he wanted Fee.

Slowly, he stood, tugging her to her feet. After what had happened at the hotel the night of the gala, he was stunned now to realize that Fiona wanted him as much as he wanted her, not that such a thing was possible.

His body was on fire for her. The hunger consumed him. Something had spooked her when he mentioned *traveling the globe*. He wouldn't make that mistake again. If Fiona was interested in hot and temporary, he would be that guy.

He knew what it felt like to sleep alone. He'd be damned if he would let it happen again. Now that she had offered an olive branch, he was determined to make the most of this extraordinary turn of events.

They navigated the narrow hallway hand in hand. It was still daylight outside. Fiona's bedroom glowed in the late-day sun, even with the curtains drawn. She hadn't made her bed that morning. The tumbled sheets were an erotic invitation.

They barely spoke a word this time. Perhaps because talking always got them in trouble.

He unbuttoned her top. The lacy bra beneath did little to hide pert raspberry nipples. She was softer than he remembered, her breasts fuller and rounder. Maybe absence truly did make the heart grow fonder.

When she was naked, he lifted her into the bed and rapidly removed his own clothes. Climbing in beside her was like coming home.

His breath came in short, jerky gasps. "I won't ask any

questions, Fee. Your reasons are your own. But know that I wouldn't want to be any place else in the world right now."

Her lips were bare. Pale pink. Kissable. Wide eyes stared up at him as he leaned over her on one elbow.

She cupped his cheek. "I was afraid you didn't want me anymore."

His rough curse held incredulity. "I'll never stop wanting you, darlin'. You're the one who seems to have a few issues."

When he reached for a condom, she put a hand on his arm. "You won't need that. I took care of things."

"Whatever you say, Fee."

When he moved between her legs and thrust slowly, the sensation of bare skin to bare skin made him shudder. "I've never been with a woman like this. It feels damned incredible."

"Yes," she whispered. She kept her eyes open the entire time, almost as if she were trying to memorize his face.

He gritted his teeth, clenched his jaw. Tried to stave off the climax that was a desperate convergence of condomless sex and long celibate days without her.

Finally, he rolled to his back, taking her with him. Now he could finger her center, send her over the edge. Her orgasm triggered his own. He came forever. Until he was boneless, helpless.

She collapsed on his chest at the end. He held her tightly, stroking her hair. "Fee..."

He trailed off, not knowing what to say and not wanting to cause another argument. Fiona seemed perfectly content when they were together like this. Why was she so skittish in other ways?

At last, she moved away from him and padded in her bare feet to the bathroom. When she returned, she had pulled a T-shirt over her head. It was long enough to cover the tops of her thighs.

Her face glowed with happiness. “It’s only eight o’clock. You want to pop popcorn and watch a movie?”

He raised up on his elbows and grinned at her. “Or have sex again?”

“Can’t we do both?” She returned his smile with interest.

“Or I could show you the new house.”

“You’ve made progress?”

“A little.”

“Sure,” she said. “Let me get dressed. You want to walk? The humidity is down. It’s a nice evening.”

“I could be persuaded.”

Fifteen minutes later, they were outside. The scent of bougainvillea and roses mingled with car exhaust and someone cooking a late-evening steak on the grill. The neighborhood was still busy at this hour. Kids on bikes. Grown-ups sitting on front porches, processing the day.

They walked at a leisurely pace. Even so, Hartley’s woebegone house was not more than twenty-five minutes away.

He watched Fiona’s face as they approached. Her eyes widened. “You’ve already closed on the property and done all this?”

“I was motivated.” And he was trying to use physical exhaustion as a sedative. Being physically close to Fiona when he was here working had taxed his self-control. He took her hand. “Come see the inside.”

When he unlocked the front door, a musty smell greeted them. But it wasn’t anything as unpleasant as mildew. More of an old-library odor combined with a house shut up in high temperatures.

“Easy,” he said as he steered her around piles of rubbish that he had already accumulated. He gave her the grand tour. Parlor. Dining room. Kitchen. An antiquated bathroom. "We can't go upstairs yet. Too dangerous."

She shook her head. "I thought when you went back to work with Jonathan you would hire a contractor."

"I will…eventually. But I needed something to keep me busy in the evenings."

She didn't react at all to his leading comment. In the front hallway, she leaned against the wall and looked up at the cobwebby chandelier. "So are you really going to flip it or live in it? It's awfully big for a guy who says he doesn't want babies."

"Not every man is cut out to be a father."

"I suppose."

Was it his imagination, or did her face look stricken? Maybe she was disappointed in him.

The golden evening lost some of its shine. "We'd better get back," he said gruffly.

He locked up and checked windows. They reversed their route. Fiona had invited him to stay the night. He wasn't sure it was the thing to do. But who was he kidding? He wasn't going to say no.

In the end, they *did* pop popcorn and watch a movie. With his arm around Fiona and her head on his shoulder, it was almost possible to pretend that everything in his life was perfect.

When it was time for bed, the tension escalated almost imperceptibly. This was the first time he had been expressly invited to spend the night. The moment seemed significant, but in light of everything that had happened, he wasn't sure how.

Fiona rounded up a toothbrush for him. They took turns showering and met in the bedroom. She seemed shy. He was torn in a dozen different directions. Tomorrow's visit to the lawyer loomed, though he thrust the knowledge away, determined not to ruin this night. He wanted her badly. Should he disguise his need until she trusted him more?

His beautiful artist made the decision for him. They had barely turned out the light before he felt her hand slide beneath the covers. She wrapped her fingers around his erection. "Make love to me, Hartley."

The sex was perfect. Their bodies knew each other now. He could make her gasp. She knew how to pull him to the edge of release and keep him there until he was ready to cry uncle. They moved together in silent yearning.

As they drifted off to sleep, he was struck by the inescapable notion that tonight was the last time. Sadness enveloped him. Giving up wasn't his style, but he sensed Fiona pulling away. Her thoughts were a mystery.

In fact, she had wanted to talk to him at the hotel, but he had shut her down.

What was the point of being together if all they had was sex? He used to think it was enough, but now he wasn't so sure…

Sixteen

Fiona awoke with a jerk, her heart racing. Someone was in the house. "Hartley…" She whispered his name urgently. When she reached for him, his side of the bed was empty.

Her heart rate slowed, but now she had a bigger worry. Grabbing up her robe, she slipped it over her naked body and belted it. For some reason, she felt the need to tiptoe in her own house.

She found him in the kitchen. He had put on his boxer briefs, but the rest of him was gloriously naked. Ignoring the ache and zing of completely understandable lust in her pelvis, she went to him and combed her fingers through his sleep-rumpled hair. "You want to talk about it?"

He shot her a tired grin, barely enough wattage to even be called a grin. "Not much to say. This is where my color-outside-the-lines behavior catches up with me. I'd just as soon not have witnesses when the lawyer reads this letter from my father, but it seems I'm out of luck."

"I'm sorry."

Hartley shrugged. "It was my choice to go to Switzerland without telling anyone. It was my choice to borrow the money."

"An incredibly large amount of money," she pointed out.

"I thought you were on *my* side."

She kissed his cheek. "I am. And if you want me with you at the lawyer's office, I'll ignore any strange looks I get from your family. But afterward, I really do need to talk to you."

He frowned. "Why can't we talk now?"

Why indeed? She poured herself a cup of orange juice, keeping her back to him as she opened and closed the fridge. "Because it's three in the morning, and I'm not coherent at this hour. Come back to bed."

He took her hand and whirled her around. "Is that an invitation?"

She wrapped her arms around his neck and yawned. "As long as you won't be insulted if I sleep through your manly moves."

He scooped her up and carried her down the hall. "Challenge accepted."

When Fiona awoke the next morning, Hartley was gone, but he had left a note on the pillow beside her.

> Had several things to do before the meeting at the lawyer's office. I'll send a car for you around nine thirty. Text me if that's a problem. When we're done there, you and I can find someplace to talk.

You and I can find someplace to talk. Innocuous words for a conversation that would change her life. Her stomach threatened to act up again, but after a cup of hot tea and some preventative saltines, she felt better.

The dress she had worn to the funeral was getting too tight around the waist. Instead, she put on a pair of the nice black pants she had bought recently—the ones with the stretchy elastic waist—and topped them with a sober gray tunic that had three-quarter-length sleeves and decorative black buttons. The dressy top hit her midthigh and disguised her change of shape.

When she added strappy black sandals and black earrings, she looked entirely presentable for an extremely serious legal meeting. She still thought it was a mistake for her to be there.

They were friends and lovers. After she told him her news, even those designations would be gone. As much as she wanted to think everything was going to turn out okay, in her heart, she knew the truth.

Today would signal the end of her relationship with Hartley Tarleton.

When the driver dropped her off downtown, Hartley was waiting on the sidewalk to greet her. He had showered and shaved and was wearing a suit that was clearly hand tailored. The charcoal-gray fabric emphasized his wide shoulders and his trim waist.

He brushed a kiss against her cheek, but he was distracted.

"You doing okay?" she asked, squeezing his hand.

"I've been better. Let's get this over with."

If any of the Tarleton siblings and their spouses thought it odd for Fiona to be in attendance, they were too well-bred to show it. When Hartley and Fiona joined them in a beautiful reception area, the other four stood and the receptionist ushered them into the lawyer's office.

Here, traditional furnishings reigned. Lots of leather

and dark green, navy and burgundy. Was the palette intentional? Meant to impart gravity?

Fiona had always reacted strongly to color and light. Either positively or negatively, the response was a function of her calling.

Today, in this stuffy, overly formal setting, she felt as if the room was trying to smother her. Maybe Hartley felt the same way, because he looked like his tie was too tight, and he was having trouble breathing.

The lawyer wasted no time greeting them. When everyone was seated in a semicircle facing the large mahogany desk, he opened a legal-size folder and shuffled a few papers.

Jonathan leaned forward, frowning. "I don't understand why we're here. I'm my father's executor. There hasn't been time for the death certificate and other initial documents to work their way through the court. Tell us what's going on. Please. What's so urgent about this letter?"

The lawyer was late fifties, early sixties. He was polite, but not warm. His nod was brief. "As you've been told, Gerald Tarleton left a letter to be read in the event of his death. He filed it with my office six months ago. Though it is addressed to Hartley, Mr. Tarleton made it clear that you and your sister were to be here when the contents were revealed."

Mazie frowned as well. "A little too cloak-and-dagger, don't you think? It doesn't sound like my father."

The lawyer bristled. "I assure you, Ms. Vaughan…the letter is entirely legitimate."

Hartley sighed audibly. "We all know what it's going to say." He shot the lawyer a cool stare. "Let's get on with it."

The man nodded. "Very well." He opened a simple white envelope and extracted a single sheet of paper.

Fiona reached out and gripped Hartley's right hand.

His entire body was rigid. This public flogging was cruel, particularly since Jonathan and Hartley had finally begun to mend fences.

When the lawyer stood, she was forced to drag her attention away from Hartley.

The lawyer cleared his throat theatrically.

"My dearest son Hartley:

"If you are reading this letter, it means that I am gone. Though I was very angry with you for leaving and taking the money, in truth, I was angry with myself for my cowardice over the years. I told Jonathan I had written you out of the will, but I did not. I never did. More about that later.

"Some weeks after you disappeared, I discovered you had flown to Europe, and suddenly I understood what was happening in Switzerland. Not the specifics perhaps, but enough to realize that my secret was out.

"I owe all three of you my deepest apologies. I have no excuse other than the fact that I was scared and embarrassed, and I didn't know what to say to all of you now that you were adults.

"I should have done the right thing years ago, but I avoided the pain and let time pass. Now Hartley has to be the one to explain everything.

"Please know that I adored your mother. Losing her nearly wrecked my entire life. I did what I thought I had to do, but I have often wondered if I did all of you a disservice.

"No father could be more proud of his children. Jonathan is the steady hand at the wheel. Hartley has the fire and enthusiasm that propels us all forward. And Mazie, my sweet Mazie, is the heart of the family.

"Whatever you decide about the Vermont situation is up to you. There is no moral high ground. Only regret and sadness.

"Hartley, I addressed this letter to you because I wanted to make absolutely sure you knew that you have never disappointed me. Ever. You have been impulsive at times, but I have come to believe that such impulsiveness is far more admirable than being stuck in endless indecision as I have been.

"Forgive me, son, for letting your brother think ill of you. When I look back at what has happened, I regret that most of all.

"Jonathan will handle the nuts and bolts of dividing the company and the estate. You will all three benefit equally from our collective hard work. Mazie and J.B. have the wonderful house in the historic district. Jonathan and Lisette are building their dream home. To you, Hartley, I leave the beach house. I pray that you will find a partner—a wife—to bring you peace and happiness and many children to carry on your passion for living boldly.

"My plea is that you keep the beach house in the family and that you fill it with joy and laughter and love.

"Goodbye, my dear ones. Please forgive your old father his transgressions and remember me with fondness.

"Much love to each of you,

"Dad

"(aka Gerald Tarleton)"

When the lawyer finished reading and tucked the letter away, dead silence reigned for several moments. Hartley was pale, his gaze haunted. Jonathan's grim expression masked a multitude of emotions. Poor Mazie wept bitterly.

The youngest Tarleton offspring wiped her face. "What money? What was he talking about?"

The lawyer stood. "I have another appointment. You're welcome to talk this over here in my office. Stay as long as you like. Goodbye..."

When the man exited, Mazie repeated her question, looking from one brother to the other and back.

Hartley rolled to his feet and paced. "I stole a million bucks from Tarleton Shipping. Jonathan was pissed, and rightly so."

Jonathan groaned audibly. "Damn it, Hartley." His jaw worked. "Tell us what the hell Father was talking about."

Mazie was pale now, too, and trembling. J.B. was none too happy to see his newly pregnant wife upset. "Jonathan is right," he said. "We need to know."

Fiona stood up beside the man who held her heart. She kissed his cheek. "It's okay," she said. "They can handle it." Then she looked at Jonathan and Mazie. "He didn't want to hurt you. He's kept this terrible secret to himself to spare you pain."

"Tell us now," Jonathan said. "Please."

Fiona nodded, giving the man she loved a reassuring smile. "It's time, Hartley. Let it go."

And so he did. For the next half hour, he talked as if he had been a monk under a vow of silence and finally released. He told them about the blackmail and the hush money and the blackmailer who turned out to be a feeble old man and a relative at that. Then he described the terrible tragedy that happened when they were one and two years old. And about their mother's twin sister. And everything that transpired in the aftermath.

He gave an accounting of everywhere he had been and

everything he had done in the past year. He told of the old man's unexpected death and of settling a stranger's estate. He explained that in a storage unit in North Charleston were cartons of family memorabilia none of them had ever seen.

The only thing he *didn't* mention was how he and Fiona had met and the fact that nine months after that crazy wedding weekend, he had come home for a fleeting visit to tell his family everything. But he chickened out. And instead spent the night with Fiona.

When his incredible tale finally wound to a close, no one spoke for a couple of minutes. Fiona could see on their faces the struggle to accept that a huge part of their lives had been a lie. There were questions, of course. It was a lot to process. Shock made the task more difficult.

Mazie seemed dazed. "So our mother is not our mother…"

Hartley knelt at his sister's feet and took her hands. "I'm so damned sorry, baby girl. You deserved better. We all did."

She shook her head slowly. "But she did care for us while we were growing up."

"I know she did," Hartley admitted. "You have to think, though, she could have injured any one of us or herself there at the end, before Father sent her away. Maybe if she'd had better doctors and treatments early in her life… I don't know. That's why I—"

He stopped suddenly, perhaps realizing at the last moment the insensitivity of explaining to his pregnant sister that he had vowed never to father any biological children of his own.

Jonathan put a hand on Hartley's shoulder, urging him to his feet. When they were eye to eye, Jonathan uttered words that weren't entirely steady. "I'm sorry, Hartley.

God knows I can't ever make this up to you. I should have known. I should have trusted you."

Hartley's face finally lightened. "Hell, Jonathan, even Fiona pointed out to me that expecting blind faith from all of you, given the circumstances, was a lot to ask. I'm ready to be done with this. It's consumed over a year of my life. I just want to get back to normal."

Jonathan hugged him tightly. For a long time. When they separated, both men's eyes were suspiciously bright. Jonathan nodded slowly. "I want that, too. This has been an awful day. We're going to be dealing with this for a long time, each in our own way. But we're family. We'll get through it."

Mazie stood up to join her brothers, the three of them standing arm in arm. She kissed each man on the cheek and gave both of them a brilliant smile. "I *hated* knowing the two of you were at odds. I'm so, so grateful I don't have to watch you both being weird anymore."

The laughter that followed smoothed some of the rough edges in the room. High emotions demanded a break, a way to let off steam after the intensity they had shared.

Lisette joined her husband and addressed the group. "You all know that Jonathan and I are still staying at the beach house for now. Why don't we have a cookout on the beach tonight? Hot dogs, roasted marshmallows. We can watch the stars come out. What do you say?"

There was a resounding yes from almost everyone.

Fiona, on the other hand, was painfully aware that her hard times were just beginning. "It sounds wonderful," she said. "I'll come if I can, but I have a couple of things in the works. I'll have to let you know later today."

Mazie was visibly disappointed. "But you'll be at my birthday party, surely."

"I'll do my best."

If her equivocation confused Hartley, he didn't show it. He hugged each member of his family one at a time and then sighed. "Tonight sounds great. But I think we all need time to debrief between now and then. Fiona and I will see you later."

In the general exodus that followed, Fiona didn't correct his assurance. Sooner or later, Hartley's family would realize that he and Fiona had ended their relationship.

Outside in the parking lot, he stretched his neck and loosened his tie. "I'm shot, but I promised you we'd talk, darlin'. Where do you want to go?"

And there it was. The question of the day. She was torn between a need for privacy and the idea that a public place might serve to quell the worst of the storm.

She glanced at her watch. "I think we're late enough to miss most of the lunch crowd. What about that new little place over near Hyman's? I hear they're giving the big kid on the block a run for its money. They have conch fritters I've been wanting to try. And the booths are comfy." Perhaps she was overselling it.

"Sounds good to me." He took off his jacket and tossed it in the back seat of the car. Then he rolled up his sleeves. To Fiona it almost seemed as if he were shedding all the stress and pain and sorrow of the last months. How could she send him back to the depths again?

But how could she continue to lie to the man by omission? How could she not tell him he had fathered a child?

The restaurant's customers, as predicted, had thinned out. Fiona asked for a quiet booth. The hostess took her at her word and seated them in a tight corner in the back of the second floor. When Hartley excused himself to go to the men's room, Fiona slipped the server a twenty and asked the young man to leave them alone once the food came.

Perhaps her face revealed more than she knew. The kid nodded vigorously. "I won't come by at all, unless you wave your glass and want more tea."

"Thanks," Fiona said.

In the end, the food was amazing. It lived up to all the hype and then some. Hartley devoured a platter of clams and oysters and an enormous salad. Fiona nibbled at her fritters and pretended to eat a bowl of seafood bisque.

She was so nervous she was sweating, despite the efficient AC.

As the minutes passed, Hartley's mood rebounded exponentially. "God, I'm glad that's over. Could have been a lot worse."

He took her hand, lifted it and kissed her knuckles. "Thank you, Fee. You saved my life in there."

His crooked male grin was sweet and sexy and affectionate.

"You're welcome," she said. "Your family is strong. I know it was a lot to have dumped on them with no preparation. But they did well. So did you."

She loved him so much it was tearing her apart. She *had* to change his mind. She had to.

As promised, the server had left them alone while they ate. But time was running out. Fiona and Hartley couldn't sit here all afternoon. After a second drink refill and a puzzled frown from the server, Fiona waved him away with an apologetic smile.

Hartley yawned and stretched out his legs under the table. "One of us was up early," he teased.

"You could have waked me to say goodbye."

"Nope," he said cheerfully. "If you'd been awake, I wouldn't have been able to resist making love to you."

His intense stare unnerved her. She knew exactly what he meant. The two of them were like magnets, unable to occupy the same space without touching. "True…" She trailed off, literally sick with nerves.

Hartley stroked the back of her hand. "What did you want to talk about, Fiona? Are you finally going to give in and let me sleep on your sofa?"

When she didn't smile at his joke, he cocked his head. "Fee?" He frowned. "What is it? Why are you so upset? Whatever it is, I'll help you fix it."

Her lower jaw trembled so hard her teeth chattered. "I'm pregnant, Hartley. I'm sorry. It must have been that day you came back from Europe unexpectedly. We were kind of crazy for twenty-four hours. I guess we weren't careful one of those times, or maybe a condom broke. Nothing is a hundred percent. I know you—"

She ground to a halt abruptly, mortified to realize she was babbling.

Hartley hadn't said a word. He was looking at her, but his eyes were blank, his body frozen.

"Say something," she pleaded. "Please."

Every ounce of color drained from his face. She knew her timing was terrible, but she had waited and waited and then the stupid lawyer letter had come. Putting her confession off for a day or a week or a month wasn't going to make this any easier.

She wanted him to yell at her or curse or lose his cool.

Instead, it was as if the man she knew disappeared. In his place was a robot.

Hartley pulled out his wallet, extracted a hundred-dollar bill and tucked it under the sugar container. Then he slid out of the booth, turned his back on her and walked away.

Seventeen

Hartley went to the cookout at the beach. It was the last thing he wanted to do, but he had caused his family too much pain to let them down in such a simple thing.

So he made excuses for Fiona's absence, roasted his hot dog and his marshmallow, and gave a damned fine performance of a man who hadn't a care in the world.

As soon as he could reasonably leave without being rude, he drove back to the city.

He didn't pass Fiona's house. He couldn't bear to go near her street. Instead, he stopped at a sporting-goods store, bought a thick sleeping bag and drove to his newly acquired residence.

Not a residence so much as a dream. A dream of what his life could be with Fiona by his side and all the secrets finally out in the open. He knew now that he was in love with her. Truly, madly, deeply. Probably had been for some time. But last night had been a revelation. Being with her again had been like one of those crazy cartoons where the character gets knocked on the head with a coconut.

His whole outlook had changed.

Even with the lawyer appointment hanging over his head, he'd suddenly known that he could deal with a dead man's letter as long as Fiona was there, too.

What a naive fool he had been. Life was always waiting in the wings to knock a guy on his ass.

His pain and terror were so deep, they consumed him. He'd seen images in Switzerland. Coroner's photographs. Things he would never be able to erase from his brain. Dreadful documentation of a suicide that took so much from so many. He would never ever reveal those pictures to Jonathan or Mazie, never so much as mention them. Even now, he couldn't forget, couldn't get them out of his head. The blood. So much blood. And his mother's face, pale and perfect in death.

Almost innocent.

He'd seen other photographs, too. That same woman as a child. Laughing. Playing. Carefree. Totally oblivious to the suffering that lay ahead for her.

The transition was horrifying.

Jonathan climbed to the second level, despite the rotting stairs and the broken glass here and there. He flung his pallet on the floor and fell down on his back, his entire body trembling as if he had malaria or some other jungle fever. One moment he was drenched in sweat. The next he wrapped the edges of the sleeping bag around him.

His maternal grandparents had lost two daughters to mental illness. How had they borne the pain? One child was still alive in an institution in Vermont, but she was a shell of herself. After her breakdown, she rarely recognized any of them. She had only fleeting lucid memories of the family she had reared.

Hartley had tried to make his peace with the past by vowing not to perpetuate it. But what now? He had fathered a child. *Sweet Jesus.* And no use asking if the baby was his. Fiona was as guileless and true as any woman who ever lived. He was the one who had pursued her, bedded her again and again, because he couldn't stay away.

He literally had no idea where to go from here.

Eventually, exhaustion claimed him. He slept in snatches, jerked awake again and again by nightmares. The stuffy house and stark, comfortless bed were no more than he deserved.

He had walked out on Fiona. Hadn't said a word.

How much of an ass could a man be and still consider himself a man?

Toward morning, he splashed water on his face and stared into the mottled mirror in despair. The figure looking back at him was a phantom, a ghost. He had searched his heart for hours on end, even in the midst of sleep.

What should he do? What could he say?

If asking forgiveness was all there was, he might figure that out. But he couldn't go back to Fiona unless he was prepared to talk about the baby. Every time he thought about a child that was his, his blood ran cold in his veins. His brain froze. He was no good to Fiona *or her child.* Couldn't she understand that?

Hunger made him faint. He stumbled going back down the stairs. When he grabbed for the railing, a piece of it splintered, slicing his hand. He stared at the blood dripping from his fingertips.

He was dizzy and weak. For a moment, his dread and pain were so overwhelming, he couldn't see a way forward. Was he like his mother after all?

* * *

Fiona had experienced grief many times in her life. Up until now, the worst was a moment long ago when she realized she was too old to be adopted, that she had missed her *window*, that she would never have the family she dreamed about.

She had been luckier than most. Her life had intersected with people who were kind for the most part. There was no memory of abuse to struggle with. No history of alcoholism or drugs. She'd simply been a good kid in an overcrowded governmental system.

Once she was grown, she'd become proud of who she was. She'd created a nest for herself, a niche. Except for brief friendships with a few guys whose faces she barely remembered, she had been content to paint and to draw and to make a living by herself.

She had learned not to dream big dreams, but instead to be satisfied with what she had…who she had become.

Until Hartley Tarleton had burst into her life like a supernova, she believed she *knew* what it was to be content. To be happy.

Like the scene in the *Wizard of Oz* when Dorothy's world morphed from black-and-white into full glorious color, meeting Hartley had shown Fiona feelings and emotions and a whole damned *rainbow* she never knew existed.

Because the climb up the mountain had been so glorious, the fall was brutal. Indescribably agonizing.

She was like two separate women. One exhilarated by the amazing new life she carried. The other crushed by a grief so all encompassing she wanted to hide under the covers.

One day passed. Then two. Then three.

She had believed Hartley would relent. But she had underestimated his pain.

One day bled into the next. She forced herself to eat and exercise and work. Yearning for Hartley was the worst misery she had ever known.

When the one-week mark passed, she knew he wasn't coming. Ever. It became harder to wake up each morning. The only thing that kept her from collapse was knowing she had a responsibility to her child.

It was ten days after the emotional scene in the lawyer's office before she saw Hartley again. By then, she had stopped hoping. She was at work in her studio. When she turned around to get another brush, there he was.

Gaunt and motionless. With a world of agony in his eyes. "I'm sorry," he said gruffly.

She gripped the paintbrush until her knuckles were white. "I didn't need an apology, Hartley. I knew what was going to happen when I told you. I knew it would be bad. I used to imagine scenarios like running away to join the circus. Or taking a different name and starting a new life on the other side of the country. No matter how hard I tried, I couldn't find a way around the obvious. A woman has to tell a man when he has a baby on the way. It's a moral obligation."

Hartley stared at her bleakly. His eyes were almost black in this light. "I'm sorry I made things terrible for you," he said. "You must have been so scared." He stood with his hands in his pockets. His jeans were ancient and torn, not at all the look of a wealthy man, one of Charleston's elite. The navy T-shirt was equally old and stained. Clearly, he had been working on the house he had bought.

"I *was* scared," she said quietly. "But you can't help your feelings. I knew the baby thing wasn't a whim. You were frightened. And rightly so."

He dropped his chin to his chest for a moment and sighed deeply. When he finally lifted his head and tried to smile, it was almost too painful to witness. "I couldn't deal with the news at first," he said. "I knew an apology was worthless until I was willing to talk about the baby."

"And now?"

He swallowed. "I didn't tell you everything. I didn't tell Mazie or Jonathan either."

Her stomach clenched. What more could there be? "Tell me what?" she asked softly.

"My uncle showed me the coroner's photographs. A crime scene. Bloody. Horrifying. Our mother, the woman none of us remember, looked so peaceful and beautiful. But she was dead. By her own hand. And then he showed me pictures from her childhood. A tiny little girl laughing...playing with puppies. A six-year-old wearing a tutu and beaming. The juxtaposition of those pictures was almost incomprehensible. That's when I knew I couldn't bear to father a child. How could I watch him or her grow up, never knowing if the illness that stole my mother lingered beneath the surface?"

Fiona trembled. "All life is a risk, Hartley. None of us can see the future. Some lives are cut short at eighteen. Others stretch out to ninety or a hundred years." Hot tears sprang to her eyes and rolled down her cheeks. She cried the tears he couldn't shed, grieving, lost.

At last, he approached her, perhaps moved by her distress. "Let's go to the living room," he said. "You look exhausted."

Hand in hand they walked down the hall. Simply being with him again was more than she had hoped for, but they were a long way from any kind of resolution.

Hartley released her and sat on one end of the sofa. Did he think she would maintain some kind of distance between them? Not a chance in hell. He was here. With her. She would fight for their happiness.

She curled up beside him and leaned her head on his shoulder. He took her hand in his. The silence was not quite peaceful, but it held gratitude, at least on her part.

She sifted through the words she wanted to say, but ultimately, the decision would have to be Hartley's. "Here's the thing," she said, praying for some kind of divine guidance. "When I was a child, six or seven years old, I lived in an orphanage. It was a nice place. Clean. Safe. But the one thing they couldn't take away was my loneliness. It lived in my bones. I painted a life in my imagination, a life I wanted so very badly. The reality was different."

He grimaced. "It hurts me to think of you like that."

"There came a time when I had to let go of my fantasies and accept that my life couldn't be the imaginary one I craved. But it could be good."

"How did you get there? How did you give up the wanting and the needing and the disappointment?"

She straightened and faced him, her legs crisscrossed. "You'll laugh. It had to do with ice cream."

He blinked. "Ice cream?"

"Yes. For whatever reason, one of the dairies in the area decided to donate ice cream to the orphanage. Every Friday at 3 p.m., a truck would roll up in the driveway, and a big carton packed in dry ice was off-loaded, filled with orange sherbet push-pops."

"I loved those," he said, his smile more genuine this time.

"I still do. In fact, if I see a kid in my neighborhood eating one on the sidewalk, it takes me back to those warm, perfect afternoons."

"I don't understand how ice cream healed your existential crisis."

She chuckled. "Well, first of all, I hadn't a clue that I was having a crisis, existential or otherwise. All I knew was that I was sad. Yet somehow, when I tasted that treat, my sadness went away for a little while. I began to understand that if something as good as orange sherbet push-pops existed in life, then somehow, someday, I was going to be okay."

"That's pretty deep for a kid so young."

Fiona shrugged. "What can I say? I was a wise old soul."

He kissed her temple. "Some of us are more hardheaded than others. I didn't want to see you again, Fee, until I dealt with my mother. I couldn't let her story define mine."

"And now?" She wanted to hold him and kiss him, but this moment was too important. Hope and fear duked it out in her chest. Right now, hope was winning. Barely.

"I adore you, Fiona James. And I won't live in fear," he said firmly. "What happened in the past was a tragedy. My child, our child, may struggle with any number of serious problems. Or maybe he or she will float through life as one of the lucky ones. Either way, I'm going to love you and this baby for the rest of my life."

"Truly?" Her chin wobbled.

He kissed her nose. "Truly. Marry me, Fee. Big wedding. Small one. I don't care. But I don't want to wait."

"Me either." She took his hand and placed it on her slightly rounded tummy. "I've already picked out your wedding gift. It's the only thing I could think of for the man who has everything."

He flattened his hand against her belly, pressing gently, his expression transfixed. "The pregnancy is good? And you? The baby?"

"We're fine. Better than fine." She cupped his face in her hands. "I want you to make love to me, Hartley. I've missed you so much. It's been an eternity since I felt you next to me, skin to skin, heart to heart."

He tugged her to her feet. "I've never had sex with a

pregnant woman." The look in his eyes told her he liked the idea.

"Sure you have," she said, laughing. "You just didn't know it."

In her bedroom, they stood on either side of the bed and stared at each other. When they met in the center of the mattress, kneeling, he brushed the hair from her face, his gaze searching. "No more looking back, my sweet Fee. I swear it. From now on, I'll be under your feet at every turn. You'll never be lonely as long as I have breath in my body."

"I love you, Hartley."

"Not as much as I love you."

He kissed her then, a kiss that started out with relief and thanksgiving for having weathered the storm, but ended up in the same fiery passion that bound them at every turn.

Clothes flew in four directions. Bare skin met bare skin. He entered her carefully, as though she were a fragile china doll.

She clutched his warm muscled shoulders, her breath coming faster, her body arching into his. "I won't break, silly man."

"No, you won't," he said, burying his face in the curve of her neck. "Because if you ever fall, I'll be there to catch you."

"You're mine," she whispered.

"Orange sherbet push-pops, darlin'. For both of us. From now on. I found you, Fee. Against all odds. I'll never let you go."

Then he gave up on words, and showed her that some happiness was even better than ice cream…

Five days later...

"Be careful. Don't tear the paper." Fiona fretted as she and Hartley climbed the steps of J.B. and Mazie's classic home. J.B. had invited half of Charleston for Mazie's kick-ass party.

But first the family was gathering to give her their gifts.

Over punch and cookies and with much laughter and teasing, paper and ribbon fluttered through the air. Lisette and Jonathan had ordered a handmade French baby doll for the woman who had grown up far too soon.

Mazie traced the doll's lifelike lashes and smiled through her tears. "I love it."

Everyone smiled. Then Hartley handed over the next gift. "This is from Fiona and me. Open with care."

Mazie's astonishment when she saw the wedding-day photograph immortalized in oils warmed Fiona's heart. "Hartley commissioned the gift," she said. "It was his idea."

Mazie screeched and hugged them both. "It's incredible," she cried.

Lisette and Mazie looked at each other and smiled. Lisette took Mazie's hand, and they stepped in front of the birthday girl. Lisette took a deep breath. "There's one more present, Mazie. But you'll have to wait a bit for this one."

Fiona nodded. "We didn't want your little one to grow up alone, so Lizzy and I are giving you two cousins, maybe even a birthing room for three if the timing is right."

Mazie's eyes rounded. "Are you serious?"

Hartley studied the pandemonium that followed with a full heart and a happy grin.

Jonathan and J.B. moved to flank him. "We're toast, aren't we?" Jonathan said. "Three pregnant wives? Whew..."

J.B. nodded. "We'll be wrapped around their little fingers. At their beck and call."

Hartley blew a kiss to his precious bride-to-be. "Any complaints, gentlemen?"

The other two shook their heads ruefully. “Not a one,” they said in unison.

Hartley felt the world click into sharp focus as joy bubbled in his veins like fine champagne. Today was a new life, a new start. He was a damned lucky man…

* * * * *

COMING SOON!

We really hope you enjoyed reading this book. If you're looking for more romance, be sure to head to the shops when new books are available on

Thursday 17th October

To see which titles are coming soon, please visit

millsandboon.co.uk/nextmonth

MILLS & BOON